Praise for The Marigold

"*The Marigold* is a tremendous book, a damning indictment of the greed that drives the suicidal hostility we display toward our own environment, and an exhilarating dive into the weird new realities that brings. Juggling multiple viewpoints and always keeping one foot on the gas, Andrew F. Sullivan has written a vicious, delightfully bizarre ecological horror story. This one's going to live with me for a while."

— **Nathan Ballingrud, author of *North American Lake Monsters*, Wounds, and *The Strange***

"In this keen and surprising work of eco-horror, Andrew F. Sullivan feeds his inventive terrors on the dark fruits of our contemporary precarity: the inequities of the gig economy, the bloated cost of urban housing, the uncanniness of climate change. *The Marigold* is a fast-paced thrill ride, populated by sharply written characters you won't soon forget."

— **Matt Bell, author of *Appleseed***

"Andrew F. Sullivan's *The Marigold* grows a terribly plausible urban future from the capitalist wreckage of the modern 'world class' city and drowns it in a tide of Boschian chaos that folds apocalypses of body horror, techno-fascism, economic, and climate collapse into one roiling, angry wave that'll sweep you away with its narrative force."

— **Indrapramit Das, author of *The Devourers***

"Andrew F. Sullivan's books delve into dark territories other writers are too timid to explore, finding nuance and emotional resonance in that stony soil. *The Marigold* has all the hallmarks of his past work while being something all its own, daunting and daring and just a little scary."

— **Craig Davidson, bestselling author of *The Saturday Night Ghost Club* and *Precious Cargo***

"Andrew F. Sullivan's *The Marigold* is a Cronenbergian *Bonfire of the Vanities*, a scalpel-sharp near-future thriller about an all-consuming city in thrall to greed and power, and the disparate creatures, human and otherwise, caught in its draintrap. Sullivan brings a pulsing urgency to his prose, a mordant wit to his unsettling extrapolations from our current technological, social, and economic plagues, and an epic sweep to his depiction of the age-old struggles between the ruling class, the arrivistes, and those who serve and defy them. A gripping tour-de-force torn from tomorrow's headlines."

— **David Demchuk, author of *Red X* and *The Bone Mother***

"Sullivan cultivates a truly suffocating atmosphere of economic and social tension, a sense that the world has moved beyond the verge of collapse and into a long, slow slide to oblivion. This is urban horror done right, layered with the cold, unalloyed terror of watching the world crumble in real time. *The Marigold* is a back-breaker for the genre."

— **Gretchen Felker-Martin, author of *Manhunt***

"As weird as it is wild, *The Marigold* is a bold eco-horror fable with biting critiques about climate change, the gig economy, and other aspects of our modern dystopia. Once *The Marigold* gets its spores in you, you'll be compelled to read to the end."

— **Lincoln Michel, author of *The Body Scout***

"A bold dystopian novel that captivates with its dread and depth. *The Marigold* is unhinged literary horror that goes right to the source of decay."

— **Iain Reid, award-winning author of *I'm Thinking of Ending Things*, *Foe*, and *We Spread***

"*The Marigold* is social critique written in the only way that makes sense right now: as delirious, meticulously planned horror."

— **Naben Ruthnum, author of *Helpmeet* and *A Hero of Our Time***

The best horror is a mirror that thrills even as we dread seeing what we look like. Andrew F. Sullivan's *The Marigold* is a fierce mirror, wide as the sky, many layered, reflecting our environmental doom and unending consumption back onto us because we deserve it. With smart, elegant prose and storytelling mastery, Sullivan blends the organic and the infrastructure of horror with terrifying results."

— **Michael Wehunt, author of *The Inconsolables***

"This impressively bleak vision of the near future is as grotesquely amusing as it is grim."

— ***Publishers Weekly*, starred review**

THE
MARIGOLD

Andrew F. Sullivan

Published by ECW Press
665 Gerrard Street East
Toronto, Ontario, Canada M4M 1Y2
416-694-3348 / info@ecwpress.com

Purchase the print edition and
receive the ebook free. For details,
go to ecwpress.com/ebook.

Editor for the Press: Jen Albert
Copyeditor: Shannon Parr
Cover designer: Jo Walker

LIBRARY AND ARCHIVES CANADA CATALOGUING
IN PUBLICATION

Title: The marigold / Andrew F. Sullivan.

Names: Sullivan, Andrew F., 1987- author.

Identifiers: Canadiana (print) 20220430845 |
Canadiana (ebook) 20220430861 |

ISBN 978-1-77041-664-2 (softcover)
ISBN 978-1-77852-102-7 (ePub)
ISBN 978-1-77852-104-1 (Kindle)
ISBN 978-1-77852-103-4 (PDF)

Classification: LCC PS8637.U54 M37 2023 | DDC
C813/.6—dc23

This book is funded in part by the Government of Canada. *Ce livre est financé en partie par le gouvernement du Canada.*
We acknowledge the support of the Canada Council for the Arts. *Nous remercions le Conseil des arts du Canada de son
soutien.* We acknowledge the funding support of the Ontario Arts Council (OAC), an agency of the Government of
Ontario. We also acknowledge the support of the Government of Ontario through the Ontario Book Publishing Tax
Credit, and through Ontario Creates. This book is also produced with the support of the City of Toronto through the
Toronto Arts Council.

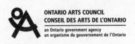

PRINTED AND BOUND IN CANADA   PRINTING: MARQUIS   5   4   3   2   1

This book is made of paper from well-managed FSC® - certified
forests, recycled materials, and other controlled sources.

For Amy

"No one, wise Kublai, knows better than you that the city must never be confused with the words that describe it."

— ITALO CALVINO, *INVISIBLE CITIES*

"Everything is fine."

— FORMER TORONTO MAYOR ROB FORD

1.

Before everything that happened, before the towers, before the site plans, before the deeds, before the failing sports bar and two-bedroom apartment above it that often operated like another, more financially successful, unlicensed sports bar until the police shut it down after that one Polish kid got strangled with a pair of pink stockings behind the abandoned Shoppers Drug Mart a block or two south, there were trees here.

Now there was only a hole. A crane perched on the edge, its lights barely illuminating the dirt below. The stooped shape of a man clambered down the sloped side of the pit, dragging a heavy burden over the frozen mud. A short shadow rippled across the dirt as he descended like a lazy bird of prey. The gardener's feet knew the way. His breath emerged in tiny clouds. No wind reached down this far, but the cold stitched itself into everything it touched. Far above the pit, towers scratched at the light-polluted sky. Most had undergone the ritual, paid their dues, if not to the gardener than to someone else with their own take on his faltering, archaic craft.

With spring, the hole would come to life again, thrumming with sweaty bodies and hungry machines, but before that happened, it had to be seeded. An aged protection spell practised since the bad old days. This was what the gardener was paid to do down here; a pile of bills in an Easton hockey bag waited for him in a vacant condo across the street. Fives, tens, twenties all mixed together. The money didn't exist outside that hockey bag. It floated in its own reality.

The gardener unrolled the tarp, let its wet contents tumble down into the low trench at the very edge of the pit. Seventeen or eighteen, the gardener didn't know. Male this time. It didn't matter. Its clothes were burned back in the ravine. A rough image of a bird was tattooed on a shoulder, yellow and orange and dead. Fingernails bitten down to scabbed quicks. The gardener knelt down in the frozen dirt, dug his thick hands into the earth. Stone, ice, and soil scooped onto the body, a patient process, ensuring the seed was fully buried. From across the street, The Marigold leered into the pit, eighty-eight storeys topped with a crown of flickering orange lights, the sister tower to what was still only a hole.

Finished with his labour, the gardener grabbed the blue tarp that had carried the heavy seed, wrapping it around his shoulders like a cowl. He turned to begin the long trek to the surface. He didn't worry about cameras catching his face. No sensors this far down, no one tracking his footsteps, recalibrating the city's functions. These matters were handled far in advance. Marigold II was supposed to reach over a hundred storeys when it was complete, another tower with a golden halo, a shining monument for some desperate legacy. The gardener put one foot in front of the other, letting the satisfaction of a task well done keep him warm. His breath followed him. There were still more seeds to plant, still more bad old days to come.

2.

Even in the wet snow, Cathy Jin refused to ride the Shit Car. Some of her kinder colleagues called it the Ghost Car. Coming from an under-financed department in the City's struggling public health department, most Wet investigators were told to provide their own transportation or take transit. Occasionally, a cop or a paramedic might bring them along, warily watching them for any sign of a cough slipping out from under the helmet. When she wasn't wearing the full masked helmet mandated by the department, Cathy wore sunglasses, mirrored and chrome. It helped keep the world at bay.

"I'm walking," Cathy said.

"We can wait for another," Jasmine said, eyes blinking through the snow. They were both old hands at this now. "Phone says next one is here in three minutes."

"I want you to look down the street there. You see anything that looks like a streetcar? Your phone lies. We can stand here like idiots or start walking."

The Shit Car sat in front of them, one of the newer streetcars running without an operator, stupid enough to almost drown itself under the Dundas underpass during the floods two years before, filled to the brim with sewage. There were others too damaged to keep in circulation. The TTC claimed to have cleaned this one out, but the stench remained. Few riders took the risk. The Ghost Car is what the news called it, a haunted house stalking the streets.

"Progress for progress's sake?" Jasmine asked, wiping melted flakes off her skin.

"I'd rather be a fool under my own power than stand out here waiting for a train that never comes," Cathy said, dragging her kit behind her, the horned helmet bouncing like it was alive.

"Streetcar," Jasmine said, following behind. She adjusted her jacket collar against the cold. It hid the public health logo on the inside. Most people didn't ask what a Wet investigator did, even when the first bodies started popping up in bus shelters or half-eaten in the sand. They didn't want to know. They weren't about to start wearing their own little masks again. Cathy knew Jasmine kept her own masked helmet inside her bag, as if people didn't know what it hid. Jasmine still thought the Wet was something you could control. Cathy wanted to tell her it was more like a weather system — something to be endured rather than confronted.

"Whatever," Cathy said, trudging along the half-plowed sidewalk. Everything melted, refroze, melted again. The Shit Car came to life and passed them down King, empty, warm, and reeking. "I want to get there before some idiot decides to poke it with a stick."

The latest case was assigned just an hour before, a notification blinking to life on her phone, Jasmine mouthing *go time* in the office kitchen. An alert in a parking garage under a condo tower in Liberty Village, a former yuppie enclave now struggling with the rising lake water.

"How bad do you think it will be this time?" Jasmine said. They used to work their own cases before people began to report some of the bodies were still alive. Cathy ran one of the safe injection sites before whispers of the Wet arrived. She didn't fight the move; it was better than getting fired, ending up on the streets with her former clients. No one knew what the Wet was at that time. They only knew something was spreading up from the lake, a toxic mould burrowing its way through the foundations of the older buildings, sometimes appearing in large splotches on the ceiling or like fingers rising from the floorboards in the rooming houses, the ones that hadn't been converted back into single-family homes for music producers and start-up investors.

"I'm sure we'll need the masks," Cathy said.

The new department was simply called Investigations. There was almost no funding. The job was solely to observe and report, tracking victims and infested sites. Like most things in the city, it only sounded simple. You came. You saw. You trembled.

"My favourite," Jasmine said. "You know I love to play astronaut."

Two cop cars sat in front of the building, blocking access to the parking garage. Real ones, not the private Threshold security some companies had taken to retaining in the other waterfront districts. They'd tried to paint over *PIG* scrawled on one of the back doors with white house paint.

One of the officers waved Cathy over. The heavy building manager paced back and forth between the cruisers, bald head decorated with melting snow. The officers ignored him.

"I don't think it's that bad," the manager sputtered at Cathy. He knew what the heavy mask in her bag meant. "Could be garbage. Someone probably just overreacted, you know?"

"We'll determine that," Jasmine said, placing a hand on his forearm. Cathy preferred to let Jasmine handle the people. She had a talent for zeroing in on people's insecurities, the weak points in their character. Sometimes that included Cathy's. "No one is going to blame you for this, alright? It's not like bedbugs or rats. We need you to stay calm until we figure this out."

He smiled weakly under Jasmine's grasp. The officers stood and watched. There was no solidarity here. The Wet investigators were considered disposable. Most public employees didn't even want to know what they did, just that they disappeared, that anyone around them might be questioned, maybe even tested and quarantined during the aftermath. Cathy pulled her mask over her head, checking the seal as it closed around her neck, locking together like a metal noose. The sensors stood up like goat horns over the massive tinted eye ports and breathing chamber.

"Can't we wait?" Jasmine said. "We don't even know if it's a false positive yet."

Cathy rolled her eyes, glad Jasmine couldn't see them. That was how most of their fights started. She did it again, savouring the moment. "Put it on."

"It's probably a level one at most," Jasmine said. "You're acting like this is my first day. I'm the one who said you'd be good at this. We are partners, right? I don't need a lecture."

"And if it's not a level one, what's your plan?"

Jasmine pulled her own silver mask out of her bag and strapped it on tight. Two shiny minotaurs now. Some of the newer masks had a matte finish. "You happy now?"

"As close as I'll get today," Cathy answered. "Let's see what they got for us down here."

It was hard to get funding for a department dedicated to a problem many believe didn't exist. This was why there was no truck, no centralized office, no real mandate beyond trying to contain this ephemeral thing that the department had taken to calling the Wet. No government above the City wanted to recognize the problem. Cathy knew they made do with the scraps the City provided, often sponsored by funds from the Threshold districts, those corporate-owned sectors of the eastern shore. Most of the money went to the masks. Expensive, fragile, and prone to malfunction, but deeply loved. Jasmine had carved her initials into the forehead of her rig.

Cathy made her way through the lobby filled with abstract orange paintings and sculptures resembling pigs without heads. Jasmine followed behind her to the service door, and they descended concrete stairs together, heavy masks blinking and whirring under the fluorescence. The parking garage walls were slick with condensation. On the bottom floor, Cathy led the way past luxury SUVs and electric cars, letting the readout in her mask guide her toward the source.

"Buddy looked like he was going to have a heart attack," Jasmine said. "I don't blame him."

Cathy knew the Wet was something people whispered about but rarely mentioned in public. There were message boards, hastily deleted accounts, owners and landlords reckoning with this new threat. If the building was officially infected, everyone would need to move out. The accusations would start with the tenants, then the management company, then eventually the developer and whoever they hired to originally build the tower. Then the lawsuits would start.

"He probably hid it as long as he could," Cathy said. "These guys are like cockroaches, they only start scuttling if you turn on a light." One of the sensors in her mask began flickering red and white, a gentle warning of spores in the air around her. "We're close."

Jasmine circled a bright red Mercedes on their right, while Cathy moved forward, her mask interpreting the world around her. It wasn't a bloom this time, emerging from the ground or the concrete walls around them, thick, oozing, and alive. This one was a body, what was once a person. The Wet fed off of it. Cathy didn't look away. Her mask read the scene, recording the data required before they took the first step to contain it.

"We got one. A body," Cathy said. "Whose building is this again?"

"Looks like a Warton development," Jasmine said. Her mask reflected the shuddering body on the ground, splaying it across her silver features. A man, maybe in his mid-forties, breathing in the spores down here in the damp. Something each woman had seen before, catalogued and quantified for those higher up the ladder. Usually the Wet went to work on the soft tissues first, working its way through the face, punching through the cheeks and soft palate. This body was a week or two old. An easy job for two people.

"They aren't going to be happy. What is it, third one this year?"

"Fourth," Cathy said, a new alarm pinging inside her mask. Then another. Each sound stacking itself on the one before it, echoes that became a plaintive buzz. "Or more."

"More?" Jasmine said.

Most cases they tried to catch early, the Wet seeping out of an electrical box or appearing in splotches in an elevator lobby. Something you could manage, spraying it down and wiping it away before it began to produce spores. This was what Cathy thought the job entailed initially — a glorified clean-up crew for the first responders.

"Look closer," Cathy said. The concrete sweat around them. Three lumps in the corner shuddered together, something like a hand emerging from the black ooze, pulsating with disconnected nerves, the smell of old, old water flooding Cathy's senses.

"I never saw one like this," Jasmine said. The body no longer held their interest. The mass in the corner shuddered again, at war with itself, alive under all the rot. "They usually don't stay up here this long. They slide back down into the ducts or the sewers . . ."

Cathy grunted, turned down the alarms inside her mask until she could hear herself breathe again. The systems were overwhelmed. "We're looking at more than one. This is just a mass . . ."

"A mass of what?"

Cathy shuffled toward the corner, the one blackened arm now free from the three piles, scrounging at the concrete, leaving behind a thick trail of grey pus.

"You know what. It was at least three of them."

Cathy circled the undulating mass. She reached into her bag for a fire extinguisher reworked with a powerful, corrosive antifungal spray. They were still trying to get the mixture right. No one had officially approved its application. "Jas, I need you to get your spray out."

She watched Jasmine's hands. They were steady. No trembling or shaking.

"Jasmine. The spray."

When the hand seized Cathy's leg, her mask lit up anew, sensors bleating in her ears. A voice flickering inside her head, trying to make itself known. The mass of bodies, a family who never returned from their road trip to Muskoka, trapped down here in the dark, all trying to speak as one, alive under the mould, shambling toward her body under the coursing Wet, a fleshy shadow rising up like a sunflower toward the light of her mask, curling toward her warmth.

Run.

The word was simple, imprinted onto her mind, a chorus of voices in her head. It spoke even though there was no mouth. The Wet clung to buildings, rotted away the foundations, peeled paint, and split wires. Cathy knew the Wet could infect a person, find a way into their lungs, weaken their immune systems, maybe hospitalize them or leave them slumped in a basement apartment over their cereal, rotting away. It was a toxic mould, unhealthy, but manageable.

Don't help.

And yet it was here, moving toward her, fighting against itself, begging her to run. A hand wrapping tighter around her leg, searching for purchase.

Run.

A cloud of white. Jasmine sprayed the air down around her, the powder settling onto the mass in the corner, drying it out, the voices in Cathy's head turning to shrieks, to mumbles, to nothing, trailing off into a dial tone she couldn't shake. She staggered away into the fluorescent lights as Jasmine continued to spray, moving in arcs around the heaving, shrieking biomass in the corner until it stopped moving, stopped speaking, until Cathy could only hear her mask screeching its warnings, overwhelmed by the presence of the Wet, of whatever it was becoming.

"You okay?" Jasmine stood over her, wreathed in floating white powder. A powerful ghost. Cathy was supposed to be the protector. That was how they knew each other. She couldn't even pull her own trigger, as if the voice was holding her back, seizing some nerve inside her.

"I'm alright," Cathy said, slowly rising to her feet. The voice could have been imagined, was imagined, a new way to process the cluster of bodies slouched together in the corner.

"It reached for you."

"Just an impulse. It didn't know what I was," Cathy said, regulating her breathing. The mask hid the fear. She pulled out her sample kit. "Like a root searching for moisture, it's natural. Did you spray down the first body? We need to make sure we got all of it."

"First body was what we expected, yeah, I got him," Jasmine said. "As for the corner . . ."

"Corner was just more than one, that's all."

Jasmine tilted her helmet, inscrutable. "Alright."

"What?" Cathy said. She walked toward the first corpse, still human even with the stain spreading through its face. She brushed small chunks of the crystallized Wet into a plastic bag, sealing it tight. "This is just more than we're used to, that's all."

Jasmine didn't argue. She gathered up other dry fragments, stuffing them into plastic bags for the overworked analysts back at the department. "What about your leg?"

Cathy looked down at the handprint, now coated white. "Could have been worse."

Jasmine snorted. "Understatement queen does it again."

Cathy smiled under the mask. "That's right."

They talked around the desiccated mass in the corner, working their way through procedure. A small vacuum attached to Jasmine's case dealt with the final bits of dried-out spores and flesh. There would be a separate collection team sent out to gather up the bags. There were only so many masks to go around. There were only so many ways to try to explain their fresh discovery down here. There was no more voice whispering into Cathy's ears.

"Jas, can you go upstairs and call in . . . whatever this was."

Another tilt of the horns. Neither woman spoke. The air between them dripped.

"Okay. If that's what you want, okay."

Alone, Cathy took her time to review the scene, examining the walls, taking notes on her phone, walking the perimeter to document each incursion of the Wet in the corners concealed by Subarus and Land Rovers. No shapes shimmered. Whatever was under the Wet was gone now, pulverized, turned to powder. Cathy headed back toward the stairs without any voices in her head but her own, telling her this was just another job. The voice sounded like she believed it.

3.

Soda learned to love the rain. Rain meant more customers, more fares, more money in his pocket or at least hovering on the screen in his hand. Digits piling up and up, but never high enough, the accumulation an illusion, one he was complicit in perpetrating every time he climbed into his magenta Camry and told himself he was going somewhere.

He only went where they told him to go. Even in the rain, streets swollen rivers, sinkholes spreading through the city like rot, he was paid to divine a sage path home or wherever the fare was headed. This was how he kept the number from falling too fast. The digits plummeted whenever the insurance company took its fee, or a customer complained, or he had to bail his father out again. Every rider offered a new risk versus reward. Soda kept on pushing the levers, sure of a breach in the algorithm he could exploit, a hidden pattern that would save him.

A hand smacked against the passenger-side glass. Soda unlocked the door. His free hand clenched a taser he had bartered for with a teenager in what was left of Parkdale. You never knew who was going to climb inside. The man was already soaked, thick beard drowned, tailored suit close to ruined.

"You know you're supposed to use the app," Soda stuttered. "It's not a cab."

"And stand out there in the rain?" the man laughed. He barely fit inside the car.

"Can you at least punch it in for me so I don't get written up?"

"I thought all you Magellan guys were your own bosses," the man said. "Be your own captain, all of that good shit."

That was the Magellan promise at first, the remnants of the rideshare companies scrambling to cover their market share after so many of the big players imploded. There would be no self-driving cars, no future. There were only people like Soda. Magellan promised to make the transition easier. They were all navigating this together, backed by the financial power of Threshold and its investors. Chart your own course. Soda had the red **M** sticker on the bottom left of his windshield. A freelancer. All he needed was a car, one they were happy to finance and then happy to surveil once all the paperwork was completed, everything signed directly from his phone. His supervisor was a voice and an email address, ticking off infractions whenever a customer complained. A gig that was meant to last a few weeks, but then weeks became months.

"It's nasty out there, man. I don't wanna risk getting trapped down on the subway for an hour. I've got a hundred bucks. Take me north."

Months became years.

"North?"

"North for now, alright? Just drive." The man dropped a single bill into the empty seat.

"You got it."

Soda left the bill alone. No point in looking too eager. He watched the big man slump down as he wheeled into a U-turn, tossing a wave onto the sidewalk. You did what you had to do unless you were down on the eastern waterfront, the Threshold district humming and buzzing with their own surveillance, making note of every fluctuation. To make a better city, a smarter, safer city, that was the line that rang through Soda's brain. A city that owned every action you took, collated, stored, redistributed, realigned, and filed it away for undisclosed purposes. It spread slowly, twisting through the concrete. Technically, Magellan's office was in one of the energy-efficient towers down there, but Soda had never seen anyone behind the desk.

North was simple. There were stranger requests. North was easy. Rogue umbrellas scrambled across the intersection ahead of him. The weather app told him to expect snow, but Soda didn't pay attention to the forecast anymore. Fluctuations came and went, taking entire gardens with them. Frost followed by five days of summer in February. The seasons tilted.

. "I'm sick of this place," the man said. "Deep in my belly, you know?"

Soda avoided conversation. He turned up the radio. After the first month behind the wheel, Soda learned he wasn't only a driver — he was port, tour guide, counsellor, sometimes a priest.

"You know why?"

"Why?" Soda said, swerving around a limping casino tour bus in Chinatown, lights pulsing red as it pumped the brakes. A man on a bike banged Soda's bumper as he nudged into the bike lane before taking off again.

"He speaks!" the big man said. "Good to know you're alive. Thought maybe it was a machine. You ever think about getting killed by one of those streetcars? Or some asshole trying to pass them?"

Soda tracked the headlights behind him in the mirror.

"I'm sick of a place where no one speaks to anybody," the man continued. Soda got lots of these lazy philosophers in the early morning, pontificating on what they believed was a uniquely troubled existence, usually drunk or coming down off a high. The man in the backseat was calm. "Like you don't even know who I am. And you probably don't give a fuck, do you? It's okay, you don't have to answer. My name is Ramji Nolan. That mean anything to you?"

Soda cut across Bloor, avoiding a neon garbage truck, trying his best not to maim students fumbling in the rain.

"Take the DVP, kid. But only if it's not flooded. They'd love it if I drowned down there, make everything that much easier for them."

"You got it," Soda said, driving down into the valley, the line of cars waiting for him. He spotted tents scattered in the trees as he descended into the clogged artery, colonies sprouting up on the higher ground. The City would send its paid squads out there again, clearing out tents and garbage and bodies, always more bodies. Soda was almost used to them.

"Everyone in this meeting today, all they cared about was the name," Ramji said. "The name and whatever bank accounts they imagine are attached. You can see them tabulating your net worth behind their eyes. I do the same thing. I was raised to do that."

"Do what?" Soda said, slinking into traffic between unsuspecting drivers on the slick road. Bright emergency lights ahead. Black smoke fought with the rain, weak flames licking at the pavement. Soda toggled off the radio to listen closer. Ramji's voice wavered.

"To take. To take what you need so you can take more and keep taking. That's what I was taught as soon as they thought I was old enough. Take it while you can, before some other asshole can take it from you. I didn't realize how much you can take though.

"Like today, while we sat there and they told us what we need to do, no, what we had to do if we wanted to succeed with the next round of development. If we want to compete with Threshold, we need to pay the old price again. They told me I would pay the same way my mother paid before me. As if I was only there to hold a place at the table. They want to fill in every little hole. They want to drain me. But they don't know what I know, what I've found."

Soda raised his eyes to the rearview.

"There are things I know. About that price."

"I know," Soda said, trying to soothe Ramji. He didn't want another broken window.

The man's eyes flickered away from Soda, taking in the scene outside. The car hadn't moved in minutes. Emergency lights continued flashing. Smoke choked the sky.

"They followed us."

"No one followed us, man," Soda said. "You're the one who wanted to go this way."

"No," Ramji said, running his hands through thick black hair. "No, this is a setup. This is how it goes. This is how they do it."

Soda considered the taser. The one time he used it the man had a heart attack and shit himself in the backseat. No charges were filed, but the cleaning bill was outrageous.

"Look, next exit, I'll get out and you do whatever you want," Soda said. "I won't even charge you for it, alright? We can pretend this never happened."

"It's a blockade," Ramji said. "They act fast, don't they?"

"Sure, but we aren't going anywhere, man."

"You're not part of it, I can tell. You really believe there is a fire up there though? Someone just starts a fire in a rainstorm? You think it just *happens*?"

"Do I believe some idiot tried to switch lanes in the rain and ended up shredded on the guardrail? Yes, it happens."

23

"I know when I'm being led into a corner. We sat there today on the thirty-fifth floor while they fed me all this shit about working together, all while the screen is telling me what we're really doing."

"It's an accident," Soda said.

Ramji laughed. "I wish it was that easy. Once you see it, you can't erase it. There are consequences to every action, even if you don't see them. All the shit has to go somewhere."

The cars lurched forward. Ramji sounded like Soda's father, so certain of the conspiracy floating around him. Soda kept an eye on the lanes, trying to judge his position. He considered riding down the shoulder, what cameras might catch him, how likely it would get back to his supervisor, and how high the fines might be.

"It's a checkpoint," Ramji said. "A chokehold."

An arm looped itself around Soda's neck, heavily muscled under the tailored jacket.

"Let me out. I don't blame you for bringing me into this death trap, but I won't just hand myself over. They will have to hunt me down."

Soda's eyes watered. His left hand fumbled for the locks. The taser was under his seat, too far to reach. Ramji increased the pressure, whispering into his ear. "Unlock the doors."

After a click, the arm pulled away.

"You keep the money," Ramji said. "And you take this." A hand shoved down his shirt, cold metal against Soda's skin, sliding down his belly. "Share it with whoever you can. If they ask you where I went, you don't know. You never knew. This never happened."

The door slammed shut. No cars moved. Soda watched the man in his three-piece suit flee through the rain, hurdling the steel barrier in one leap, legs carrying him farther and farther into the valley. Soda reached inside his shirt and pulled out a tiny steel USB key. He wanted to toss it out into the rain but recognized the name on it: *MARIGOLD-DUNDEE*.

Cars began to move. Smoke kept rising. Ramji was a speck. A siren sang out from behind Soda as another ambulance muscled past on the shoulder. He turned up the radio, a voice telling him another window had fallen off a tower downtown, plummeting sixty storeys to annihilate a couple on a blind date, right there in the middle of the street. Someone caught it all on video.

§

The house sat on a cul-de-sac, an abandoned hole beside it where some developer had given up on flipping the property. Too close to the lake and the water table kept rising. Dead piles of leaves poked through melted snowdrifts, hardening again in the cold. The garage doors were boarded over, the first-floor windows blacked out. No light in the house, but Soda knew his father was home. There was nowhere else to go.

Soda parked in the centre of the court, his Toyota mounting a berg of scraggly ice. He hadn't picked up any fares since Ramji. He still had a freelance client to get back to tonight, a logo design for a toothbrush start-up that asked if they could pay him in free food deliveries from another start-up across the hall from them in some warren of polished tiny desks down in the Threshold districts. When he sent the first invoice, they asked him if he wanted to get paid immediately by surrendering five percent of the fee. He said yes like the choice was still his.

Soda didn't bother with the front door, reinforced with metal and at least three separate locking mechanisms. He crunched over dead grass to the side of the house where the fence loomed above him, a fence his father was building piecemeal from the water-damaged houses in the neighbourhood. There was no gate, but Soda knew its weak points. He sucked in his gut, pushing his body hard against the exposed brick, shimmying past pressure-treated wood and scraping over the broken glass littering the patio stones behind it. The moon observed him.

"Dad, you out there?"

Anton "Dale" Dalipagic used to work for the City, directing the development of brownfield sites throughout the east end and the more controversial project along the eastern waterfront. He held his position for almost eighteen years, trying to rehabilitate properties abandoned by absentee landlords, numbered corporations, or long-dead owners with wills tangled up in competing lawsuits. A leader in civic engagement and the futures of cities, he was upheld as a pioneer for crafting joint projects between the private and public sectors, unlocking funds and lands previously deemed unsalvageable. For a while at least, until the tail end of some deals with a certain corporation came to light — deals with numbers that bloomed with extra zeroes as the years passed, dollars disappearing into bank accounts often affiliated with Dale's name or his wife's or his son's. When asked to resign, Dale did. Like Soda, he appreciated the illusion of choice.

"If you don't come out, I'll come in there. And we both know you don't want that."

Soda stood in the moonlight as plywood panels shuffled aside. Dale emerged with a grey beard down to his belly, a *Women's 5K Run for the Kure* cap pulled down over his bald head.

"You think I don't know it's you. No one else is stupid enough to come back here. Your mother send you over here? She still telling you I'm not a lost cause?"

They both knew she was dead. Soda didn't correct his father.

"You know what she's like."

"You telling me what I know now, eh? You my little brain in a jar now?"

"You still got a computer in there?" Soda asked. The yard was full of crumbling bricks and stacks of harvested fencing. A pile of old patio sets had been turned into a teetering scaffold for the south wall. "I think this might be something you know about."

"Something I know about? Like how they poisoned all that dirt?"

Soda didn't engage with speculation. It was what the therapist told him to do, back when he could afford therapy. Let him come to you. Sometimes Dale would sit and stare at him for hours.

"Well, what is it, Sam? You drag me out here when I'm exposed at night, which is the time when they can get away with anything, and you tell me . . . wait, you hear that? It's those raccoons again. I swear to god, they want a war, I'll give them a goddamn war. We should be wearing these things like hats."

There were no raccoons in the backyard. As part of this war, Dale burned most of his garbage out of spite, the fence stained black with smoke.

"Dad, I want you to take a look at what's on here," Soda said, handing him the small drive. "I only took a glance at it, and it all goes over my head. It could be nothing. It could be a prank. I don't know. But the man I got it from . . ."

"This more of your self-help shit?" Dale said, trying to hide his interest.

"Some developer guy gave it to me today. I recognized the name. It was information they didn't want out there. He might have just messed up his microdosing. Took a little too much acid before he spent five hours watching PowerPoint."

"They?" Dale said, examining the tiny metal fragment in his hand, running his fingers over the lettering. "There are a lot of *theys* out there."

Ramji could've said the same thing.

"You still got power? Still stealing internet?" Soda asked.

"It's not stealing when you deserve it. What do you want me to do with this?"

He hadn't started building the fences or blocking out the windows right away. It took a year or two after he resigned for the paranoia to sink in, realizing no one else wanted to hire him, not even off the books. He was a man on fire with no one willing to put him out.

"I want you to tell me what it means, if anything," Soda said. "If you can."

"Why?" Dale said. He didn't sneer when he asked. He appeared lucid under the moon, surrounded by his treasures, his building blocks and rotary saws.

"This guy was scared," Soda said. "Even if what he was afraid of wasn't real, the fear was. Maybe you'll know if it's real or not. You know the name. You know who these people are, right?"

"Okay." Dale shoved the key into his pocket, turned, and headed back into the house. "We're going to need to up our security. Get a guard dog. I can't do it all by myself, you know."

Soda slipped back out through the gap. There was no gate. Dale was building a mausoleum, not a fortress. He just didn't know it yet. Dale was the one who could make sense of all the diagrams, the floor plans, and the specifications buried in the subfolders. He would know if there was anything buried in the spreadsheets. Or it might only drive him further into his hole, deeper and deeper into his own mind, where every shadow was a threat, every note a black spot signalling his end. Soda figured it was worth the risk. It gave Dale something to live for, for now. Soda still dropped off groceries on the front lawn every Friday morning, assuming that was when most of the raccoons were sleeping. He tried to keep the bills paid. The few remaining neighbours simply ignored Dale, treated his existence like a myth. The annual floods kept the speculators away. There were stories that the old man might even be a ghost, one who only worked when the sun was hiding, building his own dark tower to blot out the sky.

Soda climbed into his Toyota, closed his eyes. The sun was still a few hours away. He wrapped himself in a quilt. From out there in the dark, he heard his father laughing. A bright and terrifying sound. It soothed Soda. The house loomed over him in the dark. Rain started to fall again, water freezing when it hit the glass. He wasn't allowed to sleep inside.

Suite 605

Malcolm Tremblay's mother told him to live without regrets.
She would've got it tattooed on her chest if she hadn't
been so concerned about what the Holy Father would have said
in the afterlife. The body is a sacred place, she told him. You must
protect it.

Eighteen years in the NHL made his body a little less sacred.
Hit after hit after hit, that's why they called him "Motown" in
Detroit, a blueliner known for crushing young guns over centre
ice — clean, brutal hits the kids shared online, ones that got sent
upstairs for review, beamed off the ice to Toronto, where some
dumb motherfucker would tell Malcolm his shoulder was a little
high. Eighteen years smashing into the boards, throwing hands,
jamming his stick into some dumb Swede's jaw — not a sacred
bone left in his body now, just prescriptions scattered around the
condo and a slipped disc shrieking every time he tried to climb out
of a chair.

"Are you going to walk me out?" Sidney said, her light voice bouncing out of the bathroom.

"And end up on tape? No, you said this was casual," Motown said, stretching out his legs, trying to gather the courage to stand. "You don't want him finding out, do you? All-seeing, all-knowing mother that he is, he probably has bugs in the walls."

"I just thought it would be nice," Sidney shouted, turning off the water. "I always leave. You never come to me. I come and go like you hired me off the internet."

Motown wasn't like his mother. He had plenty of regrets. One of the biggest was buying this condo. He wanted to blame his agent for the suggestion, but his agent was an idiot. Motown knew it was too good to be true, but bought it anyway, assuming it would just be another property to add to his portfolio, back when he had a real estate portfolio and a house in Miami, one that was now under three feet of seawater, officially condemned and written off as part of his original bankruptcy. The condo was the only asset he had left. Even the Muskoka cabin was sold, all furnishings included. Someone else was sleeping in a brass bed engraved with the number fifty-seven.

Marigold was first announced, they had a ...ing ceremony right there on Yonge Street, polit- ., developers, and media scrambling to find the right pitch e project. Some savvier investors could smell the rot. Albert old hadn't built anything new for decades; he was supposed to be a slumlord with an empire that stretched across the city, and suddenly, all the capital in the world had landed in his lap. The ads were big though, bright, warm, and inviting. The sales team focused on people with just enough money to make a mistake, but not quite enough money to afford the years of legal fees required to rectify it if things went south. This included washed-up hockey players, videogame streamers, dentists, eye doctors, and even a couple of radiologists from the children's hospital.

Such a waste.

"If he did see, would that be so bad?" Sidney said, now standing in front of him. She was forty-three but looked twenty-five if you kept the lights dimmed. He didn't care how old she looked, but he knew she did. There was no overhead lighting in the condo. Lamps only.

"Bad for me? No," Motown said, still trying to judge if he could stand. Sometimes his spine was a single nerve twitching against the open air. "But you like your life, don't you? The money, the house. I would like it too. I miss it. You really think you could go back to driving a Honda?"

"He wouldn't do that to me. He still loves me."

Motown shifted, tried rocking himself forward. "You really want to test that?"

"I know him. I've known him for fifteen years now."

"And you think he'll, what, smile and laugh?"

"No, but he'll understand," Sidney said. "He knows how we play these games."

"You overestimate him," Motown said. "I suspect he doesn't give a fuck."

"Now you're being an asshole, Malcolm." She called him Malcolm to keep some distance from his legacy. He wasn't cranking out the hits. He was muted.

"You want me to be an asshole? I can do that," Motown said. "Believe me."

He didn't realize it was a mistake at first, buying the condo pre-construction. He had the money to burn back then, six years ago. It felt like a lifetime, a nasty, brutish, and short one. After the third notice warning him construction had been delayed once again, he started to worry. After he was released from training camp

32

and diagnosed with a chronic hip injury in the press, he worried more. *MOTOWN: THE BEAT STOPS HERE* was the headline online, right up next to stories about small investors trying to sue the Marigold/Dundee Corporation for their deposits. Motown got ejected from his son's house league game, beat the ref into the pavement, mugshot spread across the world, or at least the world that cared about hockey. Electricians stopped showing up to the building site when they didn't get paid. His ex-wife Jean sent him a restraining order with a bouquet of flowers. She just couldn't trust him around the kids anymore.

Everyone knows.

When the building was finally done, relief surged through Motown. He was one of the first tenants. The ancient Albert Marigold even showed him to his suite, remarking on the beauty of the unfinished floors in the hallways, the ambience of the temporary lighting while they fixed the electrical and upgraded the elevators. The old man's mind was seeping out his ears. He called everyone *my child*.

The way Motown saw it, the son ran the show. Stan Marigold, in his early fifties, and only now taking control of his life, climbing over the shoulders of his father's warm corpse into the sun. This would be his building, his legacy, transferring power from one white manicured hand to another, slightly more tanned, manicured hand.

Motown's second day in the unit, his water stopped working. *Unit* was what they called it in the reports he and the building staff traded back and forth. Not a suite, a unit, a slot in the concrete, smaller than what he'd paid for, but had anyone actually read the contract to ensure the square footage was locked in before he signed it?

Every day he was in the building, Motown felt Stan Marigold was fucking him. When the ceiling above his head began to crack and the maintenance guy said it was a natural feature of the unit, Marigold was fucking him. When the dryer burst into flames and torched most of his good underwear, Marigold was fucking him. When the balcony doors shattered in the middle of the night, Marigold was fucking him.

"Malcolm, you talk like that to me again and I disappear," Sidney said.

And now he was fucking Marigold's wife, at least twice a week. He met Sidney at the restaurant on the forty-sixth floor, Sightlines, a name that had changed twice since. It was Hashhaus now, like they were all slumming it for fun at twenty dollars a plate for eggs and toast. Sidney found Motown trying to work his way through the gristle in his steak, making sure he got his money's worth. She placed a hand on his shoulder, asked if he still cranked out the hits.

"You understand that? I disappear," she repeated.

Maybe he wanted that. Stanley Marigold wasn't a great enemy to make, not when he was on the upswing, a hole already dug across the street for Marigold II. Motown was getting tired of sleeping with Sidney, even though she was wonderful, even though she made his heart feel like it at least had something inside it, fighting to break free. Tired because he could tell she was tired. She wanted more, wanted to take him out, show him off, explode her life just because she could.

"So, then disappear. Abracadabra, or whatever."

Sidney slammed the door behind her, a door so thin he could hear her weeping in the hallway, pounding down the thin carpet to the elevator. Maybe she really believed she was invisible. There wasn't enough inside her to sustain a person, that's what she would say, digging her fingers into his chest. Do you even feel that?

He was a single nerve waving like a weed in the concrete living room. He could feel everything, but it all registered at the same level. A cut to his pinkie the same as a migraine, pulsing through his head in the middle of the night, lighting his eyelids up white. Almost as bad as his back right now, planted into the cushion.

Motown pitched himself forward out of the chair, smashing down into the concrete floor. The pain spreading across his face barely registered. Most of his teeth were fake, ceramic and metal. Motown dragged his body across the floor. Sidney didn't know how bad it was. She never saw him curled up in a ball on the floor, his brain lighting up with old images he couldn't file, spinning him through every failure, every missed check behind the net, every time his son phoned the hotel room and he didn't pick up.

He needed another pill, something to dull the hot blade inside his spine. He pulled himself onto his knees, waited to hear Sidney knock at the door, telling him she just wanted to stay here tonight. The pills were in the bathroom, three or four different doctors in different cities. Motown dragged himself through the dark condo to the bathroom while the pain threaded its way through his body. The older you got, the more things stayed broken. Both his ankles popped and crackled whenever he got out of bed. One knee bent in on itself if he stood too long. The last time he took his kids, Kevin and Donna, on a roller coaster, he puked all over them and had to spend an hour winning a giant shark at the ring toss to keep them quiet. The shark was neon green. Motown had never seen that before.

Or maybe he had; if the pain was strong enough, anything was possible. Green sharks, purple wolves, the dead coming back alive to ask him if he really thought he could live with regret. Motown pulled himself up onto all fours and then used the knob to teeter to his feet. Inside the bathroom, he found Sidney's underwear floating in the plugged sink. He opened the cabinet in the dark, afraid of turning on the light. Sound, light, any sensation could pull him deeper into the miasma. His hands ran over the pill bottles, trying to remember by touch. Motown grabbed as many as he could before staggering back down the hall to his living room, stubbing a toe on a fifty-pound dumbbell he hadn't touched in months.

The green shark sat across from him in the living room. The kids hadn't wanted it after all. Kevin said their mom would be pissed if he brought it back to Florida. Donna kept her headphones on, even when she hugged him goodbye at the airport. The shark stayed with Motown, lurking at the periphery of his vision while he watched twenty-one episodes of *Law & Order* in a row. Sidney said it was cute. It gave the place character. The walls were still white. Most of the memorabilia disappeared during the bankruptcy.

A dead man walking.

Motown sat in his chair, teetering on his tailbone to stay alert, the fresh wave of pain giving him enough energy to focus on each bottle, shaking out the dregs of his stash. The shark grinned at him. Motown slammed a palm of Vicodin and a few ibuprofens into his mouth. Sidney wanted him to come out with her, to parade him around like a prize bull, and maybe he wanted to be paraded, to be known for something other than hitting men so hard they shit themselves. That wouldn't happen though, not the way she wanted. Someone was always watching, there were cameras everywhere in the building, pulling in little pieces of his life. It was a surveillance state. Stan likely knew more about Motown than Sidney would ever understand. He wanted them to know he knew. Motown sometimes found envelopes slid under his door, photos at the grocery store or riding the elevator. Photos with Sidney just out of frame, Motown sitting alone at the bar upstairs. Everyone knew, even the shark.

Everyone can see.

A voice in his condo, dripping out from under the sink. A voice of regret, or maybe the shark itself. Motown lurched toward the balcony, dragging the neon shark behind him, heavier than he remembered. Maybe he was weaker now. Motown pushed his way through the screen door onto the tiny balcony, a full five square feet smaller than what was promised in the original brochure. Even now, Stan was fucking him, shrinking his life down one half-assed amenity at a time.

Motown had no legacy left, just this condo, six storeys off of Yonge Street, too close to the morning traffic. He should've bought something higher up, but his life was one large *should*, the real name of regret. Motown stood on the balcony with his nameless shark, looking down on the wet street below. A stupid gesture, a failed attempt at levity to try to undo or erase something his children would not forget. The shark laughed at him again, a treacly noise. His hands shook.

Everyone knows.

Motown reared back to toss his green tormentor to the pavement below. The world swam before his eyes, the pain leaving for a brief second as he pitched forward, spinning toward the faulty metal railing like he had a left-winger lined up behind the net. He swung the shark hard over the side, all his weight following behind it. Motown didn't mean to fall.

Six storeys don't care if you mean it or not.

4.

"What we're talking about here is a new urban centre, a rejuvenated core that will strengthen not only the city but the entire region. A place that brings people together, creating connections and fostering community for the future."

Heads around the table nodded and mumbled. Well-worn, workshopped words, the kind you expected to hear in a room like this, gestures toward a kinder future, one without profit margins or neighbourhood associations. Stanley Marigold stood at the front of the boardroom, the screen behind him filled with bent glass towers sprouting out of a massive urban park, a green mass spreading over the abandoned rail corridor through the old downtown. An attempt to reinvent the public square, or that's what the marketing team told him the night before. The Marigold/Dundee Corporation was looking past Toronto, attempting to control its future once again.

"Thank you for the presentation, Stan," one of the councillors said. The stuffy room murmured its assent. Stan's assistant, Jaclyn, raised her eyebrows. "We appreciate you making the effort to be here yourself. It's definitely, uh, innovative."

"More than innovative," another man said, smiling with no teeth, shirt collar rimmed with years of yellow sweat. Were there no dry cleaners out here? "It's almost inconceivable to see that kind of growth happening out here so soon."

"It's coming one way or another," Stan said as Jaclyn packed up the laptop and projector. He didn't trust the City to have the right aspect ratio. Each transition had to be seamless without appearing overly coordinated. Spontaneous, yet structured. These presentations were meant to nail the objectives without explicitly stating motives. Usually, Stan would have sent his PR team, packed the space with supporters, brought along Hans Mantel, his security man, to ensure the right kind of people entered the room. But this meeting was an early probe, a gentle volley into the outskirts of the city, preparing for the next two decades to come.

While his father raved away in his assisted living facility, Stan wanted to make the stakes clear. Marigold was his company. Only one man made the decisions now.

"They've been saying that for years," Anna Bronson said. "There is always something coming. The same sort of patterns — towers, glass, grass, maybe a playground. The future is always coming, but we're still here either way. We aren't going to magically jump ahead with a new park. I see trees getting planted, and I know they're trying to move me down the block."

Stan turned to face the new mayor of Oshawa. She was thirty-eight, going on thirty-nine, according to Jaclyn's file. Single mother, drove a Honda, used to work Fridays and Saturdays as a masseuse while she was an undergrad. Jaclyn had underlined masseuse, as if it meant anything to him, a card to bluff with in the future. They would need more than that to do any real damage.

"I think you need to see it as a holistic—"

"I don't want you to think I'm being harsh," Anna continued, rolling past Stanley's attempt to redirect. "The fact you came down here yourself speaks volumes to me and the rest of the stakeholders who came out today. I appreciate the chance to speak with you directly. You know we have to do what is best for our communities."

"Of course," Stanley said. The room emptied out around him, a low tide exposing the chairs and bagel wrappers left behind. "We aren't here to do anything on our own."

"I'm glad to hear that," Anna said, clasping his right hand between her own. Stanley had to wait for her to let go. "Please keep me updated on your plans here."

"Yes, of course," Stan said, and then she walked out of the room. He stood in front of the empty chairs and water bottles. He counted to five. His hands curled into fists, uncurled and curled again. He counted to ten, counted to fifteen. Jaclyn waited at the door until he finished counting. The numbers kept coming.

§

"He's dead. Just like you wanted, Stan. All over the stupid internet. People texting me, calling me like they knew it was coming. He's dead. Like an idiot. A big stupid idiot. Malcolm was always stupid, and a coward, what a combination. The coward's way out, right? The way you choose to go tells everyone who you are."

Stan should've brought a driver. They were stranded on the DVP, heading south into the rain. Storms were part of his life now, coming faster and harder than before, delaying construction, occasionally killing or maiming contractors depending on the severity of the wind and quality of the scaffolding. Jaclyn sat beside him as they listened to Sidney's voice in surround sound, speakers enunciating every sigh and shudder between her words until the accusation became a naked transmission.

"Or did you kill him?"

He didn't respond. He let her scour him a little longer, a distant flaying. Part of the game they played together. It was his turn.

"He hated you, you know that? Hated your buildings and your billboards and your father. I tried to tell him you weren't like that, but maybe I was wrong, Stan. Maybe I'm as stupid as he is. Was. He was. Whatever."

A few more cars moved to the off-ramp. Stan followed, foot lurching off the brake.

"Are you even listening?"

The car crept forward. Stan spotted two naked men chasing each other in the valley.

"What do you want me to do, Sid?" he said. "What're you looking for here?"

Brakes flared, bright red. The naked men vanished into the undergrowth.

"How can you ask me that right now?"

"Do you want me to come home?"

No answer. Then a voice spat from the speakers. "Home? Where do you think that is anymore, Stan? Tell me. Tell me which house is home, but I doubt you can fucking—"

Stan ended the call with a swipe of his thumb as cars cleared out of his way. He pulled off the Bloor exit, spinning into the city. Sidney was cavalier about their arrangement. She liked to broadcast their lack of boundaries, the games they played with each other. Long leashes you forgot were there until they pulled up tight, choking you at the edge of their reach.

"I want you to take this up to Lawrence and drop it off. You can do that. I need to get out."

Jaclyn didn't argue. After three years, they had an understanding. Surrounded by towers, Stan pulled the car over to the curb and climbed out into the rain, slamming the door behind him. One of his previous assistants had lost a finger that way. Andrea. He couldn't remember the last name, just the finger. It was a pinkie. The settlement covered it. The PR firm convinced her to say it was an elevator accident in her building. It wasn't a Marigold building.

That was part of why Andrea never worked out. She didn't believe in Marigold, didn't believe in what she was selling. Even if it's a lie, you need to believe it. You have to sever part of yourself to hold two truths at once — split yourself down the middle if you must, but make sure you can exist in multiple realities. Stan was born into this split state, balancing various truths and sacred beliefs based solely on who was in the room.

Jaclyn pulled away in the black BMW, windows tinted a degree or two darker than the law allowed. No one ever questioned it, except for the cameras down in the Threshold district. The notices showed up in the email of the shell company that technically owned the car. The fines were never paid. It was the principle of the thing. He wouldn't let a computer decide what qualified as an appropriate tint, especially not one owned by the rising, faceless competition.

Stan walked through the rain in his pinstripes, letting it soak through him. Most people didn't care who he was, who his father was or had been at some point, before the old man's mind began to feed off itself. The people who loathed them — who filled comment sections and social feeds with vitriol and death threats and drawings of various Marigolds in guillotines, nooses, and boiling pots of oil — they cared. They pulled and twisted his features, exaggerating his chin, eliminating his hairline, making his eyes small and beady. They attacked his websites, set fire to his billboards, turned all his teeth black on subway ads so it looked like his mouth was just a hole. Stan welcomed the attention. They hated the Marigolds, but that hate meant they cared about the Marigolds, what they represented in a shining city like

Toronto. Old white power gone to seed, but still sputtering, spitting, and hacking on its way to the grave. A graceless, irrational, and dangerous thing, that kind of power. Hard to let it all fester unacknowledged.

Stan knew Sidney could let it all go. Maybe she married him for the money at one point, but there were richer men in the city, richer men in the world she could have grabbed. Maybe not now, but back when they first met, Sidney was the one doing Stan a favour. She didn't give a shit about being a Marigold. She passed the same disregard down to their daughter Fiona, three years spent hiding from him somewhere in Europe. Sidney wore the name loosely around her neck like a forgotten charm, a tacky heirloom she didn't need but wore out of obligation. It fit her perfectly in her continual disregard of its significance.

"Watch where you're going," a man snapped at Stan as their shoulders collided, moving against the flow of commuters under black umbrellas.

"Oh honey, I love to dance," Stan hissed into the man's ear. It was fun to pretend he was tough, the swagger of a balloon animal before the breeze hits. The man stepped back and Stan continued on his path to the subway. Sidney's words still stung, a good deep burn he wanted to savour before it disappeared. The small punishments she dealt out were subtle, delicate things he wanted to enjoy alone. He used to keep recordings of her disappointed voicemails, the ones where she mocked his nose and asked if he'd been going to the gym. They disappeared with another assistant, one smart enough to take collateral. The girl worked for a mortgage office now, a spin-off from the Marigold brand arranging financing for new buildings. Creating debt meant creating lifelong customers. Car dealerships understood. You made more from the fees than the purchase. Even when he paid the girl off, Stan kept her on a leash, slack but strong.

Stan had two phones on him. One for work, the one Sidney used, even when she was screaming about her dead boyfriend. Sidney knew she was monitored, she just didn't know how far. Part of the game, part of the taunts. He hadn't killed the goon, barely knew the man's name, but he wasn't sorry he was dead. Sleeping with your wife was one thing, complaining about The Marigold was another. The building didn't need any more bad press. They were still trying to move some suites through undisclosed third parties, disguising the lack of interest with a robust secondary market. The goon still knew some reporters, still had a few friends in the carcass of old media. A small benefit to the loss.

The second phone was private. Even Sidney didn't have the number. Stan didn't share it with anyone. He paid for it out of his own pocket; it didn't show up on the books. Fumbling with his jacket, Stan took the second phone out as he made his way down the wet stairs into the fetid subway, slipping past soaked commuters and the homeless. The smell would get worse with summer, closer to actual rot. People can rot alive. He took a deep breath, savouring the stench, old cigarettes, condoms, bits of shredded wildlife beneath the tracks. It welcomed him.

The platform was almost empty. Stan lurched from one end to the other, drawing up photos on his phone, photos of Sidney with the goon, with her old driver, with herself and no one else. He didn't touch himself, just let it grow between his legs, showing tight against his pants. People waiting for the next train ignored him, eyes downcast. He wasn't doing this for them. As the train pulled in carrying new smells and horrors with it, he paused in the crowd and slid the phone up his sleeve until the wave dissipated, leaving him briefly alone and exposed. He replayed Sidney's accusation again, pushing himself closer to the edge. Was he a killer?

As far as he knew, no, but the impulse was there, the will to throw someone in front of the next subway car. The fact she saw it in him, the fact she wanted it to be true, that kept him hard as he marched to the elevator alcove, running a free hand over dirty tile. The hand with the phone scrolled over her body. He stood facing the elevator shaft. It was broken. Every time the tunnels flooded it made it harder to recover, every new disaster unleashing a new round of impossible maintenance. Stan was safe here in his corner, but still on the edge of being exposed. Here, he could debase himself, let Sidney lash him with her tongue, her long frame spread out over another man, racked by things he couldn't or wouldn't give her.

He felt her pulling that leash again and leaned back into the sensation of being loathed, hated, and thwarted. He didn't need to be whipped or buried under latex. He needed to know he was letting her down. She wouldn't leave him. It was more than money, more than property. Blood ran between them, mutual nooses they'd crafted for each other. He wanted the high so bad he didn't worry about the bottom. Sidney was worth it.

A vibration spread through his hand as another train entered the station, heaving forward. A text appeared over her body, on the phone with a number no one was supposed to know.

We gather in two nights. Ready yourself.

They knew. It was inevitable, all part of the deal his father had committed the family to decades before. Stan understood why his father made the pact. Ethics were a frill, an add-on after the money had been made and the shadows paid. They always found him when the call came down. Using this phone was about sending a message — you are known. It could have been written in the dirt on his window. There was small comfort in that, to be known, even by those you couldn't trust. Some comfort in knowing you were finite. Stan signed, straightening his pants, pleased to find no mess. He had brought himself to the edge without release again. His robes were still dirty from the last meeting.

5.

The sinkhole was eight years old. Some of the kids in Foynes Village assumed it was always there, like the bluffs or Lake Ontario or the one swastika carved into the third-floor concrete on Tower 2. Henrietta Brakes knew better. She remembered the courtyard between the four towers, kids kicking soccer balls as hard as they could at each other, cookouts before the weather got too hot each summer, the sound of Alma's brother screaming as someone pumped a shotgun into his chest and left him spluttering in the centre of the grass, a dying star.

Henrietta was thirteen now, thirteen and waiting for anything to happen on a Saturday night in Foynes Village. The faded caution tape around the sinkhole waved to her in the breeze. There used to be fencing around the pit until it swallowed that too. Every year it expanded another inch. The tape was the City surrendering to its inevitability, giving up on an entire neighbourhood while still trying to appear like someone downtown gave a shit. A band-aid over a gunshot, Henrietta's mother said. More like an arm they refused to amputate, letting it rot in place.

"You going to pout all night out here, Hen?" Alma said. Her face hid under a scarf from the March wind. "You been out here for like an hour."

Henrietta stayed on her perch, one of the stone gates used to dress up this place like it was more than apartment blocks. She pulled a bright pink hood tight against her head, looking up at the towers lurching above her in the wind. Sometimes you could see men throwing air conditioners or TVs into the pit, caught in the light for a brief second before they exploded.

"You got something better to do, Al?"

Alma climbed up to sit with Henrietta.

"Cherry has a whole apartment to himself this weekend. His mom is going to Croatia."

David Cherry, the golden child of their grade. The good boy.

"And he told you that? Like it was a good thing?"

"He's too sweet to know better," Alma said.

"They're going to ruin that place," Henrietta said, shoving long hair behind her ears. "Did Salman tell him this was a good idea?"

"What do you think?" Alma said. "Sal is going to bring whatever his brother is growing."

"So, oregano? Or the stupid robot-dick vape?"

"Better than nothing," Alma said. There was a small cross tattooed into her palm. Stick and poke. Henrietta had chickened out that night, scrambled out of the hot fifteenth-floor bedroom, disappeared down the emergency stairs before it was her turn under the needle.

"They're going to ruin that boy's life," Henrietta said. The sky began to spit. "Let's get there before the cops, I guess."

§

47

Every surface dusted, coasters on the coffee table stacked in fours. A wall tapestry with a mouse chased by an owl across a snowy field. The TV played videos from someone's phone, a series of accidents, kids trying to jump off bungalows on dirt bikes, small children flying like missiles off hot metal slides. Cherry's apartment was a dated lifestyle feed, all muted browns and oranges, selectively ugly. It didn't match the boy.

"Your mom likes owls, huh?" Henrietta said.

Cherry shrugged. His feet shuffled, one knee pumping up and down even as his face tried to remain expressionless. They'd never really been alone together, not even in a crowd. "Yours doesn't?"

"She's more into cows. Dairy cows."

Cherry leaned back into the couch, attempting to disappear. Only a couple older kids had arrived. They sat around the kitchen table, attempting to chop up garbage weed with scissors, stuff idiots tried to grow on their balconies. Alma's grinder broke on the first twist.

"Why cows?"

"She thinks they're pure. Innocent."

"Right, the opposite of owls," Cherry said. "They poop out the bones, you know that?"

On the TV, a horse kicked a man so hard he shit himself and crumpled to the ground. Heavy bass rattled the kitchen. A few more kids came through the front door. Vera Bromley cooked up pizza rolls in the oven, while Jackie Nunes tried to make punch with vodka, Mountain Dew Passionfruit Heart Attack, and canned pineapple juice.

"So, Croatia . . ."

"My great aunt is sick, so it's not like Mom is gonna have fun over there without me. I'd just be sitting around waiting for someone to die. Only old people out there."

"Sounds like my house," Henrietta said. The beer in her hand was warm, still full.

"Oh, I didn't mean—"

The heavy door slammed into the wall.

"What up, kids? Never leave Salman out of the mix!"

Henrietta closed her eyes, waiting for Salman to pass. Salman Duron with the good weed, the kind his brother grew. Salman and his brother were part of a collection of kids who didn't use phones anymore, easier to slip through the city without being tracked, all the digital security companies working with the police to keep tabs on anyone they ever interacted with on the street.

"None of that government shit, we got the real deal bud here, buds," Salman said. He wore a bright Hawaiian shirt and flip-flops, even in the cold weather. An attempt at a moustache trembled on his face. He would never have made the cut without his brother vouching for him. He could be king for a night here though, maybe even for the summer, before the police swept through the towers again in their customized motorcycle helmets and bullet-proof vests, with battering rams following behind them.

"You realize what you've done, right?" Henrietta asked Cherry, gently kicking his pumping leg until it stopped. "You let Salman in here, you better have good insurance."

Behind Salman, a pack of older boys rolled into the apartment, high on whatever they could scrounge from medicine cabinets and backrooms at shitty jobs down in the malls.

"I think I'm just tired. Tired of how I am supposed to act," Cherry said, watching the chaos spread through the apartment. The owl tapestry vibrated as someone turned up the speakers. She knew his brothers had gone with his dad, the family dividing itself in the middle of the night while their neighbours slept. He had chosen to stay with his mother and now she had gone too. "Tired of doing the right thing, trying to be the right kind of person. Tired of being good."

"You want to do the wrong thing?" Henrietta said, placing a hand on his knee. "Right?"

"No, not even the wrong thing . . . just, like, nothing. No hobbies. No stupid little games. To not be good. To not be bad. To do nothing at all," Cherry said. He didn't move her hand.

A glass smashed in the kitchen. Salman told someone to clean it up, they were guests, this was Cherry's place, a sacred space. Laughter spilled out.

"You want to do nothing? Be nothing?" Henrietta asked.

"More like, what if I just let things happen to me?" Cherry said. "Rather than, like, trying to make things go my way, trying to mould how the world is going to happen. To stop pretending I can control any of this. Kind of let chaos take its course. You know what I mean?"

Henrietta laughed. Her own apartment was crowded with bottles, humming with fruit flies, her mother uncommunicative on the couch. "Not really. All I know is chaos."

"Oh," Cherry said, his leg shuddering to life again. "Alright, alright . . ."

"But I think I can help you," she continued, trying not to lose him. "We don't have to just talk about this stuff. That's boring, right? You wanna get out of here maybe, just for a bit?"

"I think . . ." Cherry said.

"Don't think. Don't."

"Okay," Cherry said. "Let's go."

Henrietta stood up. She was taller than most of the boys in the room.

"Al!"

Alma's head popped out from around the corner, eyes already glazed. Half her body was wrapped up in paper towels.

"Yeah, what? I'm going to be a mummy!"

"You're in charge until we get back."

She bowed deeply. "I will protect the Owl Fortress."

Henrietta didn't even let Cherry grab a jacket. They were gone.

§

If the sinkhole added anything to the neighbourhood, it was rumour. Twin boys had plummeted down into the sinkhole a week after it appeared, bodies tumbling end over end as they clutched each other tight. Henrietta never met anyone who actually admitted to seeing that happen, she just heard the stories. A television at the very bottom, trapped and playing the same episode of *Friends* over and over like a distress signal for the rest of the world, warning Foynes Village something was deeply wrong. The pyramid of mattresses and bug-infested couches lurking in its void, an altar for whatever monster lived down there. Superstition written onto the concrete walls surrounding them.

"You ever climb down here?" Henrietta said, prodding Cherry with a finger.

"No," Cherry said, staring down into the dark. "Never."

"Why not?"

"You serious? I guess I just like being alive."

Henrietta smiled. "That makes one of us. You never even considered it?"

Cherry walked around the ragged rim. They were past the caution tape. The courtyard between the four towers belonged to the sinkhole. Even Salman's brothers avoided the hole, believing bad luck lurked at the bottom.

"Maybe," Cherry said. "But you know, you hear stories, you hear stuff . . ."

"Like the mould?"

"That's different, right? Like that's real. People die from real mould all the time," Cherry said. "I don't even go into the basement in my building anymore."

"Probably a good idea in general," Henrietta said. She blew hair out of her face. "Every time it rains, everything smells like a sewer. No matter where you go."

"You've been down there?" Cherry said. "Like really down there?"

Henrietta smiled. "A couple times."

"And?"

"Hard to describe," she said, leading him to a fortified section of the edge, hidden by a few scraggly trees. An improvised rope ladder dangled down the side. "You kind of have to try it out for yourself. I can't tell you everything."

Henrietta watched Cherry bite his lip. He shivered in the wind, tried to hide it. He stalled. She reached out to him, a hand beckoning toward the pit.

"Do it, or don't. I'm going down either way. That's how you do things. New things."

There was a rumour Henrietta's father was one of the pit's first victims. Torn away from Henrietta by the ground itself giving out beneath them, shoving his daughter to safety as the earth swallowed him up with his groceries, never to be heard from again. They said they found her screaming in a ball on the edge of the pit, hands pulling the hair out of her head.

Her mother said it wasn't true at all. She told Henrietta her father abandoned them before she entered middle school. Her mother didn't know where he went, of course, the story always changed. Maybe the West Coast, maybe the other side of the city. Maybe he lived in Hawaii now, enjoying a life without them. Henrietta didn't believe her.

"You do this a lot?" Cherry said, following her down. The sinkhole was more than a single drop, it had plateaus. It wasn't totally bottomless. It only got bigger with time, spreading by inches like a new ocean prodding fragile shores.

"Maybe once a week. People throw all kinds of stuff down here when they think no one is looking. Some stuff doesn't make it all the way down."

It beat stealing money from her mom's purse. Alma had a real eye for it, knowing what they could clean up and post online. She pulled out vintage sweaters with simple stains and metal chairs with tiny flakes of rust. Henrietta was still drawn to the stranger pieces: a wooden rocking horse with its head removed, piles of extra small floral dresses from the '90s rotted together into a fabric boulder, bulky grey computer monitors flickering back to life when you pressed on them.

"You ever, like, find a body?"

Henrietta stood on a wide dirt ledge, halfway in the gloom. She sat on a barely used striped couch Alma had dragged up out of the slop below them on the next level.

"Of a person? No," Henrietta said.

"Of a person," Cherry repeated. "Right, right . . ."

Henrietta hid a smile. "Maybe a raccoon or two."

"Oh."

"They're smarter than you think," Henrietta said. "They wash their hands, they communicate, they strategize, they plan. They run this place down here. They're evolving."

"I bet. What about . . . your dad . . ."

Henrietta let the words slide past her into the pit.

"I don't know. What do you remember from when you were five? Like really? I know what people tell me. People I don't even know saying that they found me. My mom thinks he just ran away. Sinkholes aren't very exciting on their own, you know? They're kind of a nothing. Nothing is hard to talk about, so people invent stories. Some of those stories have dads."

"Like fairytales," Cherry said, eyes skittering to the edge.

"Relax, we aren't going down any further."

"Oh, you think I'm afraid of this? Because I'm a good boy? That's not very fun for me."

"I like a good boy," Henrietta said. "And you should be a little afraid. It's the people who aren't that end up dying. Fear is healthy."

"I'm healthy then. Strong even," Cherry said, stepping toward her.

"Oh incredibly," she said, climbing up off the couch. "Like an ox. Or a bull."

"Too skinny to be a bull," he said, wrapping a hand around her waist. "Or an ox."

"Give it time," Henrietta said, meeting his eyes. "Everything changes."

"I know that," he said, hesitating.

"You don't need to be afraid of me," she whispered.

"I know," Cherry said. "That's why I came down here."

The hand that wrapped itself around Cherry's foot wasn't exactly human. It shimmered, an unstable shadow grabbing ahold of his ankle, jerking him backward. A dark glistening appendage, shedding wet flakes of itself into the dirt. David Cherry didn't scream at first, lips still prepared for Henrietta's touch. His mouth curled as he tipped back, eyes wide in shock, arms pinwheeling to grab onto anything, anyone he could reach, finding nothing but dead air.

Henrietta was too far from his grip in that half-second. Another gloaming hand reached for the back of David Cherry's belt and in one swift tug, he disappeared down into the black below, a single scream, high and bright cutting through Henrietta, slashing through her brain, until she was just a void standing at the edge of a void, her mind searching for the boy who seconds earlier wanted what she wanted, gone like he'd never existed. When she finally screamed inside the hole, no one heard her. She screamed again and again, on hands and knees, looking down into the nothing, pleading for Cherry's laugh to echo out of the dark. Above her, raccoons slithered around the rim of the pit. An imperfect, silent circle gathered in some accidental ritual.

6.

The mask was broken again. Its eyes blinked purple and white.

"I need you to fix it," Cathy Jin said, swinging the mask by its horns onto the workshop table. A silver goat head. "I'm not going back out there naked."

The department office was tucked away on the eighteenth floor of a tower off Richmond and Bay, one filled with engineering firms and non-descript defence contractors who preferred to use numbered business registrations instead of names. Occasionally, visitors from other branches of the public health department would get lost, attempting to find their long-lost brethren, stumbling into drone prototype demonstrations, water filtration labs, or in-depth marketing presentations about infiltrating online anime fandoms for intelligence-gathering purposes.

"Naked?" Jasmine said, setting her soldering iron aside. "You wish you were out there naked. I know you, Cathy. You'd love that shit."

"Not on the clock," Cath said. "Not with what they pay me."

"True," Jasmine said. "Still waiting for them to fix the dish-washer in the kitchen. Tired of washing out everyone's mugs like I'm their mother."

"What would happen if we lost a mask?"

Jasmine held Cathy's mask like a specimen's skull. "Probably need to bench you for a couple weeks until they could shake down someone for the funds. You really run these things down, don't you?"

"I do what I need to do," Cathy said a little too quickly. "Sorry, I know . . ."

"You know what? You're not the only one out there risking your lungs over this bullshit," Jasmine said. Repairing their own equipment was often faster than waiting for the department to act. Even with a trail of paperwork, masks could disappear. "We're supposed to keep every little mess tidy like we're a cleaning service. Keep it in between the lines where it belongs."

"No one has even responded to the report I filed," Cathy said. She could still feel the hand around her ankle when she woke up some mornings. "It's basically just a checklist for them."

Jasmine set down the mask. It watched them through blank sockets.

"I know. But it has to pay off eventually, right?"

Cathy didn't answer. The room was filled with outdated infographics explaining the initial spread of the Wet, detailed breakdowns of hand sanitization procedures on the mint green walls. The kind of walls Cathy knew said *We are concerned about funding. We can't stop what's coming. Fill out a form to explain why.*

"Yooo," Ahmed, one of the other investigators, popped his head into the room. "You got two dudes who look like funeral directors here to see you, Jin. Very serious dudes."

"Is it about the condos? They still trying to get us to create a rating system?" Jasmine asked.

"Don't think they smile enough for that," Ahmed said. "Maybe someone more official."

"Give me a minute," Cathy said, still looking at Jasmine.

"Alright," Ahmed said. He didn't move. Jasmine stifled a laugh.

"Ahmed," Cathy said.

"Yeah?"

"In one minute, okay? Go tell them I'm on my way."

"Oh," Ahmed said. "Oh right, okay, will do."

They listened to him jog down the hall to the meeting room, a glorified collection of folding chairs with a coffee machine and a view of the concrete tower crammed next door.

"He's trying," Jasmine said. "Try to give him a shot at this. He still thinks we matter."

"Yeah," Cathy said. "He's trying something for sure."

"You were never like that?" Jasmine asked. "You came out of the womb savvy?"

"I think so," Cathy said. "My mother definitely didn't help." She laid a hand on the mask, fingers sliding into the eye sockets. "Now fix my rig, Jas. You're my only hope."

§

"We want to understand what you saw," the first man said. His sleeves were too short for his arms, wrists dangling pale above the table. He only identified himself as Robert. No last name, no title. His card simply read THRESHOLD. He wasn't supposed to be here. A curtain was supposed to exist between the city and its latest benefactor. Cathy recognized the man from back when the new corporate district was first pitched to the City. A new form of community, a city of the future built on sustainability, connection, and, most importantly, data. "We want to know what's going on in these buildings, under the surface. What you experienced while you were in the parking garage connects with our own research into the Wet here. We need a firmer grasp of how it operates, a better idea of exactly *what* you are seeing. Not just printouts or modelling analysis. Whatever it is, whatever they are, we can't rely on quantifying it anymore. We need to qualify it. We need someone like you."

"I don't know," Cathy said, one leg propped up on the table, leaning back. "You don't really want to understand me, right? Somehow our report trickled into your hands and now you want me to tell you a story about it. What I felt. You want all the details, a way to name it that won't scare your shareholders, a sequence of slides to explain it to your insurance provider, maybe a way to use whatever modelling we can create for your own needs."

"That's not quite the case, Ms. Jin. We are very interested in the health of this community," Robert said, scratching hairless wrists. "We need to know what this is beyond an abstract threat."

"Well, it kills people, I think we know that now. The Wet or whatever we are calling it this week; honestly, I stopped keeping track. Naming the thing is supposed to control it, right? What it does is change. Constantly. What it wants to do is infiltrate every building, every body, every tunnel in this city. It wants to spread. You're talking to me like I haven't been in this meeting before, like I'm an idiot. I know what an infection looks like. I know what it can do to a human body. I've seen how you people handle this kind of thing. You make it someone else's problem. What would be different this time? You're not even supposed to be here."

The two men didn't reply. Threshold was the first group to openly identify the Wet when it appeared during one of their site excavations. They were the ones who informed the City, provided samples to the universities, created the protocols for the public health department, and advised the City on containment. And then after a few months, they dropped it, moving on to bigger and more interesting problems. A simple toxic mould could only hold so much attention.

"We've told you this before," Cathy continued. "Same response every time. No follow-up. Indifference. Shrugs and runarounds. Equivocating. What's different this time?"

Robert coughed. "Equivocating is a rather strong way of putting it, Ms. Jin."

Silence hung between them.

"Just tell us what happened, Ms. Jin," the other man from Threshold said. He hadn't given a name or a card. His sleeves were tailored but fraying. An old suit. He wrote everything down on a legal pad with pencil. Cathy's department was supposed to be kept at arm's length from these types, yet they were here, asking her questions. They decided on what was advisable. The City just reacted to their whims. "We want to hear from you directly. Your own words."

Cathy's clasped hands became a single fist.

"I believe it was a man," she said. "To the best of my recollection, this was . . . is this being recorded?"

The frayed sleeves nodded. "I hope you understand why."

"Sure, we all need to cover our asses," Cathy said. The man smiled. "Okay, so since this is being recorded, I want to state on the record that everything we did down in that parking garage followed the guidelines, and I take full responsibility for whatever outcomes may spring from our actions. My partner at the scene, Jasmine, only followed my orders and instructions."

"No one is accusing you of anything," Robert interjected. "Honestly, this is solely a fact-finding mission for us. We want to skip the bottleneck. We have come directly to you as a sign of respect. We technically shouldn't be here at all. And yet, we are. We are here."

"What if you don't like what you learn?" Cathy asked.

"Then we will deal with it," the frayed sleeves answered. He leaned back, spreading thin arms wide, projecting himself as open and understanding. "We aren't the police. You know this. More than ever, we need people like you to help us understand the Wet, what it might become. We figured it was just mould before. We need you to tell us why we were wrong.

"We are here because this is what is required at this time, this is what this city needs. We don't care about your politics or allegiances. Right now, you're simply an observer. You are the eyes. The only reliable eyes we have access to in this case. We're not here for your funding. Those who sent us only answer to themselves. And we believe you want what we want, Cathy."

He turned a page on his legal pad with a flourish and continued.

"To understand. And we are going to give you the latitude and resources to do that, with whoever you need. Money, yes, but also the power to make decisions. Isn't that what your reports always say? No resources to follow up. No one to help you understand what the Wet wants. You don't need to be afraid of us. We want the same things. It's a slow process though. We can't have it appear like we are snatching you from the City. We need some assurances from you too. We need you to need us. So, I'm going to ask you again. I'm going to do it kindly. Please tell us what you saw down there, what you felt. Even the pieces you think you can't explain. All the parts that don't make sense. Tell us what you saw."

Cathy Jin opened her mouth and the whole world spilled out.

§

Sometimes she slept with the mask on. Like a baroque CPAP mask, it soothed her, kept certain dreams at bay. No matter what came through the door of her apartment in the night, she would be able to face it without fear. Sometimes she woke up with the mask pasted to her skin, sensors bleating, eyes lighting up the room purple, orange, green. Eventually, they would cycle around to a pale blue, the tiny centre of a flame. She wanted to be like that flame, necessary, insistent, ephemeral all at once.

Cathy sat alone in her kitchen, waiting. The repaired mask sat on the table beside her, mute and shining, unsuited to its surroundings. Cheap floral backsplash, laminate flooring, off-brand appliances from the landlord's cousin's import/export business that never seemed to be open. The oven only worked on the broil setting and one of the burners smoked whenever she tried to boil water. Take-out containers teetered on the counter.

Cathy kept the rent-controlled apartment in the divorce, after her husband Jeremiah fell for one of the interns in his office one summer while Cathy undertook new safe injection site training. A thing that only happened to people in TV or a movie, but not you, until it does and you're left standing in the kitchen of your ancient rental, pitching commemorative beer steins onto the floor because sometimes rage needs a vessel. For months, she saw pictures online — Caribbean wedding, new house in the mountains — until Cathy deleted all her accounts, sequestered herself away from the world. The intern was pregnant, a dream they once had that had withered, wilted. The photos said there are things you can never give, things you can't imagine. The knock at the door was expected.

"Go ahead, open it up."

Jasmine entered the rental, looked around the kitchen. Cathy was trapped here, the captured rent so low that moving would mean leaving the city all together. Jasmine knew this too. She often made this point when the neighbours were screaming or when the dog down the hall took a shit on the emergency stairs in the summer. "We need to get you a cleaning lady."

"I clean once a week, it's fine."

With delicate fingers, Jasmine picked through the half-finished take-out boxes and empty beer bottles, trying to give the stale chaos some order. "'It's fine' is what people say when it's not fine. No one says it's fine when it's actually fine. Hasn't ever been recorded anywhere."

Cathy didn't meet her eyes. She spun a beer bottle on the table. "You want something to drink?"

"I brought my own," Jasmine said, pulling a bottle of red out of her purse, a tired magician. "Not stupid enough to risk your fridge."

"That's not fair. You haven't even looked inside."

Jasmine crossed her arms and stared.

"It was one mouldy potato. One time," Cathy said.

"And why was it in the fridge? That's the bigger question," Jasmine said, unscrewing the top of the bottle. Cathy didn't own a corkscrew. "What would your mother say?"

Cathy's mother mainly lived in her phone as a series of unanswered voicemails, photos of distant relatives, and recipes she would never attempt. "Hard to say. I wanted to preserve it."

"Do you know how long it takes a potato to go bad?"

"Not too long apparently."

"A very long time, Cathy," Jasmine said. "And when it does, it smells like death. Not figuratively. A rotten potato is basically a corpse. In your refrigerator."

"You're the expert in corpses now, eh?" Cathy asked.

"You really want to split hairs?" Jasmine replied, half-heartedly looking for a glass before pulling straight from the bottle. "You think I don't see what you see out there?"

"No, you're right . . . I just . . ."

"What did those guys want with you today, anyway?" Jasmine asked, placing a hand on the mask, dimming its blue glow. "You forget to capitalize someone's name again? They want to pretend the building is perfectly fine and wash it out? Make the issue disappear."

"Well, they weren't cops. Weren't even health department. It was Threshold, sent I'm sure with the mayor's blessing. They weren't stupid. They want to protect their investment, their whole vision for the city. Doesn't matter what it says in our handbook about arm's length."

"What did they want to know though?" Jasmine said.

"How bad it is."

This was something they talked about when they were drunk together, how the world might end, or how it kept not ending. There had already been a pandemic and the world keep spinning. Maybe a flash flood out of mythology, Atlantis spread across the globe. Raging fires sweeping across the plains from the west, scorching the earth, draining life until only ash remained. Food exhaustion, disrupted shipping lines, riots in the streets. Jasmine preferred the ones with human actors like that. Nuclear detonations, followed by waves of radiation. She liked to plan their retreats. Somewhere north, somewhere with an A-frame and enough land to keep a couple of goats fed. She could talk for hours about goats. Two bottles of wine could get her to that place.

"What did you tell them?"

Cathy preferred the natural disasters, the unfeeling end of things, humanity as a passing fad on a planet that only carried them like a dog carries fleas. The weather flexed and spasmed without regard for seasons. The climate happened to you. Cathy saw it accelerating, a world reclaiming itself from people, reasserting its power like a tree pushing up through the asphalt, fungi springing from corpses, smaller, stupider lifeforms finding their place under the unwavering sun, no kingdoms left, just a rotating sphere.

"That it's not just mould. It's a fungus, sure, but not like any we've dealt with," Cathy said. "Not just affecting buildings, not just giving a few people a cough. It's spreading into people. That was what I felt down there. That was what you saw too. And it's not going to stop. The City will keep hiding it. They have no real choice. One lie reveals the rest, right? The longer they neglect it, the worse it is going to get. And Threshold, they're invested too. They want to understand it. Slow it down.

"The first body, I thought maybe was just an anomaly, a sick man or a hallucination. But I know you see what I see out there. You were the one who stepped in."

"It didn't touch me though," Jasmine said, setting down her bottle. "It touched you."

"It spoke," Cathy said, beginning to shake.

Jasmine kneeled down beside Cathy, wrapping her arms around her.

"It's alright, it's alright. You can tell me."

Cathy stopped shaking. Her beer was empty. The apartment only smelled like Jasmine now, everything else was a broken transmission. "They want me to find its source. Where it's coming from, what's making these . . . things."

Jasmine pulled away. "So, they admit someone's responsible? Even if they won't say it publicly."

"They don't know. They want to be sure. And they are willing to pay me. Pay us."

Jasmine leaned against the wall. "The department won't like it. They don't even want us speculating. This was only supposed to last for a couple years. They are winding us down. Sweeping it under the rug."

"They won't need to know," Cathy said. "Threshold will cover for me."

"For us, you mean," Jasmine said. "I know you're going to do it, no matter what I say. I hate that I know that. And I hate the idea of you down there alone, digging for them. Won't happen."

Cathy only smiled. She didn't trust Threshold, but the money was a lifeline, a way out of this place. And she did want to know what touched her, why it spoke, what she heard inside. *Run.*

She could want two things at once — to know and to leave. To be acknowledged and left alone for good. The city encircled her like a snare, but Threshold could cut her loose. All they asked was for her to remain in the trap a little longer, to get right up to the edge of that horror underneath the ground before they yanked her free.

"Put on the mask," Jasmine said. She turned off the lights in the kitchen. The wine was gone. "Put it on so I can see you."

The mask slid off the table, pushed onto Cathy's face. The eyes went purple again. The horns scraped against drywall as Jasmine kissed the ceramic frontpiece between the silver metal, pressed her tongue to its cool touch. Cathy didn't move as Jasmine pulled her shirt open. She let her work her way down Cathy's body, let her find the places she knew would light her up. The mask stayed as the minutes passed, her breath rising and falling, body bucking against the wall, eyes blinking alone in the dark even as she came.

Suite 1212

Maddy Scapes wanted to move.

show feet

    The lease was twelve months starting in December. The first few months were peaceful, but now certain clients knew where she lived. Some lurked outside the building after they finished work downtown, attempting to catch a glimpse. One was a lawyer at one of the Seven Sisters, another called himself a dynamic management consultant. One of the worst did something for a food delivery app with a neon blue gorilla logo. A beginner's mistake on her part, a piece of mail just in the frame on her fridge one day, the cost of doing business without supervision. Maddy tried to focus on her streaming career instead, avoiding the flesh and blood connections she'd established in grad school. Sometimes her life felt like it was only consequences.

Maddy ignored the flurry of messages on her screen. Feet were the least of it. Donations had peaked an hour earlier, down to a trickle now. She was done for the night. Maddy placed her running shoes up in front of the screen and leaned back, let them stare at her for a few more minutes before she went dark. Maybe closer to morning, but the sky was still black, the open pit across the road a promise of more steel and glass to block her view if she signed on for another year in this giant, leaning tower.

Lights flickered across the skyline. You were never truly alone with your thoughts on the twelfth floor, not even in a tower this anonymous. A few unknowable windows watched her back. She turned the ring light off. Maddy was twenty-six and each day seemed to add a year, bleeding into the next until the past was a shapeless thing that limped along behind her.

show feet show feet show feet

She used her left shoe to tap the mouse and the screen went black. Weeknight streams were easier. She didn't need the full array of dildos laid out on the bed behind her, all the vibrators charged and ready for action if required. Sometimes she kept the largest devices in the closet, out of sight, out of mind. Weeknights, she tried to control the tempo; let the men speak to her, share their insecurities in anonymous chat windows, and publicly flagellate themselves out in the open where the rest of the audience could see. People wanted to show you their wounds. They wanted a witness.

A thud in the hallway, two voices competing with each other.

Maddy climbed out of her ergonomic chair, pulling shorts up over her shoes and a red hoody off the couch. It read *POWER TRIP* across the front, a gift from an old client. She crept across the room to the door. Usually no one else on her floor was up this late or early or whatever you called the nonplace of 4 a.m. Sometimes it felt like the walls spoke to her. You could taste it on your tongue, a sticky treacle dripping behind the drywall. Maddy pressed her ear to the door. There was no peephole.

"This is my suite, Hans. He gave it to me!" a woman's voice barked.

"Everyone agrees it's yours, Sidney," a man said, voice too calm. "We just don't think it's safe. The suite isn't clean yet, we don't know exactly what's going on. But you can't stay here."

"I can hurt a lot of people," Sidney said, softer, retreating. "I can tell someone."

Hans's voice was patient. "Of course, you're the one running the show, aren't you? We've got a car waiting for you downstairs. This suite is off-limits. You can take it up with Stan if you want. The driver will take you back up to Rosedale."

"You think I wanna go back to that house?" Sidney slurred. "How many houses can one man have? He doesn't even know how many he has, Hans!"

No response from Hans. Maddy pressed herself tighter against the door, chewing the string from her hoodie. Nice to have a distraction, escaping into someone else's mistake on the twelfth floor. The sound of more men moving in the hallway, moving in on Sidney.

"Quietly," Hans said. "I don't want to hear about this tomorrow."

Shuffling bodies, the hiss of a radio. An elevator dinged.

"He doesn't even know who lives here!"

Another ding and she was gone. Silence for a few moments. Maddy cracked her door open. Another door was open at the end of the hall. She didn't know anyone on the twelfth floor, that was part of the appeal, why she had signed the lease in the first place. Somewhere high above the street with security and a front

69

desk for packages. High-powered internet tapped off the lakeside Threshold facilities for a steady connection during her eight-hour sessions, although sometimes flooding cut her power. She paid rent in cash, leaving as few signatures as possible. Her landlord didn't even know her real name. Sometimes Maddy even forgot it.

She took a few steps down the hall, waiting for another door to open, someone to stop her. She passed one door and then another, floating over the heavy carpet. The Marigold didn't skimp on everything; the carpets really were amazing. Maddy's unit only had bare floors. The previous tenant had left an iron bedframe behind. She adapted to it, made it part of one of her sets, rigged up in a Goth Christian affect — the watered-down American style, not the old Catholic stuff. A lot of black and purple drapes. Last week it had been a pink spaceship, beaming up her subscribers.

Worthless. You know what you are.

The door called to her in a low voice, the same voice that crept out of the crack above her bed. The door was tilted, maybe on broken hinges. Someone had to close it. She didn't spot the camera tucked under a bit of dark woodwork above the door at first. Maddy might not have noticed it at all if she wasn't used to sweeping rooms for recording devices, men trying to capture her in their two to five minutes of glory. What the camera saw, it could not unsee and so Maddy backtracked down the hall. A low moan emerged from the darkness behind the open door, deeper than the voice, a low bass note that pressed into the bottom of her skull. She'd heard this noise before, made it once or twice herself. The sound of defeat, a low note of surrender you couldn't ignore. Maddy Scapes pretended it was not 4 a.m. and that the hallway was not bright and flickering, that the carpet was not so unnervingly plush, the walls not so thin. The door at the end opened, yawned, swung wide now to deliver an absence, a void that pushed a man out from it, a man with a small black mask over his mouth.

He moved as if he was barely interested in the process of walking, drawing closer to Maddy without effort, even as she pretended to just be stumbling home in her hoodie and sneakers, entirely unaware of whatever was going on at the end of the hall, that low moan behind the door that infiltrated her mind.

"You're up late," the man said, pulling off his mask to reveal a generous smile. His bald head glowed. "My name is Hans, by the way. Everything okay?"

"Oh yeah, just needed to get some fresh air," Maddy said. Her door opened and she crossed the threshold, as if that would protect her. The man was no vampire. He would enter if he wanted. Maddy knew many men were only constrained by the threat of observation. Even men like this, with polished skulls and a swollen right hand.

"Places like this can drive you crazy," Hans said. His jacket rode up, displaying an empty holster at his waist. There were a few razor burns at the top of his chest. "You stay inside all the time, you start thinking nothing else exists."

"For sure," Maddy said, doorknob still in her hand. Hans spread his hands over the edge of the door frame, thumbs slipping inside, daring her to chop them off with a quick slam he knew she couldn't muster. "Balcony doesn't cut it."

"You're telling me," Hans said. The smile was apparently permanent, painted onto his shaved head. "I think mine is technically unsafe, but you try telling that to management."

"Oh yeah," Maddy said, wondering if she could make it the five steps to the kitchen for a knife or a ladle before he caught her and dragged her back down the hall toward that door with the tiny blinking red eye above it. "Since that dude fell though, I think they'll listen now."

"Oh, Motown? He was an idiot," Hans said. "Never adjusted when the league got faster, didn't even try to change his game. You have to adapt. Kept throwing fists even when the coaches were screaming to get him off the ice. Not surprising he couldn't hack it anymore."

Hans's thumbs were too clean. Maddy knew there were knives and a can opener and a blender she never used in the kitchen. Maybe his hands could fit inside it, their flesh turned into a slurry if the bone didn't shatter the blade. It was a fancy blender.

"Right," Maddy said, inching the door forward. "Well, it's sad either way."

"Look, anyone gives you a problem in here with whatever . . ." Hans glanced over her shoulder, taking in the living room/kitchen/ dining room/den space, all of it a blank canvas she hadn't claimed. He sniggered at the air like he knew what she was. "I want you to come and talk to me first. I know the owner. He's sort of like my boss."

"Of the unit? I thought he lived overseas — I met with a broker," Maddy sputtered, already regretting the words.

"Oh, ha, no," Hans said, at ease. He made no move to head back to the door at the end of the hall. He watched her squirm and smiled. "I mean the building. His building. At the end of the day, he decides who comes and goes."

"Oh, the old guy," Maddy said.

Hans cocked his head. "Old man is pretty checked out now. Marigold the younger is calling the shots now, probably even set up that broker you met. He's got all kinds of plans for this place, wants it packed before the new one pops up across the street. Don't worry, I'm sure he knows what's going on here. Takes all kinds to live in a city like this, Stan knows that. You know I used to be a cop? He saved me from that shit."

Maddy nodded, the same kind of tactics she used with clients who decided to dump their life story into her lap, begging her to stroke their hair.

"You ever get a namesake, you wanna protect the name," Hans said. His teeth were capped, she could tell, a mouth rebuilt from the ground up. She'd considered the same procedure. "So, whatever you think you heard or saw here tonight, I want you to know it's okay. No one is going to come around asking questions. Except for me, alright?"

He smiled on the last word, let it hang between them like a knee between her legs.

"Right."

"This place is its own little world," Hans said. "Easy to lose perspective."

With that, his painted smile disappeared behind full lips, thumbs sliding from their precarious perches inside the door frame. "We know it takes all sorts to build a community. Boss is always looking for new business opportunities."

"That sounds great," Maddy smiled. She closed the door as slowly as she could, right leg shaking as she kept the rest of her body still, teeth exposed in the grin she used even when she felt herself ripping apart. "If it ever comes up, I'll let you know."

"Remember it's Hans. Hans Mantel. Like a fireplace."

Show feet with us.

The door closed. She listened to him turn back down the hall, headed toward the low sound. When she could no longer hear padded footsteps, Maddy flipped the deadbolt and backed into the centre of her living room/kitchen/dining room/den space — it was small and now somehow smaller, not quite a cell. More like a room in a wizard's tower. A voice, the same low voice, whispered to her from the vents; she ignored it. She shut her eyes, but the pink light still found a way inside, curdling into something darker within her brain. The crack in her ceiling dripped.

Be with us, the voice said. *Worthless.*

7.

S oda used to think of himself as a competent man, someone you could trust with a pet or a child. The kind of guy who paid his taxes on time and didn't conceal anything from the government. A man who claimed every credit he could, but never misrepresented himself. A man who went twenty over the limit on the highway like everyone else, who didn't spread his legs on the subway unless he was drunk, who owned an electric iron and knew how to use it.

Time chipped away at that self-perception. Time and failure and a litany of close calls with other lives, other versions of Soda out there, Sodas who owned houses, Sodas who travelled the world, Sodas who never worried about overdraft fees or minimum payments or collection calls trying to break him like a wild horse. Soda never saw himself driving around this city for so long, fares sent directly to his phone, shuttling drunks and assholes and people trying to get to work after the subway was set alight again. He didn't see himself scraping puke out of the little runners that let the seats slide back and forth, or pissing into bottles while sitting in traffic, too haggard between fares to climb out of his Camry. It was why the other drivers called him Soda.

Everyone kept telling him self-driving cars were coming, but they didn't see all the fender-benders, catapulted cyclists, and near-death experiences that filled his days downtown. Self-driving was a fantasy, like living on Mars or owning a home in the city. Every step forward involved taking two more back, his nomad colleagues out here parked under bridges during the rain to catch some sleep, showering at local gyms that didn't check IDs, making deals with the FODDER delivery guys, who suffered even worse than Magellan drivers, swapping fries for rides and trying to make rent, even if it was just a hole in the wall of what remained of Parkdale or the far outer boroughs, isolated by the very structure of the city.

"So, you've been a freelancer for how many years?"

Another job interview. Another opportunity.

"Seven or eight, mainly just website redesigns and some start-up stuff. For a while it was like everyone was trying to start a weed company, but they all disappeared. Not great for repeat business."

"Yes, we saw your portfolio. Impressive collection," the woman said, smiling. Her name was Almond. She'd likely gone through her life besieged by baking puns.

"We do have some concerns," said the man in the glass interview room. Stale doughnuts on the table, people already so full they left food lying around. Part of your twelve hours a day in the Threshold district, grinding it out for the perks. "We have a couple of concerns about stability. One thing we all care about here is growth. Real growth. We don't have a five-year plan — at HappenDeals, it's a twenty-year plan."

"Right, of course," Soda said, trying to avoid tugging the collar around his neck. The suit was too tight. "I think the problem is it's a struggle to find anything full-time. Mainly contracts now."

"Mainly contracts?" the man said. He was older than the woman, his name was Dave, and he wore a bright pink shirt with the top two buttons undone, a shaved chest underneath. His blue eyes narrowed. "Have you considered looking at them as opportunities? You got paid, didn't you?"

"We need to understand where you're at now," Almond cut in, trying to slow the interview's descent. "And where you think you'll be if you're working with us."

Soda had to piss. This was the second interview for the HappenDeals junior graphic designer position. Before that, there was an at-home design test he took at the library, panicking as the internet slowed to a chug while he uploaded his submission. Before that, a multiple-choice questionnaire asking you to rank abstract concepts like hope, strength, and drive. Hundreds had likely applied for this position.

"You're right, I don't want to make excuses or misrepresent myself," Soda said. "I want to be honest with both of you. I do see HappenDeals as part of my long-term future, one where I can enhance my original skill set, but also expand upon it by working closely with my colleagues, learning new ways to approach challenges, take advantage of opportunities, minimize risks, and create new strengths that synergize with the company's stated goals and forward-thinking philosophy. Growth is the very nature of being, right? So why not growth at a company? I don't want to follow anymore. I want to lead. I want to work with the trailblazers."

Dave leaned back in his chair, letting the reorganized word flow of his own job posting wash over him. They watched Soda twist himself into the shape they wanted to see. Soda was running out of time for the parking spot outside, the Camry in danger of yet another tow. Threshold monitored movements to the millisecond, every square foot accounted for at all times. Dave and Almond appeared to have all the time in the world.

"That's wonderful," Almond said, keeping an eye on Dave. Soda could tell this was the whole reason she was inside the room. "Now, you do understand this is an entry-level position?"

"Of course," Soda said, clock above them ticking off seconds. He kept his phone in the pocket even as it vibrated, tight against his thigh.

"And you understand the six-month contract period to start?"

"Yes, definitely. You laid that out clearly in the first interview."

Dave snapped forward, hands sliding across the table. "This is a different interview."

"Of course," Soda said, holding his knees down to keep from shaking.

"All I mean," Dave said, "is that things change quickly in this business. Day to day, we never know what may be coming down the tubes. You need to be reactive and proactive at the same time. You ever do that, Samuel? Keep two ideas in your head at once?"

Two realities, both of them leading down, down, down.

"Sure, all the time. That's part of freelancing."

"Looks like we're out of time," Almond said, trying to smooth out the rumples in the room, to make one reality stick in this place, an emptied-out slaughterhouse that still left the tang of pennies on your tongue. They shared the space with three other companies all leasing it from one of Threshold's subsidiaries. "I want to thank you for taking the time to see us today."

"Well thank you for having me."

Soda walked across the slaughterhouse floor past rows of people five years younger. He grabbed a handful of toffee candies from the front desk on his way out. Dinner for later.

The Threshold parking enforcement officer was already punching in the ticket. The City had handed over many of its responsibilities in the district to its corporate partner, offloading services to bring down its towering budget. The mayor's office was happy to hand off the responsibility.

"Ah, excuse me," Soda spluttered, tie choking his tongue.

"You think the rules don't apply?" the woman said, mirrored sunglasses unable to hide the snarl of her lip. Her uniform was a crisp black, the Threshold logo a small yellow portcullis on her chest. Usually, they farmed this work out to subcontractors in more garish outfits.

"I'm only like a minute over," Soda said, pulling open the door and tossing his bag inside. He wanted out of the sodden suit. "I was just trying to get out of there and—"

"All day I listen to excuses, you'd think it was my job," the enforcement officer said. She was six inches shorter than Soda. Height was irrelevant. She had the ticket machine and the stun gun and the sunglasses. Most Threshold enforcers weren't allowed to have actual guns, although the City was slowly handing over those more dire responsibilities. All Soda had was sweat. "All day. Do you know what your file looks like, Mr. Dalipagic? Do you know how many violations we've let slide due to weather conditions? We've got pages and pages of near catastrophes you've caused down here. They add up."

"Come on," Soda said, failing to undo his tie. His fingers dripped.

"Too late, bud," she said. "I'm just following the rules. Collecting on the bill you've run up. You've got a job and so do I."

"I can't afford this right now," Soda said. "Can we fix this?"

She finished writing the ticket, jammed it under his wiper. "You can tear it up if you want. Won't change anything. It's in the system with the rest of your file. You'll figure it out."

That's what they all said to him, every time he tried to reach out, tried to connect with someone from his past who'd learned the secret handshake at a design shop or absentmindedly stumbled into some plum position in a corporate hierarchy downtown. You'll figure it out, Soda. You'll make it work. You can beat this. They ignored the app dinging on his phone, the piecemeal freelance gigs, the fact his car was always leaking something, that his laptop only worked when it was plugged into a wall. His phone pinged.

Dear Samuel Dalipagic,
We regret to inform you that

He didn't need to read any further. HappenDeals didn't waste any time. They had so many bodies to review, they would go with whoever bent furthest. This is what Soda told himself sitting on the hood of his Camry. This is how he kept the world from crumbling. The urge to throw the phone was powerful, even as the enforcement officer climbed into her black SUV, yellow portcullis emblazoned on the door. His hand trembled. He needed the phone. It tethered him to everything. He waited for her to leave. The rage had to dissipate.

It didn't. It collected in him like old rainwater. He grabbed the ticket off his car. It was a hazard of the job, something Magellan insulated themselves from by hiring everyone as contractors, throwing all responsibility and liability onto the drivers. There were no new ideas, just new methods to dodge regulations.

Soda stuffed the ticket in his mouth and began to chew. It tore into his gums. He took another bite, staring at the faceless warehouse filled with strivers. Growth for growth's sake until they died from the stress. The ticket in his teeth, slippery, tasting like glue. He gulped it down, let it cut his throat, seeping into his bloodstream. The enforcement officer was gone but the Threshold systems still watched him, even if the buildings didn't return his gaze. No more striving. No more dreaming of great things. The Camry was his home.

Come see the TRUTH.

Another text. Soda read his dad's message and plucked a piece of the ticket from his teeth. Ink sat on his tongue. It wasn't an invitation. It was a command.

§

Soda didn't have any terrible trauma originating from the early days of his short, insignificant life. There were no major psychic wounds planted at a young and tender age. He had fallen down the porch stairs, lost a tooth to a tree branch, slipped during an unfortunate incident with some ranch dressing in the kitchen, but none of these injuries lasted longer than a couple weeks. The things in his life that had gone wrong happened gradually, building up like so many leaves in an eavestrough.

He parked the Camry in the centre of the cul-de-sac. The houses looked the same as the week before; they didn't get worse suddenly. This too was gradual. A few homeowners pretended nothing had changed, that their basements had never filled with sewage, their attics never overtaken by wildlife. The open pit beside his father's place was now a darker shade of green, the weeds a little longer. Soda walked up to the slumped fortress. The front lawn now had metal stakes inserted haphazardly, like the old man was trying to summon lightning out of the sky. Only a year ago someone would've called a by-law officer. Soda made his way around the back of the house, sliding between chunks of corrugated tin, always prepared for a fresh obstacle.

"Dad? I know you're home. I got your text. You still keeping the phone in a can?"

A coffee can buried in what was once his mother's fire pit. Dale had to apply for a permit to get that pit approved, one that he leveraged with some force when he was at the City. Part of the downfall, another incident added to a list of petty crimes. Dale used it more like a mailbox than a phone. A series of extension cords easily revealed where it was hidden beneath dead pine branches snatched from neighbourhood trees. Not all his schemes made sense.

"You didn't call it, did you? I won't answer." The voice was inside the house. Sometimes Soda believed his father knew this was a fantasy gone too far. He held onto delusion because letting go meant reckoning with what he'd become.

"Once they hear your voice, they don't forget. They remember who you are. You live forever on their servers. They own your voice then," Dale said, emerging through the backdoor, shirtless. "They make it their property. You saw what I did out front with the poles? I don't need to explain it to you I hope."

"If you did, would I be your son?" Soda said.

Dale laughed, tears streaming down his face. Soda was used to these displays, the pitch and yaw of his father's emotional state throwing his life into chaos. It was hard to hold down a job when you spent hours each week trying to keep a man you loved from ending up in prison or the hospital. Soda had created a forcefield to protect himself from the debris, personal shrapnel that winged past his skull into the dark.

"Son, you brought this sin to me. You brought this into my home. I don't blame you," Dale said. "You just don't know what they gave you."

"Dad, how about we sit down?"

Dale took his son's face in his hands, pulled their foreheads together. "You know what a sin eater is?"

81

Soda didn't pull away. "No."

"They're doing it again. I forgot the rot runs so deep," Dale said. "They've buried it and dug it up and buried it again, but the outlines remain. The drive you gave me, if you go through the files, the story is told through the redactions, what's missing. Money in the wrong accounts. Floor plans that account for missing rooms, sub-basements, two utility closets instead of one.

"They aren't working together, but they have the same goals. Threshold only knows a little bit. The old ones remember everything, they just deny it matters. The drive only reveals half the story — where the bodies are. We need the dirt itself to tell the other half. It's worse than I thought. Everything is rising back to the surface. Everything returns. Eventually. It all comes back."

"I know, Dad."

Dale pulled away. "This is not something you can know. If you really knew, you'd be like me. And I don't want that. I don't want you to live like this."

Soda gave the old man space. "I want to know."

Dale shuddered. "Once you dig into this, it doesn't stop. It colours everything you see, every little fragment. It becomes hard to find joy. You forget things. You forget why things matter, why you should care about anything at all. And you still want to understand?"

"Yes."

The sun was gone. The yard was dark.

Dale sighed. "Then come inside. Close the door behind you."

Soda could still taste the ticket on his tongue.

8.

No one could explain the crack.

Stanley Marigold lay alone in his king-size bed. A California king was too excessive. His father had slept in a double his whole life. A king was a luxury, something to be earned.

The crack wasn't there when he moved into the second penthouse suite. The Marigold's first penthouse suite belonged to his father. It sat empty, as it had since the building was finished. They would sell it when the time came, when the elder Marigold finally threw his last handful of shit at a nurse and crumpled into dust. Stan wanted to make a sandcastle from the ashes, watch it all wash away if his siblings let him. They hadn't spoken to the old man without a lawyer in at least a decade. They only cashed his cheques, as mandated by the courts after Albert tried to dissolve the original company. Whitney and Anders wouldn't fight Stan over the company, but the ashes were different. They might have had their own plans.

The crack stared at him whenever he woke up in the suite. It was there when he slept alone, there when Sidney forgave him for an evening, there when he brought an intern home and tried to get hard while she danced for him in candy cane underwear like it was Christmas in July, melting when the A/C cut out in the middle of the night. They fixed that. The balconies too, after the glass shattered without warning. No one could fix the crack above him though. Even after tearing it all out and redoing the drywall and the ceiling, it remerged in the same spot. Nothing dripped from it. No pipe or wire lay above it. An unseeing slit witnessing all his weakness.

Sometimes Stan Marigold wondered what it was like to get in on the ground floor of something, to be part of a thing that was rising instead of falling. If you could attribute that rise to yourself the way his father had, or if there was still room inside to acknowledge the circumstances that put you ahead. Could his pride withstand that knowledge? The survivor's bias was strong with these old fuckers. They ignored the bodies around them, the dead and the missing. They ignored the human fuel for their dreams, stacked and dried like firewood. There wasn't enough fuel to make it through the seasons now, not when the seasons had no real schedule and no names that made sense except maybe fall.

Stan Marigold considered mounting a mirror above his bed to cover up the crack. He had one in his condo across town in an Eastbank building, now owned by a numbered corporation one of his lawyers arranged, a spacious one-bedroom Sidney didn't know about, and she knew about most of them by now, liked to watch him on little cameras they both pretended not to notice. The games had gone so long it was hard to tell who was fooling who anymore. The Eastbank place had a grand piano in it because it was built with one in it and they couldn't get it out after construction finished. He kept it like an awkward, ugly hostage.

Adding a mirror above his bed wasn't going to fix the crack. A weak attempt at hiding the truth — The Marigold was crumbling. Albert Marigold was never known for building the best structures in the city. Whenever a Marigold building was torn down, all kinds of garbage came out of the walls, missives from the workers slipped beneath the surface. Stanley knew almost every tower in the city had water bottles full of piss clogging up the walls.

Outside of collecting older buildings to exploit, the elder Marigold's primary goal was to get his own towers up as fast as possible and cash out before the flaws began to show. His competitors claimed a Marigold building couldn't survive the first frost of a season. They weren't wrong. Stanley was trying to change this damaging perception with the new luxury buildings, even as he battled for control of the company in court.

Stanley glanced at his work phone, the third in as many months. Only recently had the Marigold/Dundee Corporation's security team insisted he allow them to "fully annihilate" the devices — as their panicked email articulated — after one of his phones was found in the decrepit warren of the PATH system under the city, passed from a disgraced broker to a disgraced lawyer to a gainfully employed sanitation worker, all trying to crack its passcode. Whatever made the security men sleep better at night, Stan would let them have that fantasy. People wanted to believe their jobs mattered. No one at his level was clean, the stains were part of the job description. Trying to remove them only made the marks more visible. There was a calendar notification from his father. A meeting without lawyers.

Stan walked out onto his penthouse balcony, the highest suite on this block of Yonge. Naked, he felt himself shrivel in the breeze. He considered pissing off the side, it wouldn't be the first time, but he no longer found it charming, just sad. The hockey goon throwing himself over the edge had only lasted a day or two in the news. Information moved too fast, spreading in waves, fractal implosions of the story burning it out before it even got legs. If you were smart, you hired your own off-label spin doctors, people working in offices with empty names like Morninglight and Elmstone, overworked legions of people posting counterfactual information, not networks spitting out interactions to change the narrative. Sidney would take longer to convince.

Killing the goon wouldn't have made Stan's life any better. And now that he was dead, there was another empty condo in the tower, another suite in what some people called the Glass Ghost. It would need to be filled. They needed more funding for Marigold II, a second round of investors who were a little less savvy than the first. The first tower had to succeed if the second would ever survive construction. The state of the pit across the street was already dire. The initial permits for lane closures were about to run out and one of the contractors was suing, something about ongoing emotional abuse.

Maybe Stan could talk about that with his father today, dig into exactly how he thought they were going to move all these suites right as the market decided to crash. They could talk about all of the little cheats, brokers, lawyers, and public officials who still had their hands trapped in the cookie jar, who to squeeze, who to flatter, who to cajole with a combination lock in an athletic sock. Stan scratched himself and headed back inside, leaving the glass door open behind him. No pigeons this high up. Only birds of prey, waiting for their victims to reveal themselves.

§

The facility was non-descript, nestled beneath the Bridle Path, a concession to the reality that an old, vindictive generation of money was dying and the younger one wanted to keep a close eye on these barely living assets. The building was known as the Eternals Club, but the tasteful sign outside said Musgrave Living.

Stan took a Magellan, ignoring the driver ignoring him, happy to be anonymous for now. Most of the staff at the Marigold/ Dundee Corporation did not approve of these meetings. They especially didn't want them recorded or witnessed by anyone else at the company. The hours Stan spent at the Eternals Club were only visible through their absence. His calendar was empty.

Stan emerged from the car reeking of fake pine, wondered if there was ever a time people associated it with cleanliness. He used his forged pass to enter the fortress doors. The building was half-buried in a ravine, hidden from the road by thick oak trees. A lot of money went into making this place look unassuming, all of it betrayed by the quality of the door fixtures, the smooth, wrought-iron handle that was polished daily resting in Stan's palm. It was discreet in the way old money always tries to disguise itself — gently, implacably present at all times, using blank absence to clarify the power of its will.

None of the staff spoke to him. Anyone with a pass was not to be questioned. It was safer for staff, easier to avoid getting dragged into familial wars as children, cousins, and third wives battled over bodies barely kept alive by the latest medical advances the government wouldn't recognize as valid. Experimental doses of LSD, doctors who wore paisley drapes, the soothing call of a therapy cockatoo — the staff learned to let it all wash over them.

Stan knew it was best to arrive on a Monday morning, before any other future inheritors were up. His father was on the second floor, agitating every day to return to The Marigold, to sit in his regal seat above the city even if no one could see him.

"Do you know how I know it's you every time, son?"

Albert sat facing the floor-to-ceiling window, the world outside green, studded with plastic grocery bags snagged on branches too high for staff to reach.

"Because we're family?"

"Because you never learned to knock, did you realize that? Never in your life! I had to put a lock on the bedroom door when we lived on Avenue so you wouldn't keep busting in on me and Cheryl. A man forced to lock his own bedroom. What a life!"

"You always told me to show up unannounced. Catch people saying what they actually think."

"Only if you can take it," Albert said, still staring out the window. "Sometimes there are things you don't want to know."

"You're still suing me, aren't you?" Stan said.

"That's what we've agreed to, yes, keep it all tangled up in court for a few years, buy ourselves a little more time to get this building sorted out. A legacy is important," his father said, grabbing a hold of Stan's left hand, his eyes still focused on the window. "Saw a squirrel out here the other day. Big fat grey one. How does a squirrel stay that fat in March? Thought maybe I'd discovered a new kind of wildlife, but no, it's just another creature we corrupted with calories. They were scrawny when I was a boy."

"Back when the world was flat," Stan said.

"You can save the insults for the courtroom." Albert rose from his chair. Today was a good day. He was dressed. His eyes clear. Morning was the best time to catch him, when his mind was still burning, spitting out hot grease and the occasional nugget of knowledge his son desperately required.

"So, no lawyers yelling at us to be nicer to each other," Albert said. "You have something special you want today? My friends, when they come to see me, they bring me food. Muffins, doughnuts, that kind of thing. But you, Stan, you don't bring me anything fun, do you? I know you think you're helping me here, but the real fact is I'm going to die and I'd like a few doughnuts before I do. Maybe a nice bottle of real Kentucky too. I'm so tired of pretending I like scotch."

"Glad you can admit that, Dad," Stan said, taking a seat in an emerald green chair too comfortable to exist so close to death. "You're usually telling me it'll never happen. You plan to outlive us all."

"That's what you're supposed to say, isn't it? Isn't that what everyone wants to hear? If I say it, maybe I can believe it for a little while," Albert said. "Belief is a powerful thing, even when empty. Use it on anyone, even yourself if you must."

"And you must?" Stan said. His father sat down on the bed.

"Some days, yes. Some days stretch on like a desert."

"But today, you have an oasis."

"Jesus Christ, I try to say a nice thing and you go and fuck it up," Albert said, rubbing his temples. "Who gives a shit about an oasis? What do you have for me today? Someone giving us a hard time? Phone number you need? Do I need to dig up a body for evidence? Literal or figurative. I still got things you need. I still own some part of you."

"None of that. We always have problems; I deal with them. They have organized another meeting though. The old men. The circle."

Albert rubbed his eyes. "So soon? Greedy birds. Didn't we say we were slowing things down? The market cannot bear it. Twice a year. Spring and fall. When the ground is soft."

"I know, that's what they said back then, but seasons aren't the same anymore. Things are out of whack. Like your fat squirrel."

"He simply doesn't have an adequate predator!"

Last time Stan visited, his father had ranted about Koreans and the price of fresh fruit. The staff eventually had to restrain him after he found a bruise on a banana. Stan wanted to question why anyone thought giving an eighty-year-old man a whole banana was a good idea, but it didn't seem like the time to ask how his father was being fed.

"So, what should I do?"

"With what?" Albert said, digging around the sheets piled at the end of the bed. "Someone took my book. A good one too. And someone took it."

"At the meeting. With the circle."

"Some are older than me, you know that?" Albert said. "I wonder how they do it. The book was about con men. How they lived, how they lost out eventually when the government decided to stamp them out. It had to go federal. Only way to bring them down was to give them nowhere to run. Drove them into the sea!"

Stan placed a hand on his father's shoulder. "Dad, sit down. Talk to me."

"I am talking, aren't I?" Albert said, pulling Stan in close, voice a harsh whisper. "You don't think a room like this is bugged? By your lawyers? My lawyers? Maybe even the cleaners. I'm talking to you. Can you understand that? Listen."

Stan took a step back.

"In my favourite part of this book," Albert said, "they explained how a con man got people to believe him. The convincer, if you will. If I could find the damn thing, I'd read it to you, but the main point was most of these people weren't idiots. It's actually hard to con an idiot. You can steal from him, but to con him, you gotta make sure he can see his own advantage. To win him over, you have to ensure he can see, or at least thinks he can see, how the table is tilted.

"Show them the advantage. Set them up with an early win, let them win a little walking-around money. Agree with them at every turn, compliment their voices and their vices. Especially vices. Do they like women? Alcohol? Painkillers? Maybe young men.

"Introduce them to the next guy on your team, the one who can make them real money. They've already tasted it. Give them another taste. Make the payout so sweet they can't help but double down. When they lose for the first time, you lose with them. Now you're bonded together. Important to create that bond. If there is a loss, you share it. For now."

Albert gave up digging in the bed. Stan watched his father struggle back to the window seat.

"Does that make sense to you, son?"

"I think it does."

"Maybe I can loan you the book, if I ever find it."

Stan didn't bother asking for the title. It may not have existed.

"You know, I always thought I'd die in a forest."

A few birds pulled at the plastic bags in the trees.

"You've said that before," Stan said. "Near the burnt cottage."

"We rebuilt it. Always hire a licensed electrician, son. My other advice for today. A bad electrician means you're dead, not like the dead in this place though. A real death."

The birds moved on, dangling grey ribbons from their beaks. "I think about walking out there in winter sometimes. Maybe I would find a stream out there in the trees. And nature would love me like all of her children. She would not spare me. I'd die with my eyes slowly closing, nose full of the smell of those trees . . . and I think about how it's a fantasy. A sad, old fantasy."

The old man stopped talking. Stan let seconds become minutes.

"I'll remember the book."

"Yes," Albert mumbled. "You do that."

By the time he made it outside, Stan longed for the same Magellan driver to pick up his fare, the scent of that fake pine covering up whatever death still stuck to him, reminding him of bright green trees that didn't exist in forests where no one could die since they were never there at all. The new driver's car smelled like cotton candy vape. Stan didn't complain. The artificial sweetness was close enough. He knew what he had to do this time. His father made it clear. Keep going. Tell the circle what they wanted to hear, what they needed. Tell them there is enough for everyone to eat, to eat and eat until they're satisfied. Let them all gorge.

Suite 806

Sunil Tagare never admitted his mistakes. He couldn't afford it.

In interviews with glossy legacy magazines or start-up media publications that would only last six months before their funding dried up, Sunil told everyone the same polished origin story of FODDER — the app was actually his mother's idea. Yes, even as a young boy in Nova Scotia, the legendary Varsha Tagare was his greatest inspiration, the driving force behind his dominance in the home delivery market, the most powerful mind behind uncanny algorithms that appeared to know exactly what you craved in the very moment you craved it, and the root of all his sound judgement, unwavering morality, and surprising good looks.

That was the part that unnerved so many when they first met Sunil in a boardroom or the blistering heat of a restaurant kitchen. Even with sweat running down his face, his features were perfectly proportioned, his nose like a subtle blade scored down the centre of his face. A number of women had written poems about his brown eyes. A few men too, asking for a chance to show him a better way to live. He kept all those notes, let them mingle in the small drawer beside the stove behind his oven mitts, drowning out their whispers.

Don't leave us. Don't be alone.

It wasn't like he could cook in his suite. Someone had fucked up the exhaust fan over the stove; it blew the hot air back into the condo instead of out. Sunil reported it to management, even hung around one day to corner one of them in person to make his concerns known. The woman nodded and jotted down notes. Sunil spent the brief conversation trying to decipher her handwriting, wondering if she was doodling like he did during the board meetings at FODDER down in one of the timber Threshold towers, meetings that stretched on for hours as his advisors debated taking the business public, or attempting to secure another round of funding to stay afloat. Executives from different Threshold subsidiaries continued to make offers. He sat and doodled, but he didn't back down when anyone challenged his authority. He tried to remember his mother's favourite word — poise. That was all you required to survive in this world.

Varsha still ignored his calls, furious he moved out to live on his own downtown; in a tower too, not a house. Her sons needed to live in a proper home. Varsha believed Sunil should've stayed with her in Richmond Hill. For the first few months, he kept the purchase secret, referring to his appointments as meetings with other start-ups, men and women trying to develop the best way to convince you that you needed to improve all your cookware with their newer, slightly improved, and drastically marked up cookware made in the same factory in a country across an ocean, with looser labour laws.

You need us.

Sunil was one of the first to move into the building, taking possession even as the upper floors were still being finished. He told his mother it was an investment property. It would pay off eventually. It would pay off and he would buy a bigger place — maybe not a house, maybe just a bigger condo. He would escape The Marigold. His life up to this point had been defined by his stubbornness, the outsized belief he projected into the world that he was right.

A knock on the door.

"Give me a second," Sunil said. Three crisp raps, just the way the FODDER manual instructed drivers to deliver the food. Delivery had to become professional or die. This is what he believed, what he tried to sell. Why were we okay with simply okay service? Why were we letting ourselves down by letting mediocrity become the standard? Three crisp raps announced your food was here — warm, inviting, ready to eat.

The door swung open. A scrawny man smiled as he'd been instructed. He held the bag out like a present. No money changed hands. Even the tip was pre-arranged, part of which FODDER would take as a service fee for as long as they could before someone looked too closely. Sunil believed that day would eventually arrive, but for now he would push for every cent they could scrape out of the drivers. It wasn't so much about ethics as it was about profit.

"Thank you, that was a little slower than I imagined, but still pretty good for the circumstances. How was the desk staff? A lot of variables with condo buildings. It comes down to elevators, really. Were the elevators working for you down there?"

"Sure, yeah, it was fine."

Sunil took a closer look at the man standing before him, hair swept up under a FODDER cap — not a baseball hat, but a cap with the letters in bright teal. They had no marketing team, Sunil just went with what he liked. The man's right eye was smaller than the left. Barely perceptible, but Sunil still noticed. Details were part of the job, details were what set FODDER apart, after all, allowed it to survive as the competition dropped to its knees with unionizations, contractor loopholes, and the retaliation of restaurant owners.

The man wore the black vest over the black shirt as the manual outlined. Black lowered the barrier to entry, didn't show stains as quickly. The shoes were Converse, but there were no rules about shoes. His right pinkie was in a cast.

"What happened there?" Sunil said, pointing with his free hand. The food was irrelevant to the exercise. That was one of Varsha's first pieces of advice — it was about the experience, not the food. The food couldn't be bad, but it didn't need to be amazing. Good was good enough as long as everyone felt the experience was worth the price.

"Oh, just some asshole who turned into me. Smacked his window to let him know what was up, guess I hit it a bit hard. Cracked the glass."

"You did what?" Sunil said, still smiling, still holding his bag of curry or whatever he'd ordered. FODDER gave you limited options on your screen, pulled together in leased ghost kitchens down in the Threshold district. Another tip from Sunil's mother that had gone into the app. People hated making choices, especially people with money. Her first restaurant succeeded because there was a lot of butter in the sauces and because the menu was only a page, and she was there to recommend the dishes to every diner that entered. Give them a small illusion of choice. Five options a day with a special discount. Five options were just enough to get people to see the potential of what was out there, still coddled by the professionals behind FODDER who claimed to know exactly what they wanted.

"Let him know what's up. He knew what he did was wrong, man."

"That's unacceptable," Sunil said. "What's your name?"

"My name? Reza. Look, I'm not trying to cause a problem, alright?"

"Your full name."

"It's in the app, man. Light me up, I don't give a shit about ratings anymore."

"Why do you think you can talk to customers like this?" Sunil said.

"Why do I need to tell you anything, man? Get off my dick!"

"This is how you speak to your boss?"

"Oh, now you're my boss?" Reza laughed, pulling his phone up to film Sunil in the doorway. "Check this motherfucker out. My boss, just because he ordered some curry. Hungry boy now running the game out here."

"Put that away now," Sunil said.

His mother never dealt with every action documented and disseminated instantly online.

"Oh no, looks like my boss is upset. Pretty boy all upset out here."

"I *am* your boss, you idiot," Sunil said. "Do you know who I am?"

"Oh, that didn't take long," Reza laughed, backing down the hall. "Love this shit. I should probably quit, right? Go work for DoorDash or DreamDrop."

"DreamDrop doesn't even have a time guarantee! Or a uniform! They just throw your order into a queue!"

"Oh shit, for real?" Reza laughed. "This man got all the stats tonight."

"I made this company, alright?" Sunil said, shaking. The bag hit the floor. No one came out to see him screaming, but the phone captured everything. "I designed it. Built it. Gave assholes like you an option in this shithole city. You don't want to grow. You don't want to change. You want to wallow in your misery. Do you know why you're riding your bike around in the rain bringing food to me up here? Because you can't do anything else. You don't know how."

Reza's laughter slowed and stopped. His hand steadied his phone. Sunil continued.

"You've never made anything of your own, never stuck your neck out there to risk getting it chopped off. You kept your skinny little chicken neck safe. And now you take whatever scraps fall off our tables. And you should thank us for those scraps. You bend your back for us because if you don't, you have nothing. You are nothing."

Reza's phone slipped. "Well, fuck you. Fuck your company and your bullshit house of cards."

"Get out of my house, boy," Sunil said. He felt cleansed. It wouldn't last.

"You won't exist in a year." Reza tried to give him the finger, good hand holding the camera. The broken pinkie wouldn't go down. "You're just waiting for the guillotines!"

Sunil waved him off, grabbing his food off the floor.

"Also, what're you doing on the eighth floor anyway, big shot?"

Sunil almost dove right into an absurd explanation of his investment strategy, the need to own one asset before he made claims for another. No one would have heard him. Reza was gone, FODDER hat on the floor in front of the emergency stairs. Sunil left the hat where it was, slamming his suite door. He stood at the granite kitchen island he paid an extra two thousand dollars for when he purchased the unit and unwrapped his package from the proprietary plastic bag that one of his designers came up with during a late-night invention session. Chicken curry, still fairly warm. One of five choices. Sunil's phone buzzed on the island.

what were you thinking

FODDER used a series of personal questions to "get to know" their customers' tastes and desires, working out a unique personal menu that suited each person depending on the day of the week and time of day. Questions about favourite movies, sports, and celebrities were sprinkled in with spice preferences, levels of acidity, and a thorough explanation of the word "umami." All of this was designed to push the best meals toward each client, according to their marketing. A customized lifestyle, Sunil told investors. A menu that captures who you are, maybe pushes you toward who you want to be. We know what you want even before you open up the app.

r u kidding man what is thisssss, another message blipped onto the screen. It wasn't a mistake, he wanted to tell them. It was a pivot. A distraction.

now DreamDrop calling you the Food Police

The truth about FODDER was the survey led to nothing. There was no secret algorithm that precisely narrowed down the thousands of options in Toronto to the best five choices for each and every customer with the app on their phone. It was impossible, unimplementable, and extremely expensive to even consider. What FODDER did have was exclusive deals with certain restaurants throughout the city that allowed their dishes to be reproduced in the ghost kitchens, with fixed menu prices they could rely on and branding that sold people on an "experience." Varsha's food in Dartmouth had never been the best Indian food on the east coast. What mattered was how it was pitched, how it was sold. Tell people what they wanted to hear. Lead them to their own desires.

Get out of my house boy? Oh fuuuck Sunny are you
always this dumb

The data FODDER did collect was sold to certain subsidiaries of Threshold, analyzed, indexed, and distributed to firms that knew exactly what to do with it, breaking down demographics and pinpointing the insecurities, desires, and contradictions of FODDER's generally young, striving, and desperate userbase. This information wasn't a deeply guarded secret within the company, but the general optics were still not very flattering, potentially even destructive to predicted growth over the next quarter. FODDER was still losing money.

You need us.

The best way to keep information from making an impact was to create spectacle. That is what he'd tell them in the office tomorrow if anyone was stupid enough to question him in front of a crowd. He was setting himself up to take the fall, couldn't they see that? Make himself the villain instead of the company. He took a bite of his curry. It had no texture, just heat. There wasn't any nuance. Consume, chew, and swallow. This was what his customers wanted, the idea of something exotic that just reaffirmed their palates. Turning a mistake into an advantage, that was what his mother would say. She hadn't texted him yet. She wasn't online.

Please email me back. We need to control this story
NOW

Maybe he would move back to his mother's house with its eight bathrooms if you included the jacuzzi room with the toilet. Maybe he wasn't ready to be out here in the world on his own. He was only on the eighth floor after all. He was down here in the city ordering his overpriced delivery from his own stupid company, pacing inside the little box designed for him, tiles picked out from a page of twelve options, curtain rods from a selection of three, the granite kitchen island of only two The Marigold offered to its most important clients.

sunny man you stepped in it this time

One mistake could cost you everything.

haha man that fucking ruled you should do this every night!!!

Sunil didn't make mistakes. He kept eating the curry, ignoring the lack of flavour. What this video was, however it had been manipulated, was an opportunity. A new diversion from the core error inside FODDER, one that Sunil still struggled to admit to himself.

This is a huge headache for all of us.

In the morning, he'd decide. He'd move back in with his mother, her bedroom just down the hall, her life fully devoted to his, her knowledge buttressing his own belief in himself. He'd rent out the condo, price it a little bit above the market rate, make sure whoever rented from him thought they were getting some kind of special deal. He'd keep the place for a couple years, maybe wait until Marigold II was built across the street. Cash in on the cache of being part of something like The Marigold from the start, then move on to a bigger and better place his mother would approve of, one that didn't require you to open the windows while you cooked. One that didn't speak to you in your sleep, trying to tell you that you were doomed. One where you weren't afraid to be alone.

Don't leave, a voice said, a shudder from the exhaust fan. *You can't leave. You need us.*

For now, he would simply eat his meal and watch his spastic phone dance across the granite island. In the whispering darkness, Sunil would pull out the love letters hidden in his little kitchen drawer, behind the unused oven mitts, and pretend that he believed them.

She wouldn't take you back anyway.

9.

"They're saying you're a killer."

Henrietta Brakes stood on the roof of her crumbling tower, staring down into the sinkhole's mouth, pondering what would happen if she decided to jump from this high up. The rain made it difficult to see the edge of anything. She thought about falling forever — if that was possible, if eventually you died from dehydration or starvation, if you became a spirit or just a ghost, another lonely remainder.

"They're saying you had sex and then you killed him."

"What did you tell them?" Henrietta replied, keeping an eye on the hole.

"I told them you'd do it again if they kept talking shit."

Henrietta smiled, but didn't look up.

"I also told them if they want to talk about my friend like that, there's another spot down there for them and I'd be happy to drop them off," Alma said.

"You said all that?" Henrietta said. "All those words?"

"The gist of it. They got the message," Al replied, tugging her hood tight.

"I don't think I've ever seen a boy naked. Not on purpose."

"Same. Doesn't count if it was on TV."

It had only been a couple days since whatever it was had dragged Cherry down into that hole. She didn't bother trying to explain the hand she saw to the police or the social worker who interviewed her afterward, holding her hands while they asked if Cherry was talking about ending things, if he'd given away possessions, if she had dumped him that night. She didn't bother explaining that they'd never dated, she just wanted to kiss someone nice, someone who wouldn't try to push her further than she wanted to go. No one wanted to hear that.

"What'd your mom say?" Al asked.

"That we need to be careful. She knows if she starts ranting, I'll just disappear again, give her another heart attack. And I would, she isn't stupid. She just thinks the world owes her something. And it doesn't. Even I know better than that, Al."

The heart attack happened during the night shift. No one found her mother until morning, splayed out in the dairy section, mop bucket overturned, body soaked in dirty water.

"You going to come back to school?" Alma asked.

"They still going to say I killed Cherry?"

"I want to say no, but you know how it is. I can't be everywhere at once."

Henrietta kept her eyes on the sinkhole. She pressed her knuckles into her mouth until she tasted blood. The pit kept taking everything from her. It knew her.

"You going to help me then?" Henrietta said finally.

"Help you skip? Sure, what you need me to say? I can say the bus hit you again, that worked pretty good last time. The crutches were a good touch."

"No, not with school. I don't need to go back there."

Alma cocked her head. "I know we say we hate it, but you love it. I know you do. You love being in charge of a group project. And that's insane, by the way. Craziest thing about you."

"Got something else in mind. Sort of a group project, so I guess you're right."

Alma shuddered in the rain. "Can you tell me about it inside? Where it's warm and we don't die?"

"No. I need you to see what I see."

Henrietta waited for Alma to walk over to the edge. She wrapped an arm around Alma's tiny shoulders and pulled her in tight.

"We're going down there," Henrietta said. "To find whatever took him."

Henrietta felt Alma's heart accelerate. The two girls peered down into the blank maw.

"Okay," Alma said, her voice smaller. "Okay, Hen."

"You're sure?" Henrietta said, squeezing her again.

Alma laughed. "What else am I supposed to say?"

§

They gathered in the subbasement of Tower 3, the only one without any flood damage. Each tower in Foynes Village was deformed in its own way. They all bent with age, foundations mutated by time and abuse like any person might be after sixty years of being exposed to the elements and bored teenagers. Henrietta and Alma hid out here when things got too crazy on the upper floors, whenever the cops decided it was time to kick in a bunch of doors and drag a few boys out into the halls, throwing them down staircases with the cuffs on to see how they'd land.

"Are we bringing snacks?" Salman said. Alma insisted they bring him along as muscle. Henrietta couldn't see any muscles at all, but she didn't want to upset Alma. They'd hooked up the night Cherry was yanked down into the black. A lot of kissing, maybe some hand stuff. There were worse boys in the Village. Salman was all talk; all smoke, no fire. He wanted to run with his brothers but struggled to give up his phone. He couldn't disappear if he tried.

"Why are you so paranoid about snacks?" Alma said.

"I'm a big boy — if I get hungry, I get grumpy," Salman said. "Mom's the same way. Always has snacks in her purse in case the subway stalls."

The rope Henrietta found belonged to a window washing crew that used to be a staple at Foynes Village until they stopped getting funds from the housing corporation. A lot of the equipment was left behind on the roof. Her backpack was filled with water bottles, a knife her mother said could cut off your hand if you weren't careful, and three flashlights. Alma said they could use their phones, but the battery life wasn't going to make that feasible.

"You ever hear of eating to live rather than living to eat, Salman?" Henrietta said.

"My dad used to say shit like that and, honestly, it sounds horrible," Salman said. He was good at pivoting, spinning the conversation off himself onto someone else. His older brothers had taught him to be a moving target to stay alive. "Why not just become a brain in a jar?"

"Is it going to be cold down there?" Alma asked. "Packed a sweater, but do I need gloves?"

"We don't know anything at all," Salman said. He had to hunch his shoulders in the subbasement, maneuvering around retired floor polishers and snapped mops. His purple Hawaiian shirt collected grimy little smears every time he brushed against the walls. "Like, no one has ever gone down there, ever. Even my brothers say it's a no-go zone. Cops haven't been down there. Threshold dudes with their little gate badges, I mean, they don't even send drones down there. The city pretends it isn't there. Even birds avoid it. They know something."

Henrietta secured her backpack tight across her chest. "I don't care what the birds are doing. They fly into our windows all the time. They get confused by blinking lights. They eat shit. We're going down there tonight. Are you coming?"

"Of course," Salman said. "I can't let Al get one over on me here. She's not scared of anything. And I want to do something no one else has done before."

"And if we don't come back?" Henrietta said. It was easier to talk about it than to think about it, easier to forget the shadowy hand around Cherry's leg, the whisper of her father's voice in the black. She handed a flashlight to Salman. "You okay with that? We could all die."

"Always wanted to die a legend," Salman said. He placed the flashlight under his chin and lit up his face. Alma laughed. "Sign me up."

When darkness swept over Foynes Village, they made their way up out of the basement. Henrietta hid the rope in Alma's father's hockey bag, one he no longer used, body decimated by years working for the TTC in maintenance and a devastating rec hockey league hit, the collision popping the cap off his knee like it was a beer bottle.

"How long is the rope?" Salman asked. "How do you steal that?"

"Easy to steal things if you act like they belong to you," Alma said. "I do it all the time. Smile and look people in the eye like you've known them for years. If you're acting shady, they'll assume you're shady. If you're a dude, wear a suit."

"What do you steal?" Salman said. "Food?"

"Whatever catches my eye."

"And you never get caught? You should talk to my brothers."

"I'd rather get shot in the face," Alma said.

"She means it," Henrietta said.

They ducked under the yellow caution tape. Henrietta opened the hockey bag and tied the window washer's rope around an old maple tree, one of the few remaining in the square. Salman helped secure the knot, throwing his weight behind it.

"We won't need it at first, but I don't trust anything already down there to stay secure. This is our escape route."

"Literally an escape rope," Salman said.

"Shut up." Alma shivered. "I shoulda grabbed more sweaters."

Salman walked to the edge, spotted the outcropping with the couch. "You didn't kill Cherry?"

Alma stared him down. Henrietta laughed. "No, he was too sweet."

"Just wanted to be sure."

"What if she lied to you?" Alma said. "What then?"

"I can see it in her face, Al," Salman said. "If Henny wanted to lie to me, she would. But she's not. I know what a liar looks like. Everyone wants to pretend they're a tough guy, bragging about shit they never done." He shook the rope over the edge, watched it fall and fall and fall. "But this? Never knew anyone who would dare do this."

"Until now," Henrietta said.

"You're the boss," Salman said. "Show me what to do."

The two girls went first, picking their way down into the pit, sticking to the craggy plateaus they remembered, outcroppings studded with popsicle sticks and old tissue boxes. Laptops and stereo speakers stuck out of the wet dirt. Salman followed, slipping and sliding on the loose scree. Henrietta waited for him to give up and turn back, but he kept after them.

"You said something grabbed him?" Salman said.

"Oh my god, can you shut up until we get to the bottom?" Alma said. She held the rope now, letting it guide her descent.

"It's fine," Henrietta whispered. "It was your idea to bring him. I'm just glad he didn't bring any other idiots. He may as well know what I saw."

"A hand," Alma said. "What you saw was a hand. It could've been a person."

"What are you guys talking about?" Salman yelled. They were deep enough into the pit that no one on the surface could hear them. Sounds burped out of the sinkhole sometimes. People ignored its exhalations.

"Something did grab him," Henrietta yelled back. "It wasn't a person, it was, like, a thing made of wet dirt."

"And it wasn't just, like, a dirty dude?" Salman replied.

"That's what I said," Alma said. "She says it wasn't a dude."

"So, what, we're going down there to confront whatever took Cherry?" Salman shouted.

"Yes," Henrietta said. "That a problem?"

"No, just wish I brought a gun. Or like a knife. Or a taser. I don't know!"

The girls kept descending. There were rumours about bodies down here. Bodies of drunks who accidentally stumbled too many times after leaving the Elephant & Castle and were never heard from again. Bodies of people swallowed alive when the sinkhole first erupted, mothers trying to save their babies from the playground in the centre of the square. Henrietta's father had slid into the story too. People talked about them all like they were still alive down here, biding their time. Not so much ghosts as revenants, waiting to mete out their revenge on those who were supposed to keep them safe, people who were supposed to make sure things like this didn't happen in a city like Toronto. It was easier to ignore the hole.

Other sinkholes opened up. One on the island that took out a boathouse and then drowned itself in lake water. Another emerged on the rail path, taking a few cyclists on a warm June day, screams extinguished by a passing train. Or so Henrietta heard. She paid attention. Smaller sinkholes sprang up after heavy rainstorms, taking cars and garbage trucks with them. One took out part of Queen's Park downtown, dragging down the Minister of Education and a few protestors with him. Sinkholes were part of living in the city, a risk you took in an urban environment under siege from its most tenacious opponent, the weather.

Despite the proliferation of pits across the city, Henrietta knew this sinkhole was still the first and largest of them all. People whispered the cops used it for body disposal, lording it over other gangs from the outskirts with more conventional disposal methods. If you stood at the edge of that gentle abyss, looked past the mustard yellow couch and dead phones glittering like fool's gold, you might believe people were capable of awful things. You could even believe you saw a creature down there, wet and dark and reeking, with a deep voice that used to sing you to sleep.

"How much further?" Salman asked. "We're going to run out of rope."

Henrietta couldn't remember how long they'd been descending. She didn't know if they were any closer to the bottom until she felt her feet touch what felt like solid ground. She swung her flashlight around. Garbage filled the bottom of the pit. A tiny prickling of light above them.

"We're here," she screamed, a small sound that echoed back in a whisper. "We made it."

Alma touched down behind her and wrapped Henrietta tight in her arms. They stood together in silence, listening to Salman fumble and curse above them. The beams of their flashlights couldn't even make out the walls of the pit. "This is insane."

"I know."

"Like, actually crazy. We almost ran out of rope."

"And there's nothing down here," Henrietta said. That wasn't exactly true. The pit was a garbage dump, filled with old bags of trash and mismatched furniture, splintered into unrecognizable shapes after the fall. "Smells like an old dishwasher."

"You thought it was going to smell good?" Alma said. "It's basically a drain."

Salman hit the ground with a wet thud. "Fuck."

"You alright?" Alma said, voice betraying concern.

"I got too excited," Salman said, pulling himself up. "Didn't know there was a bottom."

"There's always a bottom," Alma said.

"I don't know," Henrietta said, swinging her beam of light in a circle around them, revealing a world slumped together, a place without edges. "Maybe it goes deeper."

"It does," a low, wet voice gurgled.

Salman screamed. Henrietta's beam settled on a human shape, dripping and hissing, eyes blank white stones. It grinned, revealing a long pink tongue and a few loose teeth.

"I show you," the thing said.

Henrietta took a step forward. Salman brandished his flashlight like a club. Alma raised her fists, spat into the dirt. The thing didn't move to strike. It didn't retreat either.

"I show you . . . but . . ."

Each word was retched out of its body. Black phlegm dripped onto the ground, squirming out of Henrietta's beam into the damp filth around them.

"You help me."

10.

There was no body, according to the men on the scene. Jasmine and Cathy arrived by streetcar, lugging their equipment on their backs. Most civilians assumed they were military or a bizarre branch of the police no one wanted to question. The city was filled with different security services, slowly taking on the roles of the police. There was no customer service to contact.

"You know how it starts," the lead cop said, shoulders slumped like he'd taken a beating. "Someone smells something."

"Gotta love it," Cathy replied. "That's what breaks them."

"Do you know your neighbours?" the man said.

"I wish I didn't," Cathy responded, while Jasmine opened her kit. The building was only thirty years old but beaten down by ice storms, rain that went on for weeks, and sporadic windstorms that tore up powerlines, downed trees, and rolled cars across highways. The sign out front called it The Willoughby. Jasmine said it was a stupid name for a building, and Cathy asked why she thought any building deserved a good name in the first place.

"One of mine likes to play the same Tracy Chapman songs on guitar every night."

"Doesn't sound so bad," Cathy said, pulling on her mask. The other cops shied away from the two women, unwilling to acknowledge what they saw in the apartment upstairs.

"Same two songs over and over. He doesn't get better," the cop said.

"Buy him some lessons. Anonymously," Cathy said. "Anything else I need to know?"

"This one is different. We've evacuated the first few floors and no one is allowed to use the garage. Not a simple case here. A strange one."

"All of this is strange," Cathy said, tapping the mask. "We'll let you know when we're done here. Don't leave us hanging, alright? I don't want anyone sneaking inside."

Jasmine finished prepping their tools and secured her own mask. They turned to each other and locked horns. It was strange to be a necessary tool no one acknowledged.

"You ready for this?" Cathy said. "Remember, we're keeping two sets of notes."

The men from Threshold had been clear. They wanted to know everything. There was already money sitting in Cathy's account. An inheritance from her mother, she was supposed to tell the bank. No one cared.

"I know," Jasmine said. Her mask's eyes blinked a neon green. "Document everything."

"You've got this," Cathy said.

They entered The Willoughby, door banging shut behind them, deadbolt sprung, unyielding against the metal frame. No one moved to fix it behind them.

§

A two-bedroom on the second floor, the kind of unit no one built anymore, the kind that would give most developers a seizure if they glanced at the floor plan. Four closets in total, a wide entryway that would pass for a den in most of the newer condos, and a series of nooks and crannies most residents loved and interior designers might have called wasted space.

It looked tidier than most of the scenes they attended, organized by someone concerned with right angles. The couch was threadbare, but the floors were clean. Newspapers stacked in orderly piles on the coffee table. A tower of magazines secured with twine. A massive purple dreamcatcher hung in the bay window, speckled with dead flies. The dappled light from the unwashed windows made the whole place feel sickly. No family photos on the walls.

"Two bedrooms? For one guy?" Jasmine said. "What fantasy world is this?"

"Our generation got the short end of the stick," Cathy said. She closed the busted front door, barely clinging to its hinges. "I remember when they still gave you all the appliances when you moved into a place. Washer and dryer too. Feels like a dream. Did you see anything out there in the hall? Stain-wise?"

"Just a lot of dirt in the carpet. I'm getting a few clicks here and there," Jasmine said, tapping the side of her mask. "Nothing like what we saw before."

"There wasn't a trail or anything," Cathy said. "So, where does it come from?"

Jasmine walked down the hall to the first bedroom, filled with unopened board games and old hockey equipment mounted on the walls. She moved on to the bathroom, decorated with a blue elephant theme, and then the second bedroom. A king-size bed sat in the middle of the room, empty except for pale blue walls. An island floating in the sea.

"A lot of board games."

"Don't even think about it, Jas."

"What? I know your stance. Maybe he was a reseller," Cathy said, entering the kitchen. Her mask whirred and twitched. The readout was clear. Traces of the Wet in the air. "I get what the big guy was saying outside. It is strange."

She could feel the hand wrapping itself around her ankle again, speaking through the skin.

The kitchen was narrow, more like a galley. Nothing stuck to the fridge, a blank slate like the bedroom. The old dented oven had clean burners. On the floor, there was the faint outline of a body, a thin layer of black mould stuck to the tiles like an afternoon shadow. Cathy listened to her mask whirr and hiccup, breaking down the composition of this smear. Filtered air passed through the mask, doing its best to protect her from whatever had happened here.

"Oh," Jasmine said, shuffling behind Cathy. "I see now. No body?"

"Apparently not. Can't say this work is boring."

The men from Threshold said they needed to own part of it. Alive, ideally. Cathy knelt down, noticed the cupboard beneath the sink still cracked open. She slowly pulled it open, the feedback overwhelming her mask for a moment, sending a cavalcade of numbers and colours across her eyes, a rainbow of information punched into her retinas. She gripped the horns and held tight, waiting for the surge to pass. Too close to the voice.

"You alright, Cath?"

"We're good. We're good."

Moist, damp, covered in a thin black layer of the Wet, the same smeared shadow. It pulsed as Cathy ran gloved hands over it, shuddering at her touch. The pipe from the sink ran into the wall. A hole had been gouged out beneath, leaking drips of viscous fluid.

"It's using the pipes."

"Only in here," Jasmine said. "Why?"

"It made a choice."

Jasmine laughed behind her mask. "What're you talking about? It's a fungus."

"Sure, but that doesn't mean much. They can't figure out how to culture it, as far as I know," Cathy said, climbing to her feet. "Function, life cycle, we don't really know a damn thing about how it works. Call some back-up for the kitchen here, they'll have to dose the whole thing and rope it off. Make sure they've got masks charged. Make it clear that as far as we know this is just a case someone brought home. Nothing unordinary."

"Nothing unordinary." Jasmine tilted her head, horns scraping the plaster. "Is that our story?"

"Our story is we're going to follow this trail. We're going to try and find a source."

§

There were larger forces at work, the Threshold men explained. People who were concerned about humanity's continued existence in a world spiked by a fever hoping to sweat us all out. Threshold was once a tiny data collection company, one that dealt in abstracts — risks and opportunities, strengths and weaknesses. People who were used to exercising their power from behind a series of ergonomically organized screens.

After they reorganized, purchasing so many of their rivals that multiple governments attempted to break them apart, Threshold began to realize these details still mattered, that data changed faster than they could process it, that in the process of tracking something, you might actually change its nature. They noticed the same thing happening in the dirt at the foot of the city when they came to build their neighbourhood of the future. Each interaction changed its composition. There was something strange in the moist ground, something the lake water unlocked with every flood. It had to be alive.

These larger forces wanted to understand the Wet. Or at least that is what Robert and the man with the frayed sleeves said to Cathy, explaining it wasn't a secret. They knew it existed. They knew something was wrong. They just didn't understand what it was. They needed an inside line to understand its source. They had the resources to pay, the connections to bring Cathy along if she wanted. There was an official unofficial body that spread from city hall to corporate boardrooms, all of it greased with press, public relations, and charitable donations. All it took was the right suits and smiles to convince people you were meant to be there, they told Cathy. All she had to do was provide the secret of this elixir; this dirt could corrupt an entire tower.

"It chose to stop there. It chose someone who lived alone."

Jasmine led as they made their way down the emergency stairs, avoiding dried puddles of dog piss. Cathy's mask calmed down, emitting a pale blue light from the eyes to match Jasmine's glow. They had sprayed down the interior of the cabinet, watched the breathing fungus suffocate, go white, then die. They left the black outline on the floor for the clean-up crew. It would be best to have confirmation from the larger team, especially since Cathy reported to two bosses now. It was the line about taking her with them that won her over.

Even with its crumbling infrastructure, morbid public transportation options, drowned islands, roaming coyotes, and accelerated soil erosion, Toronto was still an expensive city. The condo kept raising her monthly maintenance fees every time they discovered another flaw in the building's construction. She hadn't even wanted the condo in the first place, but when it came time to divorce, she felt like she didn't have a choice.

Escaping the condo meant buying something new and doing that in the city was never an easy task. Even saying the word "buying" out loud sounded foolish. Jasmine would laugh in her face. Public health didn't pay much. There were only so many raises on the ladder before you topped out, found yourself squirrelled away in a tower somewhere, watching inflation destroy your savings, watching the price of bananas soar as the world sweat and then shivered.

"You're saying it makes choices?" Jasmine said. They'd reached the bottom of the parking garage, familiar hunting ground. The cars here were rundown, one GMC made of rust, a fallen creature. A few still had old Ford family bumper stickers.

"It has to. Maybe not consciously, like us, but I don't know. Something in it decides where to go, who to hunt. It doesn't take the path of resistance. It needs victims."

"So what does it know, then?" Jasmine said. "That people are alone? A sense of vulnerability? You ever riding around on a streetcar at 2 a.m., figuring out who's going home alone? It's not hard to tell who's on the edge of a breakdown, who might decide to scream in your face. There's a lot of need and fear people can't help but wear on their sleeves."

Cathy snorted, her mask distorting it into a snarl. "Yeah, just like that."

"You see a guy following you home," Jasmine continued. "Maybe you cross the street. You cannot say why exactly, can't tell what he's going to do, but you have a feeling and you make a decision. You choose a path. You deviate from your course as you process new information."

Cathy leaned back against a Honda CRV that featured Calvin pissing on Garfield. "And the Wet does the same thing. And what if it remembers? What if it learns through trial and error?"

"Then we have a problem," Jasmine said.

117

"Maybe," Cathy said. "Or a new way of approaching this thing."

Her mask began to flicker; they were close to the source, wherever the Wet had forced its way into the building. Jasmine dropped back behind Cathy, readying the modified fire extinguisher, keeping an eye on the low ceiling. A utility room in the corner, door cracked open. Her mask whirred with familiar data points, but it was nothing like the wave from upstairs. An older trail.

"If it can learn, if it feels what we feel, if it knows where we are weak, then it might start to think about this whole process as more than survival . . ."

Cathy entered the utility room, eyes turning neon green. Stacks of paper towel, an old mop bucket huddled in the corner. The ceiling dripped water onto her shoulder. The Wet didn't follow any path. Its spread was controlled, maybe even directed.

A gurgling sound on the floor and what looked like a man's hand reaching toward her. The mask began to bleat again. Cathy knelt down in the dark and poked at the hand-shaped mass on the floor. The space where the wrist would be was ragged, unfinished, thwarted.

"What is it?" Jasmine said, canister primed to spray.

"It's what we saw upstairs," Cathy said "It's how they got him down here. In pieces."

Cathy pulled her gloved finger back. The mass went still. Their masks looked at each other in the dark, two sets of neon eyes.

"Give me a sample case. Biggest one you got. Come on."

The handshape slowly shuddered back toward a small hole in the wall offering escape.

"Not today," Cathy said. The sample case barely contained it. She sealed it shut.

"How are we supposed to bring this back to the office?" Jasmine said.

"We don't," Cathy said. Two sets of glowing eyes nodding at each other in the gloom. No one else could see them here beneath the earth. "This belongs to us now."

11.

"You know I actually hated hockey, right? Grown men chasing each other around on the rink to win a giant cup someone puked in the year before?"

Stan kept trying to tie his tie, thick fingers forgetting their positions for a full Windsor. He gave up and switched to a half Windsor, pulling too tight and letting it hang there for a few seconds, watching his throat strain in the mirror.

"Oh, I never figured you were into sports at all, honey."

"I played rugby," Sidney said. She was already dressed, a floor-length gown in blood red, the kind of red you only achieved with thousands of dollars on hand. She would likely never wear it again. She had to live up to expectations at these things, make sure the room understood Marigolds had money to burn. "I was the one they threw in the air. I did that for three years."

"And you never got hurt?"

"I wasn't stupid, Stan."

"I wasn't saying you're stupid, Sid. Just a dangerous sport. I knew a kid at my school, Danny something, I swear he got his skull fractured like a melon during practice. Fell headfirst into someone else's knee."

The house in Rosedale was Sidney's home base, the sun in their lopsided solar system. She waited until Stan's mother died to fully renovate the place, phoning up contractors during breaks at the wake and interviewing tile guys while they waited for a draft of the obituary.

"It's only dangerous if you think you can survive the scrum alone."

"Well, there you go, now I learned something about rugby."

"Oh, shut up," Sidney said. Her heels brought her to his eye level. "You don't need to patronize me. I know you need me there tonight. I'm happy to go. It's a good thing, Stan."

"Is it?"

"When they stop inviting you, that's when you start worrying."

No online invitation for this party existed. Nothing that could be forwarded. A small piece of paper delivered to a primary residence. It couldn't be traced to anyone. Even the printer they used to make it was destroyed after rendering its services. The ink was crimson, the invitation unsigned.

"When they do stop inviting me, maybe I'll live in peace once again."

Sidney laughed. "That's never going to be an option for you."

Stan pulled the tie tight against his throat.

§

The tower was called Babel. Yes, they were warned and warned repeatedly. The architects claimed they were reclaiming the word from its biblical origins, spinning a formerly dire warning into a statement about the joyous bonds of community, the power of multiculturalism and the unique plurality of the city's voices. Before The Marigold rose into the sky, Babel was the tallest residential tower in the city, perched off Bloor, overlooking the valley below like a wizened sorcerer reminding the villagers who owned them.

"I'm supposed to be nice," Stan said. The black car dropped them off in the private penthouse garage. Staff averted their eyes. "That's your point?"

"You're supposed to be professional," Sidney said. The elevator before them was gilded with what might have been real gold around the edges, doors an immaculate eggshell white. Stan learned all about the variations of white during Sidney's renovations.

"I'm professional. More than my father ever was."

"That's not saying much," Sidney laughed. "But you're right. They probably see you as an improvement."

The doors opened. There were only two buttons.

"I am."

Sidney chose up. Stan considered where down would take them, shifting his duffel bag from hand to hand.

"Oh, I know you think you are, that's what makes you so good at this. You believe your own bullshit. You'd tell me it was sunny during a storm and I bet you wouldn't even feel the rain on your face."

"I'll take that as a compliment."

Sidney checked her phone, scrolling through messages from someone who wasn't a hockey player. Maybe baseball this time, or another actor trying to break through, pulling shifts at The Marigold's ever-changing restaurant, complaining about the way rich people tipped.

"Maybe it is," Sidney said. "Too much doom and gloom out there. Everyone wants it to be the end of the world. Life is shit, kids are stupid, parents won't die. So even if it's relentless optimism founded on nothing, I appreciate it."

The elevator had no windows, no visible emergency button. Stan assumed it was hidden under a panel, sacrificed for the aesthetic of this metal box, simplicity surrounded by opulence. Despite its architects' intentions, Babel was built as a rebuke to the city around it, no different than the streets of single-family homes that shuddered at the thought of a fourplex. Stan believed Marigold II would embrace the city, marrying its excesses with options, overwhelming possibilities. Stan never wrote any of his theories down. They existed in his head alone. His father had no stake in this second Marigold, an attempt to undo the past. The old man only helped arrange the shaky financing.

"I'm a ray of sunshine," Stan said as the doors opened. He watched Sidney's face slip into party mode, her eyes going wide, lips sliding back for an effortless smile. He wasn't even sure if she knew it was happening. Part of the job, part of being a Marigold. She was better at it than Stan, better than his siblings, who were still hiding out at the racetracks in what was left of Florida — she didn't need it like they all did. She was a voracious force, consuming the world if it was worth her time. He measured himself against her and felt a great lack, a hole inside him never quite filled. The hole kept him hungry. The hole was where the bile seeped out.

"You're never quite late." A voice behind his ear. Sidney was already gone, disappearing into another tastefully gilded room, so restrained it screamed of wealth, all the tables adorned with singular pieces of driftwood. Every suit was dark blue. Stan didn't see any pinstripes. "You're always arriving just as everyone asks where you've been all night."

The arm wrapping itself around his waist belonged to Abigail Holstein. The building belonged to her family, but this suite was hers. Despite years of lawsuits, sexual harassment complaints, a fractured femur after a fall from the fifth floor during the construction of Babel, and three hernias in six months, Hammond Holstein still controlled the family fortune and the development company famous for its red cow logo. Abigail was happy to wait for however many hernias it took to finally bring him down. Her brothers were busy DJing in Sweden.

"It was the elevator's fault."

"The elevator's there to build anticipation," Abigail said. She wore a black dress that hid her short legs, pushed her chest up toward whoever had her attention. The top of her head barely touched Stan's chin. "It's the amuse-bouche."

"I thought that was a soup."

"Sometimes," Abigail said. "It's really just a taste."

The penthouse was filled with fresh-faced junior Holstein employees doing their best to fit in with the developer set who'd been invited, their own hangers-on already accustomed to the level of relentless excess at previous Holstein affairs. Men from mortgage firms stuffed their faces with scallops fried in brown butter and wrapped in other dead things, while buttoned-up lawyers circled the floor with fifty-year-old scotch clutched in their shaky hands, checking in with clients who could make or break their firms based on only a month or two of billable hours.

Servers in tight black shirts navigated the crowd, bodies perfectly proportioned. Stan considered grabbing a neon green shrimp cocktail off a passing tray before Abigail pulled him toward a non-descript door at the back of the penthouse, the real purpose of the party buried beneath the layers of pomp outside. The door stood out if only in its plainness, surrounded by minimalist sculptures and what looked like an original Jackson Pollock.

Stan clutched a duffle bag in his free hand, heart rate rising as they moved closer to the door. People swirled past him. Sidney waved from a conversation where she held court, a martini in each immaculate hand. A man laughed and another tried to stick his hand down a server's pants. The world shook and bucked. A glass shattered on the floor. Abigail stepped over it.

The plain white wooden door slid open. Stan slipped inside, following Abigail's lead. It closed behind them. No phones allowed. Nowhere to hide a camera or recording device. The Holsteins followed the old rules set out over a century before. A man in a black suit and no tie stood before them. He wore a tinted motorcycle helmet. He held out his gloved hands for their clothes. Usually, these events were held beneath ancient hotels or old stone buildings with labyrinthian basements. This was the first to be held in the sky. A meeting that held the city's fate by the throat, a ritual determining the arc of the future and the fate of those in its path.

Or so Stan was told.

He slipped out of his clothes. Abigail did the same. The silent man barely moved. Stan felt himself growing hard, despite the cold, eyes staring ahead, ignoring Abigail's nude form beside him. Maybe it was the fear coursing through him. He bent and reached into his bag, pulling out a long white robe. There was no hood. Stan's father had abolished the practice. Too easy to conceal yourself with a hood. You had to own your claims, had to look each member in the eye, the circle standing around the coals of a day-old fire. Without a hood, you were known.

You could be found wanting.

"Showtime," Abigail said, now in her own robe. She didn't say anything about the old stains on Stan's robe or his erection. People had all kinds of reactions before these meetings, personal distress was part of the ritual. This would be Stan's first meeting without his father on hand.

"They're waiting."

Another white door behind the silent man, another room smaller than the last. Ten other faces waiting for them, most of them old and white, but not all. One or two with long grey beards, another with an insulin pump sticking out of his side, muted screen glowing beneath his robe. Abigail was the only woman in the room.

"Finally, Marigold. You wanted us to die here waiting for you?"

"I'm here for the appointed time," Stan said. "Takes a while to change into this ridiculous shit, doesn't it? Why not just go naked at this point? Where's the new one? Ramji?"

One of the old men snorted, words layered with spittle. "Lost his nerve, I suspect. Couldn't live up to his mother. Why are we here anyway? I like a good party, but we already met this season. A successful meeting at that. Now another so soon? Not how we do things. You summon us here for what, Hammond? To show off this tower? We've all seen your dick before."

"Father," Abigail said. "Would you explain?"

Hammond Holstein was an ancient stork of a man, all bone and tendon. "I suppose we're all here because of me. I know this isn't exactly traditional." His voice flung the last word across the room like a curse. These meetings were traditional in the basest sense. "But it is necessary. What I need is clear and what we need to do cannot wait. Another year is too long."

Abigail smiled. Fine white smoke gathered in the domed ceiling, spiralling out a tiny hole at its peak. Much like a church, everyone dressed up to distract from the looming depravity.

"So, I've called upon all of you as we've always done. Even as families have joined, sole proprietors have come and gone, dynasties have ruled and failed, we've always gathered in rooms like this. I come to you with a simple request, one that by its very nature may upset your idea of balance in the city. I know we all have projects lined up. But I need to build again, now. Another tower."

All heads swivelled to Stanley Marigold. His reaction would dictate all that followed. He was the last one to pay, using his turn for Marigold II a few months before. Abigail's smile disappeared.

"Another tower?" Stan said. His erection was gone. "Now? As in this summer?"

"Yes. This summer. We've already got most of the approvals. The site has been selected."

"Have you thought this through?" Stan said. "Or are you just an old man losing his mind?"

No one answered. Stan took a deep breath filled with the fine white smoke. His father's words in his head. Remember their vices. Give them just enough to make them ask for more.

"Answer him, father," Abigail said.

Hammond hesitated.

"I'll ask you again," Stan said. "Hammond — have you thought this through?"

Hammond placed a hand in the smouldering fire and pulled out a white coal. He held it in his frail palm. "It needs to be done. If I don't move now, it'll never happen."

"Never is a long time," Stan said. "You sure that's the right word to use?"

Hammond shuddered against the heat in his hand.

"We need the money," Abigail sputtered, façade slipping. "We need—"

"Don't speak for me," Hammond said. "You don't know."

"I know enough. We need the money, Stan. Babel isn't enough to keep us growing, and without growth, they're going to start asking more questions about the money . . . we don't want anyone asking questions. I know you understand that."

Murmurings from the circle. Stan was tired of the robes, the coals, the collective's extravagant parties constructed to somewhat conceal these fetid little meetings. It was all dress-up. There was no need for any of this theatre anymore. To make money, you had to take advantage. You had to do things you did not want to do. This had always been clear to Stan, an easy, plain moral calculus he embraced as part of the job. You could dress it up with ritual, you could stand around mumbling about the price, but in the end, it was a cost/benefit analysis. Chants and murmurs were archaic versions of opportunities and challenges. Risk mitigation debated like homilies, recited like psalms, dangled before a bored captive audience. The boardroom was turned into a misguided temple, the faith they displayed for nothing but their own bottom line.

"So, you want to reach out to him again. Go against all the rules we've agreed to," Stan said. "Go against a system that by all accounts has served everyone in this room well. That's what you think is best?"

Hammond still held the coal. Stan wondered if he'd picked one from the edges, if it was even hot or if this was all a ruse to get him to bend over here with an audience. The power lay in his hands, but everyone wanted to see how he would wield it without his father's presence. Tell them what they wanted. Convince them you were on their side.

"This is what we need. Threshold outpaces us. Building their own worlds down by the water. Since you were the last to pay, we need your blessing to reach out to the gardener."

Abigail watched him closely. He could feel her eyes searching him for weakness. He waited. The Holsteins needed the money. He savoured the desperation. He waited. Outside the plain white room, someone banged out Elton John covers on a piano no one was meant to play.

"You have it. The Marigolds pass the stone to you. The circle remains whole."

Hammond sighed, releasing the coal back into the smouldering pit. His palm was raw, weeping with fresh blisters. Tell them you agree. Tell them what they want to hear.

"The circle remains whole," the group responded in an attempt at one voice, a few of the older men struggling to get the words out.

Some of them hadn't built anything in a decade but they were still here. They had paid the price. They had watched competitors' buildings crumble while theirs survived the chaotic seasons. You didn't walk away from the circle after that. Its ledger was a living thing. You were a burden that had to be accounted for at every meeting.

"Is there anything else?" Stan said. He wanted out of his robe.

"About the price," Abigail said. "We would draw it from the general fund."

"If he'll take it."

"He will," Abigail said. "He's got to eat just like we do."

Like the rest of the room, Abigail assumed everyone was driven by the same forces that drove her, the same greed, the same old hunger for more. Stan didn't argue with her statement. He surrendered the polished red stone he kept in his robe to the fire. Something his father once found at a dollar store had become part of the ritual — Stan didn't know what it was actually made from, only that it didn't melt. Hammond pulled out the red stone with the same blistered hand he used before. The old men in robes now chuckled with each other, formality sloughing off them like a second skin.

Stan had played his part. He left the room first, followed by Abigail. He stripped off the robe and collected his clothes from the man in the black motorcycle helmet, who barely acknowledged their presence. His dick stayed soft this time. Stan took his time and watched Abigail get dressed. She took her time, obviously pleased with how the ritual played out. Babel was five years old and starting to show the strain. Some of the suites still hadn't sold. One level of the parking garage was off-limits. There was currently a lawsuit with the contractors, who were suing their own subcontractors, a long line of mouldy dominoes. A raccoon was said to have taken over a suite on the fourth floor, refusing to move.

Stan pulled on his jacket, adjusted his tie. He stepped out of the plain door back into the party, where someone was still attempting to force a song out of the piano. He spotted Sidney in the middle of what was meant to be a kitchen. She held court, hands enunciating each syllable, laugh thick and throaty, head thrown back with the effort. People buzzed around her, drawn toward her warmth or maybe her proximity to power. Stan never fully knew how much of it was Sidney herself and how much of it was the glamour, if there was a veil shading every interaction, her power so vested in his own. She would be fine without it, but what would she become?

"Are we staying here for the rest of the circus?" Stan said.

Familiar hands wrapped around him again, Abigail watching his wife command the room. "Does she know? What we do in there? What it means to be invited into the circle."

"She knows it's important. She knows enough not to ask more."

Abigail squeezed his biceps, insistent. "If you say so."

"If I didn't trust her with these things, we never would've married," Stan said, moving away from the kitchen to the elevator. Abigail's grip remained. "What's the point if there's no one to leave this stuff behind for? My daughter knows that. One day she'll come back to remind us. If you're not building for the future, what's it all for?"

"Order," Abigail said. "The order of things needs to be maintained." She dragged him toward the penthouse elevator. His daughter Fiona would not want to see him now. Three years in Italy without a word back to the old man. She only kept in touch with her mother. Everyone had their own knives to bury inside you. One day, he would have to bring her to this circle. Some of the old men from the ritual now circulated the party, liver-spotted hands reaching out for handshakes and the bodies of servers, who spun and weaved their way through each untenable encounter.

"And that order just happens to have you sitting on top?"

She pushed the down button. No other option.

"It's fun to pretend you want things to be different when you're a kid," she said. "When you're a little punk who decided to go take some theory classes. Upset at Dad for a couple of weeks, maybe write an essay about the savage death drive inherent in all capitalism."

Doors opened. Abigail pushed him inside.

"But eventually, you learn you like where you're sitting. You like waking up clean and safe and calm. And maybe, you're sitting there for a reason. Doesn't need to be a good reason, but there's a reason that matters. And so, you need to ensure you maintain your position."

The doors closed.

"Or everything might fall apart."

He watched her pull open his pants as the elevator dropped. She pulled him into her mouth, already half-hard, growing harder. She looked up, eyes locking with his as the elevator plunged and kept plunging. She clamped down her teeth, letting him know who was in control in this elevator, this building, this future they had just chosen together around the coals. He let her believe that, waiting for his turn. The order wasn't what Abigail believed. She'd only seen the start of the ritual. She'd never been there at the end of a thing, only the beginning. Her idea of the price was still hypothetical, hovering in the abstract.

"Your turn," she said as the elevator touched down. She pressed up. He would tell Sidney about it all when they got home. There were no secrets between them. She would want to know everything. Her spirit was in that white room with him, guiding his voice through the smoke. Unlike Abigail, she knew the true cost of order. She knew the price wasn't a metaphor. Stan got down on his knees as the elevator rose again, Abigail's hands in his hair.

Suite 307

The family told her it would be better if she went out east for now until everything was sorted for the funeral in Edmonton. Everyone would feel more comfortable if they knew she was safe. No one wanted grief compounded. Gayle Tantallon didn't argue with them.

The suite belonged to her nephew Silas, a lawyer for a weed start-up called NorthStar, yet another Threshold subsidiary. They used an abstract constellation resembling a pot leaf as their logo. His closet was full of old hoodies with different iterations of the logo, starting with a friendly smiling star that gradually morphed into a series of lines and dots without any charm. Gayle took the oldest sweater with the smiling pot leaf star, feeling a little less alone. She could hear noise from the street below, people honking and yelling at each other, the occasional siren warning her someone was about to die or maybe the cops didn't feel like waiting for a light.

Silas said he only slept here when he didn't feel like driving back to Markham. The house was funded by the trust Gayle's father set up; every grandchild had one. Gayle suspected Silas was carrying out an affair with someone, maybe from his office or through one of those apps, the kind her sister kept showing her. *You should really meet someone*, she'd say, like Gayle hadn't met enough people to know she was better off alone.

Gayle found condoms and lubes and other things she didn't want to think about too much in Silas's bedside table when she arrived, pretended they weren't there as she lay in his king-size bed. There was a screen mounted across from the bed if she wanted to distract herself from the image of her father tumbling down the stairs, yelping like a terrier.

No one accused her of pushing him. They all knew Gayle loved the old man, stuck by him while all the other Tantallon children moved away, pursuing jobs and families and affairs and the occasional fraud prosecution. She was the one who moved into his palace north of St. Albert after he got sick the first time, prostate cancer running through him like an angry metal spike. No one accused her of pushing him, but as her sister Tanya explained, people were talking and they didn't want that talk to get out of hand, didn't want reporters coming by the house to ask what had happened to old man Tantallon and the spoils of his oil and gas empire. Gayle understood. That house tricked you into thinking you weren't alone. You couldn't keep track of where you'd been throughout the day, entering rooms with the lights still on and the TV playing a gameshow where everyone knew all the answers except you.

The condo only had so many rooms. You could keep track of where you went. The city was loud, but it let you know you weren't alone. You didn't have to talk to people if you didn't want to, and no reporters knew to look for Gayle on the third floor of The Marigold. Silas had food delivered every few days. Gayle was especially fond of chopped salads. She didn't think she'd like blue cheese, but you could wake up one day in a condo, listening to the drains, and believe you were starting over. You could hear someone calling your name, asking you if you remembered to shower the night before. *Would you like that?*

Sometimes she rode the elevator for an hour or two, watching people get on and off. They didn't know her, didn't ask how her father could have fallen backwards down the stairs, cracking his head on the hardwood. When Silas dropped her off, he told her she was his favourite aunt. That still meant something in this family, even as they gathered without her to sort out the funeral arrangements. Gayle knew she wasn't fun like her brother Kelvin, who liked to buy airplanes. His wife, Deanna, liked to travel to Europe without him, posting almost naked, splayed out in the sand like she wasn't fifty years old and getting older. Gayle knew she wasn't gifted like her brother Daniel either, who basically ran Tantallon Enterprises now, clutching it so tight people called him the Little Emperor behind his back.

To be favourite aunt meant being reliable, not forgetting birthdays, sending neatly written fifty-dollar cheques at Christmas and never even asking for thank you notes even though she would've appreciated them. Gayle never had to work, her father told her he didn't expect it, but he did expect her to marry someone and sometimes they fought about that, loud fights where he threw things across the room and she dodged them because she was still pretty nimble. Gayle used to play second base in softball during high school — an important position, you had to have a real knack for it.

Since Silas told her she was his favourite aunt, Gayle decided not to mention the dripping noise in the bathroom. A small drip, every couple seconds, you could barely hear it unless you were lying awake at 4 a.m. considering how you may have been just ahead of your father on the stairs when he stumbled, that you could've reached out to grab him, but maybe you didn't, maybe because you were so tired or because he yelled at you the night before, asking why you were still so alone, why you hadn't found anyone yet.

Silas probably knew about the drip. He flew out to Edmonton as soon as she was settled but made sure the food deliveries kept coming. Sometimes he texted, asking strange questions about her father's mansion, if she remembered turning off all the lights, if there was a reason she sent the nurse home that night. Did she remember?

It wasn't just the bathroom sink dripping. Gayle tried sleeping in the living room instead, setting herself up on the leather couch that smelled like it was recently dead. She liked it. Her nest was a hodgepodge of comforters and pillows, no taint of Silas's affair, no sex toys hidden in between the cushions.

Another drip, more rapid and insistent, kept her awake in the living room, which wasn't so much a room as part of the larger kitchen, dining room, and den area, all the walls painted the same hotel lobby taupe, featuring landscapes purchased at IKEA, old barns and fishing boats and a couple of horses pulling a hay cart. She tried turning the tap as tight as she could, the faucet waiting a few long seconds before another droplet formed. She tried pulling her NorthStar hoodie tight against her head, tried wrapping a pillow over both her ears. It worked for the first night on the couch, kept away the insistent plinking noise, let her drift away to a small place of oblivion where she wasn't asking herself why they hadn't summoned her back to Edmonton to deliver a eulogy about the great man her father had been when he was alive.

Gayle decided to fix the drip herself. As the favourite aunt, she didn't want to disappoint Silas. He seemed estranged from his young wife, Ming, who once told Gayle she reminded her of a grizzly bear. Gayle took it as a compliment at the time but was now second-guessing the remark. Maybe it was bad to be a grizzly. There were two sides to everything, Gayle knew that. It was part of why they sent her here, in case people misconstrued her father's accident.

Gayle went out and found a hardware store where everything was overpriced and they didn't even take cash. She had to use the emergency credit card she kept in her shoe. No one manned the checkout. Cameras watched her at every corner. People ignored her on the street. She liked the city even if it smelled like rot. No one wanted to know your business. She rode the elevator for half an hour, enjoying its rise and fall, the gentle chimes of its doors so different from the relentless drip inside the condo. Every chime was a new possibility.

Gayle waited until dark. The faucets didn't drip during the day. It was like they were waiting for her to try to fall asleep, like they wanted her to know they knew her habits. Maybe it had something to do with the tides, the way water moved with celestial bodies. You couldn't see stars from Silas's condo. The towers drowned them. Instead of looking up, Gayle stared down into the pit across the street, blacker than any sky. There was nothing in it but dirt and potential. She wanted to crawl down into that hole, emerge in the morning. She could hear the drip in her head, water hitting the back of her brainpan, reminding her she actually had a job to do.

Gayle tried tightening the kitchen faucet first, making sure the wrench didn't scar the metal. The best kind of favours were the ones you didn't need to claim, ones you got to keep for yourself in those small moments when you were alone outside under the sun and the air was clear and your mind was clear and all you had to do was close your eyes and remember you were a good person, maybe just for that moment.

This would be one of those favours. Gayle wasn't having much luck with the faucet, so she opened up the cabinet below the sink. She admired Silas' commitment to order, all the cleaners arranged tallest to shortest in a row, brushes and sponges hanging from little hooks. It might have been the pipes leading to the tap causing the problem, forcing water up and out into the sink. Gayle didn't know much about plumbing, but she knew the drip would clear her mind, let her settle down before the family called her to attend the funeral. She needed this space silent. The call was going to come any day now for the funeral.

On her hands and knees, Gayle stuck her head into the cabinet under the sink. Darker than the city ever got in here, darker than she realized, too late to grab a flashlight. Rot in here somewhere. Gayle placed her hand against the back wall of the cabinet, fingers sticking to a gummy black substance. The drain spoke to her.

You did it.

Gayle tried to pull away, banging her head against the bottom of the sink. The wall held her fingers fast. No pain in her hand, only her head. The wall wouldn't release her. The pipes sang, the drain above her like a mouth.

We don't blame you. What else were you supposed to do?

Gayle wanted to tell the voice in the pipes it was wrong. Voice or voices, she couldn't tell. Her head hurt, maybe she was bleeding. Her hair felt sticky, breathing rapid. Her heels kicked back at the ceramic tiles. The voice or voices tried to soothe her as she fought against the black substance binding her to the wall.

You needed to do it. We do the same to dogs.

Gayle wanted to say it wasn't that she pushed him, she'd never have pushed him, she just didn't reach out as he stumbled. She turned and saw the fear in his eyes, fear she recognized from looking in the mirror. She had never seen her father look like that before. And then he was reaching out for her.

You did what had to be done. The best thing for everyone.

Gayle tugged and pulled with her free hand, trying to release her arm. She considered screaming — the walls were thin enough, someone would hear her, but her lungs didn't have the air. She

137

coughed, hacked, breathed in the black, wet substance under the sink. It was infiltrating her body, its communal voice attempting to soothe her as it drained her will, pulling her apart in slow pieces.

The best thing for everyone.

The eulogy Gayle planned to give was thirteen minutes and five seconds. She timed it in the mirror, repeating it from memory. A brief rundown of her father's early successes, his attitudes as a father, his sorrow at the loss of her mother, all leading to his greatest triumphs, the growth of his firm into a global corporation, the expansion of his family through marriages and grandchildren and nieces and nephews, all blessed with the same last name. And all the people who took that for granted, who barely acknowledged this once-powerful man as he slipped away, people like her brothers, who took his money and spent it without his knowledge, people like her sister who pretended he was already dead, people who came and asked for favours and laughed at his liver-spotted head while Gayle was right there in the room, and she was supposed to say this was okay, to condone this ongoing circus act. Gayle's eulogy would end in a fiery accusation toward its audience, one based in love and pride, one that said she knew what had to be done and the rest were all just circling like buzzards.

The best thing.

Eventually, Gayle Tantallon stopped moving. Her shoes stopped rattling against the ceramic floor. Her lungs surrendered, her eyes closed, her hands went limp. Eventually, she dissipated. Only a wet, black stain remained.

12.

They wanted people to call it the Innovation District. No one did that.

They wanted people to call them job creators, visionaries, designers, futurists, urbanists, maybe even saviours. That didn't happen either. They wanted a world where every metric could be measured, every action indexed, every loiterer documented from various angles with a plethora of sensors, all operating as part of a larger network that could revolutionize how a city functioned, what a city knew about itself, and how it could adapt. They got a small piece of that, at least.

"Why are we here, Dad?" Soda said. "What does this have to do with anything?"

Dale sat in the backseat like a fare. He picked at dirty fingernails and surveyed the sparkling, flickering chunk of the waterfront before them. This was the home of Threshold, the hive of activity for all its subsidiaries and their workers. "It has everything to do with everything."

"That's not helpful."

Soda watched his father press his fingers to his temples before the old man spoke again.

"Do you know how anything gets done, son?"

"I've had lots of jobs, Dad," Soda said. "I've never not had a job, really."

"That's not what I asked you. You need to answer the question I ask you, not make up your own. I asked if you know how anything gets done."

They all called it Threshold, making the district synonymous with its ownership, one veiled behind a number of different holding companies and corporate entities that bloomed and shrank depending on the markets. The district hugged the eastern waterfront, still only a few promised buildings poking into the night. The two men weren't required for this place to function. They sat in silence, watching water lap against the crumbling concrete. No one would notice if Soda let the car roll into the lake. Sometimes he considered it, when the debt collectors found his new number and the credit card bill arrived on his phone, or his father stole yet another fridge from an abandoned house and asked Soda to help him move it down into the basement with all the other empty fridges.

"No, I guess not," Soda said finally.

"That's the first smart thing you've said tonight."

Whenever Soda took a fare down here, he dropped ten below the speed limit as cameras charted each turn he made. Sometimes there were competing cameras on the corner, corporations who bought up the forgotten pieces, little leftovers in the district, tiny slices of public life. Soda considered getting tinted windows even though he couldn't afford them, even though there was likely an algorithm in the works to cancel out the tint in a couple weeks. Maybe he was becoming like the old man, sure every eye was trained on him. They had a file on him, after all.

"Things only get done through negotiation," Dale said. "Now a lot of people have a very positive view of the word *negotiation*. They see it as bringing everyone to the table, a way of levelling things. But just because you're negotiating doesn't mean there's an even playing field. Just because someone sits down across from you and says 'I'm here to discuss our options in good faith' doesn't mean it's true. You know that, Sammy. You've signed a contract, haven't you? Negotiating is really just about getting someone to consent to what you were gonna do anyway. It's someone with more power than you telling you there's a choice. A false binary. There are no ones for us, only zeroes."

Threshold was supposed to change how the city functioned, offering a new way of living in the sprawling, hungry metropolis, one that actually responded to its citizens' needs. Defining those needs was the difficult part. The pilot was designed to make things free, open for everyone. Access to parks and the waterfront, heated sidewalks, sheltered walkways, a new future of urbanism accelerated with big data and AI technologies, built to make the city a more cohesive and workable place — as long as you agreed to its terms and conditions.

After all, no one was forced to live in the Threshold district. No one had to be monitored if they did not wish to be part of the experiment. No one was required to register unless they chose to enter. No one person ruled Threshold — even its location split it across the wards of two separate city councillors, a strategy to keep everyone off-balance from the outset, building an astroturfed consensus. Soda knew when you entered Threshold, you were indexed. And an index was never an objective tool. An index was informed by the very people who designed it and decided which variables mattered, which would be recorded and which would be ignored. A gated community with an invisible fence, glowing on a waterfront that now consumed it.

"They'll dress these things up," Dale continued. "They'll pretend you're included, but the decisions are already made. What I found on that little drive you gave me, that little demon drive, is nothing different than what I've seen before. There doesn't need to be a conspiracy every time.

"I know you think I'm paranoid. And I am. But the reality is power doesn't require a conspiracy to function. It operates openly. It shows you the cogs at each step, even if it doesn't name them. It operates openly because it can, because that's what power gives you: impunity."

The streetlights around them shuddered, the city struggling with another mid-March heatwave that would dissipate within a few days.

"What's on that little demon drive is the games they play with each other, the ways they dress up their crimes. If you wake up in the morning telling yourself you are good and necessary and righteous, I guarantee you'll hurt people. What lies at the bottom of all of this is how a building gets built, where the money needs to go, which groups benefit most once units are sold. Keeping it away from the old neighbourhoods, the protected spaces. And a lot of it can only be traced back to numbered companies and numbered accounts on islands we'll never see, Sammy."

Soda watched his father quietly, afraid of shattering this lucid moment. A car horn or high beams could destroy it. He tried to pretend he wasn't there, he was just another recorder in the Threshold, documenting, indexing, and defining his father without his explicit consent. They already knew him. He was the one who let them in.

"I do mean islands. Islands of their own and elaborate pens for the rest of us, two hundred and eighty square feet and a toilet in the sky. All that shit up there in the sky, sliding down the inside of each little tower. What happens when the pumps break? We both know. We all know. But we pretend they'll fix it, management will do the right thing, investors will do the right thing, board members will do the right thing. And we know they won't.

"What you have on this drive is somewhere in a little footnote, buried under hundreds of pages of floor plans and exceptions and lawyers debating what counts as a 'stove' is in the context of a 'kitchen' or a 'living space,' what you have is an admission of a very old price no one wants to speak about. A price people brought with them centuries ago, dragged it across an ocean to make it live here again."

Soda's phone pinged with another ride request, despite his offline status. Demand was high on a Friday night when the weather was too hot to stay inside. Dale didn't notice, his paranoia only held at bay by his current level of comfort in this wheeled confessional.

"If you look at this big file, you're going to see this thing on page 841 in the appendix, and maybe they had to explain it to this new kid, this Ramji. If he was new to that world, it might've shocked him. A rich kid with a conscience is always a problem — you can't undo a hundred years of wealth. Wealth is always built on bodies, on the sweat and blood and bones of others. Wealth comes from bodies. And bodies do not last."

Outside the car, Soda could hear howling.

"Now they don't have to do this," Dale said. "Some people try to get around it, using birds or cats, even livestock. It depends on the structure. The Irish still like to use a horse skull if they can find one. But here, they're still attached to those old ways, still think making it into a ceremony justifies the whole thing. A building needs blood. That's what the old ways would say. All the world over, people tell themselves this story. Saints and sinners, shamans and doctors. Greeks. Romans. Filipinos. Scottish monks. Albanians dreaming of castles. It's an old story, that's why it's useful. You acknowledge the sin without atoning. You conduct the sacrifice with a false ceremony. You pay the price without understanding the cost.

"This drive explains the true cost for a tower. It doesn't conceal it with robes or rituals. It includes it in the price as a line item. Refreshing to see it laid out like this."

Dale held up a large Tupperware container. "But those Threshold fellows, they don't understand what they have here, what rituals they've stumbled into here. They just think it's some old graves, dead bodies off boats. Something has shifted. It's spreading out into the dirt. The old offerings have shaken loose. And Threshold knows something is wrong, I don't doubt it. But not what exactly. They've found it in the dirt, but they can't really name it yet. An infection. We need proof. We need the dirt to show everyone we know what is living beneath their feet."

Dale clambered out of the backseat, disappearing into the dark with his Tupperware. Soda drummed his fingers on the steering wheel, doing his best to ignore his phone. There was no point trying to rein in his father. If he needed dirt from the Threshold district, then that is what he would get. Like abandoned fridges, cooking elements, and plywood, the dirt was an integral part of Dale's design. He just hadn't shared that design with his son.

The howling continued. A flashlight made its way toward the car, weaving along the weedy perimeter. Occasionally, another developer would take a chance building something in the Threshold district, agreeing to the hodgepodge of terms and conditions that proliferated along the shoreline. An empty lot could very well be someone else's sacred garden. A knock on the driver-side glass. Soda had to turn the car back on before he could open the window. Three more knocks, more insistent.

"How's it going?" Soda said, wincing at the light. "Everything alright?"

"You're trespassing right now. You may not know it, but you are. The signage hasn't been fully posted," the voice at the end of the light said, a familiar voice. He recognized the yellow portcullis blade on the black bulletproof vest. "You get a pass this time, but you need to leave. Now."

"This is what you do with your evenings?" Soda said before he could stop himself. Same enforcement officer from a few days before, same one whose name was on the ticket he swallowed. He was sure of it, even though he couldn't see her face. Her tone was the same, the angle of the head tilted behind the flashlight, the same sunglasses in the middle of the night. It was happening again. He was trapped in this car, this life, this city.

"Excuse me?"

"Never mind," Soda said, window sliding back up. His father's paranoia infected him. Everywhere he looked, people were plotting against him, pulling him into their web to use him up and then spit him back out. It was a gig economy after all, one built on the bodies Dale detailed from the backseat. He tried to shake it off, instead found a surprisingly strong hand forcing itself through the window as it closed, gripping him by the collar, hairy and angry. It wasn't her, but the uniform was the same. The yellow gate with its sharp teeth.

"Don't 'never mind' me. Now turn off the car."

"You don't touch him!" Dale bellowed, thudding into the enforcement officer, the man's flashlight careening off into the dark like a weak firecracker. Soda tried opening the door, but their bodies blocked it. He heard scuffling and a low grunt. The window slid all the way back down as the larger man stood and gained the upper hand, a baton striking Dale across the face once, twice, three times. A wet thud. The weight of Dale's crumpled body kept the car door jammed shut.

"Need back-up! Two of them here!" the enforcement officer barked into his headset. Soda couldn't move the car; he didn't know if there was a leg or an arm under the wheels. Dale screamed again under a new barrage of heavy swings. "He's resisting, subject is unstable!"

The words prepared everyone for what was about to happen. A distanced preparation for an eventual investigation that would lead nowhere and identify no one at fault.

"Subject is volatile! Need back-up!"

More flashlights summoned on the parking lot's edge, swaying through the long grass and bent remains of chain link from previous failed developments. The land had been flipped so many times it was likely never meant to hold anything of value beyond its existence on the waterfront. Soda yanked himself over to the passenger side, gut catching on the shifter. He pushed the door open, could still hear the steady thwack of the baton on his father's arms, the bellowing rage of a man who cannot save himself, all of it cut through by a lone howl that then became two, then three, then four separate voices surrounding them. Soda flopped out of the car onto the gravel, eyes catching yellow eyes from the other side of the lot, animals emerging around them, something like coyotes, but wider through the shoulders, unafraid of a man with a baton screeching for back-up.

"They got some kind of dogs!"

One lunged at the officer, taking hold of his arm and yanking him to the ground. Howls pierced Soda's ears as he scrambled a retreat back into the car, Dale already staggering into the backseat. The Threshold-branded enforcement officer threw the almost-coyote off him, crunching one of its legs with his boot. Soda flopped behind the wheel and spotted the rippled mass of flesh where the officer's forearm had been before, the man shrieking as he fled back toward the flashlight beams gathering on the far side of the lot. The other creatures retreated back into the grass as Soda threw the car into drive, wheels shrieking.

They fled from the Threshold district and all its hidden ways of knowing who and what you were, catalogued in a waterproof basement somewhere. A database packaged and sold, repackaged and resold, until no one could determine why the data was collected in the first place, only that it existed, only that it could further your own purposes.

"It's going to be okay," Dale said from the backseat. "It going to be okay."

"Sure, now that you got your dirt, great," Soda said, ignoring stop signs and turn signals, world whirring by in various shades of spackled grey and neon light. "They'll be looking for us now. Probably a warrant, as if they need one. And they'll find the drive and then—"

"I wasn't talking to you," Dale said, face one massive bruise. "I'm talking to our friend."

Soda smelled the new friend before he saw it, one leg still bent under its body. His father held the animal in a gentle headlock, keeping its teeth from his face. Dale purred into its ragged ear and stroked its matted chest, consoling the animal that saved him.

"There's a name on that drive, Sammy, a man you need to reach out to if you want to understand what Threshold doesn't know yet, can't comprehend. If you want to protect yourself, you need to reach out to him. I used to know his father. I never should've strayed."

Soda's mouth hung open as he climbed onto the Gardiner Expressway, the battered road still standing after years of partial collapses. He didn't bother asking about the beast in the backseat his father had adopted with absolutely no consultation. The car was already filled with blood, it didn't matter where it came from. The beast's yellow eyes watched him as he switched lanes. There was no room or time to debate the animal. Within minutes, it had become part of Soda's life. Dale did this to you. He made you complicit. He made you pay.

"Who do I need to contact, Dad?"

The almost-coyote snorted, rolling in its new father's thick arms.

"Dad?"

"Stanley. I knew his father, a mean little fuck. Hey, no biting. Email him. Little Stanley Marigold, although he's probably big now. He knows all the line items. He knows the price. He's paid it before. And from what I can see, they're about to pay it again."

13.

Time to plant another seed, but much too soon. These things took time to settle. Something the younger generation didn't understand, didn't want to believe even though it was true. The note arrived at his apartment on the fringe of the Danforth, where a few Greek restaurants still let you pay with cash. A small piece of newsprint slid under the door while he was asleep on the couch. The requests were physical things that had to be delivered by someone, ideally someone who didn't understand what they'd done. The gardener didn't believe in the internet. He had tried all that when he was younger, tried to live a life free of the compulsions he'd inherited, yet they drew him back. A mosquito bumping up against the glass, willing to die for blood.

The scrap of paper had an address for another pit that would open up soon. They would rend open the earth, reach into its bowels, pull out the hot dirt, the roots, the wires, the pipes, the skulls, and all those little pieces of the past they so despised before they poured the foundation, claiming the hole as their own, rewriting its origins into something blanker. To appease the hunger of this new place, the gardener would need to plant another seed, just as his father did.

The gardener had no sons. No daughters. His two brothers dead, one run over by a bread truck while riding his bike, the other rotting to death during the AIDS crisis. His mother withered and died on the sales floor of The Bay, her heart giving out when they told her she no longer had a position in the watch repair department as there would no longer be a watch repair department. She didn't even make it to the elevator, just collapsed between the men's shoes and the children's beach section. When they called the gardener, he asked about her discount, if it would still pass on to him after death, and he enjoyed listening to that charged silence before the officer continued his canned speech. He burned his mother and threw the ashes out of an airplane he rented with her life insurance policy.

His own father was buried under a subway station no one ever built down by the dead heart of Ontario Place, his spirit trapped there due to the city's incompetence and the provincial government's indecision. Sometimes the gardener thought about trying to dig him up, but he didn't have the tools or the permits. He had money; money wasn't the problem. Money made life easier, sure it did, it always did. He could eat that money, gorge himself on all the bills he tucked away in stacks inside his closet. Money wasn't the point.

Relations with the official city power brokers soured after the subway station faltered, his father's final sacrifice turned into a mockery of the tradition they'd carried on for over a century. The disrespect shown to the man who made so much of this city possible, that was what kept the gardener up at night. He stopped visiting the library near his building where the city's brokers used to stash their requests. He realized the subway station was never going to be built, that his father's demise might've been the city's way of permanently severing the relationship. They'd never been fully keen on the price required to maintain a metropolis; the blood needed to ensure it didn't crumble into myth.

Newcomers didn't understand it either, Threshold and their ilk. They shook up the ground, made promises in steel and glass and timber, pretending there was a way to control the surface as if what roiled beneath was irrelevant. The more they promised, the more the gardener doubted their resolve. The city had turned to these new benefactors, people who claimed they could bend the future to their vision without surrendering anything in the process. All of it hypothetical and unproven, a magic trick without a final act, just the promise of wonder on a screen.

Everything had a price, the gardener told them, one of the rare moments he ventured into the core, confronted the men on the fourth floor who never seemed to do anything, according to their colleagues. The price ain't always money, he told them, wearing his best tan suit, one he got on discount at The Bay before his mother's death was officially recorded and her name removed from the payroll. It ain't always money but it's always there. You can't run from it. The bill always comes due.

They pretended things were fine as new community centres collapsed in on themselves like rotten fruit, their decline aided by the rain and the wind, allied with the wildlife surging through the streets at night. Roads swallowed by sinkholes, construction parks turned into quagmires, and the waterfront disappearing foot by foot into the lake. The gardener watched all of this, knowing it was only a matter of time before they came crawling back to him. For now, his services went exclusively to the private sector, the men, almost always men, willing to pay him to satiate the real city, the deep hole roiling beneath it. If you wanted a "world-class" city, you had to pay.

The gardener tried to limit these bigger private jobs, aware of the toll they took on everyone. They brought a lot of attention and the sacrifices weren't always appreciated by the hunger beneath the ground. The rarity of these gifts impacted their value. The gardener's father told him there was a reason Christmas only happened once a year and it had nothing to do with Christ.

This latest request was desperate. The gardener had time to mull it over. He tucked the note into a desk drawer that held nothing except receipts for all his recent purchases, all in cash. He pulled on an old Oilers jersey and wool hat before creaking down the stairs out into the street.

The gardener walked the Danforth. He disappeared in public places, just non-descript enough to be forgotten. This was something he was taught. Too warm for the hat, but he kept it on, part of the disguise. Nothing stayed the same here, but Toronto was intent on dismantling the very idea of a *past*, of any sort of tradition. It was embarrassed by its roots, which made sense to the gardener. When your greatest glories were trapped in a puritan period of Blue Sundays and elite corruption, the past wasn't always a pleasant companion. Old things tended to resurface, marring your perfect plan for the future. This included the new development request slipped under his door.

Ever since he planted the last seed, the gardener felt something shifting in the dirt. The Wet hadn't dissipated. There were tremors in the earth he didn't recognize anymore, things he wouldn't be able to explain to his father. It wasn't that clients were refusing to pay the price — the gardener knew what that looked like, how the earth gave way beneath the structure. This was more like a violation, a rot growing inside the soil, in the sewers and the root systems, man-made and natural networks falling prey to some slow-moving, corrupted hunter.

The stooped men the gardener met on scabby street corners, the women he threw a few bucks to outside the last of the diners with absentee landlords and flooded basements, the tattooed kids who asked him to pose for a photo beside an upturned garbage can, they all whispered about the unease creeping up out of the grates, friends felled by speeding cars with tinted windows or suspect overdoses or sudden heart attacks outside what was left of the SkyDome. Deaths recorded but never investigated, bodies burned before any examination.

Most of the practitioners had given up when his father died, turned away by the city or their own reliance on the comforts of modern life. There was no one to talk to, no one to commiserate with about the reality of the Wet. It wasn't a virus. You couldn't spit it into someone's mouth or wipe it on their clothes, and yet it was still out there, waiting.

"Buddy, you can't be wearing a jersey like that around here."

The kid was young, his beard soft despite the sneer. The teeth were white, a sign this world was still new to him. He'd probably never slept in the camps, definitely not once the weather got cold, wrapped in three sleeping bags in a tent under the naked trees. The gardener could tell a lot from looking at the kid. He was an observer, a bird perched on a humming wire. Nothing fancy, no cardinal or blue jay; the gardener was more like a grackle, an anonymous mass of feathers that was everywhere at once.

"Son, I wear whatever I want."

Sometimes a kid like this would take a swing at him. The gardener accepted this as part of the gambit. He preferred to work in person. He'd surrendered his phone years ago after a city councillor called him in the middle of the night, asking for a favour. A good way to get caught.

"Oh, you're a tough guy," the kid said, smiling now. Very new, very naïve, maybe his first year. The gardener didn't feel bad, but he did feel a tremor run through him, a reflex he believed he'd killed off after the fifth or sixth seed he planted with his father. Sometimes it was easier than you expected. Sometimes you ended up in the right place to reap the bounty of a city barely able to sustain itself. "You got a smoke?"

The gardener had smokes. Different packs, depending on his audience.

"Thanks, man, doing me a solid here. Haven't had a puff in a couple days."

A lie, but not a terrible one. The kid wanted to establish gratitude without giving himself away. Men came in and out of the dive bar, the inside filled with smoke despite the by-laws. There were exceptions everywhere now, too many other problems to investigate.

"So, you live around here?" the kid said. "I ain't seen you here before."

The gardener didn't usually go looking for seeds so close to home. He often rode the subways, roamed through the parks, searching for people attempting to cling to normalcy. People spoke to him because he appeared kind. If they vomited in front of him or drew a piece of glass out of a wound, he didn't recoil. He bent his head when they spoke and smiled broadly when they made a joke. The gardener wasn't lying when he did this. He liked people. People were animals and he liked animals. When the zoo collapsed, he was one of the first to track down the rare animals, spotting giraffes in Rouge Valley and spider monkeys jeering at him in the branches of High Park, their chittering voices unaware of the real cold to come. He didn't feel bad for the monkeys, just like he didn't feel bad for the seeds.

Most people wanted to pretend the people they knew were like the people in books or shows or movies — constructions with plausible reasons for all their actions, compulsions, and desires that fit neatly into charts to be parsed for tropes at a later date. Real people, though, were rarely driven by any specific force. The gardener knew they were infinitely complex and unknowable, products of nature and nurture no analysis could untangle. Ambiguity, the gardener's father said, is what makes us powerful. The inability to be known, the desperation for a reason, any reason, is what drove a ritual.

"I live close enough," the gardener said. If a seed presented itself, he would take it. "It's a good neighbourhood. Used to be I knew everyone around here. Things change so fast I lose track. Things keep happening and you stop keeping up, you know? But I'm still here."

"I feel that for sure. Used to live up, like, Bathurst and Finch, right?" the kid said. "But then that got so fucked, my buddy kept letting all these freaks crash there. I couldn't take it. Every morning we'd have no spoons in the house. I can only eat so much cereal with my hands, right?"

The gardener smiled. He lit up his own smoke. It was going to rain again.

"I been there."

The gardener wasn't concerned with the kid's morality. He may have qualified as a saint. It never mattered once they were buried in the earth. What the gardener looked for weren't sinners either, even though he'd take them in a pinch. Baby killers and con artists all served the same purpose, offerings to older things no one named. All the seeds only had one characteristic in common; they were loners, not by choice but necessity. People who'd been hurt so many times they withdrew into themselves or who hurt others so badly they now pinged through the universe untethered from empathy. They all came to him in their time of need, hands outstretched, desperate for someone to witness them as they were, to admit and acknowledge their existence.

"You know I been sleepin' at this one guy's place. He wakes me up at like 5 a.m. to watch soccer games," the kid said.

The gardener laughed. "Probably calls it futbol, right?"

"Fuck, you know he does! He has all the scarves and everything."

"He buy you a scarf yet?"

"He keeps threatening to, I think."

Rain trickled down. The kid finished his smoke, eyed the men cheering and laughing inside the bar. His shoulder slumped before he shook it off, preparing himself for whatever lay ahead.

"You don't have to stay there," the gardener said. "I got a room if you want to change things up. No pressure or anything, alright? I been in your position before. Just figure you could use a hand."

"Oh, you do, eh?" the kid said, guard back up. Sometimes this dance went on for hours, days, weeks. The gardener let it play out. They all withered eventually; they came back when he needed them. "What're you saying, huh?"

"All I'm saying," the gardener said, "is that you got a choice. That's all."

The kid laughed but didn't go back inside the bar.

14.

The first time Henrietta Brakes tried a tomato she threw up. She was five, her father attempting to expand her palate in the No Frills. A cherry tomato, the kind they grew in industrial greenhouses and shipped across the country in the dead of winter. The texture of a burst eyeball in her mouth — even though she'd never tasted an eyeball before, she knew what it was.

"I show you things."

She liked tomatoes now. It took years, but eventually Henrietta learned not all tomatoes were created equal. Some grew in vast industrial facilities, used in sad little salads and dishes behind the sneeze guards at Subway. Some sprouted on city rooftops in the summers, clinging to life above the smog, battered by pigeons and seagulls. There were Cherokee purples brought in from the farmer's markets across the city, even in Foynes Village, where Henrietta was finally won over after Alma challenged her to eat an entire purple tomato like an apple. A ten-dollar bet. She couldn't turn that down.

"You trust me. You help me."

The thing that stood before her was asking for a lot more than ten dollars. It shuddered even as it tried to stand still. The eyes were almost human. The flaps of the mouth still made words around the strange pink tongue. It didn't retreat from their flashlight beams. It kept speaking.

"I show you."

Henrietta held up a hand. She would give it a chance. She had to try. "We're listening."

The thing gurgled and spat. "Follow."

"No way, no way, not happening," Salman said. He still believed he was in charge here, Henrietta could tell. A big mistake. Alma tucked herself behind him, shaking her head but saying nothing. The blackened thing glistened in their beams. The stench deadened the receptors in Henrietta's nose.

"Guys, look at me," Henrietta said. "Look at me. I know this is messed up. I know none of this makes sense. I know that. You don't have to come."

"Fuck that," Salman said. "We aren't leaving you with that thing. Whatever it is."

"Cabeza," it said.

"Cabeza," Henrietta said, sweat gathering on her neck. "See, it has a name."

"It means head meat," Alma said, squeaking out the words. "Roasted head meat, Hen. It probably learned it from a taco shop."

Salman shuddered. "I'm gonna puke."

"Don't you dare," Henrietta said. If he started, she might follow.

"Am I the only one smelling this?" Salman said. "My nose burns. Like I snorted cinnamon. It burns so bad."

Cabeza made a noise like a laugh.

"He says he can help us," Henrietta pleaded.

"And I got a bridge to sell you," Alma said. "You believe that too?"

"Fuck off, Al," Henrietta said, rage snowballing inside. "We're at the very bottom. I'm just trying to adapt to what I see. Who are we supposed to go back and explain this to without getting sent to the hospital?"

It was only a couple years after her father had disappeared that her mother claimed memories of that day were mere hallucinations, Henrietta trying to make her life into something larger than life. She wanted a magical daddy, her mother said. She wanted a man to come save her. Reality had a far duller edge. There was no big secret to hide. There was just the limp reality of existence, every room the same, every day emptied of surprises.

"How about we calm down?" Salman said. "What if we all—"

"Shut the fuck up," Henrietta and Alma said in unison. Henrietta didn't talk about her father disappearing at school after that. She knew what not to say to counsellors, how to avoid confrontations with her mother. She let the edges of her father fade, eyes going vacant, beard disintegrating into wisps. She got used to squeezing her nails into her palms, how to stop just before bleeding. Cabeza spat another black mass, one that skittered away from the lights.

"Alright, alright," Salman said, hands up in surrender. "Not my place."

Cabeza dripped and hissed. It was patient. Henrietta had no idea how long it had been down here. It could've been forever; it still knew it had been someone. Time didn't seem to exist at the bottom of the pit, if this was the bottom. The earth was spongy underneath their feet, more loam than soil. It was a place where things were remade, part of a larger cycle. You could rationalize it away, forget about the smell, forget about the length of Cabeza's tongue, the teeth that remained.

"I'm not leaving Cherry down here," Henrietta said. "If this thing is the way to find him, then I will follow this thing until we do."

Cherry was the reason she was down here, the boy she barely knew, but wanted to desperately believe knew her, could know her. Could change everything for her if she let him. She had opened up a door, he had reached inside. And then he was gone too.

"Cabeza. Call me Cabeza."

"Right," Henrietta said. She got used to things changing quickly. When the schools sent most of the kids home with computers, she adjusted. When her mother discovered a stash of love letters to another woman her father left behind, Henrietta destroyed them immediately, burning them in the sink while the tap ran cold. She could handle the unexpected. Given time, you could accept anything. A gooey corpse wasn't so different from a person. At least it was polite. Cabeza could have attacked them if it really wanted. Henrietta had no idea of its capabilities down here in the dark. They were in the predator's den, barely more than living snacks. Cherry's kidnapping made that clear. "My mistake."

The thing made something like a smile, seeping gunk crinkled around its eyes. "Okay."

"You're both crazy," Salman said.

"Alma?" Henrietta said. "Talk to me. What're you thinking?"

"You know what I'm thinking, Hen."

"This is stupid, yes. I know you know that," Henrietta said. "But . . ."

"It's the only way to move forward," Alma said. "And the only way to find Cherry. And if we don't find him, if we do climb back up outta here empty-handed, everyone still thinks you shoved him down here, no one can prove it, and you spend the rest of your life as a scapegoat for everything bad that happens in Foynes unless you decide to move away, but even then . . ."

"You know what I have to do," Henrietta said. "I need to bring him back."

"I know," Alma said. "And I don't like it."

"You don't need to like it, Al, I just need you to do it."

Cabeza rubbed what was once a stomach or maybe its thigh. Pieces slid around in their own sickly rhythm. It had no coherent existence. "I help you. And then . . . you help me."

"What do you want?"

"Find my body . . . real body, before Cabeza," it slurped. The tongue ran over half its face, searching for dust and debris that it flicked back into the dark. "Old body. Old bones."

"After you bring us to our friend," Henrietta said. "The boy. We need him first."

Cabeza squirmed a nod out of its shape. "I can bring you to him. I can bring you there, where it takes them all, in all its shapes, all the shapes it takes. But then, you help find me."

Alma shook her head. "How does that even work? We go looking for another pile of shit?"

"I exist more around others." The dripping sound of its form filled the absent air between them. "Exist more when observed . . . when part of something bigger than just me. Otherwise, I slip away, melt back to jelly, to only some small remembering . . ."

Henrietta attempted to touch the body. Cabeza shimmered away from her finger, afraid to let the flesh touch its outer layer, the danger of a finger probing its sentience.

"On the beach. In the sun. I remember. Old bones. A scar down my chin. Small shoes despite my height."

Henrietta nodded at it. "You take us to the boy, we will take you to the water. To the beach."

It made a smile with its tongue. Henrietta wished it hadn't.

"So, now we're looking for two dead people?" Salman said.

"We don't know Cherry's dead," Alma said, too quickly.

"Not dead, not yet," Cabeza gurgled, circling around them, gathering confidence. It had a pulse that moved in time with the group, as if they were all breathing together. "Takes time."

"Show us," Henrietta said. "Show us what you know."

Cabeza flicked its decaying limb toward a tunnel. "Follow. They all go the same way here. Down and down into the core, swirling around."

The thing shambled off ahead, confident they were now part of its larger form. Creaks and groans emitted from the blackened world around them, air cold and moist, the smell of Cabeza drowning out any other aromatics they might've noticed, mushrooms and trash pocking the walls, old bike tires spinning in strange breezes. A queen mattress embedded in one of the walls, spray-painted with *DON'T CALL ME ANYMORE*. A pink carousel horse leered at them from the low ceiling. Wires dangled down into their hair.

"Remember sand," Cabeza said haltingly. "Cold. Cold water. I remember beaches. Sand against my face. No beaches down here. Growth slow. Forgetting slow. All so much slower here. Hard to pull it together and keep it together. Hard to keep each piece. So easy to lose all at once."

Henrietta kept her beam on Cabeza's back. This was its territory, its home. It moved without thinking, its voice shuddering to articulate each word. Henrietta looked around for bodies. This was a tailing pond of human excrement, the fear, the hate, the fluids, all dripping out of the walls around her. Was her father in the walls? Cabeza may have been like her once, may have been someone she knew. Why did she trust this dripping thing? Why did its voice soothe her, even when every cell inside her screamed to run, flee back to the surface? Forgetting is slow, the thing said. Could she make it remember?

"I want to see beaches. Bring me to the sand. Dirt sand, don't care. You show me . . ."

162

Henrietta could hear Salman trying not to heave behind her. The underground wind sang.

I never left you.

Forgetting was easy above ground. Forgetting meant the voice could have belonged to someone, but it could also just be a dream, a desperate lurch toward finding something good down here. The earth could just open up and take things from you, scour your family until there was only raw flesh left behind, nerves still bleating.

"Is that all you remember?" Henrietta said. Maybe this was what anyone became down here, if they stayed long enough. Her father shambling down some other corridor just out of sight. Cherry molting into some new, drearier shape until they couldn't recognize him beyond his gait.

"Never want this for anyone," Cabeza gurgled. "To be like this. Can't be others. They all become part of it instead. All part of it, draining down into it. There are other ways to end up down here. Not breathing though. Shouldn't have taken him breathing."

The tight tunnel opened up onto a spacious cavern. Henrietta couldn't track the walls, but felt the air spread around her, the dampness subsiding as she moved past stone markers in the loam. Henrietta felt dead leaves brushing against her feet, fluttering down from somewhere overhead. Her father had loved fires, built them in the centre of the park before the sinkhole appeared. He knew how to evade the by-law officers if they came around. A fire always starts small, he said. If it doesn't feed, it dies. You're like a little fire, Henrietta. To grow, you need to feed. Not just your stomach. Your soul too. And all the other parts of you. You need to breathe in everything.

I would take you with me.

Around them, there were bones. Human bones and caskets, the leftovers from graveyards that had been subsumed by this under-world. A creeping wetness pulling them all down, just like it pulled down Cherry. Henrietta and her friends stood in a tight circle, trying to avoid the femurs poking out of the dirt around them. Cabeza slumped down onto a larger boulder, its various masses rearranging, crawling over one another.

"Too old," it said. "Fresh ones carried further down. Follow."

Salman mumbled a prayer under his breath.

"Ah, ah." Cabeza strained to shake its head. "That won't help. Only hurt down here. Don't teach it. Don't let it know. Don't let it know you. You know only me. Together."

Henrietta drew her beam over old stone markers, chunks of skulls, and shattered coffin lids. Bodies, flesh, all dragged down into the soup of the pit. A form of sustenance for whatever lived down here, whatever took Cherry off the edge.

"Fresh ones?" Alma said. "You make it sound like we're walking into a slaughterhouse."

Cabeza hissed and smiled. "Living ones. They don't . . . don't take so often. I never saw it take them so alive." It gestured at the distant unseen walls, implying the size of a stadium. "It has so far to go. And further, further still. It takes them down through this way. Go further."

A new smell cancelled out Cabeza, an old smell, a sweet rot, the kind that lived in drains, that gathered in the bottom of things. The same smell that took Cherry. The same smell that dripped inside her dreams. A reminder of the pit. But now she was there, following a voice in the dark.

"Further."

They were standing on bodies, surrounded by death, death so old it no longer smelled like death, only sweet earth, the decay that eventually became renewal if you waited long enough. Renewal for what and for who, Henrietta didn't know. Cherry was only at the beginning of the cycle. Her father somewhere further down, still holding out a hand, asking her to taste, to try something new. Could the dirt bring someone back? Could the ground itself remember?

"Come here," Cabeza said. It seemed to remember. Maybe it would tell her more. "I am older than this, older than this new shape it takes. And I don't know why it takes. But I know where."

A chittering sound echoed from the tunnel behind them. Cabeza perked up, its body sloshing into action. "Ringed ones. They feed too."

"Raccoons," Salman said. "Down here?"

"They feed too," Cabeza burped, revealing some teeth and the bright pink tongue. "Move."

"We're going to run?" Alma said. "That's honestly your plan?"

The chittering turned into screeching, growing louder in the blank, wet air around them.

"Fresh ones," Cabeza said, a tiny flame of panic under the slurry of its words. "Further. Before they get to them. Deeper. I will show you and then you will find me. Find me whole."

"Deeper it is," Henrietta said. There would be another tunnel. And another tunnel after that, filled with the stench of everyone above them barely filtered through the soil. Henrietta knew eventually this world would seem normal to her. You learned to like tomatoes despite years of trying to avoid them. You forgot about the groceries he took with him when he fell. You found a creature who smelled like the drains and reminded you of a man everyone said was dead.

"How cold was the water, Cabeza?" Henrietta asked. "That you remember."

It attempted its smile again. "So cold."

"And the shoes?"

"I stole them from the kids' section."

Something like a human still in there, straining toward them, taking its cues from their actions. Henrietta tried to smile, even as it ran ahead. "We will find it for you. I promise."

Cabeza gurgled again. "No promises. A pact. I show you. Then you find me."

"A pact," Alma panted. "Great."

Henrietta punched her in the arm. They scurried after Cabeza, Salman already digging into his snack stash, leaving a trail of crumbs, as if that would guide them back to the surface. Alma kept tracing the tattoo at the centre of her palm, a reminder of the last time she was brave, braver than Henrietta had ever been on that night, someone who could look pain in the face and swallow it whole. Down here though, the stakes changed. You had to accept something like Cabeza was not dead, not alive. You had to accept that even a cross might not save you. That there were things beyond your understanding.

"A pact," Cabeza said. "Only way to know we are one and the same. Seals us together."

Cherry would live, Henrietta told herself. Cherry would be okay, unlike Cabeza. There were no beaches down here. No sand. Cherry was still waiting for them, a fresh one. All she had to do was believe in this monster that named itself after a taco. It could always be so much worse.

Suite 4004

Up this high, air felt lighter. It wasn't, but it felt that way. Forty storeys up, you better be feeling something new at least. WonkaKong90210 aka WonkaKong aka on3shotkıll4h aka Travis Budden had paid for the unit in cash after his emancipation was finally completed, the lawyers taking their fees and disappearing from his life with little more than an invoice. He appreciated their business-first attitude, tried to bring their quiet competence and studied disinterest into every aspect of his rapidly expanding streaming empire.

The following month, WonkaKong took out a restraining order against his father, even going so far as to provide the uniformed, humourless men who manned the front desk downstairs with photos of the old man — with and without his broom moustache. WonkaKong's dad was never a handsome man, but he looked better with the moustache, less like a rat, more like a beaver. Both photos were mugshots. The elder Travis Budden enjoyed looking through his neighbours' windows at night.

WonkaKong had few male role models in his short, erratic life on and off the internet, a product of forums and streams and scrolling, all fuelled by the raging id of the perpetually online. Even his childhood doctor betrayed him, forwarding his bloodwork to a gossip site. Now the whole world knew about his diabetes. WonkaKong's fans sent him insulin with their love letters, offered up their young pancreases as tribute if only he would have them, while his haters attempted to have chocolate cakes delivered to the condo. WonkaKong sued the doctor with a different lawyer, a woman named Marge Homily who made her living suing the police. She feared no one and never confused the significant differences between Type 1 and Type 2 diabetes. Marge was the closest thing WonkaKong had to a mother at this point in his brief existence.

You have to take care of yourself, Travis.

The texts were complete sentences. She kept them short but direct, like the motion she'd recently filed against the Marigold/Dundee Corporation when they refused to fix the sink he'd clogged with a batch of scrambled eggs mixed with Rice-A-Roni. WonkaKong had a new obsession outside of his various lawsuits, something better than the latest FPS or the resurgence of the unforgiving MOBAs of his youth, which drove so many of his subscribers to tattoo his name across their chests and build him elaborate shrines in digital worlds their parents would never see. He had no time for streaming tonight. Tonight, WonkaKong's brand-new telescope had finally arrived.

Not just any telescope. No, this was a Celestron 11098 NexStar 11SE, featuring the classic orange chrome tube design with all the updated features to provide the best stargazing experience in a confined space, such as a condo unit on the fortieth floor of a building that was possibly tipping out over the street below. WonkaKong put much more effort into this small purchase than his box in the sky with its temperamental windows and rotting caulking.

The five-inch aperture provided excellent light-gathering ability, offering WonkaKong impressive views of the moon and planets if he so desired, along with deep sky objects like the Orion Nebula, reminding him just how small and insignificant he actually was, which would come in handy if anyone ever hacked his email account again, spraying his nudes across global message boards. He didn't need his father's help to escape into the sky. The single fork arm design and sturdy steel tripod all broke down into separate components for easy transport and quick assembly, which helped when WonkaKong moved it from the bedroom to the living room and back again, tracking the movements of his targets.

WonkaKong wasn't as interested in the stars as he used to be. Instead, he looked for companionship, people who had no idea who he was, or that he was even there at all. That's what he told himself, sitting behind the telescope pressed against the glass. He wasn't like his father, a man who loved to watch, according to the prosecutors in several cities across the province. He could have had his pick of admirers, the ones who flooded his talent agent's office with fan mail, baked goods, and novelty gorilla-themed knick-knacks wearing purple top hats like his online avatar. They all knew him as WonkaKong. They didn't know Travis.

WonkaKong's telescope roved across the glass towers surrounding him. There were rumours people were dying in this opulent, over-stuffed building, their bodies removed under the cover of darkness, a handshake agreement between the police department and the management company, which was actually a subsidiary of the Marigold/Dundee Corporation. There was a video of the hockey player who threw himself over his balcony, his body hitting the street with a thud that made WonkaKong wonder if it sounded any different when you jumped from the fortieth floor.

Don't be reckless, Travis. We are worried about you.

Another text to ignore. WonkaKong scrolled his telescope across The Bahareque, its rooftop barely rising to the edge of his window. Most of the windows were shut, lights off, blinds closed. Maybe he'd chosen The Marigold because of its height, the way it imposed itself onto the skyline, but what was the point of owning a unit that wasn't even halfway up the tower if that was true?

No one except his inner circle knew he lived here, except maybe for his father. His lens travelled across the stumpy Madonna tower, and the Andrew Lloyd Webber Presents The Phantom, a garish collection of white and black boxes stacked up to sixty-five storeys on the other side of Yonge. He roved over the old bank buildings and courthouses in the middle distance, each of them in a constant state of restoration and repair, the scaffolding a second skin never fully shed.

WonkaKong spotted a body on the thirty-eighth floor of the Mason's New Lodge, a development only a few years older than The Marigold. The body was a man, a shirtless man attempting to lift a medicine ball over his head, twenty-eight pounds hovering over his head under nine-foot ceilings while he watched a documentary about NASCAR racing. WonkaKong watched the man complete three strenuous sets before losing interest. Scrolling down the side of the lodge, he watched a woman eat a plate of fettuccini alfredo, her tongue scraping the last bits of sauce off her fork. He was there, sitting across the table from her. He could see the textures of the noodles in between her teeth and he wondered if he was destined to always eat alone, his FODDER delivery bags clustered around the front door like a depleted mushroom farm.

An alarm jolted him away from the telescope. Time for another insulin injection. He ignored it. He went to the fridge, pulling out what had been a chicken parmesan sandwich, part of a pop-up a restaurant chain called Mother Hen had co-produced with WonkaKong's production company, WK Innovations & Libations. Marge hated the name, but he didn't pay her to like it, just to file the paperwork. There was a hair in the sandwich. WonkaKong paused and swallowed.

The garbage can was full. Despite the high-end aspirations of The Marigold, it had a series of garbage and recycling chutes like any other, chutes often clogged by out-of-season Christmas trees, hacked-up dining room tables, and the occasional dead pet. WonkaKong knew he had to hire a cleaning service, but he also did not want to be seen and so he stayed in here with his garbage, adjusting to the smells. No one could see the smells during his streams. The neighbours hadn't complained about him so far, although he wasn't sure if he even had neighbours on the fortieth floor. He listened to his sink gurgle.

He's waiting for you.

Stomach sated, WonkaKong returned to his telescope, swinging it down toward the street level. If he wanted nudity, he could find it online. If he wanted to see people in the middle of their most intimate acts, there were services for that, an endless stream of bodies in any position he could imagine or desire, even those who didn't consent to being filmed if you went deep enough. He wasn't like his father though, he wanted to explain that to no one and everyone.

WonkaKong lived in fear that one day some of his fiercest critics like SpiciBoiz and TheonETrueSquirtle would discover his true origins, the son of a man with a rap sheet that included a variety of low-level sexual offences and maybe something worse. He didn't want to end up like the CEO of FODDER, his entire life splashed across the internet in real-time. He needed to control the outcome, the shades of WonkaKong he was willing to share to over twenty million hungry sets of eyes, five to six nights a week, four hours straight at a time. Threshold had recently bought his streaming service and presented him with a very healthy contract. All he had to do was sign.

We're waiting for you.

WonkaKong slid his eye along the sidewalk, spotting women headed out into the unpredictable weather with layers of coats. He observed vanity licence plates on stretch limousines that read *BIGSPENDA* and *CLSR2GD* and the fresh curses carved with keys or pocket knives into the sides of Magellan-tagged vehicles by the vestiges of the broken cab companies. WonkaKong's telescope crept along the sidewalk until it reached the pit where Marigold II was supposed to sprout; at least three years of construction across from his unit, an eternity of cranes and concrete trucks endlessly churning.

For now, it was just a deep, dark hole, so deep even his telescope could not pierce the void. They said this pit was for all the parking spots. It would be the tallest building in the city, a staggering achievement if it was ever completed. WonkaKong wondered if it would be finished before the first Marigold collapsed. His vision went woozy for a second as he examined the cranes around the worksite, imagining bodies dangling from the hooks. There were protestors who climbed cranes across the city to set themselves alight, bodies covered in gasoline burning like torches as they tumbled into the streets below.

We need you here with us, Travis. He needs you.

Another text buzzing against his leg, probably from Marge again. He ignored her pleas. The pit drew him in, his eyes now scoping out its edges, spotting movement, dark shapes burbling along its edges. Maybe he could record something down there, send a stream from a place no one had ever been before. He only needed his phone. Something was happening down there in the dark, but his lens couldn't see.

WonkaKong pulled on his fanciest driving gloves. He had never learned to drive. He wrapped a branded Nintendo mask around his face, the fabric decorated with Mario's moustache. Sunglasses and a plain white beanie completed his disguise. He slipped out of the condo, the door locking automatically behind him. The elevator chimed immediately. WonkaKong didn't believe in fate exactly; his father had told him there was no such thing as god, only opportunities, but the ride down felt fated. No one else joined him on the thirty-nine-floor descent.

In the massive marble lobby, the doormen nodded in his direction even as he ignored them. WonkaKong stepped outside into the cool air for the first time in three months, breathing through his Mario mask, taking in the smell and the taste of wet pavement, cigarette butts, and chicken bones. WonkaKong didn't bother walking to an intersection or waiting patiently for a light to change. He hopped and skittered across four lanes of traffic, narrowly missing a cyclist with three food orders on her handlebars. The pit called to him.

We need you to show them all.

Marge liked to say her young charge was deeply, maybe even pathologically, goal-oriented. It was how he'd found success at such an early age, breaking down the algorithms of what was popular on streaming sites; the games, yes, but also the attitude of the personas. He'd shaped himself, made his life into a spectacle while slashing through fantasy realms or shooting thousands of aliens through their bone-crushing mandibles. Ten thousand subscribers, then one hundred thousand, soon a million. But goals could shift and change, especially as he got older.

Travis, it's time for you to go to bed. Please. I'll call you in the morning.

WonkaKong made it to the edge of the massive construction site. The darkness provided him cover as he slipped under the fence, walking around the perimeter's edge. He could stream something from here, maybe even deeper. No one would know where he was, they would just know it was something new. He considered climbing one of the cranes around him, scoping out the best place to film. A shape moved from somewhere in the pit, something like a human shape, waving up at him. WonkaKong hesitated. Maybe he was too tired. The sunglasses obscured things; made them look unreal.

We need you with us. He needs you.

The shape beckoned, a hand reaching out toward him. Its face slipped in and out of the lights that dangled from the white and red cranes around them, a face like a rat or a beaver, all teeth and hair. It smiled at him, held its shambling arms open, spoke without speaking, a call that thrummed in his skull. There were no stars down in the pit. Abandoning his phone to free his hands, WonkaKong90210 began to descend, picking up momentum, running toward a shape he recognized, a figure he needed but couldn't name. The pit would provide.

Travis. Remember that I love you.

15.

"You think they'll just take you onboard? You'll have your own little office, and you'll attend little meetings with your own presentations? You can't be serious, Cathy."

Jasmine was over at her place again. She still had one roommate who was a second cousin, a girl from Syria who woke up at 3 a.m. to travel to her job at a bakery on the other side of town, dodging three sinkholes along the way, riding buses that died at random in the middle of intersections depending on the humidity. She had no time for Jasmine's love life.

"What am I going to do? Stay with the City? They couldn't give a single shit. And if I brought them the sample? The hand? They'd stick it in a locker somewhere and forget about it or decide I'm crazy and try to get me locked up."

A half-eaten pizza sat between them. Mushrooms, banana peppers, and soppressata. Cathy picked off all the mushrooms, a new development. She usually ate them by the handful.

"Am I wrong?" Cathy continued. "If I'm wrong, tell me why; otherwise, I'm going to stick with the plan. They have a spot for me. For us. That's the promise. You know how much money Threshold pays, fuck, I mean even the health plan. You know what it's like to not be afraid?"

Jasmine's plate was empty. She didn't pick off the mushrooms.

"Did they actually say us? Or you?"

"I'll get to dig into why this stuff happens, actually work with people who know what they're talking about."

Jasmine laughed. "That's an interesting answer."

"I promise, you're coming with me."

"And you're a comedian," Jasmine said. "Or you just think I'm really stupid. You won't even let me move in here. How many toothbrushes do I have to leave around here?"

"It's terrible here. You deserve better than this place. If it wasn't so cheap, I'd have left years ago. Look, the department, they don't know shit. They don't even want to repair the masks. They see everything we do as a waste of time. They barely keep tabs on us. Why do you think you're working, like, ten hours a day as a full-time tinker? The masks are from Threshold. The knowledge is at Threshold. The fucking money, Jas, the money is at Threshold. Don't you want to be part of that?"

"And you trust them? Really?"

"Ha," Cathy said, reaching for another warm beer from the case on the floor. "I don't trust any of them. We need the cash. We take the money, take the money for as long as we can stand it. And then we go, just like you wanted."

"You really don't want to answer these questions, do you?" Jasmine said. "You're so high on the dream you haven't looked to see if there's anything even holding it up."

The hazy plastic container sat beside the pizza, a dark shape at its centre.

"Look, we don't have a lot of options here, alright? I have to play this out my way," Cathy said. "And I know I'm exposing you a bit here too, but we're already exposed. I messaged those Threshold suits. Discreetly. They want to meet with us tomorrow at a 'secure location.'"

Jasmine laughed. "They sound like they're trying a bit hard. Where is it?"

"Oh, you'll love this. Centre for Collaborative Insight. Used to be a ceramics museum."

"So, it's a front. Another front. And we're going to just hand this over? The sample."

Cathy swirled her beer. "I don't know yet. I will need to see some paperwork."

"You don't know?"

"Jas, I'm just saying we will see what they have to say. I'll want it all in writing."

"So now you don't trust them," Jasmine said. "Good. Cause you're telling me the department is a joke, and I agree with you. You're telling me we're going to go meet with these guys in secret, and I agree with you. And now, we're going to hold them hostage at the last second? Then what's the plan? Go our own way? Run forever? I'm not an idiot, Cathy."

"I want to see how they react to the news first, see if they are committed. They barely understand what they are asking for right now. They want us to introduce them. We both know the Wet is conscious of itself. It thinks, it plans. You and I have both seen it is aware."

"If it's that dangerous, you have to tell them either way," Jasmine said. "If you know how terrible it is, Cathy, you shouldn't even have it in the same room as us. You shouldn't be acting so nonchalant. Why is it sitting here on the table? Why am I even sitting here anymore?"

Cathy shrugged. "I put my life at risk every day when I go down there. And so do you. And I trust you one hundred percent whenever we put on the masks." Cathy snatched hers out of the bag and banged it on the table, eyes bright orange. "Don't you trust me? You have to trust me."

"Sometimes I forget what a bitch you really are," Jasmine laughed, rising from the table. "This is why you're alone so much, Cathy. Because you know best. What happened to leaving? What happened to doing something else with our lives?"

"You seriously want me to walk away from this? We have something they want," Cathy said, slapping the container against the table. The glass rang out. She could barely keep hold of it with one hand. "Do you know how rare that is? To be in this position? Even for an instant, for half a fucking second, Jas, we have some control here."

"I'm done talking about this," Jasmine said. "You keep telling me how things will be, but the story changes every time. I thought we were going to leave. Now you're talking about years and years here, working for someone else but doing the same shit over and over again, putting your life and mine at risk, and for who? For what? You can't really tell me outside of money and I'm telling you there is money other places. There are other ways of being in this world. And you don't want to know that. You refuse. I'm going home."

"The subway isn't even running," Cathy said, voice softening. "Another flood down there. Shut down until morning at least."

"I'll order a car," Jasmine said. "I don't need to be here."

"Yes, you do. I need you. Even just for tomorrow, I promise they'll take us both. I promise if you hate it, you can leave. We can leave. Together."

Jasmine looked at Cathy, eyes starting to drip. "Why are you like this? Every time?"

"Like what?" Cathy said, glaring at the bottle in her hand. "I just want the best for us."

"Nevermind," Jasmine said, stalking off to the bedroom. "I'll go with you tomorrow. But I can't listen to any more of this right now. You're already planning out my life all over again."

Cathy didn't move for a few minutes. The same fights, the participants only changing slightly, words pulled from the trash, sentiments recycled. She got up and turned out each light in the apartment. She shuffled out of her work outfit. The blanket on the couch smelled like potato chips and sweat, comforting enough in the dark. She could hear Jasmine in the other room, her voice making some kind of keening sound, held behind her teeth. The fights were growing closer together, little eruptions that used to take a month now popped up on a weekly basis. Cathy wanted to blame the job or the city itself or even the beer, but she knew the only variable that each fight had in common came back to her. She wanted to be right. She had to be right.

Cathy pulled on her mask, felt the horns burrow into the pillow behind her head. The eyes glowed blue as she drifted off, a world where she was safe for at least six hours before she woke. On the table in the cold, dark kitchen, the dirty container shifted slightly, its contents quietly searching for weakness in the seal.

§

The former ceramics museum, now the Centre for Collaborative Insight, sat at the top of Queen's Park circle, surrounded by decommissioned university labs and dormitories that were either luxury condos or abandoned to squatters who refused to move. A sinkhole had swallowed part of the circle where the provincial legislature stood, a few trees still clinging to life around its edges.

There was a small monument built afterward for the victims that stood at the southern foot of the pit, until that monument was swallowed too. It wasn't replaced. People still wondered why the whole building didn't fall in while the politicians were in session. A missed opportunity. On major holidays and long weekends, people drove around the pit in circles, firing Roman candles down into the blackness. Sometimes a car would get too close and tumble down.

"You don't have to do this with me," Cathy said as they emerged from the rerouted subway tunnel, masks pulled tight over their heads, horns glistening. "I know you don't love confrontations. You can wait out front if you want."

"I know," Jasmine said. "But I saw what you saw. And I can't sleep at night if I don't do something about it. I think about all the times I should have done something . . ."

"I know what you mean," Cathy said.

"I used to date this dude in high school, this rich boy," Jasmine said. "Maybe I told you this story. His family was lovely, and he was sweet enough. But, ugh . . . this is stupid."

"It's alright, we got time." Cathy wanted to delay this meeting, maybe even cancel it. She felt too eager to meet, too eager to share this knowledge. It felt like surrendering herself.

"They had this poodle, this big black dog. And this guy threw a brick into the pool, told the dog to go and fetch it. And the dog did. It jumped right in, kept diving down and down again. And he was smiling the whole time and I stood there until his dad came out and stopped it."

"And you don't want to just stand there this time," Cathy said. "Right? We've just been standing there for years, checking the temperature of the water. Threshold will help us though. All we need to do is give them a taste of what we saw."

"I can't unsee what we saw down there. I can't keep it to myself."

"Alright, let's go then," Cathy said, trying to convince herself. They hadn't talked about the fight, got dressed in silence, rode the subway without speaking. Maybe Jasmine understood now. This wasn't a way to live, trapped in the city, barely able to stay above water. There was a way out. Cathy was only now struggling to believe it. "Remember, we aren't promising anything. They only know what we tell them. They owe us. We need to get some of this deal in writing."

"I hear you," Jasmine said. "We stick together."

The top of the circle was empty. It was cold again, the tiny heatwave abandoning the city as soon as it arrived. Cathy heard crows in the trees as she climbed the steps into the empty museum, past the abandoned security desk, through the cavernous coat closets, and into what was once a showroom. A table and four rickety chairs sat in the middle of the room under a massive, incandescent bulb that occasionally buzzed, an exhibit someone forgot to remove.

"This is the Centre for Collaborative Insight?" Jasmine said. "A single bulb in a room?"

"We appreciate your promptness," Robert said, sleeves still too short for his arms. The man with the frayed sleeves stood behind him. "But do you need the masks?"

"You mean these?" Jasmine said, cocking a finger to her temple. "It's our policy across the department. We're too close to a pit for us to remove them safely."

"I've never heard that," Robert said. "Our group has researched the sinkholes, you know. We've sent a few drones down the one in Foynes Village. Are the pits themselves that dangerous? We haven't considered them as vectors. Please, enlighten us."

"It's primarily a precaution," Cathy responded, taking a seat at the table. They didn't need to shake hands. This was more than business; it was something far more urgent and insidious. She wanted to scream, to press their faces against the glass box and shriek. Instead, she folded her hands on the table. "Tell us what you've learned, and we'll tell you what we found."

"I don't know if you fully understand how this works," Robert said, pulling out a tablet. The man with the frayed sleeves still had his pencil and legal pad. "If you're serious about actually joining us, you have to understand there is a hierarchy to these things. A chain of command. We won't be hunting you down. We don't need to do that. We need to know what you see."

"Oh, I understand," Cathy said, still trying to keep her tone light. Men curdled so quickly under scrutiny. It took a measured and gentle approach to make them comfortable. They had to believe they were in charge even when they already held all the power in the room. You had to put a finger on the scale. "You need us. We need you. I know what a symbiote is. I read comics."

"Okay," the frayed sleeves said. He was haggard, rundown and haunted after only a few weeks' absence. "Alright, let's talk, Cathy. We're excited about your future here, you know. Our people have been learning a lot. We believe you can lead them to some further insights."

"You have other people?" Jasmine said, mask's eyes flickering green.

"Of course," Robert said. "We need to understand this phenomenon holistically. It's part of our environment, part of a larger interlocking set of factors. Even the negatives within a biome contribute to its overall state. We can't just remove one piece and assume all is well."

"Right," Cathy said, patting Jasmine's arm lightly. "Covering all the angles."

They were all seated under the massive lightbulb. The man with the frayed sleeves nodded. "It's not an equal opportunity offender. It seems to only target certain buildings, or it has so far. We've seen it spreading further and faster, leaping over certain benchmarks we assumed it would hit. We have run our own ecological models, but it changes too fast for us to keep up. It doesn't behave in any rational manner. We are acknowledging our failures here to you. The patterns we predicted are not appearing, the assumptions behind our decision-making are flawed. There are pockets emerging outside of downtown, usually near the sinkholes, like you've noted, but nothing definitive in that regard.

"We have some contacts in the City. They all say the same thing — it's no longer under control. We have our data collection methods and our security forces but they aren't enough. Your department continues to take samples, continues to report on the scenes that are reported, if they are reported. What we are concerned about right now is what goes unreported. The vast majority of these cases. The landlord's secret."

"The phantom cases," Robert said, wrists glowing pink under the light. He ignored his tablet. "What some might call the silent majority. What you told us last time intrigued us. We need to know more about how the Wet is behaving. What it is or what it is threatening to become."

These men stalked around the truth, manipulating each interaction into a confession. Still, they offered more transparency than public health's disorganized bureaucrats. They couldn't even handle bedbugs. The Wet was beyond their abilities, easier to deny than resolve. It remained a rumour, which was the more politically expedient route. It didn't affect the affluent for years, until it finally did. Threshold offered a way to make a change, a real one.

"You can look, but I wouldn't touch," Cathy said, pulling out her sample box and setting it gently on the table. The black mass played dead, trying to hide its intent. "It's more intelligent than we thought."

"You mean, you have a chunk of it?" Robert said. "This is alive?"

Jasmine put a hand over the glorified Tupperware. "It's more than alive. It plans. It plots."

183

"We had some indications," the frayed sleeves said, hesitating. Robert sighed, shrugged, and then let him continue. "We'd noticed some of the episodes were happening in some buildings more than others. You start to see patterns. We collect data in our own way, pulling from sources you may not be able to access so we were able to pull a bigger picture together."

"And what're you planning to do with these new revelations obtained through surveillance?" Cathy said. She stared at the scribbled notes on the other side of the table, attempting to decipher each scratch and dot.

"We need to study it further. It's probably got some learned behaviour . . ."

"You're saying it's a tool," Jasmine said. "Someone designed it."

"Not quite, no," Robert said. The massive light buzzed. "Not a tool, more like a natural pesticide people might learn to direct, or at least redirect."

"Something like an English garden," the frayed sleeves said, continuing to take notes. "Controlled chaos."

"So, you know who is redirecting it then?" Cathy said.

"We charted some correlations between building permits and investors, the kind of projects allowed to go ahead. Whoever started this didn't intend for it to go this far."

"Like adopting a baby alligator," Cathy said. "Starts out so small. And then suddenly the sewers are full. You want to believe this version of the story is true, don't you?"

Robert rolled up his sleeves to reveal veiny forearms. "You actually think this is something we'd invent? We're here in good faith, Catherine."

"Sounds like damage control," Cathy said. "There are no correlations. Maybe some mistakes resurfacing. This started with the lake, with the water, with whatever is buried under the ground. All those old little dirty secrets bobbing back up to the surface.

Neighbourhoods that don't exist anymore, corpses appearing out of wet ground. Camps and ghettos, repurposed, replanted, revitalized. And now whoever sent you here is trying to restore some order."

"You think we want to claim this?" the frayed sleeves yawned, notes trailing away. "I assure you, we are on the same side here. I thought you wanted to help us."

"A nefarious purpose is still a purpose," Cathy said from behind her mask, the hand on her leg again, telling her to run. A decaying hand reaching for her face. "It still gives you some agency, gives you some power over whatever is happening here. You retain control even in the fallout if you can lure everyone into forgiveness. What I saw in that basement didn't belong to any person. It wasn't taking orders. It wasn't obedient."

The frayed sleeves snorted. Robert snatched the glass container off the table. The light hissed above them.

"What are you doing?" Jasmine said.

"You said you'd help us," Robert said, pulling the lid back. "The spirit of the agreement remains the same, don't you think? We will share what we've learned together."

The black mass inside the container didn't explode out of captivity so much as it lurched into Robert's palm before lunging up his forearm, shedding a cloud of spores into the air. Jasmine and Cathy's masks immediately flickered and screeched, the readings overwhelming their senses as the Wet spread into the air, flecks landing on the face of the man with the frayed sleeves, his scream swirling the spores into his mouth. The Wet worked its way through the frayed man's face rapidly, sensing some weakness in him, holes it could swiftly penetrate and then proliferate. It was angry.

No absence.

This spastic Wet moved with a purpose, distending the man's sunken red eyes, flaring through his crumbling nose and mouth, turning his old gums black. He crumpled to the floor, his chair skittering away. Unable to help his partner, Robert tried to resist the pressure from the chunk of Wet now clinging to his face, shoulders spasming as it worked its way across his features, a large globule pulsing in and out with his frantic breathing.

Only presence.

Jasmine staggered back from the table, screaming through her horned mask. Cathy reached out and grabbed the largest chunk of the Wet off of Robert's crumpled face with her gloves, stuffing it back into the cursed container, jamming the lid shut as it fought back against her, making a high-pitched keening noise. She then snatched frayed sleeves's notes off the table. The light above them shrieked with a renewed vigour until it shattered. Shards of glass rained down. Jasmine shuddered in a ball on the floor until Cathy yanked her up. Robert's moaning howl followed them as they fled the building, neither woman looking back.

§

Fungi change and adapt based on their environment. Cathy knew this. They're shaped by experience. Their growth is reactive, not passive. They share this with humans.

"Jasmine, look at me," Cathy said as they emerged outside into the cold, grey world. "Look at me. Whatever happened in there, you need to push it away. For now, push it away."

Jasmine tried to shake off Cathy's grip. Cathy latched on tight until she got an answer.

"Okay!"

"Listen to me, look at me," Cathy repeated. Mask to mask, they stood together. "Things are not going to go back to normal after this. There's no more explaining these things gently to anyone. But you are more than this, okay? You are more than the worst things that happened to you."

Jasmine's mask nodded. The eyes went blue. Tiny raindrops began to fleck against the metal casing. The sky rumbled above them before it opened, a cold and relentless rain.

"Follow me. We aren't coming back."

They descended the stairs to the subway, moving past terrified commuters and confused children, dragging their kits behind them, bumping through the turnstiles and broken escalators. Thunder crashed above them, the storm moving deeper into the city. Cathy tried to make sense of what she'd seen. A naturally occurring biological weapon, one humans could never hope to control, designed by no one and beholden to nothing but its own propagation. This was the Wet.

Threshold wanted it for themselves, Threshold or whatever head of its hydra had sent Robert and the frayed sleeves after them, so gently at first. She had their notes now. A hard copy. Nothing anyone else could claim. As rain gushed down the subway steps, Cathy and Jasmine clambered down off the platform into the subway tunnel. No one tried to stop them. People went back to their phones, waiting for the next wheezing train to enter the station. A raccoon chittered as it sorted through the platform trash, yanking out wet morsels for itself.

16.

According to the latest set of floor plans sitting in Stanley Marigold's disastrous inbox, Marigold II would feature at least three restaurants on the premises once construction was completed.

"Jaclyn, who makes the best sashimi around here?" Stanley said. "I don't want whoever's best in Toronto at all, actually, that's like fishing for trout off the Queensway. People want authentic, don't they? Who's the best in Vancouver? I want a list of names as soon as possible, a real list. See about LA too, we'll tell them we'll pay them in American dollars. I don't think anyone from Japan will come. Maybe see if we can get a fried chicken competition going."

Three restaurant concepts, to be specific. Stanley would retain ownership through a numbered company set up by his lawyers, shifting each establishment to respond to the untidy whims and desires of his clientele. Toronto was a city that loved to chase its own tail, a place that never saw a line it wouldn't join. For a few years, it was doughnuts, then ice cream, then artisanal cheesecakes, then fried chicken sandwiches. Sometimes poutine would make a sudden resurgence. Something cheap you could throw a few shallots onto for the upsell. There were restaurants selling grocery store chickens like they were dry-aged steaks and wine bars convincing clientele to spend twenty dollars on a mortadella sandwich. Glorified bologna. Stanley admired the hustle, and like anything he admired, he wanted to make it his own.

"What about you, Hans? You like sashimi? You a big fish guy? I never know what people like to eat, I guess that's my first mistake. Or I see what people like to eat and I don't believe it."

"I like fish," Hans Mantel said. Head of security for The Marigold, Hans spent a lot of his time sitting in the building's restaurant, which was on its third rebranding and still technically owned by a group of investors who hadn't been fully bullied out of their shares yet. His constant presence was a reminder of who actually owned the building. He and Jaclyn sat across from their boss, now on his third bottle of Riesling. "Especially when it's fresh."

"We'll have someone fly it in, people love to hear something just flew in," Stanley said. He could see Sidney on the other side of the dimly lit restaurant, sitting across from a man who's face remained a mystery. She'd ordered a Western omelette with freshly chopped shallots and back bacon from ethically raised Lacombe hogs from a farm outside the city. They used whatever was available at the supermarket if they ran out of the ethical bacon.

"Why three restaurants?" Jaclyn said. "This one still isn't . . ."

Stanley smiled at her. Diners around them shifted slightly, conversations puttered to a stop, even the music faded out. Hans coughed.

"Still isn't what?" Stanley said. "Go ahead. Tell me how we're disappointing you."

Hans shrugged. "She's not wrong. No one wants to ride up forty storeys to eat eggs and potatoes. No one sane. Getting deliveries this high up is a headache. You know how many creeps try to sneak up on those service elevators? I keep finding dog shit inside."

"Add more cameras," Stanley said. The man with Sidney turned. Nice eyes, straight teeth, but a small bit of mucus hanging out of his left nostril. A disappointment. If she was going to cheat so flagrantly, as they'd agreed, she needed to put more effort into it. Stan required competition.

"But back to the question from our favourite assistant," Stanley said. "Three restaurants work because then we can establish varying levels of exclusivity. One we run as something like a pop-up on the first floor. We run different people through it, keep the media coming back. Every six or eight months bring in whoever the next up-and-coming kid is, doing deconstructed kimchi or telling everyone she reinvented the burrito."

He missed the hockey player. At least he'd been able to mess with that guy. Stanley didn't know if Sidney's newest toy lived in the building. Hans would have a new task tonight.

"We run a second venue maybe two floors up, something seafood-focused but totally over the top. Maybe we claim to be a Portuguese place, taking all the best elements of Lisbon's cuisine? Or we try to bring back some classic dishes, give people nostalgia for a time that never existed, food that should've never been made — a lot of aspic, maybe some lobster thermidor, throw in a Baked Alaska. I like fire, don't you? Pretend we're a hotel that never left 1948."

Abigail still texted him. With all the permits and approvals settled already, The Holsteins wanted to break ground on their new tower as soon as possible. Stanley had already paid the price for Hammond; they were just waiting for its delivery. The note was accepted. Abigail wanted to see him again. She sent him photos. There was no discretion. Abigail had never needed to use it.

"And the third?" Jaclyn asked.

"The third one? A private supper club. Members only. You pay a yearly fee for access. It's hidden somewhere on, oh I don't know, the twelfth floor. We can get people in and out a little easier. The point is we make it too small. We're overbooked. We don't answer our phone. We don't rebook reservations. We call it something like *Fide*."

"Loyalty," Hans said, smiling. "So, you're naming it after me."

Stanley barely acknowledged Hans. Good practice to make his subordinates fight for his attention. "The point is to dangle it in front of them. Only pull back some of the curtain. We aren't selling something. We're making you an offer."

"There's a difference?" Jaclyn said.

"If I'm trying to sell you something, there's an implication I'm the one in need."

Hans jumped back into the fray. "Don't want to make it too easy."

"I want them to want me," Stanley said. The man with Sidney held his fork like a shovel, working his way through the Tater Tot log house like he was digging a trench. The hockey player stuck to burgers. The actor before that preferred walnut and spinach salads with an organic honey and citrus dressing Stanley later had forcibly removed from the menu back when the place was called Escalera, two concepts ago. "I don't need their money. People want to feel excluded."

"You fool!"

Stanley's shoulders tensed. When he was ten years old, he broke his foot trying to jump off the roof of the guest house into the family pool. Albert said the same thing then when he heard his youngest child's agonizing scream. It required a plate and six screws to repair the leg. The bones still sang whenever the pressure sank, turning Stanley into a bionic weathervane.

"How did he get in here, Hans?" Stanley hissed. Jaclyn pretended nothing was happening, focused directly on her three hardboiled eggs, each wrapped in a subtle variation on prosciutto.

"How is this my fault—" Hans stuttered. Stanley brushed past him through the dining room. Sidney and her date were now watching, everyone was watching. There were too many mirrors.

"Dad, I didn't realize you were feeling so much better," Stanley said, hooking his arm through his father's elbow. His voice dropped. "We aren't supposed to be in public together."

"You made a grave error," Albert said. "You've called in another favour."

Neither man was supposed to acknowledge the other in public. As far as the wider world knew, they were still locked inside a bitter lawsuit over control of the Marigold/Dundee Corporation. This kept the rest of the family at bay, along with former investors and contractors who were waiting on an outcome from the lawsuit before filing their own.

"Grave error?" Stanley whispered, dragging his father to the table. Their roles slid back and forth, father and son operating on a sliding scale of influence. Sidney and her date watched. "You sure you're not talking about yourself?"

"Son, I would hit you right now if I had a stick on me," Albert said. "Knock you flat on your ass here so the whole world can see. You made a critical error."

"I did what you asked."

They flopped down into the leather booth, the elder Marigold crashing into Hans.

"You did nothing of the sort. You were supposed to lead them on. It's too soon."

"Jaclyn. Hans. Can you give us a few minutes here?"

Hans climbed over Albert, who refused to move. His bald head glittered in the mirrors of Hashhaus. Jaclyn quietly placed each hardboiled egg in her purse before leaving. Stanley waited until they exited the restaurant. He heard Sidney laughing, a glass shattering in a corner he could not see.

"You never should've put this restaurant up so high," Albert said. "Takes forever for anyone to get here. People are either late or early for their reservation. A total bottleneck."

"This was your idea!" Stanley said. "You wanted it to spin in a circle."

"And does it spin? No, so what's the point of being this high up?"

"Why would it need to spin?"

"Do you know what the word panoramic means, son? People pay for the view, but the view gets old if it's the same buildings two hours straight. We're too high up to even look into most folks' windows. No one wants to pay a premium for this."

Stanley grabbed his father's shaky hands from across the table. "Why are you here?"

"You overplayed your hand. You shouldn't have actually gone to him."

"To who?"

"Who? You say that to my face? You've upset the balance," Albert said. "We did the right thing with our new project after this disaster. Don't you learn? I wanted you to sell them on the idea, not follow through. Let their building fail."

Stanley leaned back. His father was here, undoing years of careful planning, undermining their entire plan to disorient and disrupt the transition of power, providing cover for Stanley to continue enacting the same policies and investment strategies his father established.

"You don't actually believe in that shit," Stanley said. "We had nothing to lose, it's the same old system. Something goes into the ground so something can go up. It's hocus pocus. I play the game, I bring the dollar store props. Everyone pretends we're all powerful when it's just hazing."

"It's a necessary tool," his father replied, his words slurring together. "A tool we need. You've pushed it too far, too fast."

"I paid him the price."

"You don't understand. The price is the body," Albert said. "What goes into the ground. But too many too close together . . ."

"It's not real, Dad. It's how you justify what you do. And when someone new comes along, it's how you bind them to you. We're all buried out there. We drove Ramji crazy when we tried to bring him in, he's just disappeared. It's a sacrament to ensure silence, that's all."

Albert's eyes darted around the restaurant. His son recognized the look overtaking his father's features, a numbness that started in his eyebrows and worked its way down.

"Dad, it's going to be alright. It's one guy. Hammond Holstein is an old man. He can't keep up with you. He'll be gone so quick. Okay?"

"You should never have paid for two towers so quickly. He won't like it. He'll lash out."

"I'm going to call a car."

Hans and Jaclyn were gone. There was no one to smoothly transition his father out of the building, maybe even throw a coat over his head. If he appeared too invested in his father's wellbeing now in front of this eclectic and gossipy audience, the whole charade would fall apart, leaving him exposed, opening him up to all kinds of liability.

"You think you understand."

"Dad."

His father's hands trembled against the table. Lips moved without sound. A denture slipped.

"Dad, I don't want to do this, but . . ."

Albert Marigold couldn't make it through a day anymore, his hours disappearing into minutes inside his head, the years collapsing onto each other until all that remained was some spite and the puddle of piss beneath him. Grimacing, Stanley shoved his plate of hash browns into his father's face from across the table. The old man sputtered, barely resisting the attack. Stanley ground the potatoes into his cowering father's nose, covering his eyes and mouth with mush.

"I don't want to see your face in here again," Stanley bellowed, making sure his captive audience heard each word. "You want to see me again, I'll meet you in the cemetery."

Stanley erupted from the table, hiding a smile. There were decades where he'd dreamed of doing this. It was too bad the old man couldn't or wouldn't fight back.

"Stan," Sidney said, appearing by his side. "What do you need?"

He kept walking. Servers skittered out of his way. A flash went off behind him. More evidence for the crows online.

"Take him downstairs," Stanley whispered. "He'll listen to you. If he says you're Margaret, then you're Margaret. Whoever let him out of the home tonight, I swear to god."

Sidney nodded. Her date had disappeared.

"Where'd your man go?" Stanley asked.

"He's washing up. Do you want me to . . ."

"No, you can tell me about it all later. I'll have Hans meet you downstairs. That bald idiot should have known something like this would happen. I should send him back to jail."

Sidney smiled. "I'll make sure it gets done."

"That's why I love you," Stanley said. "Even if you like hockey."

She pretended not to hear him, turning back to deal with the old man weeping alone in his leather booth. The bartender tried his best to find a song. Stanley wanted to buy the room a round of drinks, but the cost was prohibitive. They could have the story instead, a dynasty crumbling right in front of them while waiting for a pancake dessert with three layers of Italian ricotta.

Stanley escaped into the lobby outside Hashhaus, ignored by most of the guests stepping off the elevator. He took out his phones, trying to track down Hans to ensure no one tried to speak with his father on his way out of The Marigold. There was a text from Abigail, asking to come visit her before they broke ground on the new tower. She'd attached a number of photos. Jaclyn had outlined his meetings for the next day, those highlighted red were mandatory. Most were red.

Someone wanted to buy his boat, *The Last of the Brohicans*. He'd tell them it was contingent on keeping the name, see if they were serious or not. Someone else wanted him to buy their plane as if he didn't already have one. Another elevator arrived. He stepped on alone. He considered sending Abigail a picture in return but didn't have the energy to undo his pants. Another notification caught his eye as the doors closed. He didn't recognize the name. *Alvin Simon Theodore*. Fake, potentially more spam. The subject line read: *Ramji Nolan's Devil Drive.*

17.

Happiness was the problem. No one wanted to admit it. An absurd agreement to pretend discontent was anomalous, strife and sorrow somehow discrete moments in life rather than the forces that shaped it. Soda considered this as he attempted to wash out the backseat of his Camry at a fast station near Moss Park, the water doing its best to remove the almost-coyote urine stains from his decaying upholstery. A familiar ritual. He pretended it was any other Sunday morning, that yet another man in Converse and a blazer had puked in his backseat.

"You got fired? Soda, you don't make it easy on yourself, buddy."

A couple other Magellan drivers hung out at the same gas station/coffee shop/burger joint, the kind of place that made your burgers while you watched them work behind the glass and gave you extra pickles on the side if you asked nice. It was spared from becoming yet another tower by the presence of the gas station, the chemicals and hydrocarbons in the contaminated soil making it far too difficult to pass an environmental assessment; a small and

197

at times volatile refuge in the core, one Magellan drivers used as a floating office space. They knew someday someone would ignore the cost of rehabilitating the land and annihilate this place.

"Blame those Threshold gate guards," Soda said. The firing arrived in an email, outlining his ongoing violations, part of a larger package his supervisor, an AI system named Horatio, had put together, underlining each failure in a gentle burnt sienna, pointing out how far below the norm he fell on a number of colourful charts used to cull the least efficient Magellan drivers each month to ensure their ongoing destabilization. Soft teals and pinks pointing to underwhelming numbers, vermilion squares for the more vicious customer complaints employing asterisks to lightly censor the more offensive language.

"I lost a full star when I refused to take a chick down there," one of the other drivers said, shaking his head. "My phone's already a direct feed. Like, it's not worth it when they're spitting all that info right back to the bosses on top of that."

"They don't want to know us," another older driver chipped in before taking a long deep pull from his vape pen. Cotton candy filled the air. "They just want our data."

"Which they then sell to someone else," Soda replied, turning off the pressure washer. He was careful with the settings. Too many drivers lost windows or ruined paint jobs during clean-up jobs. "It's a circle. It goes around and around until everyone is fed."

"Disgusting," the cotton candy driver said. "But not wrong."

"Definitely not."

Soda bent over, trying to peel the Magellan sticker off the inside of his windshield. The app was uninstalled from his phone and he'd removed the tracker they forced him to keep in the glovebox. He was supposed to mail it back to headquarters for a deposit but dropped it down a drain instead. They had video footage of his *reckless driving* in the Threshold district, a detailed rundown of each minor by-law he violated, all caught on cameras and sensors that tracked his speed, distance from the curb, lane drifting, and the tightness of his turns. There was no mention of the security team they sicced on him, or the strange animal in the vehicle, which was prohibited for drivers despite an ongoing lawsuit about an emotional support pug all the drivers called Ugly Humbert. There were certain things Magellan didn't want to feature on the official report. Similar tactics were used for drivers convicted of "minor" sexual harassment offences. If it was never officially recorded, they could later claim they were "never notified of the situation."

After a strong tug, the bottom chunks of the **M** still clung to the glass. Soda swore and climbed into the driver's seat for a better angle to pry at the gummy remains.

"There's one positive here, Soda, you won't have to piss in your car anymore. You can—"

A rumble cracked through the parking lot.

"Oh my god!"

The world filled with a long, high-pitched screech like a singing saw, before the ground opened up beneath the only diesel pump on the lot. Ground was there and then gone, the light blue Volkswagen at the pump plummeting down as the structure crumpled around the hole.

"The whole thing . . ."

The hole spread wider, taking down another pump that screeched as it was sheared away from its roots in the pavement. Drivers began to panic, spinning their wheels, fighting to escape from the tiny parking lot that was quickly turning into a deep, dark hole. Horns blared, punctuating the screech of another pump before the larger roof of the gas station collapsed.

Soda watched a Honda tip backwards, the Magellan sticker on the windshield catching the light before it disappeared. There was no crash, no scream, just an absence. Soda slammed his door shut and shoved his foot onto the accelerator, blasting over multiple curbs before he reached the road, smoke billowing into the sky behind him as gasoline spread into the streets, a single spark turning the block into an inferno. Sirens wailed as he navigated between cyclists and pedestrians fleeing from the city's freshest wound.

Soda's hands flickered over the console, jumping from one radio station to another, as more updates spat into the car. The hole swallowed the entire lot, churning up the edges of the intersection. The fire was still burning.

Soda careened down toward the waterfront, prepared to escape back to Mississauga, finally, truly grateful for a suburb where the rot was still undeniable, but moving slower, happy to infiltrate basements at a gradual pace. The trunk of Soda's car was filled with groceries, including all the expiring meat he could find. His father needed to eat and so did their spontaneously adopted pet. The city would recover. They didn't need a witness. No longer tracked, monitored, and indexed, he told himself. The last of the **M** still clung to his window. It was a good lie, a kind lie, the sort of self-deception that would last until he made it home.

§

"It's the city's fault," Dale said. Soda was in the backyard, now fully encased with old plywood, corrugated metal, and harvested front doors. He could taste the rust in his lungs. "They think they can keep opening up the earth like they own it. They think they own everything, even the air. It's just retribution. As natural as an ulcer. We do it to ourselves and then try to curse God."

"Are you sure this is safe?" Soda said. The almost-coyote was chained to a refrigerator. Every few minutes, it strained against its harness and the doorless Maytag shifted an inch or two. The creature calmly gathered its strength before the next lurch. "It looks pretty pissed off to me."

"Just hungry. You know how I get when I'm hungry. He and I have a lot in common."

"Him?"

"I checked," Dale said. "He has a name now."

"You're not going to tell me?"

"He hates Mondays."

Soda winced. Sunlight did its best to penetrate the structure. The only real illumination came from a few stage lights his father had stolen. "Tell me you didn't name it Garfield. Please."

"No, of course not. His name is Odie."

"Of course it is," Soda said. "Does he have a last name?"

Backlit by the harsh stage lights, Soda's father stared while taking a long sip of tea from his vintage Muppets mug. "Now you're being ridiculous."

Soda didn't mention he was fired, or his concern about how they'd pay the property tax bill on the fifteenth. The world was bigger now, a pockmarked landscape where power did whatever it wanted. There were larger forces at work that he could finally believe in, slipping into his father's delusions and finding they fit. It was a bizarre inheritance. Dale wasn't even dead yet.

"You're right, it is ridiculous. Do you think Odie understands us?"

"He knows we aren't like him," Dale said. "Imagine he's loyal, but we'll put that to the test."

Dale got up from the picnic table and shuffled over to the corner. He unlatched Odie from the chain but left the improvised harness in place, a motley collection of belts and suspenders. Odie revealed his teeth and backed up to the edge of the dome. Dale took another step toward him.

"You know, I emailed that man."

"You did what?" Soda said. "You don't have a phone, you don't even have a fucking email."

"Stanley. I can still use a computer. It's the devil's machine but we use their tools to protect ourselves. I told him about you. About that demon drive. The one the man gave you. Ramji."

"Dad, I don't need that kind of attention from anyone right now."

Odie snarled as Dale took another step forward. Soda remained frozen on the bench.

"Better than doing nothing. I know they are coming for us. That soil holds their secrets. Sometimes you must make the first move, even when it is difficult. He wants to meet you."

"He wants to meet?"

"Stanley, yes. He thinks you could help him. I don't know why, but I think he meant it. I think he is very alone. His father was like that too. These people are islands. When you know their sins, they think you know them."

"Dad, what are you—"

Odie let out a high yip, pouncing forward. Dale raised his left forearm, letting the creature sink its teeth into his flesh. With his other hand, Dale grabbed Odie by the throat, staring into the animal's yellow eyes. He whispered and cajoled the creature until it released him, leaving behind deep punctures. He wrapped his arms around Odie, holding him against his chest. Blood poured out of his arm. Soda yanked off his hoodie and ran over to his father. Odie growled.

"Dad, what're you thinking?"

"He needs to know whatever he does, he has a place here. That whatever he does, he's still one of us," Dale said, running his hands through Odie's matted fur. His body shuddered but he held the animal tight to his chest. "He doesn't need to be afraid. He doesn't need to keep running forever. The running stops now."

"It's a wild thing," Soda said.

"He," Dale said. "He has a name. Odie."

Soda wrapped his sweater tight around his father's arm, watched the blood pool and drip through the fabric onto the patio stones. Odie watched him carefully from inside Dale's embrace.

"You have to go to a doctor, Dad. This is insane."

"I need you to stop arguing," Dale said. "I need you to listen for once in your life, since your mother cannot translate for you anymore. You remember what I said? About power showing itself? About what a negotiation looks like?"

"Yes," Soda said. The bright lights made the blood too real.

"You have to see this man, this Stanley. Before they come to collect their dirt. They'll figure out why I took it. You have something he wants, and he doesn't want Threshold to get it. They'll take everything when they arrive. And they are coming. They will say it was an altercation gone wrong. They will say I was a mentally unstable man struggling with an episode. Maybe I will fall out a window. Maybe I'll burn alive. There will be a cover story. There always is. They investigate themselves, a council of foxes deciding what makes a henhouse safe. I can feel it in the air. They are coming. Their teeth, that yellow gate slamming shut. They don't want anyone to know what they found. You have Ramji's drive. Take it. You know what the price is."

"I do?"

His father grinned, releasing Odie, who wandered away from them into his corner and lay down. Dale wrapped his son in his battered arms, the gummy hoodie resting against the back of Soda's sweaty neck, the fluids running together down his back, trickling between his shoulders.

"It's blood, son."

Odie howled, a mournful note. It found no exit.

"It's always blood."

18.

Salman screamed so high he summoned rats out of the dripping walls. "My foot!"

Henrietta cranked her flashlight, flicking it past scurrying, sniffling bodies. Alma knelt down in the muck of the tunnel, trying to lift his weight. "He messed it up good."

"I didn't, augh, that hurts, Al!"

The foot swayed when they pulled him up, the limited-edition white-and-yellow Adidas swivelling with its own rhythm. Henrietta winced as she and Alma tried to lift the heavier boy.

Cabeza cocked its head. "Slow us down."

"Can you put any weight on it?" Henrietta said. "Can you try and . . ."

Another scream. A whimper. A sigh.

"He's done, Henny," Alma said. "How do we get outta here, taco man? There's no way he can keep going on this foot."

Cabeza burbled under the goo. "Can't leave."

"There can't just be one way down here, Cabeza," Henrietta said. She missed the sun. "You know this world, not us."

"Don't leave me," Salman said, sweat pouring down his features. "I'll get eaten alive."

Cabeza gurgled. "Yes."

The shambling creature had led them through the underground, past crumbling foundations and augured holes punched through the earth. Tiny specks of light occasionally slipped down, bouncing off old mirrors and shattered bottles sifted over the decades into the urban sediment along with cigarette butts, disposable coffee cups, and an endless supply of chicken bones, fatty knobs petrified. These were paltry offerings to the hunger of the pits, open wounds left to fester.

They had spent four nights so far underground, attempting to sleep in a circle. They travelled beneath highways and through sunken housing projects no one remembered, flashlights uncovering names and dates from the long forgotten. Cabeza didn't sleep, guarding the edges, attuned to the vibrations in the tunnels, the squelching and shrieking. Most weren't threats, just the ground shifting under the weight of a new building or the collapse of another when the money ran out.

"Further to find," Cabeza said. "If still alive."

"Cherry," Salman groaned through his teeth. "All of this bullshit for the one good boy who Hen *definitely* didn't kill when he shut her down in the pit. Imagine if we did anything else instead of this stupid shit."

"Salman, shut up," Al replied. "Just this one time, shut your mouth."

"He can't stay down here," Henrietta said.

"Out to the valley," Cabeza said, voice nearly human for a moment. Its skin hovered like oil over a puddle, barely congealing over the grim hard bits beneath, what might have once been organs or bone. It existed in a constant state of flux, barely coherent to the human eye. Henrietta did her best not to stare too long, afraid she might lose herself in its murky cosmos. She knew the slouching thing could speak, but the effort took a lot out of the creature. It burbled and hissed before more words emerged. "Another hole. Go up. For a little while. Next part harder."

"We trust you," Henrietta said. She tried not to think about Cherry under the same ooze, if he was already progressing through the same transformation. A dripping, living thing, but not human. They hadn't seen others like it so far on their journey. Cabeza's voice was too familiar when it could get the words out.

Salman laughed. "Trust? Do we have a choice?"

"Follow."

Henrietta kept pace behind Cabeza, trying to keep her gaze off the dripping and pulsating mass. They moved in silence, the two girls supporting the weight of the boy between them. Salman did his best not to whimper, but Henrietta still wanted to hit him. Time slipped away from them, minutes no longer relevant. Would Cherry be doing this for them? She didn't know. Was Cherry even a person she knew? Henrietta didn't examine the questions too closely, their edges too sharp to hold.

Cabeza raised a shuddering arm into the air to bring them to a stop. The tunnel ahead split into three directions. A great whistling sound swept around them.

I wouldn't leave you.

"Follow this path . . . here . . ."

"Are you coming with us?" Henrietta asked, resisting the impulse to reach out and touch the creature spasming with each breath it took. Alive and dead at the same time, a memory of a person scrawled over a skeleton and filled with some meat jelly. Maybe that was Cherry now, no longer a pile of pressed shirts, dog-eared books, and delicate movements. Maybe he was like her father now, a slurry at the bottom of the pit, dead without a grave. There was no tombstone, no memorial except what she carried inside her. "We still don't have Cherry. This isn't what we agreed to before."

"I wait," Cabeza said. "Still need to find old me. First me."

"How long will you wait?" Alma asked, shifting her shoulder under Salman's armpit. He barely spoke now, murmuring into her hair.

"Time not anything," Cabeza said, plopping to the ground, collapsing in on itself, losing the outline of its human self, becoming something darkly viscous and unknowable. "Come back. Please. I wait. Always wait. Please."

Henrietta nodded at the bubbling mass and turned.

I would take you with me.

When they emerged from a humid crevice in the Don Valley, the swathe of green and highway that cut through the city like a jagged ribbon, Salman dropped to the dirt and kissed the ground, immediately pressing his lips against a grocery bag full of old clothes hidden in the scraggly weeds. He shrieked and scrambled, his flopping foot bending in impossible directions.

Figures emerged from the trees around them, weather-beaten faces that scowled without revealing their teeth, eyes alert or looking right through them. Tents and lean-tos were camouflaged in the trees and the lush, fetid undergrowth. The ground sweat. Henrietta quickly became aware of her own smell, the ripe rot of the underground, a sickly sweetness. They hadn't journeyed as far as she thought. The world under this place disorganized your brain, made you forget what distance was or meant. She was years older. Cherry was still inside her head, still the same age, still asking for her help. He was dangling in her brain, a link to who she had been only a few days before.

"How deep did you go?" a high voice called out from the trees. "All the way down?"

"That's no place for girls like you," another said, laughing.

"We're full up," someone else barked. "Back to the pit."

Henrietta could make out bodies in the trees, doing their best to blend in with the valley. She knew about the city's sweeps, the tents piled and burned, the dumpsters filled with entire lives. It moved like waves through the parks regularly, a constant churning, Threshold subsidiaries taking contracts to play along with the police, whacking heads so hard against the concrete they left little wet pieces behind. The valley was one of the last safe places to hide from their purges. And now Henrietta and her friends had arrived, bringing old death with them. It clung to their skin.

"We know what's down there," another lower voice said. It was like the old oaks spoke. "Leave them alone. If they lived, they can stay. If they saw what we saw . . . they know."

"Our friend needs help."

Salman wept silently in the grass. They might need to remove the foot. A few days ago, Henrietta might have puked at the sight. Now she was only annoyed. Feet shouldn't bend like that.

"Please," Henrietta said. "He just needs to go home."

Another high-pitched laugh. "What kind of home is that?"

A sunset illuminated the valley with a hazy purple light, glinting off shopping carts parked inside brambles. Water jugs were stacked on top of each other by a low, smouldering fire. A series of piñatas dangled from another tree, each of them bleeding candy onto the ground, swarmed by ants. Henrietta stopped herself from grabbing a handful despite her hunger. Salman wasn't as picky, crawling over the burnt grass. He grabbed pieces, unravelling their sweetness.

"Don't go back down there," he murmured. "This is just an ankle, but there is so much worse down there. You heard it, didn't you?"

"I did," Alma answered. "But we have to go back down."

Salman shuddered. "Don't."

"I can't let her go back alone."

Henrietta watched Alma strut toward the fire, daring the shapes in the trees to show themselves. "My dad lives here somewhere," Alma said. "Or he used to at least. They chased him from place to place, running him down, making him start over. The city hates everything about him. And you're going to tell me you don't help each other? That you can't look out for one another? I know that's not true. I know you all better than that. I know."

Bodies revealed themselves slowly, emerging from the green.

"You're going back down there," a man's voice said, harsher and deeper than the others. "I know what's down there. At least part of it."

The man's once lustrous beard was filled with dirt and burrs. His three-piece suit was torn at the ankles, fraying at the wrists. Once tailored to his body, now it hung from slumped shoulders.

"My name is Ramji. I need you to take me with you."

"Who brought their lawyer?" Salman said, trying to regain a piece of his swagger even as he fought with ants over the candy. Henrietta watched his chest puff up like a balloon animal. All it took was a needle to pop him. "You drown your Lexus in the river or something?"

More peals of laughter from the trees, more bodies emerging. Punk kids and small children with burn scars on their faces. Women in eight-inch heeled sandals, old men wrapped in Disney sleeping bags like robes. Soon they were surrounded. Ramji reached out to Henrietta.

"I know you think I'm crazy for asking. I need to see it for myself."

"What do you know about anything?" Alma said, unimpressed. The time underground hardened her. Henrietta was barely familiar with this outline of Alma, one that only appeared when the lights went down and her shadow swelled to ten times its size. "What do you think is down there? You don't know anything at all, man."

Ramji scratched his neck, revealing monograms on the cuffs of his jacket. "Offerings."

Was that what Cherry was now? An offering? Henrietta didn't know to who or to what. They could stay up here with Salman, maybe call a Magellan or wave down one of the last cabbies struggling up the side of the valley. Retreat, leave Cabeza down there in the tunnels, dripping and murmuring. Head back to the towers, pretend nothing happened. People would still whisper she was a killer, but who said she wasn't? She had brought Cherry to the pit after all, even convinced him to climb down with her. Maybe if she was lucky, she could forget the smell.

"What do you mean *offerings*?" Henrietta said. "How do you know?"

Ramji leaned over Salman, inspecting his foot. "A bad break, man. How do I know? I know because I know who puts them down there. At least some of them. Maybe most of them."

Henrietta glared at the bearded man. "You don't know what it's like down there."

"No, I don't. You're right."

Salman groaned. They would need a replacement.

"You saw what happened to him," she said. "Why would you want to come?"

Ramji didn't answer. The other campers in the valley began to lose interest and drift back into the trees, back to their homes. Henrietta kept her gaze locked on Ramji, until he looked away from her into the low, trembling fire.

"You want to see what you've done. You want to know how bad it is."

His gaze flicked back to her. "Yes."

"Okay," Henrietta said, collapsing into the grass beside Salman. "You can come."

In the waning light, Ramji and Alma scrounged up water bottles and granola bars. One woman offered a stash of technically expired Mini-Wheats boxes; Ramji traded his watch for most of the skid. Sitting around the flames, the group unpacked plastic sacks from the boxes and taped them to Ramji's back, turning him into a pack mule. This was part of the bargain. They found fortune cookies in fresh garbage bags residents rolled down into the valley, correctly assuming no one policed illegal dumping anymore. The City had larger concerns.

"May you live in interesting times," Salman read his fortune. Ramji had applied a splint to the foot. They even discovered crutches in a garbage pyre no one had got around to burning yet. "It's not even a fortune, is it? Just a weird curse."

"Read it either way," Ramji said. "No matter what, it still comes true."

Henrietta watched the bearded man carefully, unsure why this new ally would trust two teenagers to lead him down into the earth. His suit was all that separated him from the others in the valley and he clung to it. His shoes were spattered and creased from this new life he'd built here, but they signalled a lot of money somewhere behind this mess. Maybe he had lost someone to the pit too. A girl could lose a father and then a friend to the hole. A man like Ramji could have lost anyone. Maybe he wanted them back too. Maybe he wanted to know for sure.

"I've experienced enough interesting times," Salman said.

Henrietta watched Alma rise from the fire and make her way over to Salman's slouching shadow. Raccoons chittered and squealed at them from the brush.

"You're the only one who knows where we went, okay?" Alma said. "That's still important. We need someone to tell everyone we didn't run away. We had a purpose. Can you do that? You can tell them we went to Montreal. Tell them we aren't really gone."

"You want me to lie?" Salman said. A tear hissed into the fire.

"I want you to protect us," Alma said. "Convince everyone we're doing something amazing. If we don't end up back at the towers, at least we aren't trapped underneath them forever, right?"

"You'll come back," Salman said. "You always come back."

§

They left in darkness, Salman an outline by the fire. Alma led the way to the crevice. Henrietta followed. She knew the world was designed to break her, to remove people from her life one by one. She had a chance now to snatch them back. She wouldn't waste it. Henrietta saw the gently steaming hole in the earth, prepared to enter again with full knowledge of what awaited her.

"How bad is it?" Ramji said, gesturing back at what remained of Salman. "Seems like he's a bit broken. I don't just mean the foot."

"Not as bad as you think," Henrietta said. Alma sniggered.

"The fact you're saying that . . ."

"Means we don't know," Henrietta answered. "We've only seen the start."

Ramji didn't speak. They pushed through the brush, nettles stinging.

"Why didn't you go down there yourself?" Henrietta said. "Alone."

"It's stupid," Ramji said.

"Well, this is also stupid," Alma said. "This is like the stupidest thing we have ever done."

"I don't like the dark."

Henrietta laughed. "Sure."

"I didn't want to be alone," Ramji said.

"You're not alone now," Henrietta said. The crevice lay before them, a familiar rot.

"Oh my god, you weren't kidding about the smell," Ramji said, following Alma into the crevice, disappearing from view. Henrietta then dropped down, a flashlight in the dark.

"Hello," Cabeza said, limbs sprouting from the pile of black sludge into an outline of a person. "New . . . new friend?"

Ramji screamed, tried to run, fell, scrambled to his feet again. He was trapped in the crevice. Mini-Wheats rained down into the goo around him. Alma yanked on his arm, holding him back. "Jesus, fuck. Fuck, Jesus. Fuck, what is that? This?"

"This is our guide," Alma said. "This is what you wanted to see, right?"

"This is a person?" Ramji stuttered. "You trust this thing?"

"We trusted you, didn't we? You get used to it," Henrietta said, listening to Cabeza drip and hiss. A few teeth and a tongue tried to approximate something like a smile. "All it takes is time."

Suite 3003

Marcos Marcos didn't sign up for this shit. Technically, he didn't sign anything at all.

"Jeanie, people are dead in here. No exaggeration."

When he first tried to create a unified tenant organization in The Marigold, management sent one of their bald goons to meet him in the lobby, offering to help with his mortgage if he agreed to stop posting fliers in the mailroom about collective action.

"Jeanie, I'm serious, they're straight up covering up deaths ever since the hockey man decided he couldn't live with himself anymore. I couldn't either if I was him, to be honest, but I don't want anyone to actually die. Just a little ego death, maybe. That would be healthy for everyone. Kill the cop in your head, right?"

The second time they caught him in the elevators putting up fliers, using liquid glue from his friend Cavan Silencio, a print artist Marcos met at an underground art gallery that also served as storage for stolen bicycles in what remained of Kensington Market, a few stubby buildings under the towers of Spadina. Cavan put up

214

posters all over town, shellacking walls that hid construction pits with fake touring bands, imaginary album releases, and disgusting fragrance launches — Cotton Candy Diesel or Dog Ambergris. In Cavan's tiny apartment in an old tower by the Lakeshore, bonding in the homegrown weed smoke, Cavan told Marcos he needed to bring the building down from the inside if he wanted to enact change. Living in The Marigold, you knew there was no prince coming to save you. You had to climb down using your own hair.

The unit was technically owned by his father, but Marcos Marcos lived here. He was the one who discovered the condo board was a sham, a number of people who didn't live in the building, but all appeared to have connections with the Marigold/Dundee Corporation and their various subsidiaries, which included label printing, milk product exports, and a syndicated mortgage company that changed its name every eighteen months. They controlled the contracts of property managers, cleaners, and security staff, all tied together like a rat king, all begging to be fed.

One of the biggest problems was absentee owners serving as proxies for the board, providing signatures even as their empty units decayed and maintenance fees rose. Maybe four people actually lived on Marcos's floor — two never left the building, everything was delivered to their doors. He never saw their faces, only cases upon cases of apple juice at the one door and a series of stuffed animals outside the other. The two other units were leased, doing their best to survive on whatever money was left over after they paid rent. The one girl said she worked at a bank, the boy in law school. Both pale and somehow always dirty, fingernails too long, dandruff gathering in the folds of their clothes. The air-conditioning didn't always work this high up, cutting in and out in the middle of the night with bangs like shots in the dark. Sometimes the dirty kids stole from the apple juice deliveries. Marcos Marcos didn't blame them. He knew some poor people.

With the sinkholes, fewer units filled up with tourists, no longer drawn in by the temptation of shareable small plates in low-lit bars across the west end, even with a weak dollar and a police force supported by various by-law enforcement affiliates dedicated to eliminating the homeless from view. Some of The Marigold's units were never intended to be inhabited. They only existed as supposedly sturdy investment vehicles for overseas buyers. Even the ones who did live here didn't seem to understand — they believed this building would last.

Marcos tried to explain it to his father once, how an abandoned luxury condo unit eventually loses any semblance of luxury, turning an investment into a liability. They were on a video chat, his father planning to fly back to Copenhagen to speak at a conference about the resiliency of cycling infrastructure during the annual floods plaguing most of coastal Europe. Marcos ran down what he'd discovered with the support of Cavan and their friend Jeanie Calypso, a tarot specialist and registered astrologist who lived in her own tastefully appointed concrete box.

Without tenants or owners living in the units, appliances caught fire, pipes exploded with no HVAC support, and mould grew along every dark surface because the fans were turned off, or stopped working, or circling back to the first point, had already caught fire and been removed. Taking twenty-nine flights of stairs down to the ground during yet another fire alarm made their frequency very clear to Marcos. His father only asked how much the maintenance fees were projected to rise before ending the call with his third and final son.

"Jeanie, can you come over here so I can feel a little less crazy? I'll pay for the Magellan, alright, even the female driver upgrade, okay? Please? I know I sound crazy right now but it's so much bigger. They know I know what they do here."

Notes were slipped under Marcos Marcos's door, some from the management company. Management were unfailingly polite, reassuring Marcos that his concerns were valid; he was both being seen and heard. Since he wasn't technically an owner, he couldn't run for a position on the board. If his father was interested, they were open to talking with Mr. Adam Moreland as soon as he answered their emails.

"You can smell it in the building, it's like when you don't clean out the washing machine. Little bits stuck in the rubbery part, right? Oh, don't give me that, Jeanie. Yes, I do my own laundry!"

He would've called Cavan, but Cavan was still in jail, refusing to pay their bail and holding out after leading a rent strike in their apartment building. Marcos wanted to be like Cavan, if only for a little while. Cavan was the one who told him it was okay to give up his family name, to cast off the Moreland mantle and strike out on his own, to build his small fashion empire with a few social media accounts and a website that processed all the orders, shipping his visions from countries he'd never visited across oceans he'd never see.

Marcos mainly worked with patterns he designed himself, dragging and dropping little icons onto his screen. He was very into pirates at the moment, a lot of skulls and crossbones, but with neon highlights. A death that glowed is how Cavan described it before the Threshold security team entered their cramped apartment, four burly men dragging Cavan in their dress and heels out into the hallway, Marcos on the other side of the screen watching his friend shrink until only the empty apartment remained, the sound of a taser going off three times. Marcos shut the screen.

"Jeanie, don't tell me I'm being irrational, okay? If you want irrational, step outside. I saw a raccoon in the elevator the other day. It smiled at me. No, I did not get on the elevator with it. Jeanie, they're not our friends! Have you seen their hands?"

The other notes that slid under the door were less official. All capitalized, the tone direct. **STOP**. Marcos Marcos kept these letters, sure they'd help his cause eventually. The building forced him to pay for the elevator clean-up, which required his father to release more funds. Sometimes Marcos wondered what it'd take his father to say no, if a limit was possible. His older brothers both followed the family business, obtaining engineering degrees and wives and positions in Moreland-Sterling Engineering, overseeing their father's attempts to rewrite the world according to his vision. Marcos was the one who remained on the outside.

"So, you'll come, won't you? Jeanie, just say you'll come. Look, I'm already ordering you the car. Can't undo that now, can I? That bald guy they love to send around, the pretend cop, he's the one sending these letters you know, he's the little lapdog. No, I don't have a camera. I know what a footfall sounds like, do you under-stand? He walks like a toddler, big steps. I will see you when you get here. Your place has silverfish, don't even dare me to go over there! They're not your friends! They're silverfish!"

Maybe it was the darkness on this side of the building, the windows pressed up against the grey façade of the old skyscraper next door, a blank slate so slim no one even bothered to graffiti — there was no audience. Any unit on the south side of the building, below the fortieth floor at least, only had a view of this wall. The wall supported no wildlife. It looked slightly darker when it rained, whiter when it snowed. The alley below was just wide enough for a garbage truck to pass if the driver was experienced. Marcos learned to use earplugs on Wednesday nights when the shriek of metal on concrete reverberated up the canyon between the buildings. Another complaint he submitted to every possible inbox.

Marcos used one of the bedrooms as a work room while the den became an altar, a place for him to relax and meditate, with a futon for anyone who stayed over. He had a life-size cut-out of

Janet Jackson in one corner, circa her "Together Again" video, a gift from Cavan last year. Janet was surrounded by extremely powerful lightboxes for Marcos's seasonal affective disorder. Cacti and other dead succulents covered most flat surfaces, their rot covered by various applications of incense, Febreze, and a box of baking soda on the kitchen counter.

You lost them.

The latest letter slid under his door was not an official document from anyone. ***STOP BEFORE YOU HURT YOURSELF.*** It arrived while he was napping, in the middle of designing a romper featuring two pirate rabbits in pastel yellows and greens, a slightly rebellious Easter theme. Calendars still counted days, clocks still managed minutes, all inescapable and immutable unless you were in a place without time, a place with only a single slate of grey to judge the weather.

The letter was shoved with enough force to make it under the towel he kept against the bottom of the door. It was like they knew what went on inside his suite. He traced the walls with his fingertips, looking for cameras or bugs inserted into the drywall while he slept. Jeanie would be here soon to lead him on a guided meditation. Together, they'd pull back each layer and find the truth, even if it meant having to redo the entire interior again.

You could have saved them.

Sometimes when he stared out at the grey wall across from his unit, Marcos Marcos heard a voice slide into his ear. Familiar, confident, slightly imposing. It spoke like it knew him, like it was part of him. It wasn't his father's voice despite its paternal tone.

They needed you.

Marcos wanted to tell the voice it was wrong, the voice lingering near his guest bathroom, the one with a Japanese toilet that no longer functioned. He duct-taped the lid shut so guests would stop using it. The flushing mechanism required a software patch, but he had to update the drivers first, and the toilet wasn't compatible with any of the cables he had. The sink was still usable, but Marcos didn't like to enter that room. He wasn't even able to fix a bathroom, never mind the condo board, never mind the political framework of this city that was happy to strangle anything that grew a little too tall. He couldn't even save Cavan.

After they dragged them out, the police alleged Cavan assaulted two of the officers, striking one so hard that he had "a serious concussion" according to media reports. Marcos had never seen Cavan throw a punch before. He didn't even know if they could make a fist. The one phone call Cavan used went to Jeanie, who immediately started a fundraising effort to match their bail. She asked Marcos to provide testimony, maybe even video from their final chat, if he could somehow find the file, if he'd been recording it. He had not.

They still need you.

The right thing to do would be to cover the cost of the bail himself, to truly step out of his role as an observer and become an actual activist. Cavan needed support, needed money, needed a lawyer, but a small voice, a meaner voice than the one he heard in the suite, asked Marcos where it would end. Would they all end up coming to him for money? It wasn't his money after all. And what if the money was pulled away? What if he was forced to choose?

The fundraiser picked up steam at first, but soon slowed down to a trickle as more and more activists were yanked out of their apartments, thrown from windows, dragged through barricades, jaws dislocated, arms shattered, eyes pulped by rubber bullets. Cavan's name slid further and further down screens, still many thousands from their goal.

You could make it all go away.

Marcos never fully made the jump into Jeanie and Cavan's world, the bitter underbelly they clung to so viciously, even as the city refused to love them back. He still appreciated having the doormen downstairs, the delivery drivers who weren't afraid of his address. Even if the tower was decaying, it was better than what remained of Parkdale. Even if it was corrupt, it was a home with semi-functional AC and hot water. No silverfish crawling over his body in the night. Small comforts were still comforts.

A hard knock at the door. One of the bald man's favourite intimidation tactics. Jeanie didn't knock like that; her hands were too small. He ignored the knock. Cavan was in a smaller cell, but weren't they both trapped? Weren't they both haunted by a place? He shook his head. It was sickening to think that way, sickening to pretend this was anything like the South Detention Centre. Marcos felt bile rising in his throat. Jeanie would be here soon, and they would plan together. He wouldn't die in this place and Cavan wouldn't die either.

Another hard knock, a voice mumbling against the door. Marcos fled to the bathroom with his useless Japanese toilet, closed the door behind him, sat in total darkness with his phone in his pocket, waiting for Jeanie, for anyone to call. He puked in the sink, a thin gruel that burned his lips.

You could have helped them.

A whisper from the drain, speaking through his own spittle, rising up before the mirror. A physical thing, a pulsing mass emerging. There were so many bodies in this building, so many bodies in that jail. Cavan deserved better than a friend like Marcos Marcos.

You can join them, the wet, dark whisper in the sink said. *Join them.*

"Okay," Marcos replied. "Okay."

The drain gurgled out a laugh.

19.

The augers brought him peace. Even with the latest sinkhole in the east end, work continued. The sinkhole was blamed on an ongoing transit project, the improvised product of a number of PR teams scrambling to unite behind a single story. A subway renovation/tunnelling exercise gone wrong. The story was a tourniquet, settling the rumblings that spread through the city. The rise and fall of these augers centred Stanley Marigold, allowed him to forget the earth was ultimately unknowable, his existence a blip. Coupled with the cranes clustered around the fresh site, the thud and shriek of the augers allowed Stanley to see futures beyond futures, a city that stretched past the clouds, roots planted so deep no shift in the earth's crust could bring it down. A blip that kept repeating was no longer a blip, it was a pulse.

This spot, overlooking a drowned swathe of High Park, would become the latest Holstein skyscraper, all of it financed with the discreet support of Heritage Lands Development, a subsidiary of the Marigold/Dundee Corporation. Albert remained unaware of the novel arrangement, the details too complicated for his mental state. Stanley believed his father would have approved. There were commission fees of up to 15 percent for every investor directed toward HLD by various brokerages across the country, those investments then funding another round of development once the commissions were quietly skimmed before anyone even applied for permits. Not even the other Marigold siblings knew about the arrangement, but Whitney and Anders were ghosts to Toronto now, flying off to Japan for new cybernetic implants or Turkey for factory-pure MDMA. Sidney said they understood how to be rich.

The struggles of his first flagship tower were still raw whenever he woke up in his suite, staring into the crack above him. Only a last-minute concession by his father in the darkened subbasement saved the project, leaving a slight tilt in the final structure as a reminder of Stanley's hubris, his attempt to reject the building's seed. They paid the appraisers a little extra to ignore the uneven floors. One girl in the office spent her days deleting comments about rolling chairs and dressers tipping over in the middle of the night from official media channels, fighting a slow cold war against owners and increasingly frustrated tenants.

Dirt becomes a hole becomes a foundation becomes a tower becomes a rupture in the skyline. There were people who compared the towers to cocks, somehow certain they'd never grow soft, never crumble. Stanley saw them more as an attempt to outdo trees, to reach as close as they could toward the sun. This new project didn't have a name yet; the seed hadn't been planted. The talk of cocks in the sky made Stanley think of all the quiet little homes in what was supposed to be a city, the single-family units clinging desperately to the idea they mattered.

There was desperation in the phrase "world-class city," even as Paris burned, San Francisco disappeared into the ocean, and Tokyo turned against itself. A prudish sensibility held firmly at the heart of this city, a long snide look down its patrician nose at any attempt to do anything different, bigger, or denser. It was easier to write a new development off as a sexual aberration than confront the overwhelming evidence, gathering in the ravines and beneath the bridges of each borough, that there weren't enough places to live, that the city could not contain its multitudes and would rather have them rot than see them housed.

Stanley stuck with the image of a tree in his mind — a money tree as long as you escaped the pit intact, as long as you poured the foundation correctly. The hole before him was only fifty or so feet deep, a benign impression compared to Marigold II at this stage. Each morning he woke up and looked down into its gentle abyss, the concrete trucks running at all hours around its puckered edges, turning what was once an expensive dream into a precariously valued reality. Hans kept telling him there was a wet spot at the bottom that wouldn't go away — a pool of fluid that wasn't rain. They were learning more about its contents.

Now under the heat of the sun with his mandatory hard hat, Stanley prayed this new Holstein building wouldn't be given another biblical name. There were rumours the Holsteins wanted to go with Gethsemane. When it came to biblical names, Stanley preferred the kind that didn't involve betrayal, especially if you needed to sell every unit during pre-construction to keep creditors off your back. You could only deny a debt collector so many times before the cock crowed.

"So, is it worth it?" Abigail said, wrapping her arms around Stanley's waist. Her hard hat brim bit into his back. "It's going to be amazing. We'll have two towers, playing off of each other. Did I show you the rendering? They're absolutely wild. They won't stand up during the design committee, but for now they look impressive. We're going to try and present the land between the towers as, like, a public park. The towers don't actually connect until the fifth floor, but it still gives you the impression of that solid wall, like a gentle kind of fortress, right? I wanted something welcoming but also protective. You can see yourself in there. Word the marketing girl used was *ensconced*. People will be ensconced. Can you see it?"

Stanley didn't ask what the architect cost. The Holsteins had their own money to burn if they wanted. HLD would continue to collect commissions. Holsteins move too quickly, Albert told him during a brief lucid moment at the Eternals Club in yet another secret early morning conference. Holsteins act without thinking, without planning.

"Ensconced, eh? Please tell me you didn't use that word in your public meeting."

Still better than Threshold, that corporation believing in nothing but its own mantras.

"No, we called ourselves a neighbouring start-up," Abigail said. She was facing him now, hard hat grazing his chin. "There is so much negativity around us. You get the same response every time you come into a neighbourhood. The big bad gentrifier . . ."

"Every development you've completed has been a luxury building, wouldn't you agree?" Stanley said. The pit appeared shallow enough to jump. Multiple teens had split their heads open when they attempted to infiltrate the original Marigold site after the pit was opened up, crashing into the side of a dump truck after overestimating their own leg strength. All their lawsuits failed, but lawyers still charged by the hour.

"It's pejorative," Abigail said. "I'm sorry we're improving your terrible neighbourhood, I guess? I'm sorry we're planting trees and creating livable spaces."

"You just don't like being the bad guy."

"I don't have the flair for it, unlike some people I know."

Stanley looked down into the hole. He wanted to bring Sidney here, show her how far his influence reached. She was still sending him photos from another suite somewhere in the building, underwear hanging off a door handle. He appreciated the composition of the images, if not the content. The walls were blank, the paint job obviously still the original sloppy coat completed by the last crew of contractors he refused to pay. She needed to find better partners. Maybe someone who could decorate or at least had the money to hire a decent interior decorator. He'd even accept a collection of action figures or a large virtual reality den instead of a bedroom. Something with character. Their games weren't fun when they were so one-sided.

"What's next for you then?" he said. "You start calling renters 'members' instead of tenants? Maybe install a convenience store on the first floor but call it a bodega? Capitalize the B? It's about the aesthetics. I get that. We dress it up. Bike lanes are universal. Trees are positive, adding to the natural environment, strengthening the soil, providing more oxygen. Ten percent of this building will be affordable, right? So, you sell them all these things that will eventually price them out. Your trees are harbingers, no different than a reaper. And they begin to see that as the end goal — a removal. Some people might even call it a publicly funded renoviction if the City decides to chip in on expenses. Who doesn't want to cut the ribbon on a new urban green space named after a dead minority?"

"I didn't realize you were such an activist," Abigail said.

"Honestly, I couldn't give a shit either way," Stanley said. "I'm not going to pretend I'm the nice guy here. I annihilate the past, just like my father before me; only he did it in places no one cared about, in a time when you could pay someone off a little easier. And you do it too. There's no history here. I'm not helpful. I'm not in this to improve anyone's quality of life."

"Very brave," Abigail said, giving him a light shove. "Didn't realize there was such an easy path to valourize becoming an asshole."

Stanley watched the cranes swinging overhead. In a couple weeks, he imagined another teen would throw themselves off the top into the darkness below. They all gave their gangs little names. The West End Phoenix, the Humber Humberts, the Woke Stasi. All of them eager for a chance to burn out on camera rather than live on the periphery.

"I never said it was a good thing, just how I choose to run things," Stanley said.

"Well, you're a man, you get a little more latitude when it comes to being a prick," Abigail said. "I don't get that luxury."

"Girl boss manifesto. Blame it on your old man then. Blame it on the times."

Abigail stared into the hole. "How much deeper does it need to go before we can rest easy?"

"Based on my limited experience, he usually wants the pit to be about a hundred feet down before he shows up. My old man figured it was an arbitrary number. I think it's practical. No one's supposed to be around when he shows up, part of the deal. Privacy is the number one thing. He doesn't even have a phone. Next couple days is likely. He's patient."

"Have you ever met him?"

Stanley removed his hard hat, scratched his head. The sun was out again. "Only once. It was dark. He didn't say much. It wasn't how it was supposed to be done. We were making amends. My father was trying to fix my mistake. I didn't realize it mattered."

"Does it matter?"

"The price?"

"Yes," Abigail whispered.

"I don't know," Stanley said. "But if you're wrong, it costs you more than money."

Abigail stared down into the pit with him again, likely imagining the price they were all so happy to pay when they didn't have to see it. A phone, a home, a lamp. Someone else paid.

"Jaclyn, can you get me some copies of the marketing materials?"

Stanley called out to Jaclyn, turning back to Abigail. "You're really going to go with Gethsemane?"

Jaclyn picked her way across the site. Stanley had considered bringing Hans, but The Marigold had enough issues at the moment. People were starting to spread rumours about bodies in formerly occupied units, the other tenants only alerted to their presence by the smell. He'd need to hire more cleaning crews, strengthen their NDAs, maybe even offer to hire them on at the Marigold/Dundee Corporation to ensure control.

"Yes, it implies resiliency, survival, rebirth — all that good stuff. People love that shit. Overcoming adversity. A dark night of the soul leading to a clear morning."

Jaclyn didn't fall so much as tip over the side, losing her balance in the loose dirt along the edge of the pit, leaning out into the air until she disappeared. Stanley could only watch from the corner of his eye. The scream went on for longer than he expected.

"Oh my god!" Abigail shrieked, fleeing toward the foreman's trailer, hands covering her face. Stanley crouched, leaning over the pit. A tuft of blond hair stood out in the dirt below. A collection of white helmets scuttled toward it, mumbling concern. Someone fired off a siren. Heavy machinery hissed to a stop. He watched the white helmets pull her body upright, watched the tuft of hair sag back down. Sweat ran into his eyes. Stanley pulled out his phone, texted Sidney.

Know any good assistants?

Sidney didn't need to know all the details. He didn't want to upset her. They were supposed to have dinner tonight with her sister, where he would ask the right questions about breeding cocker spaniels and drink at least three bottles of wine. The place, Wontons, served deconstructed tacos, just ingredients thrown haphazardly on a plate. It would be a shame to ruin dinner. Stanley stood up and wiped the dust off his knees. He'd need to call the dry cleaner. And the barber. And the restaurant to ensure the reservation was still on for tonight, in case Jaclyn hadn't done that already. The list of assignments grew as he tallied them in his head.

Abigail disappeared inside the trailer, her weeping blending in with the rest of the chaos. He'd phone her later to apologize, offer to pay for the therapy. Maybe even a weekend away together. He needed to remember the name of the motel in Prince Edward County, the one he went to last summer with that DJ who wore a set of elf ears in bed. And there was still the email about Ramji's drive, sent by one of those old city cronies his dad used to golf with up in Muskoka, all those secrets waiting to be spilled. He would need to get back to that old man, make his case clear. Threshold wouldn't be allowed to win again. They never understood the price, never even tried to pay it. They were making things unstable. Stanley sighed deeply and walked back through the dusty site to his car before realizing Jaclyn still had the keys.

20.

They weren't going rogue. They just weren't answering emails. Cathy and Jasmine stopped to reconsider their options in a struggling Starbucks, tucked away from the rest of the customers in their own tiny glass pod off College. Their heavy masks were hidden in their bags to avoid suspicion. There were six missed calls from numbers they didn't recognize and a series of official department emails fluttering through Cathy's phone, vibrating it across the table. She pinned it before it plummeted to the floor.

Cathy stared at the notepad she'd snatched off the table after the Wet exploded in the ceramics museum. All in shorthand, the notes spiralled around each other, each acronym estranging her from the next. Frayed sleeves had doodled in the corner, little trolls clambering over each other, thunder clouds firing lightning bolts down half the page. There was a list of developers on one side of the page, the names running into each other, becoming something like a song, all of them eventually circling the same name toward the centre of the page, a full stop to his crescendo.

Marigold

Most of the developers knew there were two routes toward making bank in their industry. You either went after the rich or you went after the poor. If you wanted to continue pulling in money year after year, the poor were the easier option, as long as you weren't getting your hands dirty. Lawyers and managers waded into the muck for you; money drifted back up to ownership.

That was what those old Marigold towers in the east end were like, with names like Duke's Terrace or The Chancellor, lumpy piles of bricks operated by a series of opaque management companies who specialized in not having websites, email addresses, or working phone numbers. They made periodic repairs and raised the rent annually, doing their best to subvert government regulations where possible. Lower property taxes and operating expenses kept things affordable for the owners. It wasn't very glamourous, but it was steady money. People had nowhere else to go. You learned what they were willing to suffer. Cathy had seen this first-hand, spelunking down into their basements, searching out the mould that was eating away at their infrastructure.

"Who are we supposed to go to now?" Jasmine said, rage and fear battling behind her words. "Who's next on your list of little helpers? How do we explain this?"

The next page of notes listed Cathy's own accomplishments, or lack thereof. Had they really been considering her as a candidate? Or was it all just a fancy carrot until they needed to bring out the stick? There appeared to be no institutional support behind the notes, just sprawling theories.

"We don't tell anybody anything."

Jasmine's phone buzzed. She looked Cathy in the eye.

"Don't."

Jasmine checked the screen. "I guess the department really doesn't keep tabs. They've got a new one for us. Reported by the residents. A number of complaints. Almost all anonymous."

The third page was a rough map, a sketch of the city's core, harsh squares or diamonds drawn over the new development, the open holes in the earth. All of their internal systems and this Threshold man was still keeping his cards to himself, tracking the pits in the city by hand. The sinkholes appeared as literal black holes, ground into the fine paper. The freshest square was only a few blocks away, a new hole for the next Marigold tower, the fabled Marigold II.

"I'm going to respond," Jasmine said, tapping out a text. "Keep up appearances for now at least. Until you decide to join the world of the living again."

Another ping. Cathy looked up from her map. "I'm not going to Scarborough again. I am not going across the Don Valley for anyone."

Jasmine rolled her eyes. "You can't even escape your own area code. You're going to die here. Why don't you just quit? Take your little box and walk out of here, go see if they'll hire you at the front desk down at the Threshold office. Show them your little monster instead of a resume. How does that sound? I'll pay for the car."

"You're not a little bit freaked out?" Cathy said, trying to keep her voice low.

"I'm fucking terrified," Jasmine said. "But you've basically got a biological weapon in that bag right there, and you don't seem too bothered. So, I'll just keep living my life. Punching the clock. Pretending this didn't happen. Pretending you and I just work together. Colleagues. And that's all it needs to be, right? That's all it ever needed to be."

"Jas . . ."

"Are you going to come with me?" Jasmine said, shoving her phone back into her pocket. "One last ride where we can pretend all of this is normal. Because I am done, Cathy."

"Done?"

"With this job, with this half-assed life you're trying to drag me into. You realize how much trouble we're in right now? We watched two men . . . well, whatever happened there. And then we took the weapon that did it with us. We took the evidence. We watched and then we stole. We're basically carrying around a murder weapon."

Cathy rolled the notes up, stuffed them into the liner pocket of her jacket. There was still so much she didn't understand. The Wet wasn't only learning — it was extrapolating and accelerating. It was circling the city like a noose. If you could name the shape shambling toward you, then maybe, maybe you could learn to destroy it. Threshold seemed more interested in monitoring it, rather than wiping it all out at once. They wanted to see what it could do, maybe how it could be put to use. The notes hinted at new applications for the mould. The temptation was there, the power inside each cell, untapped, unceded. The sample was still in her case. It wanted out, wanted blood, wanted dominion.

"I'm sorry."

A flood of teenagers entered the coffee shop, high voices breaking the tension between the two women. Jasmine tossed her cup into the trash but missed. They watched it roll in circles.

"Please," Jasmine said. "Let's just do our job. One last day of pretend. That's what I want."

The Marigold stood in the middle of the list. Threshold's surveillance networks picking up all the cases no one wanted to claim. A case they could both agree on pursuing. There were even notes on the suite numbers, a growing tally that might have been a body count.

"Well, you'll be happy about this then," Cathy said. One last job on her own terms, to see what Threshold claimed to know, see it for herself. Then she could decide if she was willing to stay, maybe even show them all what it could do. "We can walk. No streetcar. No Magellan."

"It's in the core?" Jasmine said. "And who told you that?"

"It's in The Marigold. Twelfth floor."

The name on the page in front of her. All signs pointing in the same direction. Even with Jasmine's rage boiling across the table, Cathy still welcomed the chance to confront the Wet again. Maybe it would speak to the sample she had in the case. Was it one? Was it many? The frayed sleeves's notes asked the same. She would confront it with itself.

§

They entered The Marigold without masks. Cathy knew it was a risk. That's what they were now, wild cards without any chain of command. Cathy and Jasmine didn't speak on the walk over. There was too much to say, too many images still floating around in their heads, the light bulb shattering as the Wet flexed its full potential, displaying its hunger. There was a desperation she could feel creeping in around the edges of her brain, that she might actually need Jasmine more than Jasmine needed her, that Jasmine could just walk away after staring down that horror. Jasmine knew what she saw, understood the threat it presented. She didn't need to diagnose it.

"Can I help you?" the man behind the desk said, uniform freshly pressed. "Do you know who you're here to see?"

"Oh," Cathy said, moving across the polished floors like she belonged. Anonymous calls were usually investigated discreetly. The lobby was enormous, all marble and mirrors with a few solid gold French bulldogs scattered across the floor like potential lawsuits. In one corner, a janitor's bucket caught the dripping juices of the air-conditioning. "Just meeting a friend upstairs. Hope you have a nice day!"

"Oh, you'll need to fill out a form," the man said, rising from his chair. The lobby was close to empty. A couple of stooped people lingered by the doors, eyes watching for whatever vehicle was promised on their phones. No pedestrians outside. Across the street, the pit for Marigold II was alive with yellow machines. "Everyone has to fill out a form before they head upstairs."

"I'm sure we can handle it on our own," Cathy said.

"Won't get anywhere." His golden name tag said *Clarence*. "I control the elevators."

"Oh," Jasmine said. "That sounds absolutely fascinating."

"It's not," Clarence said.

"Of course not." Jasmine smiled.

"With those bags, it looks like you're here to sell stuff," Clarence said. "We don't allow solicitors inside. Had a man in here the other week trying to sell perfumes in the lobby."

Cathy was bad at playing the actual renegade; she needed procedure if only to buck against it. There had to be other ways inside, especially in a building this big and ugly.

"No perfumes," Jasmine said. "I promise."

Clarence was immovable. "Wonderful, then if you'll fill out these forms . . ."

"Are you giving these women a hard time, Clarice?" a man's voice said, a smug smile waiting for when Cathy turned around. She recognized the slouch of a former law enforcement officer, cop shoes that undid the power of the suit, bald head shaved each morning. "I admire your dedication, but I'm sure they don't mean us any harm."

"Whatever you say, Hans," Clarence said, wilting back into his chair. "Rules are rules, but do what you want."

"Thank you, Clarice. My name's Hans, by the way, and you're . . ."

Cathy watched Jasmine turn several different colours in quick succession as Hans shook her hand. His blazer was a blinding white, barely concealing a steroid-fuelled chest.

"Sadie and Tammy," Cathy said. "We're visiting a friend, he told us to come on up."

"And Clarice over there decided it was his time to shine, eh? No problem," Hans said, flicking his fingers toward the elevator. "I can overrule him. Head of security here, actually for the whole Marigold enterprise. We do have quite a few folks pretending they live here. Adds to the prestige, I guess. Where are we headed, girls? You've got an escort now."

"Twelve," Cathy said quickly. "Thanks so much, I know it seems stupid."

"Not at all," Hans said, scratching his skull. The jacket rode up to reveal an empty holster. The elevator dinged and the three of them stepped into the steel chamber. Hans flashed a key fob and hit a few floor buttons. "It's sad we have to have this level of security, but you heard what happened at the Bijou didn't you? Two Croatians showed up to buy some limited-edition Jordans, ended up shooting the dude through the door. Can't have that."

Cathy felt Jasmine sweating, even though she couldn't see it. "No, definitely not."

Another ding and the doors opened.

"Twelfth floor. Honestly, not much to look at here. If you girls want to show me what's in those cases later, I'm up on the thirty-third floor, suite number 3303, alright? Have fun at your party."

He didn't have to wink.

"Thanks," Jasmine squeaked as the doors bounced shut behind her.

"Disgusting," Cathy said. "Glorified security guard."

The walls were bare, thick carpet already exhibiting wear and tear down its centre. The light fixtures hummed. Cathy got down on her knees and opened her bag, pulling out the mask. She flicked it on, watched the eyes blink a bright green and then go white. "Get yours out too."

"If people see us . . ."

"They'll run in the other direction if they know what's good for them. And if they don't, we tell them we're here on official business. Act like we're supposed to be here."

Jasmine yanked her mask over her head. "If anyone even shows up."

Cathy realized the twelfth floor was a ghost hotel, unlicensed and unregulated. Someone buying up an entire floor of units. The Marigold should have been too new for this, and yet the signs were everywhere. The blank doors and quiet halls, accompanied by strange stains on the carpets and an underlying tinge of ammonia. Despite whispers of the Wet and constant flooding, people still came to Toronto, putting their own lives at risk to observe a city in managed freefall.

"You picking up on anything?"

"Yes," Cathy said. Through the mask, she found the trail, a faint hint of the Wet toward a darkened corner. She moved slowly. A pale purple flickering on the floor, particles floating through the air around her.

"Damn," Jasmine said. "If it's already up here . . ."

"I know," Cathy said. "But the masks don't lie."

The trail led to a door. Cathy tried the knob. Locked. She reached into her bag and pulled out a small crowbar. Technically illegal, the department provided them after an officer ended up trapped in the basement office of an infected tower in North York, found in the morning by the cleaning crew. Cathy leaned on the crowbar until the door popped open. It should've been harder to get inside, especially in a newer building, but everyone cut costs somewhere. If the owner wanted a more secure door, they could upgrade at their own cost.

"You smell it?" Jasmine said.

The unit had obviously been inhabited by a young woman who spent her life onscreen. Piles of small shoes on the floor, underwear stacked on the low coffee table, florid backdrops arrayed against the far wall for streaming. One was a castle dungeon, another filled with clouds and flocks of doves. There were multiple monitors set up by the window, heavy blinds keeping out the streetlight. A single ring light hovered above the monitors, still lit, the only light in the suite. Jasmine turned it off with a quick flick of her fingers. They didn't need a spotlight for this. The presence of the Wet was close to overpowering Cathy's mask's sensors. Jasmine dropped her case and pulled out her extinguisher. Cathy set her own bag down in the spartan kitchen, staring at the outline on the kitchen floor, a small human body rendered in black mould. The doors beneath the sink were open. A keening sound reached out from the darkness.

Cathy reached into her bag and pulled out the container. The blob inside slammed against the lid, a high-pitched shriek matching the noise from beneath the sink. Cathy's and Jasmine's masks whirred and hissed as she opened the lid and the blob sprang out, still retaining some of its original form — a human hand. It skittered under the sink.

Jasmine shone her flashlight underneath, the black residue around the pipe moving as if it could breathe. The hand pressed itself into the shuddering mass, embracing it. The keening increased. The mottled shapes became one and then two again, dancing in the cabinet. Transferring knowledge, speaking in high-pitched tongues. It did recognize itself, or maybe its selves. It longed to be reunited with the whole. Cathy watched as the hand-shaped blob then moved toward another larger hole eaten away in the cabinet's bottom, threatening to escape. She seized it in her gloved hands before it could drop out of sight, and the mass under the sink undulated in sympathetic pain as she yanked it back into the container, shoving the lid shut, snipping a piece of the blob off that inched back toward the larger trembling darkness.

A small metallic click, a gun barrel tapping the back of Jasmine's ceramic mask. Cathy turned slowly, the world shuddering out of focus.

"Glad you found your party," Hans said. His own mask looked like a rabbit's freshly skinned skull, white with long ears instead of horns. Its eyes were purple, just like theirs. Two other figures stood behind him, blocking light from the hall. Their masks were white too, their meaty hands covered in latex gloves. Hans laughed gently and took Cathy by the hand, until her mask pressed against his own, respirators hissing on and off, out of sync. "I'd love it if you came to ours."

21.

A sacrifice had already been made. The gardener smelled it when he arrived at the appointed site, blood still present somewhere at the bottom of the hole, drifting up to touch his nose. Blood was his trade. He could tell it was human. He knew it likely belonged to a young woman, a slim woman, a woman who didn't have enough iron in her diet, likely losing her hair every time she showered. A drain clogged with straw. They weren't his type — more his father's style, or their old competition in the west end, the arborist who swam out into the lake and never came back. This blood meant the ritual was ruined now. Another betrayal, another costly mistake.

The gardener sat on the bumper of his van, a gloriously ruined Dodge Grand Caravan purchased at a police auction ten years earlier. Navy blue with tinted windows, it was very good at being ignored in almost any neighbourhood. A little rust around the wheel wells and a couple dents made the van look like it belonged to a contractor when he visited the more elevated bits of old Toronto, venturing up to the Bridle Path or Rosedale to be a little closer to some of his clients, people who didn't fully know where their money went most of the time. No way to sustain that level of wealth without blood, he wanted to tell them. Bodies fuel your fortunes.

And now he had a useless body wrapped up inside a bright blue tarp in the back of his Caravan, a body alive less than twelve hours before in his apartment, a living and breathing human being who only wanted to talk about hockey and drink the gardener's beers. The gardener kept the kid around long enough to learn about his history, the familiar notes all playing out in the same sequence — a distant father, a divorce, an angry or ill mother, maybe both, a new man entering the home, a power struggle over her love and affection the kid was bound to lose no matter what he did, a growing sense of unease as the kid discovered his own tastes in love and affection might not be conventional, the inevitable discovery of his pornography habits on a screen somewhere, whether it was a phone or a laptop or a television buzzing at 3 a.m. after he passed out in front of it, his entire body contorted by his need.

The spiral of self-loathing, the sensitivity to loud noises, slammed doors, men's voices, the blare of a car horn running through him like a hot wire when he woke up in the middle of the night naked and afraid, curled up into a ball on the hardwood floor, his heart shuddering like a bird trapped inside his narrow, sunken chest. The drinking that started with his mother's vodka and then led to the man's whiskey, and then when those bottles were too exposed, too dangerous to continue diluting, moving to harder things that friends who were more like acquaintances provided during skipped classes that became skipped days that led to abandoned semesters, drifting in and out of social circles that expanded and contracted based on what you could provide them, how tender your heart was, or whether they felt like turning on you once you revealed your weakness, your need.

If the gardener knew one thing, it was what people needed. He nourished the desperation, let it flourish, nursing his victims toward acceptance, reconciliation with themselves, and ideally, resignation to their fate at his hands. Of course, not everyone handed themselves over, not when they saw his eyes flicker, empathy draining out, the settled logic of his end game playing out for them swiftly with a rope around their neck, or a rolled-up T-shirt, or a bedsheet. His father preferred to cut them, but the gardener never liked the mess.

Cleaning up meant throwing things out meant getting caught. He didn't want to get caught — not now, especially when he was the last one still following the rules, still planting the seeds when summoned. The last one who understood the real price of progress so many in this world appeared to have forgotten, unwilling to admit the human cost of their endeavour, writing it all off with suspicious scaffold collapses around the holidays or crane malfunctions that dropped a ton of concrete onto some twenty-two-year-old who could barely hold up a sign that said *SLOW*.

That wasn't how it was meant to be done. You needed to start with the foundation. You had to acknowledge the price you were willing to pay. Incidentals and disbursements incurred along the way were irrelevant. You put blood into the pit and then you watched it grow.

This pit was ruined before it even had a chance to flourish. Beyond the hubris of this belated request, the gardener's fury was directed at the carelessness of the site itself, the flagrant disregard for safety protocols so prevalent in construction across the city. Despite the power of his senses, the gardener needed to see the blood before he abandoned his mission. Every minute, the body in his van grew colder, the seed losing some of its vital essence to the relentless villain of time. He picked his way past rickety fencing and backhoes parked haphazardly at each level of the pit, dodging loose stashes of rebar and overflowing porta-potties.

There were still bits of stray hair where the woman had struck her head on the way down, clinging to the metal with bits of scalp attached. Someone had kicked dirt over the blood, dragged a tarp over to hide most of the crime. They wanted it to go away. The gardener pushed his hand into the dirt, let the gummy blood gather in the dirty webbing. He probed a thumb into his mouth and shook his head. More than enough had been spilled to spoil the site, but without a body, it wouldn't take. The building was doomed before it even began, according to the code he followed. The gardener's belief wavered at times. This work was never something he imagined doing forever; it was an inheritance, more like obligation than vocation. He wasn't a preacher, and it was difficult for him to articulate the cause aloud. The true practitioners were doers, not talkers. They did what was necessary even after the rest of the world moved on.

Sometimes the gardener lay awake for days in his walk-up, watching cars pass outside his window, the traffic light changing throughout the night. To live in a world we don't understand, his father told him after their first kill together in the basement of a shuttered Greek restaurant, we must build structures that permit understanding, even if it's misguided. We must build to live.

People tried to work around the system, pretenders who drowned cats in burlap sacks and stuffed them into the foundation of new homes, half-committed men who raided the morgues of hospitals, coroners who looked the other way when the right amount appeared inside an envelope. They propped up the ruptured retail plazas with embalmed hands, did their best to restore convenience stores with lengths of intestine harvested from biowaste dump sites, presented pig lungs like they were human to the architects who finally decided to build their own family home, unaware of the flawed magic they purchased. If your child fell down those basement stairs, was it an accident?

Or a late penalty on the debt you never paid? The earth didn't like instalments.

This Marigold kid though, he'd been warned by the gardener himself, told what would happen if another mistake was made. The gardener thought they understood each other after the foundation of Marigold II, restoring order to their struggling relationship with an easy transaction. Everything had gone to plan. It may have been a different name on the branding around this new spoiled site, but the money all came from the same place.

The last time the younger Marigold tried to cut corners, the older one had only just saved him in time, made a last-minute deal with the gardener down there beneath the parking garage to salvage a tower already threatening to topple. And now with the old man faltering, the younger Marigold had gone back to his old ways, trying to grab a discount for this Holstein woman, making a mockery of the only meaning the gardener had anymore. He couldn't let this seed go to waste.

The gardener looked up from the bottom of the shallow pit, tracking the moon through dangling cranes. There was a balance to this practice. If the first Marigold could come down, the second would never even have a chance to rise. All it would take would be a shift in the earth beneath that troubled first tower. A second seed fighting for its position against the one he'd planted before, a battle for sustenance that would disrupt the foundation's stability. The van still had gas. The seed wasn't dormant yet. The gardener had a new plan. To reaffirm the old rituals and restore any honour his father might have found in this cursed vocation, he'd have to shatter the pillars from inside the temple, and bring them all down into the cold, wet earth with him.

§

After yet another Magellan driver came flying up out of the underground parking garage beneath The Marigold in a burnt sienna Subaru, the gardener slipped his battered van into drive and chugged past the guard at the top of the slope, careful to conceal his face from prying eyes. He wore an old gas station hat with the brim yanked down to his nose and a skateboarding hoodie stained with bleach, the kind he could burn quickly after the job was done. As he rounded the first corner, the seed slid out from its position in the back of the van, the tarp unfurling to display what was left of the boy.

The gardener pitied his seeds, but only before they died. He saw them in their moments of weakness and embraced them during periods of great despair. He didn't know many others who would be so willing to open their hearts and their homes. It wasn't easy to live your beliefs. He'd met too many people who spoke of helping those in need who then went home to empty houses, beds unused, fridges too full for any one person to empty. They spoke of giving, but it was on their own terms, a dollar here or there, always with a tax receipt.

They weren't worthy. That's what the seeds told themselves. They weren't valued. And the city reinforced that, crushed them down into smaller and smaller spaces until they weren't quite people, but weren't animals either. People pitied animals, rescued them, took them off the streets, and made them part of the family. The seeds would never find that love. They couldn't reciprocate it, people said, but a cat couldn't either. A bird could learn your name and then outlive you. He didn't trust birds.

He continued deeper into the parking garage, luxury vehicles tightly packed together, an insurance company's nightmare, a sea of red and black and silver SUVs begging to scrape against one another, gracelessly shredding their bumpers on hidden railings or concrete pillars painted a bright yellow warning. He circled and circled into the underworld of The Marigold.

It had been years since his last visit, in the same van. The seed back then was a young woman he met outside a karaoke night on College Street, her hair a faded purple at the fringes, her teeth showing too much wear compared to the glow in her features, the healthy, tender feel of her skin under his hands. His father had told him about other practitioners who slept with their seeds before they planted them, men who consummated their practice. He had tried it once or twice, but could never follow through with the ritual afterward. The gardener had to leave some part of them untouched, if only to comfort himself when staring at that traffic light, saying in a low voice that he didn't take everything; he left some part unknowable.

The deeper the van went, the emptier the parking garage. Five or eight spots in a row without a vehicle, and when one did appear, it was an older model, slightly battered. Dark water dripped from the ceilings, mixed with oil and wiper fluid and whatever else trickled out of vehicles in the dark. Lights flickered as he passed numbered spots without owners. A pick-up truck trundled past him on one level, the driver hidden behind tinted glass, the license plate reading R34V3R. The gardener shook his head, disgusted with the flair, the excess. Why draw attention to yourself? Why bring the wolves to your own door? He turned the wheel again, headed toward the very bottom of this place, and listened to the seed shift again, unrolling itself from the tarp.

The girl he planted here with the Marigolds, she had stayed with him for a few weeks, kept trying to get in touch with an aunt who she said lived over in Cabbagetown. Every night, he watched the light go from red to yellow to green to red again, hoping she would leave him, that he'd wake up one day and she'd be gone. She stayed though, and when the elder Marigold called with a solution, the gardener didn't hesitate. His hands were rough. He watched her in the mirror as he did it, the light so bright in the bathroom, her eyes so wide, the whole room erupting in a scream around him before her neck finally broke and he was able to turn off the hot tap, wipe away the steam to see himself standing there naked.

When he arrived, the younger Marigold had already dug the hole under his father's orders. The elder Marigold knew the old ways even if he was a cheap huckster. He understood there were tolls you couldn't avoid. The seed was swallowed, the concrete poured over the body in that dark underground. They had saved their project from disaster, but it would never be fully secure. It would always leak, always tremble in the wind. It was a stopgap solution. The gardener explained this to the Marigolds when he took the hockey bag full of bills. The price is non-negotiable. The price does not respond to supply and demand. The price is fixed. No discount.

He reached the bottom. A few busted sedans lingered in the dim light. The gardener climbed out of his van, opening up the hatch to pull out a pickaxe and a shovel. His father's tools had never gone out of fashion. There were no cameras this far down. The elevators didn't even go this deep. No one would find him here. A new task to drive him forward. His seed would find its home. He carried his burdens with him, found the unsecured maintenance door to take him down to the very limit of this place. At the very bottom of The Marigold, the gardener began to dig.

Suite 2809

Winning ruins lives. Golan Modan knew this now. It only took twenty-six million dollars to make it clear. Twenty-six million dollars to discover everyone who ever loved him did so with conditions he was never privy to, conditions that may have never even arrived if it wasn't for the twenty-six million dollars that supported the generous real estate empire the appointed financial advisor had set up for him after he won Lotto 6/49, the winning ticket purchased as a bitter joke on his fiftieth birthday — the same day the bank had foreclosed on his home, a terrible pink and grey split-level haunted by its original owner, a woman the neighbours all referred to as Big Donna.

Big Donna liked to play practical jokes, yanking the sheets off of him at 4 a.m. or running the hot water all night in the kitchen sink, leaving him to shower in the cold in the morning. He didn't bring the men he met downtown back to the house, fearing the ghost of the old woman would embarrass him with another fit in his kitchen cabinets, if chipped wood panelling in his bedroom didn't do it first. His sisters didn't need to know what he did with his life either. They lived around the corner, both widowed after their husbands tried to swim across Lake Ontario on a bet with each other.

After his big win, Golan's aging parents assumed he'd take care of his sisters, who both refused to work after their traumatic loss. Their house's trim was a decaying yellow instead of pink and the windows were covered in striped bedsheets. Big Donna would've approved. With his winnings, Golan paid off their mortgage, purchased them a used Elantra, and sent them on a cruise around the Mediterranean, where they both got food poisoning twice.

The knock on the door was expected. Golan answered, a thin young man waiting for him, leather messenger bag draped over cowed shoulders.

"Irving?" Golan said. "Come on in."

"Thanks, thanks so much," Irving said. Golan had found him online, recommended by one of the LGBTQIA2S groups he'd joined anonymously after he moved into the condo. Most of them were so young, so desperate for connection, it hurt Golan to read their posts, watching them reveal themselves so openly, without shame, until they suddenly disappeared.

"Have you done this before? It's all about the vibes," Irving asked. "I've got a few clients who see me, like, every other month or so. Some people are addicted; they think it's going to be different every time."

Golan gestured toward his living room. Most of the furniture was selected by a designer his original financial advisor had recommended, a lot of metal and leather with driftwood scattered on a credenza. He didn't look at the bill. He would change it again once he got bored. Other tenants complained about the building, the coldness of it, the way the fixtures all faded after only a few months of use. But Golan liked the anonymity. He liked to hide how much money he had. People treated you differently when they saw eight figures dragging behind you.

"I'm still trying to find the right fit," Golan said. "It's difficult to match the energies. They want to jump right in, but it's unhealthy if we're not coming from the same place."

"Of course," Irving said, flashing white buckteeth. Golan took a seat on an elaborate stool that made him feel like an exotic bird. He kept all the blinds open. Fifty years of doing his best to hide who he was had been washed away by the money, allowing for a small spurt of happiness in the moments between the self-loathing and the dread, the weight of this surprise wealth heavy on his shoulders. Irving took a seat on a leather bench across from him, emptying his bag onto the steel. Golan needed to replace that table. It was a dead thing. It brought the wrong energy into the room.

"Now, the deck I use isn't very conventional," Irving said. "I know I messaged you about that, but I've had a couple run-ins recently where the client expected me to be like some kind of mystic wizard. That just isn't my vibe. This is fun for me. It's part of why I'm only charging a nominal fee. I want this to be a learning experience for both of us."

Irving spread his tarot deck out over the autopsy table, the back of the cards a bright red that clashed with everything in the room. Golan had gone through a number of tarot readers and astrologers over the past two years. A deep fear he couldn't shake — this windfall was actually a curse. No one at the bank wanted to discuss it. His parents sighed and told him to donate the money if that was how he really felt. They didn't want to know what he did, didn't want to name it. It was the kid who delivered his fridge and slept with him in the same night who suggested he try reaching out in a more spiritual direction, providing him with a couple contacts more interested in burning incense than telling him about the cruel hand of fate. Golan kept trying. He could feel Big Donna with him, watching each move, waiting for him to slip up. He was sure she had come with him to the new building, the only woman who actually knew him, who saw through the butch façade he put up whenever he stepped outside.

"I want you to be as open to me as possible here," Irving said, shuffling his cards. "I need you to meet me at the same energy level. Let me know what you're sensing and experiencing. If it's a bad fit or if you're uncomfortable, I need to know immediately."

"I understand," Golan said, scratching his freshly shaved chest. "You're the guide here."

"I can only guide people who accept guidance," Irving replied. "Let's begin."

The first card flipped. Cher stared back at Golan.

"Is that—"

"Yes, I use a diva deck one of my friends in Montreal put together," Irving said. "Adds a whole other level of recursive thought. Like any reading, it's about collaboration. What do the cards bring out in us? What sort of images do we see?"

"What I see is Cher. And she's blowing a trumpet? So, she's Judgement? I don't know."

"That's one word to use, yes," Irving said, fingers hovering by his temples. "Judgement. What does that summon in you? What frames of reference do you have there? You don't need to answer right away. Take your time. Examine your biases. We're not in a rush."

Golan did his best not to think about Big Donna, the voice calling to him in the night, asking him why they let her die in a house like that, trapped behind all her furniture on the second floor. It was the entire reason he'd been able to afford the cursed house. The neighbourhood was terrified of her presence, even after death. Big Donna had been known to throw cans of kidney beans at children who came by for Halloween. Part of the deal when he bought the house was that he would assume responsibility for all the contents. She had nowhere to go after the developer who bought the old house tore it down.

"Judgement has something final about it," Golan said. "An endpoint."

"Is that where you see yourself?" Irving asked. He smelled like old frying oil, like he'd just got off his kitchen shift. "At an ending? But you're still alive, aren't you? You're still here. In a courtroom, you're not dead after judgement."

"If not an ending, then what?" Golan said. "Don't give me that circle of life stuff, okay? You want me to sit with myself, but that's all I do day after day, I sit with myself. And I find nothing there. Nothing!"

Irving raised perfectly maintained eyebrows. "I'm going to let that one go for now."

"I'm sorry," Golan said. "I get tied up in my head. I circle and circle."

"I can see that," Irving said. "There's a lot of old pain in there. You let the same currents carry you down the same channels. You need to steer yourself out of that pattern. When I see this card, and when I see Cher, what I see isn't an end of something, but the potential for reinvention. The cards aren't always about the exact image you see. It's not a one-to-one correlation. I know this isn't your first time, right?"

The money changed a lot of things for Golan, made his life better in so many ways, and yet it also emptied him out. His parents would never know him as long as their faith remained paramount in their lives. Even his sisters couldn't fully embrace who he was. He didn't want to ply them with cash. Every interaction with old friends or lovers he met off dating apps had an underlying desire — for more of his time, more of his body, more of his money. Golan was expected to give and give. His winnings only reinforced that point. And so, he stayed perched halfway up a tower, spying on the street below, all his major decisions made by financial planners, lawyers, interior designers, and occasionally, the ghost of Big Donna whispering in his ear, asking him if he ever thought about what it meant to die alone and unloved, turned into a story rather than a person, a cautionary tale.

"You're right. Cher is the master of reinvention. And successful at it too. And yet the world still treats her like a joke."

"She's too powerful," Irving said, wiping sweat off his forehead. "The jokes, the sneering, it's all fear of a woman who has strived to control her destiny. The fact that she is partially robotic now, I mean, it's honestly so aspirational."

"So, what is this saying about me?"

"You've been through a series of ruptures. You've seen yourself from the outside, and you know how much damage each change brings to you. I think you have another big change coming, but it's going to be internal."

Golan reached out to touch the card. He wanted to touch Cher's black wig, maybe summon her into the room, all the human parts between wires and fluid sacs.

"I would prefer if you didn't touch the cards," Irving said. "It's part of my process."

"I understand," Golan said. He wasn't sure how much he was supposed to pay this kid. Golan already knew everything this card was supposed to represent, knew his future like he knew his own palms. Some nights, he swore the lines on his hands changed, altering his course in life, but there was an endpoint no matter how his fingertips swirled.

"Thank you," Irving said, turning another card. Dolly Parton appeared on the top of a log cabin, bosom overflowing.

"And that is . . . that is the High Priestess? Reversed?" Golan said, trying not to judge this deck too harshly, trying to give this boy his shot. Maybe a thousand dollars would make him happy.

Sometimes he wanted to give all the money away. Sometimes he considered burning it here, letting the whole tower catch fire, cameras catching people leaping like cinders.

"No, no, no," Irving said. "I'm glad Dolly didn't hear that, can you imagine? I don't think they even let her into church anymore. Guess it depends on the denomination. My father was a preacher. He still thinks I'm going to the Pentecostal every Sunday."

This didn't surprise Golan. Many of his tarot readers were the children of other faith leaders, desperate to carve out their own practice, a ministry by any other name, bringing the same structures of in and out groups with them.

"If she's not the High Priestess," Golan said. "Then who is she?"

"The tower. Reversed."

An object thudded into the window. Irving screamed. Golan watched the bird slide down the glass, a thin red trail behind it. "It happens sometimes. I've complained to management, they say it has something to do with the lights. I tried putting stickers on the glass, but it didn't seem to make a difference."

"I can't do this," Irving said, sweeping up Dolly and Cher into his deck of divas. "The energy of this place . . . not you, you understand? Look, you don't have to pay me."

"I understand," Golan said, rising to shake Irving's hand. "There's a spirit in here with me. I feel she might be bound to me now. She has no home to return to anymore."

"I don't deal in spirits," Irving said, pulling his hand away from Golan. "I don't mean any disrespect, I cannot . . ."

"You saw one too, didn't you?" Golan said. "Not here, but in your life."

"When I was a boy," Irving said quietly.

"It's written all over you. I want you to see something," Golan said. "Can you bear witness for me? I want you to know that I trust you."

"Bear witness?"

"Come with me," Golan said, leading Irving to the guest bathroom. "I want to know if you see what I see in this place. If the presence I see is the same one you do."

"And you'll . . . you'll still pay me?"

"Of course, I don't want this money. Money is a curse."

The tower could stand for many things. Misery, distress, calamity, disgrace, deception, ruin.

"Only rich people say that," Irving said, trembling receding, trying to laugh.

"You're not wrong," Golan said. "But I want you to go in there and turn on the light. Tell me what you see. If you see a woman there, ask her what she wants."

"And if I see nothing?" Irving said, confidence returning. "You still pay me?"

"I'll write you a cheque," Golan said.

"I prefer cash."

"Of course," Golan said, opening the bathroom door. This was where Big Donna spoke to him, her voice rising up out of the drain at night. This was where she told him how the world worked, what it did with the people it deemed unfit. This is where she offered him a deal.

"Smaller bills too," Irving said, stepping into the dark alcove, hand reaching for a light switch that didn't work as Golan shut the door, standing with his back against it.

"I don't see anything. And there's no—"

A loud shriek quickly muffled by whatever lurked inside the drains, the substance speaking in Big Donna's voice whenever Golan entered, promising love, community, a sense of togetherness, all while creeping toward him. He felt Irving's hands pound against the door, wondered what voice the wet blackness in the drains used on Irving, if it was actually Big Donna, or some other voice speaking to the kid, his cards unable to warn him.

Soon.

"I'm not ready yet," Golan said, speaking to the writhing wet on the other side. "Not yet."

The tower reversed was not calamity, but it wasn't joy either. Golan knew the cards. All it offered was nullity, apathy, a sense of nothingness. When the door stopped shuddering, Golan pulled out his phone and ordered a chicken shawarma platter, making sure to leave a note for the delivery kid that he didn't need any plastic cutlery. He would eat it with his hands.

22.

"Every city has a heart beneath it," Ramji declared. The march continued. Trying to be friendly, Henrietta had mistakenly asked Ramji what he believed lay beneath them. "A series of pumps. The closer you get to the core, the less dirt you find. It's all infrastructure, concrete and data nodes. Networks of pipes connecting everything under the surface, wires and cables tethering it together. We end up reproducing the systems inside us. That's part of what I realized. We shape the world into our image, even if we don't know it. The city is one big body."

Henrietta was calm, now used to the stench of Cabeza and the narrowing walls around her. Salman's snapped ankle was a minor crisis, but one she could solve. Cabeza had waited like it promised. Cabeza didn't require food or water from what she could see. It lived off the underground, melding with the dripping walls, its body always in flux, continually struggling to maintain a human shape. It found sustenance in the dirt itself.

"And that includes shit," Alma said. It wasn't just dirt. The human waste trickled around them, a funnel for the surface.

"It does, doesn't it?" Ramji said. "Your friend might know something about that."

"It calls," Cabeza gurgled as it continued sliding toward the dark at the end of Henrietta's flashlight. The cranking noise kept her awake, her wrist growing tired. "Closer. We are closer."

"Closer to what?" Henrietta asked.

"The ones you want."

Cherry's face before he tumbled down the pit, shock and want pinging across his unblemished features. Her father smuggling grapes inside his coat from the grocery store, feeding them to her frozen on the roof of the old building. A man who her mother said just got up and left one day, left them both with his debts and all his old basketball jerseys in the closet. Henrietta had never really believed it. She could still see the outline of where he stood in the square, before the earth opened up. She was tired of pushing it down, swallowing the old story.

"We want Cherry."

"The ones you want," Cabeza said. "It knows. The ones."

"What does it know?" Alma said. Her enthusiasm had waned without Salman here.

"Who you want," Cabeza said. "What you want. What I want."

"I know what you want," Henrietta said. "You want your old self."

Cabeza shook its head. "Not old, no. Just me. And you will find what you want. It will know you. It knows us. Knows me. But it won't say. You will have to show me. Take me. After I take you to see what you want." It gurgled and spat again. "If you still want to see it. To know it too. Once you know it, you will know me. And you will find me out there."

The tunnel narrowed. Cabeza squelched itself smaller, losing its human form for a few seconds before emerging into a wider cave on the other side. The kids hunched their shoulders.

"I think I know where a thing like that comes from," Ramji said, squatting low to follow them. His face was covered in dirt now, the suit disintegrating every time he brushed against old lead pipes and harsh stone. He didn't seem to mind. Henrietta believed he still thought this was an adventure. "How something like your gooey friend here happens."

Cabeza's stride stuttered. Rogue teeth and the long pink tongue roving for the word. "How?"

Closer to downtown, under the Bloor line, occasional gusts of air brought the smell of grease, road salt, fresh urine, French fries and street gravy, reminders of the surface. Ever-present rats shifted around them without fear or curiosity. This was their territory. The few raccoons were different. They watched. Henrietta no longer questioned why they were down here, so far from the trees. They kept their own counsel. She was a trespasser, a temporary inconvenience they tolerated for now.

"How?" Cabeza said again.

"I had a lot of time to think about this," Ramji said, leaning against the damp, mottled wall. "Sitting down there in the valley, watching how things fall apart. They showed me at the conference, I just didn't understand at the time. All I could see was the budget, you know? A lot of money for one little item. You see the pieces, but not the whole. Not right away. Maybe you pretend not to understand. I think that's how my mother coped with it, how she made it through each day. You look right past what you know is true."

"Jesus Christ," Alma said, pulling a long strand of something from her hair, flicking it into the dark. "Who gives a shit? Cabeza says we're close. Let's go."

Henrietta laughed, but Cabeza had stopped moving. It stared at Ramji.

"How?"

The low walls rippled and murmured. Henrietta heard voices reaching out to her, old voices with words she couldn't quite process. The way the air moved down here, the moan of the underground turned into its own human dirge, low notes under the high-pitched whistle.

I didn't leave you.

"Any time you tear open the earth," Ramji said, "they say you need to pay a price. The way they read it here, or at least the established families, is that it's blood, ideally still in the body."

A distant constellation of memories prickling inside her skull, lighting up one by one. Basketball games in the park, men screaming her father's name. An air conditioner plummeting twenty storeys, her father shoving another man out of the way. The rain beating on the car while they waited for her mother to emerge from the clinic, dead eyes in the rearview mirror. There were ways you could protect yourself, to build up stories you knew weren't true. You told them until they became real, then stopped telling them. You let the details crumble into so much ash.

"This is some fairytale shit," Alma said. "Cabeza, let's go."

Cabeza dripped, did not speak.

"I'm saying it's what's done, not that it's true. Back in the day, you were guaranteed to get some blood on a job site. Whether the scaffolding gave way, or somebody got drunk and took a tumble on a Saturday morning overtime shift. Some guys would just throw a cat in there. Or, like, a rabbit. But when there are millions at stake, you don't want to leave that up to chance. A rabbit is not enough. So, you take a body. And you put it in the foundation."

They took me. I didn't leave you.

"So, it's the mob," Alma said. "Who gives a shit?"

"No," Cabeza said, waving her off as she tried to pull at its jellied shoulder.

Ramji's eyes glowed, feeding off of Cabeza's undivided attention. Henrietta tried to listen, even as the image of the pit pushed back into her mind, her father's hands reaching up out of his mass grave, calling for her, a rerun, a recovered image splattered against the inside of her skull.

I wouldn't leave you. I would take you.

The city never committed to naming who the pit swallowed. There was no official list of the forsaken for the Foynes Village hole. It never even got a name. Only caution tape, spreading like a vine as the hole gradually expanded. No one could ever prove he fell down there. No one could say who remembered. No one could trust the word of someone so young.

"They would say they aren't monsters. The system works out, so their hands are clean. In the past, people were walled into these places alive. Now when they do it, they'll say it's humane. These people don't care, and they want you not to care either. Everything you own comes from bodies and blood, one way or another. Your phone. Your clothes. The good things you have are primarily drawn from the misfortune of others. Blood, sweat, and tears. All of it literal."

People disappeared all the time. Had the sinkhole really claimed him? Her mother would never admit it, pushed it down, told her to stop thinking about it. And yet, the man and his groceries, walking across that square. Sweat ran down her back, dripped from her elbows. Four bags of groceries in his hands, weighed down for the weekend, sending her on ahead.

I would take you.

"That's you," Ramji said, reaching out now to touch Cabeza, his finger slipping into the body, his eyes growing wider and wider. "One of those bodies."

I would know you.

The wailing wind grew louder, the drain stench suffocating. Alma shuddered.

"You know . . . you know what I am?" Cabeza spoke, turning its white eyes on Ramji. "You know where they put me? You know."

"I can't know that," Ramji said. "We never saw that part. There were no names. No faces."

"You know," Cabeza said, an urgent rattle under its phlegm. "You . . . must know."

"The cost of doing business. That's all you are. Don't you see it?"

You would be with me again. With us. Only an us down here.

Ramji laughed, sliding back against the wall. Cabeza gazed at the hole Ramji's finger had pushed into its undulating mass. "The floods set you free and now you're roaming around on your own, still trying to get home, get back to where you were going before you died. And they don't know! No idea!"

Only a squelching sound from Cabeza.

Bodies gathered under the earth, bodies speaking to her now, the words feeding her paranoia. She was only talking to herself, imagining the man with his groceries, with his hard hands, with his voice in her ear telling her there was no sunshine when she was gone. No light. No warmth. He was walking home and singing, and the world was still unmade, still open to her.

"They think things will stay the same forever."

Henrietta watched the wall reach out a tendril and drape it over Ramji's shoulder. She tried to speak, choked on the words. He had breached some barrier, tried to merge with Cabeza without realizing what his touch had done. The earth was jealous.

Only an us.

"The only thing constant is change. My mom used to say that. I thought it was stupid. I gave her such a hard time. She was never open about any of it. Old secrets, buried under concrete. All of it eventually finds a way free. There's always a crack. A fissure."

I would take you. I would know you.

A shape darker than Cabeza pulled itself free from the walls around them, a thick mist in the air flooding their senses, wrapping tendrils around Ramji's torso, hand-shapes emerging to pull at his face, plucking his cheeks, penetrating each pore. Cabeza snapped out of its reverie, shuddered at the very presence of this thicker, more viscous version of itself. It repelled Cabeza, oil and water in this tunnel, the host rejecting a failed graft.

I would know you.

"Run," Cabeza burbled.

Ramji couldn't scream, the Wet forcing its way into his mouth, his ears, his eyes, undulating around his skull. He looked like he was laughing, his body shuddering with the effort. There were no more rats in the cavern. They knew. Henrietta could only stare as the Wet pulled itself around Ramji's body, slurping into its larger self. The same fluid shape that had snatched Cherry. It took what it wanted.

I would take you.

Alma yanked her away from what had been Ramji, following the scuttling form of Cabeza, somehow still free from the whole, a mind that had escaped from the larger consciousness down here. Ramji swallowed by his own monster, but it could have been her. It could be Cherry. How many bodies had Ramji's mother buried under the earth?

"Close," Cabeza bleated, scurrying further ahead; rats plowed out of its way, bodies popping beneath its weight. It moved like every step might be its end. "The pool. The light. Close."

Alma's fingers tight against Henrietta's wrist, bruises already forming.

I would take you.

A true human scream behind them finally, then a guttural shuddering sound, like a new god being born from an old wound reopened, pulled out in one piece and set free in these capillary tunnels, the stream of the city itself. A gurgling, churning sound — a variation on a theme they had heard before in the walls around them as an echo, now fully present, surrounding them.

I would know you.

Henrietta pushed the voice out of her head, eyes closed, and let Alma pull her further into the dark, rats skittering between her feet. Four bags of groceries plummeting down into the pit, tomatoes, apples, two sides of bacon. The had always made too much bacon, the fridge filling up with mugs of fat, sparing the pipes. She was running again. No sunshine down here. He was gone, he was gone and yet was still speaking inside her head, the words simple and direct. The heat of Ramji's consumption roiled behind her, his own voice just a high keening noise. Cabeza spoke of the pool, the light. A hand reaching out from the sinkhole to the towers above, a hand she knew, a hand she held in her own before he told her to run. A heart beating under the city, pumping it full of bile and old blood, diseased and alive and wanting, always wanting.

I never left you. I waited.

23.

Maybe Dale was a prophet. Maybe he could see what was coming. It didn't mean he could change it. Soda knew that now. It didn't matter what you knew. The future was owned by someone else, someone bigger than you, someone or something that didn't even pay taxes.

The boys from Threshold didn't knock so much as smash through the front door, shattering the frame in the process. They had new toys to use, all of them technically non-lethal in the most abstract sense. One of them hit a booby-trap and went up in flames on the linoleum while the others pushed past him into the house, already consigning his impending loss to the cause. The yellow portcullis on their chest was the only loyalty that mattered in these situations.

Soda's old man was prepared. Despite layers of the latest riot gear with hastily applied logos, unidentifiable behind black masks, heads covered in surplus police helmets, these were big, soft boys.

They cursed each other, slipping and sliding across wet tile. The one on fire rolled back and forth until he put himself out, the fire spreading to the walls, catching on the dusty curtains.

"They'll figure it out eventually," Dale said, smiling at the flames. Soda watched from the backyard through dirty windows as his father picked up an aluminum baseball bat with a metal ring duct-taped to its shiny end. They took down most of the plywood on the windows after Soda told Dale he was followed home from the grocery store, the SUV racing to keep tabs on his whereabouts. The old man's fantasy was coming true, flames feeding into his extended conspiracy. His old friends were paying him a visit. What was once a drop of truth inside a delusion was now a full-blown prophecy, melting the house from the inside out. The men inside barged through the home, room to room, tripping over wires. Odie snarled, hitting the edge of his chain. Dale tugged the beast back, handing the chain to Soda.

"Your mother wouldn't want you to go out like this. She thought you'd be better. Wouldn't it be nice to be better than what came before you? I like that idea. Progress. It's fake but I like it."

The Threshold boys started yelling to one another as the smoke spread, obscuring their view. Soda's father yanked boards out from the fence, tossing them into the middle of the concrete yard. Odie howled while Soda struggled with the chain, the links biting into his soft palms.

"Saw this coming," the old man said. "Always going to come for me first. Ever since I signed that deal. Should've never gone down there for the dirt, but can't change that now. Once they have your face, they know you. Unless you cut off your nose. Can't have anyone looking at that soil. I need you to find Marigold. He knows you're coming. Give him what we found, okay?"

Another scream from inside.

"The dirt in the jar. It's in your trunk. Make him see what he's done, what he needs to do different if he wants to survive. Smell that? Someone is burning. Go through the weeds."

The old man tore down a sheet of plywood, exposing the thick bramble covering the yard behind them, an abandoned two-storey with a three-car garage. The Jansens had moved out a decade ago; no one took their place. It was the beginning of the drift, the lake waters rising. There was still a family back then; Soda still slept here, his world was this neighbourhood, filled with everyone he needed. He was still trying to figure out which university would take him.

A rubber bullet thudded into the fence next to his father, then another, and another. Soda tried to breathe slowly, the old chain tearing at the flesh of his hands as Odie howled. His father wanted this. He needed it to be true, and now it was all falling into place. His eyes were bright. It was all happening, just as he'd told his son. The stars aligned. They came.

"Don't take no for an answer. Not after everything else they took. I only have you. I have you, you understand that? That's all I need. To know you will do the right thing. Cause I still can't. I never could." He coughed. A piece of the roof crashed to the ground beside him. He didn't move. More screams from inside. Dale had been planning on this for a decade.

"You keep choosing certain gates as you go, but what you don't know is those gates close behind you. Refuse those gates. I know what you are. You aren't me."

Another explosion from inside the house, another scream. Smoke spread out the shattered windows, trapped under the trembling roof over the yard, barely held together with twine and clusters of carpenter clamps. Soda didn't question his father even as Odie fought against the chain. He dragged the animal through the hole in the fence into the thorny nothing.

"Don't worry about me," Dale said, slamming the plywood back into place. Now he was only a voice again, calm and certain. "I know this place."

More rubber ricocheted off the tin. Dragging Odie behind him, Soda moved low to the ground, slowly edging along the huge exterior fence, the yard like a barn with its tin roof and mismatched walls. Soda heard the solid crack of an aluminum bat against a skull, then a shriek as someone else was electrocuted. Heat radiated off the fence as he slid along the perimeter, pushing through towering weeds. A window exploded from the pressure inside the house. Burrs bit at his neck. Crabgrass stabbed his ankles until he emerged onto the front lawn.

"Stay where you are."

The woman in black wore the Threshold badge on both shoulders. She hadn't bothered to enter the bushes or the burning house. She lounged in the centre of the cul-de-sac, leaning back on an SUV parked beside Soda's Camry, so close you couldn't open the driver's door, paint jobs touching. Three other large GMCs with tinted windows and chrome grilles blocked the road behind her. No logos, just anonymous hulks. Only one streetlight was still alive.

"And the dog too. I have no problem taking out an animal, you hear?"

Soda didn't slow his approach. An explosion rocked the house behind him, shaking the earth. Probably the propane tanks rigged up in the basement. A cloud of smoke gathered high above them, trapped in the humid air. Rain began to fall.

"Old man Dale really think he was gonna sneak you by us? Get on the ground."

Soda released the chain. Odie was faster than anyone standing in the cul-de-sac imagined. He went right for the unarmoured neck; a rookie's mistake to keep it uncovered. Soda waited a few seconds before yanking the chain again. The guard was still alive, each breath pumped more blood out of her throat. It wasn't the same woman who'd given him a ticket, wasn't even one of the guards who'd tried to stop them collecting dirt the other night. Just another body thrown in his way, a depleted resource.

He stuffed Odie into the backseat of the Camry and then opened up the trunk. The jar was waiting for him. They hadn't searched the car. Too lazy or too stupid, it didn't matter. He grabbed the jar then slowly climbed in from the passenger side. He applied a seat belt to the jar. Odie whined in his ear. The house was fully alight in the pouring rain. Certain gates were closing. There wasn't time to fully mourn. He would live up to his end of the deal he didn't understand, the arc he had never agreed to set in motion. Soda drove away in reverse, watching it all burn, watching the last Threshold trooper shake on the asphalt until the roof fully collapsed, and then he turned toward the highway, tires screaming against whatever metal they'd lodged inside the rubber, hoping they could slow him down.

With the pouring rain, most people tried not to take the expressway in the dark. The wipers whipped back and forth. Soda let his mind click back and forth with the hazard lights of the other vehicles around him, all doing their best to stay in their lanes. The expressway dipped down low as it changed from the QEW to the Gardiner, cars slowly changing lanes around him. He watched a Honda dragging a trailer slowly spin out in a wide arc behind him in the rearview mirror, furniture flying off into the other lanes. Soda tried to keep his hands at ten and two. This would be his last drive in the car, all the way to The Marigold. He'd only ever dropped off fares there, never picked them up. Soda switched lanes, trying to ignore the shriek of his wheels, unsure of what the Threshold team had done to his tires.

Soda wanted to feel fury. The house had finally met its fate, the one his father had wanted, building his own world inside its walls.

He had crafted his own apocalypse when he discovered the world could go on without him, would in fact neither rejoice nor grieve in his absence. You only existed in as much as you were observed, loved, and acknowledged.

Although people swore this was the end of the word, Dale knew the truth — the world was only flipping the mattress. There was no true apocalypse. People went on living and dying even as horrible things happened to them, even as they were abandoned and neglected, even as they disappeared down holes or fled into the forests, or disappeared into their offices downtown. There was no end of things, only an end of the self, a collapse barely worth acknowledging.

And so, Dale crafted his own end.

Tires screamed again as Soda tried to change lanes, the shriek matched by Odie's howl in the backseat. Soda's father had built his own temple to accompany his self-destruction and like Samson, old Samson and his blind eyes, he brought it crashing down on himself. It was the story his mother had loved most, what she once called the most human story in the whole Bible, and Soda wanted to believe his father's final act was a tribute.

He wanted to believe it so badly that he didn't see the van slam on its brakes ahead of him as he tried to shift onto the Queensway, the car spiralling out of control, the doors singing against the concrete barrier before shuddering to a stop. No cars were behind them, and the van was gone. No one was pursuing them out here, but it wouldn't take long for someone to notice the Camry blocking a lane. Soda tried to reverse. The car shrieked again in protest.

"Let's go, Odie, come on. Come on, baby, calm down."

Breathing slowly, Soda patted down his pockets, ensuring he had the USB drive on him. The jar of dirt was still safe, belted into the passenger seat next to him. Soda's phone buzzed against his thigh. He scrambled to pull it out, the number only identifying itself as private.

"Hello?"

"Hi, I'm calling you from Talcum Recruiting. You'd filled out our online form and I . . ."

"Can I call you back?"

"Excuse me?" the voice said.

"Kinda an emergency going on here. Not your problem, I know."

"Mr. Dalipagic please, this will only take a couple of minutes. As you know, Talcum is all about connecting employers with talented individuals like yourself. There's a position at a brand-new content creator platform, NillyWilly, that we think you'd be great for. We've noticed you answered 'not applicable' to a lot of the mandatory questions, which has brought up a few concerns that need to be addressed. They want to ensure anyone we're sending them is a good fit for their culture."

Soda climbed out of the ruined car, examining what remained of his front right tire. The headlight had imploded and the bumper was torn in half. He kicked the sideview across three lanes of empty asphalt, watched it ping off a streetlight pole. Pelting rain continued. Cars rushed past.

"I saw the emails, yeah."

"We are truly excited you've signed up with Talcum, but we need you to take these questions seriously. Every connection we make is between people. People first, always."

"What're the questions again?" Soda said. In the distance, he could see a streetcar approaching. Its blue lights soothed his rage momentarily. Odie could sense it. Soda could get downtown, it would just take a while. There would be no app to reject him, no explanation to some gig driver about why he had what looked like a wolf on the end of a chain.

"How do you think you align with the NillyWilly values?"

"Values? Like their mission statement or something?"

"Yes. How do you believe you align with their mission?"

The streetcar appeared empty. Soda reached into the car and grabbed his jar of dirt. Odie hopped out of the backseat, barely pulling on his chain as Soda led him to the streetcar stop.

"I align with their goal to commodify every aspect of the human life, to denigrate anything and everything we make by affixing a value to it that will rise and fall depending on trends in the marketplace. Is that accurate? They host other people's works and take a percentage, right?"

Silence on the end of the phone.

"We're pretty aligned at the end of the day. We both need to eat, right? Even if it's scraps."

"Why did you sign up for this program, Mr. Dalipagic?"

The streetcar skidded to a stop. As the doors opened, Soda realized his mistake.

"Seemed like a good idea at the time," he replied. "I had a future ahead of me. You did too, you know. I bet you had a future once."

"Sir?"

He threw the phone as far as it would go. Soda knew it wouldn't take long for them to find him again. It was too cold and wet outside to wait for another streetcar. Soda did his best not to breathe. There was no driver, just an automated computer behind the wheel. He was on the infamous Shit Car. The familiar, putrid smell permeated everything; the windows fogged up with the residual humidity inside. Soda released Odie and let him roam the car. The beast sniffed each seat, overwhelmed by the aroma. Soda crumpled into a seat. A single raccoon sat in the back of the streetcar, propped up like a person, watching them. Odie ignored it.

Certain gates closed behind Soda, the world shrinking with every decision. There were so many lives he knew didn't exist for him anymore. He knew there was no risk of anyone else attempting to board before they reached their destination. He held the jar of dirt in his hands and closed his eyes. He tried not to think about torn-out throats and melting flesh. The Shit Car was his chariot now. Stanley Marigold would have to tolerate the smell when Soda finally arrived.

24.

You don't set out to do the wrong thing at first. It accumulates over time.

Stanley hadn't even wanted the family business. His daughter didn't either, she'd made that much clear. It was supposed to go to Stanley's brother Anders, the eldest who wore suits on weekends as a child, the kind of kid who had preferred tailors depending on the season and the fabric. His sister Whitney was supposed to step up when Anders disappeared into rehab for the first time. She ran off with a girlfriend instead, the only evidence of her movements found in credit card statements as she bounced from one Mediterranean resort town to another, working on her music. Anders and Whitney reconciled after she got addicted to sleeping pills, passing out in airports and cocktail bars and police stations across Europe.

The burden finally fell to Stanley, an afterthought from a third wife who cycled through nannies on a regular basis. The first thing the elder Marigold did once he decided on his youngest child as his successor was to bring him along to an eviction. They sat in a car and watched as a young family's possessions were dragged out of one of the Marigold low-rises in Rexdale, the furnishings stacked under pounding rain, the mother screaming at a man with a clipboard, children clinging to each other. Stanley's father made him watch while he sat up front, smoking. He had no driver back then, no assistant, before they started building luxury towers, back when this was a good way to make a buck — buying up old rental towers and rebranding them as Marigold Properties, squeezing the poor for a few more dollars each year, raising rents with lobby repairs while refusing to fix any of the actual units. Soon doing the wrong thing was just how things were done. You got used to cutting corners, cracks still creeping across the ceiling.

"I knew it would end up like this eventually," Stanley said. No one else in the room noticed the crack in the ceiling. He had someone from IT trying to hack into Jaclyn's email; she changed the password without informing anyone before she took that header in the Holstein pit. Stanley hadn't found a replacement yet. He refused all new meetings, ignored calls, and tried not to ask Sidney for help. She wasn't prepared to see him this weak. That wasn't how their game worked.

"We were on the lookout," Hans said. Two security guards with him, all with white rabbit masks pulled down over their faces. "Word got out. Word always gets out. I still blame that hockey guy. I was thinking we'd actually find some Threshold muscle, but no luck. Just these two, wearing Halloween costumes."

The two small women wore shapeless coveralls. Their masks were on the table before him blinking and ticking. Old Threshold prototypes, outdated models gifted to the City.

"You found them where?" Stanley said. His face was bare, skin still raw from his morning shave. It had been three hundred days since he'd last nicked the skin. He kept a little counter on his

275

phone, something else to explain to his new assistant. "One of the contaminated units?"

"Twelfth floor," Hans said. "Should consider sealing it off. Couple units with no responses when we knocked. A few people complaining about smells, though we've got a crew dealing with that now. And then the empty ones . . ."

"Empty ones?" Stanley said. "Hans, what have we talked about?"

"We don't say empty," another security man said, words muffled under his mask.

"He can answer for himself," Stanley said. He considered calling Albert, but once noon hit, the old man forgot too much, speaking in riddles Stanley used to think held answers. Albert didn't see any of this coming. It was time to change the Marigold business model. He was still quibbling over electric bills and how long a tenant could go without a refrigerator before a new one could be installed. He never saw Threshold coming into town, buying up the waterfront, implanting it with their sensors, struggling to surveil a city that didn't want them while failing to confront the rising water levels that would annihilate half of their buildings within a few years. Threshold didn't know about the price; they only knew there was something in the soil, eating away at all their attempts to control the flow of information. The age of development was ending. Stanley would adjust. He had a new business model, an organic IP.

"Right," Hans said, running a hand over his bald skull. There were small nicks toward the base of his neck. It was hard to find people who cared about the details. "We don't say empty, we say unoccupied. Or between owners, or ownership groups, or estates. Or it's a pied-à-terre."

"I knew you'd remember," Stanley said. "Empty implies this building wasn't a success, that we didn't fulfill our obligations to our investors, that the Marigold/Dundee Corporation may be struggling to cover its debts while building another tower across the street. And we don't want that, do we? Because if that happens, you become ghosts. And I become something else."

The women remained silent, kneeling on the floor.

"This is ridiculous. Get them some chairs."

Chairs appeared, off-white, perfectly balanced.

"Alright, so who sent you here? Our friends down on the waterfront? Or did the City finally decide to take a look on their own?"

"IDs say they work for the City. Public health. Cathy Jin and, uh, Jasmine Hassan."

Stanley laughed. "Oh, public health. That charade still functioning, eh? Figured you guys mainly handed out condoms. Should've stuck to doing outreach, don't you think?"

"We also found this," Hans continued. "Seemed important."

A glass container with a plastic lid. A dark black goo throbbed inside it. Hungry.

"Collecting samples, huh? I didn't think it would move this fast. Those Threshold kids wish they had this stuff, I bet they wanted you to tell them what it was. Couldn't stick with the old ways. Although I guess it's not their fault, is it? It's the floods, feeding them. Whatever's in the lake, working its way through the underground. Doesn't matter now. It's spreading, isn't it? Someone lost control, somewhere. It's easier when you don't see it."

Stanley picked up the glass container. He poked at the lid, watched the older woman shudder.

"Cathy, right? Look like you've been at this a long time," Stanley said. "What made you go rogue? Public health doesn't jump unless the mayor's office tells them to jump, and Wilma Ford isn't making many decisions without the input of my friends. Did someone make you an offer?"

Cathy shrugged.

"You probably saw it back when it was a fungus, didn't you? A little bit of black mould. Back in the old days, it was in a bunch of my father's buildings. He did his best to wipe it out once the bodies started showing up. No one wants to kill all their tenants. We're in the business of making money, not killing people. I don't need a semantic argument about how those are the same. The thing is, we're going to need to pivot. And something like this, well, the world would pay quite a pretty penny, don't you think? Who cares about a building? Better to own something universal. Better to own an idea, own the potentiality of a thing, don't you agree?"

The Marigold/Dundee Corporation never killed anyone themselves, not outright. Most of the other developers held a similar code. That was the gardener's job. Albert had preferred driving some irate tenants out into the countryside in the winter, leaving them there to find their own way home. Occasionally, they tossed men off boats in Lake Ontario to see if they could swim. Never women — the old man's rule. Stanley saw no difference. Everyone still had to pay.

"Let's make this fast," Stanley said. "Hans, please grab my mask from the bedside table."

Hans disappeared into the other room. Jasmine began to cry, tears slowly sliding down her cheeks. Cathy remained stoic. He imagined she sat through board meetings worse than this, found bodies in places no one else looked. Stanley admired her resolve.

"You know what they want, don't you?" Stanley said. "The men who sent you on this little quest? They want to turn us into a resource. A collection of numbers. And they're willing to do whatever they need to achieve that, even if it means a few of us die along the way. They don't actually understand what they're dealing with. It's like their algorithms. The systems become so large they begin to defy human understanding. They may be able to explain the core concepts, but they don't know how it works. Just like this stuff. This Wet. You have to give up control. Let me show you how we do that. Give up that control for one second."

Hans returned with a sleeker version of the goat masks still laid out on the table. Stanley snatched it and pulled it over his skin. A light silver layer covered his face but didn't wrap around his head. The eyes were pale green sockets.

"Now let's see what it does. We can experiment together. A new business venture. Hans, grab her mask."

Cathy didn't fight Hans as the mask was snapped back over her head.

"My father always used to talk about Pandora's box every time we started a new excavation. Depending on what we found, there would be archaeologists and heritage specialists to pay off, or an engineer who might need to reroute a couple sewage lines without informing the city. Only way to find out was to put a shovel in the ground."

Stanley opened the container. Through the pale green lens, he watched the black goo rise slowly, reshaping itself into a woman's hand, creeping toward Jasmine's face. The tears continued. One of Hans's men puked inside his mask. You had to have a stomach for this work.

It was an old rot that had festered for decades, but it was familiar to Stanley. His father had shown him what the price was when they had to open up the subbasement of The Marigold. This is what it had become, what it was becoming. He watched the blackened hand-like shape squirming up Jasmine's chest, headed directly toward her pleading face.

"What happened when you brought your little sample to those guys? Is that why she's so afraid? Talk to me. That's the only way you get out of here."

Stanley held back, waiting for Cathy to speak. No words at first.

"I don't know . . . I can't explain. It's not that simple. It's not something I can . . ."

"That's not good enough," Stanley said. "You know better than that, don't you? Maybe you need some kind of incentive. I always hated incentives. Do it or don't. But desperate times . . ."

Jasmine eventually screamed; the sound muffled as the black mass entered her mouth. Stanley watched Cathy, waiting for her to try to do something heroic, something beautiful and ultimately useless. That's usually what these public service types were all about, weren't they? Cathy didn't move. She kept her mask on, even as sensors screeched and eyes flickered.

"You need to be careful with this stuff, eh?" Stanley said. "They had no idea."

"They?" Cathy asked, mask unmoved. A new kind of weapon. A new kind of life. Stanley understood he could finally abandon the towers. Let the old man die. Become something new.

"Threshold. The City. Everyone, really," Stanley said. "Even me. She still alive?"

Jasmine's eyes closed. The skin of her face was ashen. Still human, but changing.

"It should've . . ." Cathy started, before stopping herself.

"You saw what it did before? Maybe it learned something since then, huh? Don't go underestimating the Wet. Who knows how many people are in it," Stanley said. "That's what it is, you know. Bodies. It's a collective. A plurality. And it's poisoning my building. You know. You want to tell me why?"

"I don't know," Cathy said. He believed her. She was defeated, listless. "I don't know."

"Take her down to the new pit," Stanley said. "We've got what I would call a wading pool down there. Maybe you can help us figure out what's gone wrong. Send this Jasmine down the hole too, maybe she can communicate with it now that it's inside her. Maybe we can use this for something good. Even just as a little threat. Walking around with a gun while everyone else has a knife, oh yes, that must have been what that old bastard Oppenheimer felt out there in his desert lab, unmaking the universe. It's exciting and horrifying in equal measures. You can feel your heart reject the very premise of it, and yet, I can't stop thinking about it. An unmaker. A remaker. We've got a lot of changes coming, Hans. We're going to be distributors."

Hans nodded behind his white rabbit mask. The men dragged the women after them, Jasmine still quaking and shaking as the Wet made its home inside her. Stanley turned back to the windows, massive rain clouds rolling in off the lake, cancelling out any hope for a dry season. The soil was already clogged, so much of the old dirt paved over. Water had nowhere to go.

"Someone call Abigail Holstein for me," Stanley said, before realizing the room was empty. They'd have to plan for next steps, an orderly retreat to move their assets. Sidney would follow him, but he wanted more, needed the challenge to sustain himself. The old man couldn't help them anymore. He could be left behind, left to join with whatever the Wet became. It was weaponizing itself. Stanley walked into his bedroom, ignoring the crack, searching for his phone. Sometimes you had to do the hard parts yourself.

"Abigail? Come on now. I know you're upset. I know. It's a bit more complicated than that. I understand. I swear, okay? I need to see you. We need to talk."

It was time for the Marigold/Dundee Corporation to diversify once again.

Suite 1710

Empty. No one ever lived here. No one ever would.

25.

Wanting was a curse. Cathy knew that now; reaffirmed with every step she took on this journey into the Wet, scrabbling alone in the dark, clinging to anything that might provide an answer. Wanting led you to open doors that should've remained closed, to ask questions that should've gone unanswered. Wanting dragged those you loved into your orbit and then kept them there at the edge of your reach. Even catatonic, Jasmine still held bits of her inside.

None of the men acknowledged Jasmine shuddering between them in the elevator, her skin already taking an oily sheen as the Wet spread through her. They had seen things like this before or were too afraid to show weakness in front of the others. Cathy put it at an even split. The private elevator plummeted down and down, Hans's veiny hand on a little red key in the corner.

They took away her phone and tools, everything that was in her kit, but they let her keep the mask, yanking out most of its sensors. They were running their own experiment. She was a Wet test dummy. They wanted a demonstration of whatever they had down in the pit of Marigold II. Jasmine, or what was once Jasmine, continued to hiss in the centre of the elevator. Her eyes were blank, massive black pupils. Her teeth chattered inside her skull. The Wet learned from its past mistakes. There was no point in destroying the host before you figured out how it worked.

Plastic zip ties around Jasmine's wrists, and then again around the elbow joints. Small, discreet, likely painful. Hans was efficient. The city had been crumbling around Cathy for years and she hadn't wanted to acknowledge the signs, convinced her zealous, simple mission was enough. Public health could make it on grit and honour alone, but she now knew structures crumble slowly at first, just like buildings before the full collapse.

Love was the same. The collapse happened faster than she fathomed, but she was now alone, even with the body that was Jasmine beside her in this elevator. There were words you said and words you meant, and Cathy knew those had rarely aligned between them. She was never going to leave this city, even as it choked her out, trapped her in that rental, staring out over flooded streets and burning highways, unable to flee further afield, unable to see a life without the bonds of this place that had come to define her. Jasmine was the one who wanted to free her from its hold, never fully comprehending that Cathy had swallowed the key years ago and let it dissolve inside her. The city and Cathy became one and the same, a single circle, scorched and suffering.

The escape was Jasmine's fantasy, detailed and documented in emails, texts, and mood boards full of A-frame cabins. There were lakes untouched by motor oil, chickens roaming over a single acre, leaving eggs for each day's breakfast. She didn't let the dream overcome her reality though. She could build things, fix things, rearrange the world until it felt like home for them both. Sometimes the dishwasher leaked. Jasmine could fix that. A mask would blow a sensor. Jasmine again had it under control. She bent the world to her whim so easily, so smoothly that Cathy continued to abdicate her responsibilities, let herself fall into Jasmine's welcoming care, a warm blanket she never imagined would be yanked away like this. But there was always a seed inside her that refused to surrender, a piece of Cathy rooted somewhere outside the words they shared in the dark, their panting faces buried in each other. The elevator shuddered to a halt.

"Alright, ladies, let's move," Hans said. This was the other side of The Marigold, all exposed cinderblocks and piping, the heat of overworked on-site commercial laundry rooms, prep kitchens, and massive water pumps that fed up into the eighty-eight storeys above them, a precarious network of pipes, wires, and various adhesives clinging together.

There were no restraints on Cathy. They assumed she was beaten, or at least defeated enough to follow without question. Who could she run to? Threshold likely considered her a collaborator at best and the department would be happy to let her burn. There was no authority to point to, no single place to lay the blame. It was diffused across the entire structure and diluted through that process.

"The door," Hans said. "Pretend it's another eviction."

The group emerged, droplets of the coming storm pinging off of Cathy's mask. A horn screeched at her as two of the security men hustled Jasmine across the street, their stance implying she had some greater fame, a more glamourous reason for this entourage. Hans slammed his palm on the hood of a Honda with a Magellan sticker, and then dragged Cathy after him. Another opportunity to run, and yet she kept her captors close.

She needed to know what they wanted from her. If she understood their desires, maybe she could play them against each other. That was a lie, a good one, one that might have been true a week ago, maybe even a few hours. It was Jasmine she wanted now, a life she wanted to save. There was still so much they didn't know about the Wet. Maybe you could bring them back. Maybe you could find a loophole. That was the truth she recognized, the same thing that kept her from fleeing this city, a sense of obligation to the systems and structures that protected her, who gave her someone like Jasmine, who didn't ask for what Cathy couldn't give her. There was no authority to appeal to here though, no law to rage against. Nature took what it wanted.

"Welcome to Marigold II," Hans said as they entered the construction site, bodies now hidden by the clapboard and scaffolding. "Supposed to be taller than the CN Tower when we're done. Thirty elevators. Although I guess that's over now."

A world without rules wasn't actually without rules, it only provided a smokescreen for those who wielded power under a haze of undirected actions. It was what made something like this pit possible. Digging so deep solely to prove it could be done. The group moved deeper and deeper into the pit, circling around the edge, the walls rising until all Cathy saw through her mask was dirt and sky crowded out by cranes.

"You probably think he wants to kill you down here," Hans said.

Cathy let him talk. It was the best way to learn.

"I don't think he's ever killed anyone himself. No denying he's careless. But he's not a killer. He's a doer. He makes things happen, even when the powers deny him. I undo denials."

Learn whatever she could before they got to the bottom of this pit, before Jasmine was put through yet another test by Marigold's crew.

"Once you're down here, no one on the surface can hear you," Hans continued. "But you're useful, right? Stanley thinks you'll understand what's at the bottom. It's coming up from somewhere deeper into our foundation. This little wet spot."

Cathy recognized the smell through her deactivated mask. Most of the pit was dry. There was rebar and concrete around the edges, gravel in piles. At the edge of her vision, a scummy black pond against the far side, almost underneath the road, a rotten cave beyond beckoning her forward. They released Jasmine, who shuddered toward the edge of the water. It looked more like an open grave, forms resembling bodies shimmering in the thick black fluid, barely human and yet achingly alive the closer you got to the shallows. The slurry moaned, a guttural sound.

"You see our problem, don't you?" Hans said. The Wet had found a home out here in the open, exposing itself to the sun. "Every morning it's like this. We tried filling it with sand. We tried using hoses. It's persistent, I'll give it that much. And now Stanley thinks it's our future."

Jasmine waded into the slurry. Cathy resisted the urge to pursue her, every muscle in her body screaming, her brain trying to find some logic for her muted stance. The men stood back from the edge of the black water, watching Jasmine wade out into the centre of the pool, communing with it. This was not the Wet as Cathy knew it; this was something that defied her worst-case scenarios. Hans sighed deeply behind his mask. Was this their grand experiment?

"You know how much this is going to cost to remediate?"

Cathy knew she still wanted things. She still wanted that future Jasmine detailed at night, a place so far from cities that you could read the entire sky as one story, constellation after constellation. Cathy considered shoving the men one by one into the slurry, watching them scream as it sucked them under. The satisfaction of their faces slipping between the living glop down there, their voices joining the larger chorus whispering in her ear. Would that be enough for it to let Jasmine go? Would that make it happy? Did it even understand happiness?

"And now we've got a tunnel under the road. Fuck, every day something new down here." Hans pointed to the far edge of the pit. "Goddamn it."

Cathy didn't want to take her eyes off Jasmine, now up to her waist in the slurry. Hans yanked her arm. "See, it's feeding into our building now too."

"It knows what it wants now," Cathy said. She was a willing part of the experiment. It was what the Wet wanted, to exploit the bond. It knew her now. "It's speaking to them, asking them to join it. Look at her walking . . . that's not the girl I know. It's all the lives gathered together, disassembled and put back together. An organic cult."

"So, they all want to be part of this?"

"Not all of them," Cathy said. "I've seen what it does when it takes by force. But it's learning. The willing are easier prey."

Jasmine was now up to her neck. Cathy didn't move to save her. She kept her composure, even as her partner sank deeper into the Wet. There were no heroics for Cathy.

"And if you're not willing?" Hans said, his voice faltering. "If you resist?"

"It may take you anyway. It's more of a preference than a requirement. Do you eat meat, Hans?" Cathy said. There was so much she still had to say, so many apologies Jasmine wouldn't hear. There was no point in articulating them to this version of her. The pond continued to groan as rain pelted down. The security men grumbled and shuffled, trying to control their disgust as Jasmine's mouth sank below the surface. No sputtering — she reunited with her new essence. She was part of the Wet.

"Yes, I do," Hans said. "What man doesn't?"

"You don't want to kill an animal in distress. It spoils the meat," Cathy said. "Easier to incorporate the willing or the dead."

The pond sloshed as Jasmine disappeared, a thin gurgle of bubbles. Cathy kept her face blank. A security man threw up, the glop nearly forcing his mask off. Hans was unmoved.

"And those Threshold guys, they had no idea?"

"Ignorant as you."

"It's not going to stop flooding this hole, is it?" Hans said.

Jasmine was gone, a non-entity. "It wants more. That's why it's made a little tunnel into your building there. It knows there's bodies inside."

Cathy didn't know if this was true, but it would buy her more time.

"You mean people."

"All it cares about are bodies. Lonely bodies. It needs to keep growing and it found a source to do so. It works its way up and in, just like a fungus through a tree. It's starting in the roots."

"Why're you telling me this?" Hans said.

"I saw what you did to my friend."

Over Hans's shoulder, the two other security men waded into the pit, their masks behind them on the ground. They had no trace of the Wet in their faces, but they were compelled to enter. It was speaking to them too.

We could have a life together.

Jasmine's voice in her ear now, pushing into her head. It learned so quick.

We could be together in this.

Hans suppressed a shriek as he watched his men abandon their posts as a collective, wading into the muck, drawn toward the hole in the wall of the pit, leading toward the base of The Marigold. They flopped down into the muck, embracing it, pulling it into themselves.

Together.

Cathy wanted to take her mask off. She took a step toward the pool as the other men sank beneath its opaque, oozing surface. They disappeared faster than Jasmine, fully accepting the embrace of the Wet. Cathy could feel their voices joining the collective in her skull like a pulse.

Both of us.

"No." Hans yanked on her arm. "No, not you too. Can't have that. We still need you."

All of us.

White bobbing corpses. Hans dragged Cathy with him around the edge of the pond, his strength unnerving. He picked his way around the dirt and gravel, pulling her along the slanted shore of the pond toward the rough tunnel in the wall; a low moan emitted from its entrance.

"I need you to tell me what it wants from us."

Hans pulled her after him into the dark, dripping space. His phone lit the way.

Both of us, Cathy.

"Stan won't want me coming back empty-handed. Now let's go."

All of us.

Cathy let him lead her into the dripping dark, searching for the heart of the Wet, the dripping mould that had festered in her dreams for so long. She needed to know its heart. Jasmine would understand. Hans continued marching forward, alone now without his masked entourage.

Together.

Somewhere down there in the pool of melded flesh and ash, Jasmine could wait for her.

Penthouse B

Abigail Holstein almost bought a unit in The Marigold, back when it was just a model sitting in the middle of a hotel ballroom, wood and glass under subtle amber lighting, the kind of light that practically never graced the city itself. She stood in front of this model and tried to imagine herself way up on the eightieth floor, a clear view across the city, taking in all the neighbourhoods she would never visit, the shambling towers pocking the horizon to the east and west and north, the crumbling glass fingers stretching for the sky down by the lake, a space where the view went on forever. Abigail still wanted to believe in that forever. If you could imagine the right future, you didn't have to acknowledge the present. You could simply wait it out, keep your eyes on the horizon and avoid the horrors ravaging the streets below.

The elevator shuddered to a stop on the eighty-seventh floor. Very few people had access to The Marigold's penthouse elevator. It had its own alcove in the lobby, the passcode a heavily guarded secret. It didn't exist on the official fire plan, only in the nether-world enjoyed by the ultra-rich and slightly paranoid, in league with private supper clubs and hidden bars three storeys beneath the earth and members-only rural hunting lodges where the only things that got shot over a long weekend were clay pigeons and the occasional valet.

"Ah, I see you're fancy now," Sidney Marigold said, surrounded by packing boxes and ancient oak furniture. Dust fluttered in the brightly lit space despite the rain outside. Abigail could barely detect the veneers in Sidney's generous smile. "Did he text you the code or do you have your own?"

"Uh . . . he said he needed some help."

She was a decade older than Abigail, which Abigail only knew after digging up as much information as she could about Stanley's family — the ongoing lawsuits between his siblings and his father, and the potential for a prenuptial agreement that might cause him to reconsider pursuing a relationship or whatever this was between them.

"This was his father's space, you see. There was always this dream that he'd move back in here, the two of them looking out over the city together. But the decline came fast."

Abigail set down her bag. The elevator clanged shut behind her.

"First he started forgetting what day of the week it was. Then he missed sitting down in a chair when we were out for dinner. Shattered the right hip. And it just kept spiralling." Sidney grabbed some packing tape and another box. "He passed this morning, apparently."

"Oh, I'm so sorry for your loss," Abigail said on instinct. Stanley had summoned her here, providing few details beyond a request for her immediate presence. They'd barely spoken since his assistant had tumbled down into the Gethsemane pit. It wasn't his style to offer up sympathy.

"Oh, I wouldn't call it mine," Sidney said, still smiling. "If anything, probably more of a relief. Stan has big plans. He no longer needs to look over his shoulder for approval. He can be whoever he wants now. There's no mantle to uphold."

Ever since that day at the pit, nothing had gone right with the site. The city was fining them every day for blocking the sidewalks, despite assurances from the local councillor they'd obtained the correct permits. One of the cranes had crumpled overnight the week before, its cab set aflame by some kids who stuffed it full of old newspapers and uploaded the video to a number of anonymous accounts her team struggled to trace. Every time they took it down, another one popped up. Every video had a soundtrack of trumpets — big band, classical, free jazz, atonal ambience that shook the speakers, all of them in on the joke.

"Do you need me to call anyone? Are there certain protocols for the funeral or . . . ?"

Sidney smiled and set down the tape. "Oh no, honey. We're over that. The whole family thing is done, I think. All that song and dance . . . Stan has been waiting for a reason to let go of that mantle for a while now. And he's found a new obsession, something his father can't say he built. Not that I blame you for asking, I could never imagine the pressure you two are under in that world, all the legacy issues, family honour . . . you know what I'll end up inheriting if my parents are kind enough to kick the bucket before I do? Debt collectors."

Abigail laughed, trying to stay calm. Stan was supposed to meet her here.

"At least our daughter can rest easy. Fiona won't talk to him anymore, but I still get her emails about grandpa. I think she would like you. If the three of us could get together some day . . . now that would be real power. Stan loves to ratchet up the tension, you know. He didn't tell me you were coming, but I should've expected it. The trick is to find things that get under his skin, but don't necessarily leave a mark, you know? That's what Fiona learned. Hold him at a distance and he'll keep asking for you. Do you want any of this furniture? It's going to consignment otherwise. Albert always had to have the biggest, heaviest pieces. What does that say about a man?"

"He has trouble letting things go," Abigail said, slowly regaining her confidence. Sidney didn't appear angry. She was mellow, a satisfied cat languishing in her new domain. Abigail might be a mouse to play with for now, but she was okay with letting the older woman believe that. It made things a little more exciting if this became a long-term arrangement.

"That could be it," Sidney said, now measuring one of the credenzas. "Something about permanence too. As if you can outlast your own mortality, live a little longer through your things, through your buildings. I've seen enough estate sales to know that's a lie. Some great deals though. Really great deals. The trick to negotiating is to come in at half on the first offer."

Abigail didn't say anything about the hockey player, or the rumours about the Wet. The Marigold had been a success eventually, hadn't it? Its initial struggles were legend among the other developers, but could any of them claim they would've done something different? The Marigolds had stepped out of their comfort zone and they had paid for it. But now there was a spire you could see no matter where you went, its crest glowing yellow and orange in the gloom.

"I don't mean to be rude," Abigail said.

"Oh, I'd prefer if you were, I think," Sidney laughed.

"Well, why am I here exactly? If you're here . . . and I'm here . . ."

"Stanley has some new ideas."

"That's right." Stanley's deep voice behind her didn't sound bereaved. He walked past her to open a window, the kind that wasn't supposed to open this high up, according to the regulations her own architects kept shoving in her face for the Gethsemane. It was so obvious and yet she knew she couldn't break the pattern. If you denied Abigail something, she would only want it more. She didn't need a therapist to explain that to her, the evidence was littered throughout her childhood and teenage years, the need for attention, the drugs, the random excursions to cities she'd dreamed about, her father's bag men in suits appearing to collect her like clockwork.

"I'm glad you made it," he said, sticking a hand out to feel the rain. He was shirtless, but still wearing suspenders, the edge of his gut hanging over his pants. His chest hair was shaped like a bull, one horn shorter than the other, like it'd broken off inside of him. "Used to have them buzz me when someone was taking the elevator, but that kind of ruined the surprise."

Sidney shrugged. "She's not going to believe that."

The bright overhead light made his age show. Hair thinner, shoulders less defined, like bits of him had winnowed away, the world grating him down into something more manageable. Maybe it was the grief he was hiding. Abigail wasn't sure if she'd ever seen him fully naked — it wasn't how they liked to meet each other. Clothes made things more interesting, brief revelations instead of full confessions. Her gaze travelled down to discover Stanley held a glass container in his hands, black substance inside it beating against the glass like a heart. *Thunk*.

"I was sorry to hear about Albert."

"Oh, right, yes, that was a surprise, but not a shock, I guess. Does that make sense? I'm sure you'll feel the same way once Hammond decides to return to his crypt."

Sidney laughed and continued measuring furniture. They were wasting Abigail's time.

"You probably think I just brought you here to act all maudlin," Stan said. The container *thunked* again in his hand. He set it down on a massive orange ottoman, almost a couch. "Come and see the man brought low by his own emotional attachment."

"Pointing out your flaws before the bully can," Abigail said. "I'm familiar."

Thunk.

"Were you the bully? Or were you trying to stay one step ahead?"

"Probably the bully," Abigail said. "I was bored. I think most bullies are bored."

"She makes a good point," Sidney said.

"She does. I was definitely a victim most of the time."

"You expect me to believe that?" Abigail said, trying not to stare at the container. Sidney didn't seem to care about its presence.

Thunk.

"As much as you believe anything else I tell you," Stanley said. "Yes, I was a victim. I am a victim. I've just learned how to spin that position to my advantage. I can decide when it starts and stops at this stage in my life. Like a tap, I determine the flow."

"What's in there, Stanley?"

"Oh this?" he said, waving around the container with its little black heart. "This is just the future. Probably. Not that I'm an expert on these matters. This stuff is why I'm bearish with buildings now. The start of a whole new world order. We can probably thank our fathers for that. They know not what they do, right? We can forgive them once we see some profits."

"What do you mean?"

"Hard to explain," Stanley said, trying to find a place to sit amongst the moving dollies and haphazard furniture. He settled on a wheeled bar cart. "You ever think a ritual might cover up some kind of darker truth? That we might create a ceremony to absolve ourselves a little? Every little thing we do is buried under the surface. But what happens when it comes back? And it always comes back, Ab. That's what I'm learning. Nothing stays buried."

"Stan, did you smoke today? Are you drinking again?" Abigail said.

"I wish," Stanley replied. "Killing yourself slowly, that's real power. Deciding when to go . . . you know Albert wanted to die in the woods? Just wanted to go out into the dark and fall asleep."

Thunk.

"Maybe you need more sleep."

Sidney laughed, wrapping up a vase in butcher paper. "I said the same thing."

Stan laughed. The bottles around him shook. "Wouldn't that be nice? I wish I could sleep. What I've got in this little container here is the future of us. Me and Sidney. And you, if you're interested. What I hold here is what happens when we die now, in this place, isolated, alone, alienated, and afraid. This thing, this substance, this . . . Threshold and their lackeys at the City like to call it the Wet, and maybe that's the best thing to call it, right? The source of life itself."

"You mean . . ."

"What they thought was a fungus, what's ruined property values across our fine, shining city on a drowning shore — yes, it's alive. It's us. And it can undo everything."

"Us?"

"It's what comes once we are gone. People are choosing it. It's the new Pepsi. Or having it forced upon them — I guess that happens too. All very interesting in a morbid, abstract way. But there's nothing abstract here, Ab. The worrying part is someone tried to harness it, probably our Threshold friends, and things got a little out of hand. Or maybe it was nature finding a way. The thing about innovation is it's not just for people."

Thunk.

Abigail didn't hear any voice coming from the Wet. She only heard its hunger.

"If I opened this up now, it would speak."

Thunk.

"Do you want to hear what it says, Abigail? Do you want to listen? I've been told it's very convincing, that it's amassed all the fears and hopes and dreams and little nagging concerns of the bodies it has swallowed, the brains it has consolidated into some floating mass under our towers, using us like fuel, burning us up to live. The Wet runs on us."

Abigail took a seat beside Stanley on the couch. "I thought you said this was a new business direction."

Sidney laughed. "Oh, it is. But we can't do it alone. We need some capital."

Abigail could see Gethsemane clearly now, an abyss for all her dreams, nothing but a hole. She wouldn't bother filling it in, let it remain like a scar stitched into the city, a reminder of what happened when capital went on strike, when the money removed itself from the equation of a future for everyone. Let them burn her cranes. Let them deface her billboards. Let them drown.

"The end of one thing and the start of another," Stanley said. "The floods are coming back again. You can see all the bodies scurrying down there in the streets, fleeing north. No more towers. We're on the edge of a new frontier now. One that requires some direction. All frontiers are built on bodies, the kind you don't ever see or talk about. The kind a victim would know."

Sidney wrapped an arm around her. The lights shuddered on and off, the electrical system bucking inside the walls. Abigail smiled, finding her place in the chaos. "And you need a bully."

Thunk.

"We need your insight," Stanley said, grinning. He snapped his suspenders and slammed the container onto the table. The glass held. His teeth were yellower than she remembered. Sidney opened up a bottle of ancient scotch from the bar cart and then drained it in front of Abigail. When she wiped her mouth, she kept her teeth out.

"We need to know how far you're willing to go."

Abigail grabbed her own bottle. She could carve out her own place in this penthouse. This couple didn't know what they had just offered so eagerly. Both their necks exposed, their entire future summarized inside a little glass box, one that spoke only to her, the way a heart did, the way blood did, a relentless march inside her skull. Abigail could smell the weakness, taste their fear and excitement in the room like musk. "I mean, Hammond is already unsteady on his feet."

Thunk.

Albert Marigold would've been proud.

26.

Henrietta used to bury toys in the empty lot outside the Village, finding hidden corners to dispose of dollar store dolls and plastic dinosaurs. It felt good to dig. It felt good to hide things only she knew about, secrets shared with someone else she'd never see, someone else curious enough to question what lay beneath the dirt.

"I don't want to die," Alma said. "It would kind of ruin my life."

"And I do?" Henrietta responded, trying to find her friend in the sludge.

"I think you're more likely to accept it," Alma said, her body invisible to Henrietta in the tunnel. Their voices were hoarse, sonar signals in the ooze. They had run for hours, following Cabeza's low voice through the tunnels, trying to outrun whatever Ramji had become. "I think you'd be okay if you were just like a skeleton, you know? You'd find a way to make that work."

"Like a lich."

"Whatever you want to call it," Alma said, hacking up phlegm. "A skeleton queen."

Henrietta pushed the voice of her father out of her head, the one the Wet had learned to mimic so well the longer she was exposed to it. Not things he ever said, just the things she wanted him to say. She could have warned Ramji there in the tunnel, but she hadn't, the voice in her head too insistent, too charming to be ignored. He was gone now, just like Cherry, the same sequence occurring all over again. Maybe she was a killer. Or maybe something even less exciting. Maybe Henrietta Brakes was just a lure.

"Come." Cabeza's voice almost human to her ears now. It was real, a physical thing in the air between the three of them. A crack of real light up ahead, the promise of a surface. "We find your friend at the pond."

Cabeza had been rejected by the Wet for some reason. It didn't explain why. She had watched the mass coiling around Ramji recoil from Cabeza's touch, unable to incorporate its being, the teeth and tongue still so human inside the sludge.

"I don't know if I want to see him again," Alma said. "There can't be much left . . ."

"Some go slower," Cabeza said, pulling together the splattered version of itself as they emerged from the slick crevice into a construction pit, their bodies flopping down into the dirt and gravel as rain pattered over their bodies, the smell of the fresh air almost winding Henrietta. Salman was right to kiss the dirt in the valley. She almost wanted to do it here, press her lips into the stones, taste the cool rain. Every inch of her body was covered in the loose ooze of the underground. The path they followed was greased with the hundreds of bodies that came before them, drawn to this place, this attempt at building yet another tower.

"They saving Cherry for something special?" Alma said. "He going to be their new spokesman? Was that your old job?"

Cabeza made a shrugging motion. Its body didn't respond well to the light, even with the cloud cover above. Henrietta watched its form contort with each movement, cycling through its cells out in the open. Would there really be anything left of Cherry? Who was Cherry anyway at this point? She had thrown herself into this idea that she could save him, and yet all she knew was the barest outline of the boy, the way his neck went red when he couldn't answer a question after the teacher called him, the smell of his breath when he spoke too close to her face. The small trail of skin tags on his right arm, like he'd been snatched away from a twin in the womb. His mother in Croatia, or was she flying back now that he was missing? Missing or dead, they meant different things. Maybe missing was worse. It was easier to assume her own father was dead, not alive, not a part of the Wet, speaking to her in that dripping dark, asking her to join him one last time, asking her to forsake a life lived on the surface and a mother who forgot her.

"It decides," Cabeza said. "Who it wants . . . to speak to . . ."

The decaying flesh moved in a frenzy as they got closer to the pond, surrounded by heavy construction equipment. Henrietta could see bodies bobbing on the surface. There was no breeze here. The rain was almost gentle. Cabeza's body trembled and flared like static, an old television burning out its screen, the cells rabid, chasing each other across its frame.

"Wants us to be part of the whole. Sometimes calls. Sometimes takes."

Alma grabbed Henrietta's hand, trying to slow her down.

"We shouldn't be here."

Henrietta sneered. "It's too late for that, Al. I need to see. I need to know."

"You don't need to do anything," Alma said. She was too small to slow Henrietta down, all her bluster deflated out here in the open. The yellow earth machines dwarfed them.

There is no alone here.

The voice in her head once again. The pool before them decorated with the remains of security uniforms, drifting around its surface. Cabeza circled it, looking for shadow from the light, a safer place to stand.

"He is in there . . ."

"He doesn't exist anymore," Alma said. "Think about Ramji. You saw what it did to him. What it took from him, Hen. It swallowed him up."

"I didn't see him die."

"You didn't see him die because we ran, Hen! We ran and we didn't stop running until we couldn't breathe. Because there was nothing else to do. Even the rats ran. Even Cabeza ran. And if Cabeza is running, I think that's a sign something is pretty fucked up, don't you?"

Henrietta didn't care what Alma said to her. Cabeza had fulfilled its part of the bargain. She was at the pond, at the source, according to the gurgling promises of her guide. Ramji was part of the toll she paid. Salman had been spared. She walked up to its edge, immune to the smell, immune to the pieces of flesh and organs she saw bobbing in the slurry around the leftover clothes. She stared down into its shallows. It refused to provide her with a reflection.

"Hen, you won't find anything in there. You won't find him there. You won't find anything except more fucking corpses!"

Together.

Cabeza shuddered in the crook of an excavator, concealing itself from the light, desperate to return beneath the surface. She still owed it something. She had to know.

"Cherry?"

The shallows bobbed with bits of fat, yellow and white in the black ooze.

"Cherry, if you're in there, I guess . . . I just want to say I'm sorry."

I would take you.

A face formed in the ooze. Not her father, not Ramji. A young face, a smile already on its lips. When it spoke, the words didn't play in her skull. It rose up to something like a human shape, the body rippling like Cabeza's, but organized and focused. It was rooted in the pond. It smiled at her, like Cherry did at the edge of the pit. It smiled without teeth, only a void.

"You came back for me," the thing said with Cherry's voice. It spoke like Cabeza with actual words dripping out of it, actual words that could only come from Cherry, it had to be. "You came back to get me. I told them you would come."

I would never leave you.

"Cherry . . ."

The shape moved toward her, unable to pull itself out of the pond yet. The pond fed into it, kept it plump and almost human. It still struggled with anything below the waist, sputtering to form the correct shapes, but the hands were there reaching out for her.

"You let them take me," Cherry said to her.

"I know."

"You let them take me. And they wouldn't let me sleep."

"Stop it, Hen," Alma said, attempting to pull Henrietta away from the edge of the pond. "It's not real! It's no one!"

Henrietta shoved her aside, the smaller girl pinwheeling into the rocks. Alma always wanted to be tough, but she couldn't see the truth. She didn't know what this actually was, what it meant. She wanted to go back. She wanted to unsee what was plain before their eyes. Cherry alive.

"It's not real," Alma whimpered from the dirt. "It's not real, Hen!"

"You let them take me," Cherry said again. "You told me not to be afraid."

"I didn't mean—"

I would take you with me.

The voices fought inside her, the one in her skull like a warning. Cherry sounded just like Cherry and he was still here, still whole. He wasn't like Cabeza. He hadn't forgotten who he was. She could bring him back. She could pull him out. He just had to remember.

"Your mom loved owls, you remember that?"

Cherry nodded, barely dripping, cohering into human form. She just knew it. Henrietta was used to being alone, pretending she didn't miss her mother when she stumbled into the apartment at 3 a.m., pretending her father was still alive out there in the Kootenays. She knew connections only existed to be severed, wires snapping under the pressure of their very purpose. Frail, fragile things, wires and people, and buildings too. They didn't last, they only endured. The Wet wanted you to celebrate that entropy. Its voice was a world, a portal with its own siren song.

"She did. And yours . . . loved . . . cows."

He was in there. Henrietta stuck a hand out to Cherry, his smile welcoming her. She wanted to embrace him. She could pull him free, she could save him from all of this pain.

Not alone. Never alone.

It felt like Cherry's hand in her hand if she closed her eyes. He had so much time ahead of him, time she could give back. Time that Ramji and Cabeza didn't deserve, time her father wouldn't know how to spend.

Not awake. Not asleep. Only presence.

"Come on, Cherry. Let's go home."

The figure hissed and shuddered again. "No."

"No?" Henrietta said, opening her eyes. Cherry was larger now, something like her father but mutilated, a mass of flesh, pocked with pieces of cloth and the fatbergs she'd seen floating in the ooze. A larger hand clutching her own now, pulling her forward, a gentle insistence turning into something else, older and desperate.

"You come."

Henrietta tried to yank her hand free. Cabeza mewled from its perch, unable to reach her.

"You come down with me," still in Cherry's voice, pleading. "Like you promised."

"I didn't . . ."

Another arm springing loose from Cherry's spasming side, swinging out to pull her beneath the shallows into the Wet's tailing pool. Cabeza never warned them about this. It didn't know.

"No!"

Alma's tiny body thrown in between them, taking the brunt of the swipe, swallowed up by the blackness and dragged away from Henrietta, who stumbled back into the gravel, outside of the pond's reach. Alma laughing, her face disappearing into the fist of the shape, the shape that had been Cherry, then someone else, now nothing but a gurgling noise. No voice. Henrietta wanted to scream. All that she found was a whimper. It couldn't have been her. It wasn't her. She climbed to her feet. The top of the pool was quiet again. There was no movement.

"Alma!"

"Gone," Cabeza murmured.

"Shut the fuck up! Alma! Al! Come on!" Henrietta screamed from the shore, preparing to wade in herself. "Alma!"

Cabeza hadn't moved, still human under there. Teeth and tongue roiling in its face, the pain of the light still worth its presence beside her.

"Alma, come on!" Henrietta screamed again, a hand splashing into the Wet, a chunk trying to cling to her hand. She smashed it onto the ground, watched chunks retreat back to the pool, felt the blood run down her knuckles. "Al, you can't do this."

You buried things so you could dig them up again. You buried things and hoped someone else would have that same sense of discovery, welling up inside their hearts, hands tearing at the earth. You buried things to pretend there were worlds before and after you, when all you were given was a history and told to believe it, a history that didn't acknowledge you or didn't even realize you existed in the first place. It didn't matter. You could bury things solely so someone else would find them and know that you were there once.

Not alone. Never alone.

The pond sang to her. She saw Cherry's face burble to the surface again, pulled into the pond. Henrietta tried not to let the pool have faces or names, tried to hold on to what she was, even if she couldn't quite remember it all at this point, the details of her life drained away after hours without sleep or food or warmth. Stripping the world down into wire mothers, unable to protect her. She wanted to fall down, to sleep.

Only presence. No absence.

The Cherry shape was rising up again, gathering strength. It would try again.

"You can't win."

Maybe she didn't remember his voice after all. This sounded like a grown woman. Maybe she didn't remember his face either. Maybe there was nothing left except an idea of the boy.

"You can't win like this," the woman's voice again, calling to her from past the pit. Cabeza snapped to attention. A human on the other side of the pond inside the mouth of a cave, its head covered by a silver goat helmet, eyes a bright and unseemly purple. "It will come back for you. It will use everyone against you. Anyone and everyone. Whatever it takes."

No absence, said the voice in her head. *I would never leave you. Just presence.*

The pond swirled again. The Cherry figure now had two faces. Alma's was in there, struggling to find a way to express itself, morphing into something sympathetic.

"It will keep trying," the goat head said. "I know."

"What are you?" Henrietta screamed. "Some kind of fucking zookeeper? Its owner?"

The goat head laughed, shaking its horns. A man in a rabbit mask emerged behind her, gun in his hand. "You can bring your monster, girl. We need to make sure we have everything before we go back upstairs. Come on now, before it convinces you to join up. It's good at its job."

The mass in the pond started to laugh, Alma and Cherry and her father all mixed together.

"It knows," Cabeza said, trembling, finding more words in its teeth. "You love."

"Your monster's not wrong," the rabbit man said, tapping his gun against the back of the goat's head. He seemed very calm despite the floating charnel stretched out before him. "You can join the others, or you can come with us. It's a choice in the narrowest sense, but a choice."

"It always wins," the goat head said, defeated. "It knows. What's your name, girl?"

Henrietta heard the rabbit cock the gun, watched it swivel in her direction. Cabeza shrank away but didn't flee. She still owed it. This wasn't over. The bodies were still hiding from them in the Wet. Cabeza could find his old self. Maybe she could do the same for Alma, for Cherry . . .

"Henrietta."

"Us or them, Henrietta," the rabbit said. "Don't let the Wet decide it all for you."

I waited for you.

Henrietta didn't answer. She put one foot down into the earth, shuffling with her back stooped, moving in synch with Cabeza's squelching mass. Sometimes you buried things to hide them from yourself, to make sure you didn't wake up with them staring back at you, beady eyes and plastic buttons in the half-light, calling out to you. Sometimes you buried things and they still came back on their own, as if rejected by the earth. They weren't finished.

"Cabeza, are you going to . . ."

The rabbit tapped the back of the goat's head again, a crisp metallic note that rang out over the air. The pool swirled behind her. Cabeza groaned but didn't leave her. It kept on pace, headed toward the cave's entrance. Back into the earth again, back under the buildings.

"Where are you taking us?" Henrietta asked. Over her shoulder, Alma and Cherry spun and split from each other, dripping attempts at human clay, reeking of all the rot inside the hole. She stopped looking back, stopped listening to the pit's laughter, the wet, satisfied sound.

"The root of the thing," the goat said, almost with a laugh. "This is just its waiting room."

"The source. No one goes home until we can name it. I need a full report of what we have down here, bodies be damned. If we own it, we need to know what we own. If we sell it, we need to know what we're selling. You understand?" the rabbit said. "Now start walking."

No absence. Only presence.

Henrietta could barely move. Cabeza went first, shuddering forward into the tunnel, followed by the goat. The rabbit sighed, prodded Henrietta with his gun. He turned on his flashlight, lit up the way ahead. No voices before her, only the call of the dead behind her.

I waited for you.

"It might've been easier if you gave up. You could have joined all your friends," the rabbit said, keeping pace. "It takes the weak, you know that? Weak in spirit. Weak in body. Weak in mind. That's what I know. So, if you resisted it, what does that tell me? You just haven't been broken yet. Well, we can fix that. Now move, before it finds a new voice to convince you."

Henrietta started to shuffle a little faster.

Only presence.

"Before you decide maybe it's worth it after all."

I waited.

27.

Soda expected some resistance in the lobby. What he found was chaos.

Doors wide open. People ran past, clutching suitcases, garbage bags, and antique lamps. Sirens wailed outside while Magellans fought over fares, waving phones at each other. No one even noticed Odie, trailing behind Soda on his chain. Soda had wrapped it around his belt to ensure the almost-coyote couldn't escape. Over the course of their ride downtown, Odie tore up most of the seats on the Shit Car. The raccoon spent the ride watching, attentive and unafraid. When they climbed off at Yonge, Soda could've sworn it waved goodbye.

"Man, hey you," Soda yelled, trying to get the attention of the doormen behind a huge slab of stone festooned with screens. "I need you to send me upstairs, I got an appointment."

They didn't even notice him; eyes glued to their screens. Soda saw the veins in their temples throbbing. Something was happening, maybe another sinkhole in the core swallowing another parking lot. He didn't care. Soda reached over the desk to grab the younger one by the collar.

"Look, you need to send me upstairs."

"Whoa, hey, let go of me."

Bodies streamed past.

"As soon as you send me up to see the big man, I'm all good. Send me up."

The older man looked over, reconsidered intervening.

"Big man? Look dude, I don't—"

Odie put his front paws up on the counter, snapped his jaws.

"You don't what?" Soda said. "Send me up to see Mr. Marigold."

"We're not allowed to . . ."

Soda gestured around the lobby, rattling Odie's chain. "You think *allowed* matters right now? You've got bigger problems than me. Send me up. I know the big man here doesn't take just any elevator. I'm patient but my little buddy here doesn't have the greatest understanding of time."

The two doormen exchanged sweaty glances. Odie growled.

"Alright, I can send you up, but I can't promise what'll happen when you get up there," the younger doorman said. Somewhere above them, a siren began moaning a deep bass note.

"I understand," Soda said. "You're the gatekeeper. And I'm the keyholder. So, open the gate."

Piss in the air again. He wasn't sure if it was Odie or the doormen or if the Shit Car itself had blessed him on his way out. "Take me to the elevator. I want to see what he sees."

Odie howled. No one could hear it over the cavalcade of horns outside.

§

312

Soda knew his father would've told him he was an idiot. The kid from the front desk used a heavy-duty pass key to summon the secret elevator, hands trembling while they waited for it to arrive. Soda snatched it off him before boarding the steel box. It was a struggle to drag Odie inside, scrabbling before he tumbled through the doors.

An idiot entering the lion's den without a plan. Stanley Marigold was still more like a myth than a person in Soda's brain, the son of an older, plainer evil, now king of a sinking kingdom. Even here in his steel box, Soda could feel Threshold searching for him, eyes in every corner, surveilling his movements, collecting all his minor crimes to build a dossier of failures. In the elevator, Soda Dalipagic allowed himself to finally cry, whether for his father or himself he couldn't be sure. It was easier to say it was for himself now, car destroyed, phone shattered somewhere out there in the weeds. A sickly kind of freedom, the kind that removes you from obligation to those around you, the freedom of the cast-off, the beaten, and what his father would have called the municipally damned. This was what the old man had felt, a great severing that silenced a connection to that older world where power held him aloft.

Soda's father was a warning of what happened when you played the game so long you forgot there were still stakes, that you could indeed lose, and once you did, there was no promise you'd be allowed back to the table. This was the old man's return to the game, refusing to engage with Threshold, headed to the other end of the table, where the old rules might still be applied. Soda held two cards in the elevator, both gifts. Ramji Nolan's Demon Drive, the last inheritance from a broken man. The other, a little jar of corrupted dirt his father was sure contained the future.

Soda wept standing upright. He let it roll over and through him, let it shake his chest and pound through his temples. Was the world this clean, this antiseptic, this removed from reality? Maybe he preferred the Shit Car. Maybe he preferred to be down there in the street, manholes boiling over, air full of exhaust and screams and endless rain that tasted like oil. Maybe that was his home now. The old world was a burnt-out husk. No security. No structure. The world spun on more than one axis. Soda wiped at his face, began to catalogue his demands for Marigold. The floors clicked past them. Odie curled up in a corner and waited for the ride in the skybox to end.

§

When the metal doors opened, Soda didn't bother restraining Odie. The creature took off down the hall. Soda followed, listening to the rattle of the chain. He held the drive in his hand, unsure of how to present it when he did meet the man behind the towers. The contents provided context, but it was his father who had explained the full story, the very human cost of opening up the ground. Under the mix of gaudy light fixtures and minimalist paintings on the walls, Soda reminded himself there was no need to show his hand during the first round. He shoved the cursed drive back into his pocket as he passed through an open door, blond wood, heavy brass, a strange combination like a portal to the past. The carpet was plush under his feet. The drive's false heat thrummed his thigh, a treasure map for all the corpses folded into its storage capacity.

He entered a kitchen; he was almost certain he had the wrong floor and that he was in whatever Marigold had decided the restaurant would be today. It appeared to change every few months as another chef de cuisine was fired. There were rumours it would be taken over by FODDER, whispers between the old Magellan drivers that Marigold was sticking it to Threshold and their fallout with the FODDER board. Soda glanced around the gleaming room. An industrial space, a sink for drowning, a fridge for bodies.

Everything was larger than it needed to be. Monsters didn't keep bodies in the fridge. They had assistants for that. They had staff. Real money didn't show itself on the street. Real power didn't flex itself; it barely lifted a finger.

A scream, a woman's scream, higher and higher and then nothing.

"Odie!" Soda said. "Odie, come here!"

Rounding the corner, he found Odie rolling back and forth on the thick, orange carpet before Stanley Marigold, the man himself kneeling down, hands rubbing the creature's belly like they were old friends. The carpet was ruined. The room was full of gigantic oak furniture and packing boxes. Bottles of scotch were scattered around the room, some empty, some shattered. Two women crouched behind the couch. One was Stanley's wife, a woman Soda recognized from press releases and the charity functions and the limited run of NHL-themed handbags she tried selling before the league began to implode. She only raised an eyebrow in his direction. The other one was younger, her clothes a little nicer, face somewhere closer to a sneer than a smile. She offered a tentative wave from her fortified position behind the massive couch.

"This belongs to you?" Stanley said. "What is it, a husky? Can't say I'm a fan of the chain, but it beats a prong collar, doesn't it? Supposed to be illegal, but think anyone follows the law?"

"I don't know what he is," Soda said, trying to reevaluate his approach. It wasn't supposed to go like this. "Be careful, he bites."

"They all do," Stanley said. "That's what they're designed to do, right? No matter how you train them, they're killers. Eating to live. Takes more than a few centuries to break that instinct. So, since you've interrupted us with such a lovely furry friend, who the fuck are you? You eating to live, son?"

Soda played his first card. "You got an email from me."

The women behind the couch laughed.

"I get a lot of emails," Stanley said. "Why should I know about any specific email? Was it about this dog? I'll buy it off you right now. How much you want, kid? I can go up to twenty, but that's all the cash I've got. If you take e-transfers, you can fuck off and I'll keep the damn dog."

Soda should've brought a knife or the brass knuckles he'd bought as a joke in high school, still far too big for his hands. They were in his Camry.

"I've got this," Soda said, pulling out Ramji's hard drive.

"Oh, that email," Stanley said, stretching to his full height. He was only wearing dress pants and suspenders. "You're Dale's kid."

"I'm Soda."

"Well, we do have something to talk about then. Although whatever you found on that drive, no one will believe it. Or if they do, they won't be able to prove it."

"And yet, you're still talking to me."

"I'm talking to you because you want something, isn't that right, Abigail? Sidney? You know Abigail Holstein, a good friend of mine. And my wife, of course. We're here planning for the future. Abigail's having some problems with her little project over by High Park."

"I don't—"

"Man," Stanley said. "Relax. You already made it up to the penthouse. Try to enjoy that. You got past the guards, though I suspect a number are dead now. You see a bald guy down there? Face always looks like he's pissed off."

"No. Just people running out of the place like ants."

"You ever pour hot water into an anthill? It's satisfying. Alright, well, you didn't go to the media, because you know no one believes anything anymore. Fake news, fake news, the angels are singing. The men like me, we're laughing. Unless it's about a dead girl, they love shit about dead girls, don't they, Abigail?"

Abigail sighed and came out from behind the couch, playing with a silver mask on a table. Sidney went back to packing up knick-knacks scattered between the bottles. "Unfortunately, they do. They love a dead girl."

"But more than one, or god forbid, a bunch of nameless bodies, buried under buildings that are decades old, the kind of bodies that don't have friends or families or recorded histories? Soda, let me tell you this — no one cares. You know that. And yet you come here, and I respect that. Even if it was your dad who sent the email, I respect it. In this room, we've all got dads who overreach. Or had dads. Even your little doggie here."

Stanley turned around, a small glass container with a blue plastic lid in his hand. A black chunk beat inside it like a heart. Abigail winced when she saw it, like a bad dream returned to the room. Sidney laughed and began dragging a bookcase away from the wall. Soda noticed the window open, black clouds rolling over the city like a weighted blanket.

"This stuff is really what that little hard drive from our mutual friend Ramji should be about. The extract of those bodies," Stanley said. "Imagine a living extract, life that only desires more life. Imagine if you could bottle that. Or imagine if you accidentally created that, that you knew about it and tried to hide it. Hunted it down, tried to control that narrative. Can you imagine?"

Soda pulled out his own little container. It looked the same, but it didn't beat like a heart.

"I think I have something like that."

Abigail drew in her breath. Sidney continued to drag the bookcase. Stanley cocked his head. Odie rolled around on the carpet between them. The room smelled like him now.

"Not as advanced as mine, but happy to see you've some idea of what we're up against," Stanley said. "More than a little email, hey? Where is your old man?"

"Threshold didn't like us taking the dirt, so they took him."

Stanley laughed. "That's bold. Stakes keep rising, don't they? Rising and rising. By took him I imagine you mean by force. Their security team? They have no idea, do they?"

"Something like that."

Stanley walked over to the window, smacking the container with his open palm in time with its beat. "This thing is worming into every building you see out there. Look outside. It's out there and it's infiltrating us. It is us, really, a new version of us. A fungal humanity."

Abigail snorted. "Is that how you're going to brand it?"

"Let's talk about the root of all behaviour," Stanley continued, ignoring her. "The root of everything we do. Every living thing too, even whatever's in this container."

Soda set his own container down on the couch. Nothing had gone to plan. This wasn't any different. They were both playing with things they didn't understand. "I'm listening."

"There're three reasons behind all mammal behaviour in this world. Maybe all living things. Let's see." Stanley's hand, beating against the plastic lid, keeping time with the black heart.

"Getting enough to eat, now that's one. Obvious, but important."

The black blob inside like his father's dirt, but now alive.

"Number two is therefore, avoiding being eaten. Again, not a surprise, but relevant to our current situation."

Abigail yawned. Sidney tried dragging the bookcase a little further, but it wouldn't budge. She took a break and poured another drink. "Just get to the point, Stan. Moving truck will be here in a couple hours and I need you to decide what stays and what goes."

"But the real big one, let's call it the third prime directive — well, that's reproduction."

Stanley set the container down and pulled on the silver mask. It hid his features, so only a voice emerged from behind the veneer.

The thin horns crackled with static, the eyes went a bright green. "So, which one is it, son of Dale? Which one drives you? Is it hunger? Is it fear? Or do you want something more? Something you haven't seen yet?"

Soda wanted to answer him. No words came out. Odie grunted.

"What I'm asking you is: do you want a job or not? Abigail has the old money. Sidney and I have the empire. And you have the knowledge, don't you? At least a little bit. At least enough to make my life difficult if you took that knowledge somewhere else. Tell me what you think."

Soda watched Stanley Marigold pry the lid off the container. He didn't realize it was going to be a job interview. Odie tore up a strip of the carpet like loose skin.

"You decide. The future hangs before us," Stan said. The bookcase crashed to the floor. He didn't flinch. Sidney laughed, pulling out her own goat mask. "As it's prone to do."

28.

Buildings grew from seeds. Single, perfect little seeds planted in the foundations before the towers sprouted. A simple system, easily replicated. Everyone understands what a tree is, the gardener's father told him once, the two men knee-deep in the mud, a wet bundle in a blue tarp between them. We're planting for the future, acknowledging the wound we're creating and offering up part of ourselves in the process, our blood soothing the earth. You cannot take without giving. It catches up with you.

The gardener's tools opened up a wide hole in the bottom of The Marigold. He'd never done this before, but his father told him stories about other practitioners who'd revoked their seeds after payment terms weren't followed to the letter. One snuck into churches whenever they were sold for condos, removing what he considered sacred seeds, fragments of bone and hair and dust. Dust was human. We breathed each other in every day, clung to the insides of our neighbour's lungs. Adding another seed though, that was something you only did when you wanted to upset the balance, to make a point. It was often too risky to pull off once the building was completed, leaving certain practitioners unfulfilled as towers rose that betrayed their original design.

Adding a second seed before the building even settled could only spell disaster. The gardener knew this, even as he worked deeper into the ground, shovel clanging. The Marigolds hadn't listened at first, Stanley believing this was just an archaic bit of theatre. He only began listening to his father when men started tumbling off the scaffolding and windowpanes shattered on arrival. Investors began to pull their money and journalists began to sniff around the Marigolds' first grasp at luxury development. And so, the younger Stanley returned to the fold, joining his father in the half-finished parking garage, a hole in the ground for a seed that would never fully settle. It was better than nothing, the gardener told them. And at least I know you won't make the same mistake again. We're trying to grow trees here, not weeds.

Join us.

A voice down below. The gardener grabbed his shovel off the concrete and yanked the seed in the tarp after him into the hole. Two seeds competing for the same resources promised a rupture somewhere higher up the tower. His father was clear about making sure the price they paid was singular. One body, one building. Part of the old math he didn't understand.

You fed us. You made us. You are us.

The gardener turned on the light strapped to his work jacket, sliding further into the cavern he'd created only a few years before. It had vastly expanded since then, stretching further than his light travelled. Down here, a vast, dripping pool of fluid, the stench of so many seeds freed from their moorings, a hidden sea of flesh and lake water combined into a slurry that gathered around his knees, clinging like a second skin. This was not what the gardener intended. There was no rationale for what he saw. He clutched the fresh seed against himself, listening to the fluid dead speak inside his head.

You made us.

He wanted to explain it wasn't just him, he was part of something bigger. An ancient vocation almost forgotten, like the cobblers and the butchers and the hatmakers, skills passed down from fathers to sons, old tendrils of the patriarchy erased by their own futile nature in the face of progress. The gardener was the last keeper of an esoteric knowledge the Marigolds and their ilk needed if they wanted this city to stay upright longer than a season.

"It's spread out here," a woman's voice said, monotone. This one wasn't in his head. "Not as strong, only up to my ankles. Can't we go back? Tell him what we saw."

"He knows you're holding back. Keep moving, Cathy, I know it's down here, it has to be. He wants the core of it," a man's voice barked. "He wants the source."

Cathy's head was covered in a heavy metal mask with horns attached, the eyes glowing a light purple as she pushed through the muck. The gardener turned off his light, watching these figures from his perch just below the fresh hole, hidden in the cloying shadows. The man wore a white rabbit mask, ears slicked back over the head. The gardener recognized the mask, the contempt in his voice. Hans himself, the Marigolds' errand boy. The gardener had no mask.

"I don't hear any voices," Hans said. These new ghosts were illuminated by their own little lights, fireflies in the swamp. After Cathy, what looked like a child and a decaying seed, shuffling together, wrapped into one another.

No absence.

The voices were doing their best to imitate his father, but they didn't have his words. He was likely in there somewhere, a strand of flesh inside the stew.

Just presence.

322

"Consider yourself lucky," Cathy said. "It will come when you feel there's no other way."

The other bodies shook in agreement. The gardener watched Cathy run her hands along the support beams. He wanted to tell her it wasn't supposed to be like this. The world she saw down here was an aberration, an insult to the old ways. He wanted to show her this was an art, not just a biological accident that was now something else entirely, a sentient hunger — a devouring.

Just presence.

"Where is it? If it's still speaking, tell it we want to join," Hans said, voice higher and hoarser. The glint of the gun in his hand, flashlights sputtering across his mask. "Have the girl ask for her father again or her friends. Bring it back."

"It's not a dog, it doesn't do tricks," Cathy snapped back. The gardener's seed began slipping from sweaty hands. Cathy turned toward the sound. "It changes. It adapts. It strategizes. The idea it might even have a source . . . that just can't be true."

Hans tilted his mask. "Why not?"

"Each expression of it contains the whole. It's a fluid consciousness. There's no source. No brain," Cathy said, nodding her goat head. "The mistake is thinking it's like us. It's not. And you destroyed how many . . ."

"I didn't destroy anything," Hans said. "I did what I was told to do. You've done the same."

"And what did you find?" Cathy said. "What did you think you were going to find? A pulsing brain? A pile at the centre of the map? The pile is everywhere. It doesn't need a source. It lives at any size. It consumes. And then it knows. It knows. It knows you and me — anyone who touched us, it touched too."

"I don't care!" Hans said. "I need something to bring upstairs. Show me what I need to take with me, or I'll leave you both down here. Show me a fucking result or you'll join it."

The gardener slipped on his perch as he tried to creep further back into the darkness.

"Did you hear that?"

Hans spun toward him. The seed's tarp slipped out of the gardener's grip, sloshing the body down into the goo below. The gardener was only a few feet off the ground, hands outstretched, caught in the act.

"You little freak, what're you doing here?" Hans laughed, clocking the gardener's empty features. "Trying to get rid of the evidence? The scam you have running on all these guys, man, I wish I thought of it. You feel me?"

The gardener didn't believe there was anything interesting about himself. He was a tool designed for a specific process, forged and moulded into the traditions. His kills were practical in nature, rarely ever evolving into pure bloodlust or desire. He had a fondness for his seeds.

"I'm trying to fix it," the gardener said.

"You already dropped your payload. Come on down, we've got stuff to show Stan now, don't we? You fucked up big-time, buddy. You got him talking about biological weapons. He's gotta get down here and see this nightmare for himself, don't you think? Maybe get a refund."

The gardener swung the shovel. You weren't supposed to interrupt him. Hans staggered, blood pouring out of his left ear, one of the eyes in his mask dangling loose. The gardener hit him again. There wasn't a great angle. The first shot should have taken him out immediately. He felt his father breathing down his neck, nostrils flaring in disappointment. The Wet in his ear, asking him why he failed.

You had so much promise.

The goat mask watched him but didn't move to help. Neither did the girl. She was captivated, so distracted she didn't notice the fresh bodies rising behind her. They carried no lights — they were one with the Wet itself, moving through it like well-honed predators who hunted with sound instead of sight. Creatures that only existed in the underground, moulded into warriors by whatever hive mind this goop possessed. The gardener stood over Hans's scrambling body, watching his light fizzle in the ooze, the Wet claiming him like a shallow bath, drowning in less than six inches of slurry. What knowledge would Hans bring? What memories could he provide? It made the gardener sick to see that individuality drained away, even from a bent little man like Hans, the body becoming fuel for someone else's pyre.

Alone. Always alone.

No one asked to be part of this collective. No one asked to die one hundred feet beneath the earth, drowning in your own blood. The gardener used his shovel to steady himself, watching the larger shape move past Cathy and the girl, a creature made almost purely of the Wet itself. His seeds got more respect in death than the Wet would ever offer. The weak light strapped to the gardener's chest revealed the dripping mass had been a person once, or a collection of persons. Pieces slid and slopped over the bones, realigning into faces he could recognize.

"You . . . made me," the shape said.

The gardener considered climbing back up out of his hole. He'd dropped the seed down here somewhere. The tower was already doomed, the Wet working its way up the structure's innards. There was something familiar about the thing's head, a vision on a subway platform blurring into an impression of a person.

"Yes, I made you."

Behind the thing, Cathy and the girl huddled together. It should've attacked her, dragged her down into the muck. The creature spoke again instead, showing a pink tongue. "Who was I?"

"I don't know your name," the gardener said. It spoke like they were old friends. "I don't like names, they confuse things. You served a purpose."

"Who?" the shape spoke again, chunks dripping from what had been lips.

"The question you're asking is where, not who," the gardener said. "I can remember . . . I never thought I'd see one of you again. This isn't how things are done."

The shape nodded, chin plopping off into the goo before another chin sprouted to replace it.

You made us too.

So many buildings, so many towers. He'd planted seeds all over the city, rumbling around to building sites in his van, gently depositing his bounty in the earth. He didn't remember names. Addresses stuck. He gave up on the smaller buyers after a while, plazas, grocery stores, car dealerships. They didn't understand what they were buying. It was the towers that needed his gift. Each burial was notched inside his skull.

"157 Queens Quay West, I think they called that tower The Ambition. What a name."

The shape moaned or laughed. The gardener couldn't tell. "Ambition?"

"Didn't say it was a good name. I don't name these places. Names change even when addresses remain."

You are us.

"How'd you get free?" the gardener said, resigned to his position. The voices of the Wet crept into him in a low chorus. It believed he was the creator, the origin of its intelligence. He wanted to explain he was only a bag man, a functionary. Nature was the one who made them, tearing his careful gifts from their special tombs, spinning them through the guts of the city until they were a slurry of souls. They pulled at him, asking the gardener to join Hans, to submerge himself inside them, surrender his voice to the whole. The floor burbled around him.

"I woke up in a tunnel . . . dead."

"You were, Queens Quay," the gardener said. "I remember. A long scar along the jaw, you said it was from a baseball bat. Your mother stitched it up for you in her kitchen. Feet too small, said you bought all your shoes in the kids' section. I remember. I always remember each one. Had to burn those shoes in the ravine. You were dead. You still are."

"I am," the shape said, "Cabeza."

"Alright, Cabeza. Doesn't matter, does it? You're still dead."

Cathy and the girl crept around the edge of their argument, eyeing the hole behind the gardener, the only available escape route from the Wet slowly filling the cavern around them, speaking in its own tongues his brain couldn't hear.

"Not dead. Not alive."

Other shapes rose out of the Wet, other seeds for buildings he could recognize, rippling masses responding to the faint light. 827 Wellington Street West, a girl, one who smiled a lot to show off the gap in her teeth, hated the Blue Jays. 900 Niagara Street, an elderly man who asked for mushroom soup every day until the gardener finally ended his life with a plastic bag in the shower, holding him under the water until it ended. 2810 Islington, a boy who had a tattoo of a tiger wearing a crown of thorns on his neck, who took the gardener to church the morning before he died, a quick snap of the neck at the kitchen table.

You made us. You are us.

"Are these all your friends?" the gardener said to Cabeza.

"Not me," Cabeza gurgled. The girl and Cathy behind the gardener now, almost within striking distance. "But wants me to be."

The gardener realized Cabeza was right, the other shapes weren't as defined as it was, they shuddered and splattered into one another, struggling to hold cohesive forms. He glanced down at Hans, saw the Wet already working its way through his eyes and mouth, filling him up, emptying him back out, integrating him into the whole.

327

You made us. You join us. Us.

They weren't all lives he'd taken. Too many he didn't recognize. The Wet gathered every body it could reach in the wet earth, harvesting from unmarked graves, sanctified cemeteries, family crypts, and mausoleums, to become a new kind of life, rejecting human narrative.

"You," Cabeza said. "Their . . . architect."

"No," the gardener said. "You do not get to do this."

"You no longer make the rules," Cathy said, lifting the catatonic girl through the hole behind him into the tower's gut. A potential seed. Another missed opportunity. "That part is over."

"You," Cabeza said, gesturing with tentacle arms around the massive subbasement of The Marigold. "I am . . . not ready."

Us.

The gardener didn't fight the shapes. He let 525 Lawrence Avenue West and 328 Morningside Avenue wrap their shuddering limbs around his neck. Under the slurry, it was warm. He watched Cabeza slip away, up and out of the hole the gardener had created. More viscous shapes piled on top of him, blocking his view, filling his eyes and ears and mouth with a sickly-sweet fluid, drowning him in their want, their need, their singularity. The gardener gave in willingly, losing his voice to the Wet, the constant mantra it repeated. It took everything he knew. He had no father now. He felt his heart flutter and then stop, felt each node inside his brain click off in sequence, felt it all until there was only one feeling left, a sole imperative to transmit from his husk down here in the darkness, calling out through The Marigold's pipes.

Us.

29.

Stanley saw the appeal of horses now, why they enchanted his siblings, leading them so far astray. Horses allowed you to invest all your hopes and dreams inside a living thing, all your rage and your inadequacy, and then set it loose to outrun time for a little while, potentially making some profit in the process. And even when it died, when its leg shattered due to a millisecond of. hesitation, there was always another horse to replace it.

An animal's life was finite — horses were expected to die in pursuit of their goals. It was built into the sport, outside the racetrack in the form of veterinarians' teams waiting to pump the animals full of chemicals to put off their fate a little while longer, injections for their joints, steroids for their constant pain, running until they collapsed for good and were carted off into the dark. A brutal, useless business, but everyone understood its losses were inherent.

No one wanted to admit a building could fail, not unless there was something bigger and better to replace it. The world of towers didn't allow for failure. Failure meant death for someone, not just a horse. A tower that fell removed itself from the skyline. A tower that fell was a judgement. Like a bridge or a tunnel, you did not build a tower so it would crumble, even though one day you knew it would. You built a tower to outlast yourself. And so, what happened when those towers became burdens, when the Marigold empire was more rot than growth, ceilings collapsing on tenants and roofs leaking through the winter months, the mould growing so quickly you could trace it hour to hour, its hunger so similar to a human's, its need to expand, to consume, to take over like looking in a mirror to find your basest impulses, the twitch in your eye before you struck your prey. What happened then, with your father dead and everything he ever cared for crumbling in your formerly capable hands? What did you do then?

Horses couldn't solve this.

"Do you want the job or not?" Stanley said from behind his silver goat mask to Soda. He wondered if he should've put on a shirt. Soda made this more interesting, putting Abigail's position into question. What did she really know? How much did they need her money, all tied up in family estates? Soda's father knew all about the bodies, all about sacrifice. He would have passed it down to the boy. There are secrets only meant for fathers and sons, Stanley knew that well. He was alone now. He needed an apprentice. Sidney would critique his choices later, from behind her own silver mask, the horns curled like a ram's. She wasn't expecting a fourth party.

"It's a simple question."

The age of the tower was coming to its end. The Marigold/Dundee Corporation needed to diversify, needed to expand its reach. The process would remain the same. Like any landlord or developer, Stanley had to find market inefficiencies — gaps he could identify and then act to close them, buying land with potential while it was

330

cheap, selling it off once the higher value was commonly acknow-ledged. When the economic landscape changed, you changed with it. When the value disappeared overnight, so did you. "I don't actually care if you're good at it or not. What matters to me is loyalty. Prove you're in for the long haul."

He opened up the desk in front of the window, pulled out a second silver horned mask. The floor was covered in water from the rain. The mask looked sadder than the one he wore, the lips turned down into a frown. It was supposed to be for his father. Too late now though, plans were changing. The Wet was here inside the tower, it was no longer a rumour or a ghost. A great and powerful thing. A collated collection of souls and memories, all bleating to become one.

He watched the chunk of Wet burble on the desk before him. A wave of alienation and isolation underneath the fragile bones of the city now made into something not quite flesh. Was that really a voice you heard in the pipes, calling you to join them? Was that really a spore travelling up your nose? A parasite, but a human one, or at least one that had once been human. Amorphous, amoral, ahistorical — an abject thing that required only one of those three primary directives — reproduction. Unmitigated growth.

"Which of you wants the mask? Only one left to go around."

Abigail reached to snatch it from his grasp, tripping over her own feet. Soda smashed his own jar on the floor, sending Odie, the beautiful wild dog, into a frenzy. Sidney tried to hold it down, dragging her body across the floor. Lamps shattered and ornate chairs selected by Sidney so many months before disintegrated under its touch. Her mask barely clung to her face.

"I don't know how long they'll continue to work," Stanley said. "The Wet is always learning, don't you think? That was what Threshold couldn't understand. You don't control it."

The mask dangled from Stanley's finger as the black heart thudded and beat on the desk, spreading across its surface, searching for people to incorporate. The dirt on the floor responded to its call, threading through the carpet. He watched the two sources seek each other out as Soda jumped over the coffee table to grab the mask, taking a firm elbow to the chin from Abigail. Sidney's mask blared like a smoke alarm.

"This isn't a game, Stanley!" Abigail said. "This stuff will kill us."

"I know that," Stanley replied. The masks were prototypes. They'd need to be continually refined. You had to mute the monster. Another revenue stream, another way to maximize return on tragedy. A building wouldn't do anymore. The very act of holding onto a property was immoral. He reconciled himself to that years ago, welcomed his role as the villain. To be an owner, to be a land-lord, meant someone had to be subjugated. The other developers who talked around those facts were kidding themselves, doing their best to put some polish on an ancient profession. Humans couldn't survive without a roof over their head. A building gave you more time, sometimes decades. To deny anyone that, well, you'd need to be a monster, wouldn't you?

"I want to see it in action," Stanley continued. "It seems to change, every time. It seems to know what happened before. What do you do with a parasite that remembers?"

It's important to know what you are, his father said. You're not a hero. At your heart, to succeed in any business, you need to be a good liar. You need to find something other people don't have and trick them into wanting it. Or, even better, take something you know they need, and offer them only a taste.

"You stupid fuck," Soda said, doing his best to shove Abigail to the floor. "You're going to get us all killed. Did you . . . let go! . . . Did you know that?"

Sidney's helmet continued to bleat and screech. She was trying to pry it off her face even as it malfunctioned, bucking against her fingers. Odie whined and skittered away into a corner.

"Maybe," Stanley said, stepping away from the window, the one remaining mask still clinging to his fingertips. "I've definitely been known to make reckless decisions. I like risks."

The pit where Marigold II was supposed to grow was filled with this stuff. He kept an eye on the two grappling bodies, Abigail's rage somehow giving her the upper hand for a second as Soda struggled on the floor, unable to hit her as hard as he should. A sentimental boy. It might be useful to have that kind of help. He was brave or dumb enough to bring that drive with him, to try to force Stanley's hand. Ramji was weaker, had cut and run instead.

"Stan, don't do this to us," Abigail begged, grinding the Dalipagic boy's head into the carpet. She was all teeth and nails, blood dripping from the corner of her mouth. They were rolling in the Wet now, it clung to their bodies wherever it found purchase. "Give me the mask."

Sidney was now trying to smash her mask off against the furniture, a new development. The dog barked and circled her body. It could smell the distress.

"It's not so much the mask as the position, Abby," Stanley said. "We need to have a whole new outlook here. We need to think about using this stuff as a tool. How do we export it?"

This was what he had learned from his father and the gardener in the upside-down world beneath The Marigold, the tarp-wrapped body descending into the blackened earth under the harsh beams of their flashlights. Bodies were tools. So was the Wet, even in this newer, vicious form. You used the tools you had to benefit yourself, whether it was an interest rate or an act of god exception in your insurance policy. You found the advantage and you pressed it, like

Soda was doing now, hands locked behind Abigail's right knee, bending it against its nature.

"You don't have to kill each other," Stanley said. "Maybe it won't consume you. Maybe you'll be able to reject it. I've heard crazier things. It needs you to need it, maybe?"

Abigail bucked Soda loose, delivering a few decisive kicks to his throat. This was better than his usual competitions with Sidney, maybe something new they would take up after they fled this city. She almost had the mask off now, its alarms ringing right through him. A defective model.

It was clear the Marigold/Dundee Corporation would need to realign itself around a new product. Land was only reliable as long as it was stable. Stanley had heard whispers here and there, his own father telling him to finance the towers of others, collecting his own fees in the process, leaving them to flail once the projects began to go belly up. The ground was rotting.

Soda hooked an arm around Abigail's leg, bringing her crashing to the floor. The Wet continued its progress, moving across their skin. They didn't seem to notice or care. Stanley Marigold continued to waltz around the outer perimeter of the room. He placed a hand under Sidney's mask and began to pry it off. She stopped lashing out, bent to his will. Maybe instead of a penthouse, he'd go live in a forest somewhere, acknowledge that nature had the upper hand.

"You stupid child," Abigail snapped, digging a spiked heel into Soda's chin. "You don't even know what you're playing with. Give me the goddamn mask!"

"Oh, you're talking to me?" Stanley said from behind his own mask. "I like that, Abigail. Your aggression always impressed Sidney. Right, Sid?"

Her mask refused to come off. Sidney's body stopped fighting, and sat down, defeated.

"Oh, looks like we'll have to get the maintenance guys."

He'd never be satisfied by the trees though. He knew that. If the Wet was the new material condition of this place, then he would be its master, just like Threshold had tried to do down by the water. He wouldn't try to understand it; wouldn't try to pretend he knew what it wanted.

Stanley didn't know how to build a tower either. He had never operated a crane or poured a foundation or killed anyone with his bare hands, and yet, all of those steps were necessary to construct a building. He only wore a hard hat on the site because it was mandatory, but the building was his at the end of the day. He wasn't the architect or the engineer or the labourer. The tower didn't belong to them, despite all their best efforts. It was The Marigold, his namesake, even in this tilted incarnation. His money, his palace, his flower glowing over the city, only surpassed by the flimsy toothpick of the CN Tower. Sidney could join him if she wanted. She would need to bring something better to the table than Abigail, rolling in her own filth. Stanley didn't need to know or understand the Wet at all, he only needed to direct it, make it his own, claim and name it. Bottle it, sell it, refine it.

A human poison to be deployed around the globe, to rot out cities from the very ground beneath, rearticulating the structure of the world, sending ancient centres of commerce and human creativity into a deep, dark depression from which they might never emerge again. The possibilities flowed before him, even as he watched the two bodies struggle with each other through the portholes of his mask, their skin on skin, their blood on blood, mixing with the Wet on the orange carpeting. This was a fallen place. He would never tear it down though. Leave it like a cursed temple, its endless uninhabited suites, its unsold floors, its broken tiles and misaligned bathroom pipes. Let future explorers discover what it meant to challenge the sky, the cost of what it meant to dig so deep into the earth that you had to paint the foundation in blood.

When Stanley Marigold turned back to the struggling bodies on the ground, they were no longer struggling and no longer on the ground. They were practically next to him, two hungry faces with blood and dirt smeared into their skin. The dog howled with the storm outside.

"We've learned a lot," Abigail said, spitting blood. "Don't you hear it?"

"The voices," Soda said. "They know what you are."

Stanley didn't hear it, not with the mask over his face. Abigail wrapped an arm around his neck and yanked the heavy mask off his head, slapped it on her own face. Soda leaned his full, heavy weight into Stanley's body and removed the other silver mask from his hand, yanking it over his own bloated features. "We need these."

Stanley tried to fight back, but their combined weight was too much. Sidney slumped on the floor, her mask blurting red then orange, then yellow, a pattern of distress. They dragged him over to the open window. The floor was wet and slippery; he lost his balance and slammed to the ground. They backed off, two horned silver masks without expression, still wary of one another. Blood ran down Abigail's shins. Soda's throat looked partially slashed. Stanley didn't realize Abigail's fingernails were that long. He'd underestimated her. It made him smile.

"We decided to make an executive decision," Abigail said. "Sidney will understand, I promise. She just needs to get used to the mask. This is how we live now."

Odie approached and began licking his face on the floor. In Stan's head, a voice gathered, trickling into his ears, the black heart he'd thrown to the floor now speaking a language beyond words, one that penetrated to the centre of him. Stanley couldn't allow this.

No absence. Only presence.

336

A voice attempting to lure him into its collective, to subsume himself into the whole.

Ours.

The words sickened him there on the floor, his body rejecting their claim, even as the Wet moved toward him, its tendrils seeking out every orifice. It wanted him to join, to release himself from his single self, to surrender fully and completely. He would dissipate and become part of something bigger, something stranger.

Ours.

His masked betrayers stumbled back when he rose to his feet. He could feel the Wet insisting, probing at the edges of his consciousness, looking for a weak spot, an old memory, a failure to exploit, anything to deny his sense of self. It dug deep, clambering into his childhood that was more like an abattoir. Sidney couldn't help him here, trapped in her own mask, her own delusion.

Us. Ours.

No escape. The Wet was inside him. He turned toward the open window. This was not what he had planned, but being a Marigold meant you kept your options open. Abigail screamed behind him as he let go of the window frame, body plunging down through cold air, the Wet unable to compete with the sensation of falling. Stanley's life didn't flash before his eyes as he tumbled toward the street, shirtless and without socks. He didn't cry out for his dead father to save him or his concussed wife to forgive him. Stanley fell from the top of his namesake with one thought in his mind, one mantra running like a ticker down the centre of his brain, even as he plummeted to his final resting place, skull colliding with a black GMC's engine block.

Mine.

30.

Once Jasmine asked her what a world might look like without obligation. They lay together in the apartment, moonlight streaming through the window, the chug of the highway and the hoot of trains fading into the background like the sound of their blood, the rise and fall of their chests in unison. Usually, Cathy was the big spoon, but this time, Jasmine's arms were wrapped tight around her. Imagine a world where you owed no one anything, she said. Imagine a world with just me, outside this city. Imagine a place so far from everyone that when we die no one even knows it happened. That is what I want, Jasmine said, pulling Cathy's neck tight against her lips. To only be obligated to you. To only know you. To leave this city and all its tiny tethers in the dust.

I want that too, Cathy said, pressing into her body, absorbing her warmth. These were the few hours outside reality, sketches of ways they could be. Cathy didn't know if she believed it.

"You can't slow down."

Cathy had never been hunted before. Men had pursued her, women had stalked her, but this sensation consumed her, filled her with a boiling dread that didn't settle when she stopped to catch her breath. She followed the shambling creature before her, a mass of gloppy pieces that called itself a person. Her mask was heavy and cumbersome, but it made the world tolerable for now. She pretended what she saw wasn't real, only an elaborate hallucination, even as the Wet consumed the city around her, pouring like a wave down the streets, dragging civilians down into its depths. After it absorbed the man below The Marigold, it was like the entire city surrendered to its embrace, the Wet pushing up through the soil and the concrete, shattering water mains and tearing cables loose from the ground. The man down there, a blank little man, he recognized so many faces in the Wet. She had watched them call to him, watched him embrace them willingly.

Sidewalks, bike lanes, official parking spots — none were spared. Bodies floating beneath the building, limbs and lips and other unknown parts bobbing in the slurry, asking for her to join them. Hans's face appearing to sneer at her, the men from Threshold dangling their hands out as if to pull her up and out with them. The collective memory of a place draining down into a single impulse, a mass of longing. She hadn't slept in two days. Her legs shuddered when she thought about them too much, as if her calves acknowledging the effort was harder than the act itself.

"I can't do this by myself. If I can keep going . . . you have to do it too."

The girl said her name was Henrietta, like she was some ancient time traveller stranded in this drowning city, unfazed by the horrors of the future because the past was still somehow worse. Worse than this — could such things exist? She didn't seem to need a mask. The Wet couldn't convince her to join it, or maybe it had something else in store for her, a crueller seduction.

It wore you down. It showed you all you lost.

After she ran her first marathon, Jasmine claimed humans were the original persistence hunters, said this while on the toilet, talking to Cathy from the other room. How they would follow animals until their hearts gave out or they died from exhaustion, implying she too could do the same. You had to be incredibly naïve to believe that, Cathy told her. The Wet didn't care about marathons, half or otherwise, split times or shoes or whether or not the events were too corporate these days. There were no days for the Wet, only a now, a persistence that had nothing human in it except its inability to turn back. It trudged forward, occasionally casting up human shapes, faces closer to approximations than reality, the lips and teeth just holes where the screams came out in little ruptures. Cathy saw shadows of Jasmine in its spastic form, but she was sure the others didn't. Jasmine asking her to please slow down. The Wet became who you lost. It threw shapes after you, shapes you knew. The Wet knew which wounds to press.

Cathy and Henrietta followed the shambling creature that called itself Cabeza, its voice a nightmarish sound that scraped back and forth across Cathy's brain, pinging off every sensation of revolt and disgust that she owned, reeking of the dead, more vivid than the grey slurry. But Cabeza was not dead and not undead, a bug trapped inside a light fixture, rattling around. It still knew what it was to live. There was no crude approximation.

"It hungers . . ."

This was the theory. The Wet needed to consume to live.

"My mom's probably somewhere in there," Cathy said, trying to throw out names and ideas, anyone but Jasmine bobbing up beside her in the crush. It was like the running of the bulls, but in slow motion. The cruelty was approximate. "Everyone I ever knew is probably in there."

Henrietta laughed, rage bubbling beneath. There was so little Cathy could offer her, barely able to keep up the pace. "Me too. It'd be nice to see some of them again. Cherry, you fucker, come out of there. Show me your face again! Speak to me, tell me what I'm missing!"

A death march. To stop was to surrender. Henrietta pulled Cathy along by the hand, leading her down toward the lake. What was once the harbourfront was now sunken landscape. Front Street, that last outpost of resolve against the rising water levels. Sirens rang in the distance, dogs screeched, police cars attempted to drive through the Wet and floundered in its slushy embrace, the fluid seeping up the windows, searching for openings, entering through any crack to offer up a new way of being, a simple surrender or a death by drowning. You decide.

Her phone still worked, texts and emails fluttering into her hand as it vibrated. The office trying to reassure everyone even as the centre of the city belched up its innards, even as more towers began to teeter and lean out over the streets, their roots corrupted. Behind them, the Wet created more simulacrums, people weeping, people begging them to join. Like they had with that man beneath The Marigold, their original creator, the gardener of forgotten graves.

Graves were old scars reopened. It was Jasmine who told her about the scurvy cases that cropped up sometimes in the older apartment buildings in the north end, or in the student housing with the more solitary boys. It wasn't only teeth and gums that fell apart. Without the right nutrients, the lack of vitamins led to formerly healed scars transforming back into open wounds, fresh opportunities for reinfection and potential amputation. Sometimes they found them in time, a neighbour who was a little too nosy poking their head inside a door. Sometimes it was too late, especially with the elderly, the bodies roasting in their own juices in the summer months until someone complained. This was the story that Cathy knew, but Jasmine gave it a human face, one that tracked down next of kin and explained what happened, walking that tightrope between compassion and practicality Cathy could never master.

No absence. Just presence.

It still tore at her ears through the mask, low, level whispers that massaged her brain, tried to tell her it was okay to lie down here in the street, to make peace with all the paths her life could have taken. They would all lead here anyway, right? A long wait for the same end.

"I used to pretend if I climbed down one of those holes, I would end up on the other side," Henrietta said, squeezing Cathy's hand, reminding her they were still here, still together, walking past burning storefronts and flooded condo lobbies, people gazing down at them from glass cells above, afraid and uncertain. "I didn't think I was going to end up in China, I wasn't that stupid, but I thought there might be another place at the bottom. A hollow earth. An older place."

"But there isn't," Cathy said. "I know what you mean."

Somewhere, another explosion, a chorus of screams that rose and fell and rose again. They continued walking. No one else outside. The grey slurry followed, hungry, searching for new sources of energy. They caught glimpses of the human shapes it made behind them. Cathy spotted old friends from grade school, her first supervisor in public health, his bald pate unable to shine under the rain. She only saw reflections — the real thing remained behind her. Cabeza hadn't slowed. It plodded forward, setting an example. Henrietta's grip tightened as the rain continued, road slick with garbage.

No absence, just presence.

A truck overturned ahead. No people, only what they'd left behind.

No obligation.

Jasmine pushing through the noise.

I don't blame you. You always tied yourself to this place.

Jasmine's face a real shape before her, rising like a snake with a column from the concrete, wrapping itself around her brain, slipping its tongue inside her ear, clutching her body tight.

I don't blame you for offering me up.

"I didn't offer you up."

I was a risk worth taking.

"I didn't . . ."

I am still a risk worth taking.

"Please."

Jasmine's image shuddering, the mirage unsustainable. *No obligation. No expectations. No absence.*

Cathy crumbled to her knees, tried to hold the goop against her chest, felt it worming against her chin, attempting to find a way inside her. It circled her leg, the same spot it first grabbed her before Jasmine interfered, breaking the tether between the two, setting Cathy free, and for what?

Just presence.

"Come on," Henrietta said, turning back, slapping a hand against Cathy's mask. "It's not whoever you think it is. Don't look back now. We can stay out here for a little while. As long as you got that mask on, I'm assuming you still want to live, right? If you didn't, you'd take it off."

No obligations.

They waded out into the shallow waves of what had once been the Queens Quay, the freezing water smashing against their shins. Cabeza led the way, its shambling form already deteriorating in the unsteady surf. Its left shoulder disappeared, the glop unable to reconstitute against the concussive force. The lake was eating up Cabeza, piece by piece. She could see white bone poking through its gooey corpse, even in the dark. The bone glowed as if radio-active. The exposed piece was like a lure and they were prey. She moved against the instinct that told her to back away from Cabeza, that told her the water was too cold and she wasn't a good enough swimmer. She pressed forward, leaving the city to shriek behind her, buildings tumbling, bodies wailing, the Wet swirling in search of a drain. It was so much easier when it was only a fungus.

No absence. Just presence.

"Don't wait for me," she said, but then Henrietta grabbed her hand again and pulled her forward. She wouldn't relent. Jasmine's voice was barely present, now just listing off all the places they dreamed of travelling together, all the homes they would never own, the pets that would die on them over the years, a small graveyard of their own. Jasmine describing their mutual decline, their home in disrepair, garden overgrown. Henrietta dragged Cathy deeper.

No absence.

Once they were close to twenty feet away from the misshapen shore, they turned to look back at the grey, slouching wave that had followed them, the cars and mailboxes and broken tents the Wet carried with it. Human bodies in the wreckage, old flags, signage, the occasional yelping dog, birds' nests, fire hydrants, electrical wires hissing and snapping at each other in the grey mass, a bubbling expanse with human faces that looked right through them, unable to move any further, unable to consume them and incorporate their bodies, their minds, their memories. It lurched along the edge of the water.

"Fears the lake," Cabeza said. It shrank with each lapping wave. "Dilution . . ."

"You believe that?" Henrietta said, lungs struggling to get the words out. "I don't."

Cathy didn't say anything. Her toes barely touched the ground.

"Still speaks to me . . ." Cabeza burbled.

"And it's telling you it can't join you?" Henrietta said, teeth chattering.

"Says killing myself."

"But you're already . . ." Cathy said, before closing her mouth.

"Killing myself for good," Cabeza replied. Water took more of it away, exposing more bone.

No absence. Just presence.

Jasmine's voice still ringing in her head, faint now, a squirrel trapped inside the walls, rasping against the wood on the other side, desperate to get in again. *No obligations.*

"First found me, I remembered the surface was like. Remembered sun. Remembered the beach. Whatever old me was . . . loved the beach . . ."

Cathy wanted to reach out and touch Cabeza. She couldn't make herself do it.

"Henrietta . . . say this is a beach?"

Henrietta laughed, staring at the horrid shore. "It's something."

"Henrietta . . ."

"It's a beach, Cabeza," Henrietta said. "And you're in the waves."

"I am."

"You are."

"Good," Cabeza said. Water crashed over them. The left side of what was its face sloughed away. Cathy refused to watch the dissolution. More chunks dripped and dropped into the water. Soon there was little of the mushy flesh substance left. It made a motion like smiling.

"This was all I wanted," it said.

A skull floated in the waves before it disappeared too. Then only Cathy and the girl remained, eyes fixed on the shore, waiting for the Wet to extinguish itself. It screeched in hunger, unable to maintain its mantra.

No absence.

"Is it over?" Henrietta asked, swaying in the water. "I want it to be over."

Only presence.

Cathy placed a hand on the girl's small back. "No."

"Are we deep enough?" she asked, trying to regain her composure.

"I want to say yes," Cathy said, staring at the towers, watching the top of The Marigold flicker yellow and orange, on and off, until it went out. A great thrumming passed through them, like another sinkhole opening, the tower's foundation slipping down into the slurry, swallowed.

"But you can't."

"I can't," Cathy said, running a hand through Henrietta's thick hair. "I want to, but I can't."

"I know," Henrietta said. "I know what's down there. What's waiting for us."

Cathy grunted. Her mask still covered her face. Henrietta couldn't see the tears.

"Can I ask you to do something for me?"

"Yes," Cathy said, her legs gone frozen in the cold water of Lake Ontario. "What is it?"

"Can you tell me that we're safe? If you're going to do anything."

Cathy floated beside her new friend, this shuddering girl who had outrun a wave of mutilation, this person who pulled her up out of the rubble and told her to live. She didn't know who else was still alive in the city. Her phone displayed a NO SERVICE alert. On the distant shore toward the port, Threshold facilities were on fire. That was the only light she could see — clouds hid the moon and the stars, denying them any reassurance of some astral continuity.

"We're safe," Cathy whispered, her mask humming against Henrietta's skin. "We're safer than we've ever been. We're not alone. We're waiting for the storm to pass."

"Okay," Henrietta said, stiffening against Cathy's touch. She didn't pull away.

"We are standing in the eye of that storm," Cathy continued. "And we are waiting for it to pass. The eye of the storm is always calm. It's the place where you ready yourself for what's to come. You tell yourself in the eye that you survived the first half. And when it hits us again, we'll be ready. We'll wait it out in the water. Together."

"We'll wait it out," Henrietta said. "It can't last forever."

"Yes," Cathy said, trying her best to believe the word. "Eventually, it'll stop."

"Eventually."

"And we will go back," Henrietta said. "We will go back."

"Yes," Cathy said, shivering. The water slowly rose around them. "That's what happens. Someone always comes back."

"I know," Henrietta mumbled. Her body was cold in Cathy's embrace, even through the public health coveralls, pockets filled with useless tools, mask still clicking like it could save her.

"I know you know," Cathy said.

"They come back," Henrietta said, quiet now. Another building fell somewhere in the distance, lights sparking and hissing before going dark. Cathy tracked its fall by the cloud of dust erupting behind it, quickly quenched by the wet air. "Because if they don't come back . . ."

"I don't know," Cathy said. The rain continued to fall. The water continued to rise. Cabeza's skull bobbed to the surface, glowing. She barely felt her fingers. "But I want to say I do."

Suite 1301

Ceaseless chittering. Squabbling and hissing, pissing and snapping. Suite 1301 was a party in full swing, sacks of garbage dragged in from the clogged chute down the hall. The tower didn't collapse completely. It leaned over the street, slumped against the shorter towers across the way, a precarious sculpture, its very existence a provocation against the laws of physics.

The Marigold belonged to the raccoons now, their swollen bodies moving from suite to suite, pillaging broken refrigerators and busted pantries, chasing the last of the forgotten dogs and cats out of their new home. They gathered in circles and cooed and moaned at each other, unaffected by the Wet. It didn't speak to them. They had inherited a city full of garbage and this was the first of many feast days. A calendar of feasts without true days or months or years, just the sun rising and falling, their sleep cycle only interrupted by the larger coyotes who had bred with dogs and were beginning to stalk the streets in packs, howling for one another.

Raccoons scurried up and down the hall of the thirteenth floor. The Marigold/Dundee Corporation had done away with superstition. There was a fourth and a thirteenth and more. No one was coming to remove the animals. They entered closets and pulled out clothes, shirts and pants and boxers and bras wrapped around their thick necks, small hands pulling and stretching each other's garments, shrieking in delight. They were the new owners of this tower, all of it torn open. They sang and swilled from bottles they found hidden in closets and stacked on balconies, dropping glass down onto the road below, the night verging on eternal.

Concrete would crumble. Glass would weaken, fall and shatter. Towers would topple to the earth. The decay would continue unabated. It would subsume everything. It would flourish.

Acknowledgements

This book is about Toronto, a city that exists despite itself. Its geography is always in flux, and I have played with it as I saw fit to serve this story. Thanks to my various former apartments scattered across the city, especially 35 Jane Street. May you stand forever.

Thanks to my generous and thoughtful editor Jen Albert at ECW Press, who shaped this book into the best possible version of itself. Your vision was essential to this process. Thanks to the dedicated ECW Press team as well, including Jessica Albert, Shannon Parr, and Jennifer Knoch.

Thanks to my early readers, including Naben Ruthnum, Georgia Luyt, and Diana Davidson. Your insights helped guide this book to its final form.

Thanks to those whose words, art, and conversations helped influence this book, including André Forget, Franz Stefanik, Craig Davidson, Dominik Parisien, Jordan Ginsberg, Rick Meier, Bhanu Pratap, Pasha Malla, Daniel Scott Tysdal, Affinity Konar, Michael

LaPointe, Daniel Mittag, David Bertrand, Matthew Trafford, and Kris Bertin.

Thanks to my family for their enduring support. Special thanks to Dick Jones for use of the desk.

Thanks to my tireless agent Stephanie Sinclair for believing in my work and the entire CookeMcDermid Agency for supporting my efforts.

Thanks to the Toronto Arts Council, the Ontario Arts Council, and the Canada Council for the Arts for their generous support of this project.

And finally, thanks to my wife, Amy Jones, first and best reader, wiser than I ever will be. And Iggy, the bread dog, who knows nothing but rage and love in this world. There is no in-between.

Andrew F. Sullivan is the author of novels *The Marigold*; *The Handyman Method* (co-written with Nick Cutter); *Waste*, a *Globe and Mail* Best Book; and the story collection *All We Want Is Everything*, a *Globe and Mail* Best Book and finalist for the Relit Award. He lives in Hamilton, Ontario.